God's Mountain

McLaughlin's Valley

Joan M. Kay

HERITAGE BOOKS
2012

HERITAGE BOOKS

AN IMPRINT OF HERITAGE BOOKS, INC.

Books, CDs, and more—Worldwide

For our listing of thousands of titles see our website
at
www.HeritageBooks.com

Published 2012 by
HERITAGE BOOKS, INC.
Publishing Division
100 Railroad Ave. #104
Westminster, Maryland 21157

International Standard Book Numbers
Paperbound: 978-0-7884-3280-4
Clothbound: 978-0-7884-9428-4

In memory of James Lee Gray McLaughlin,
my Dad,
and for all the military men and women who have served this nation.

And "Thank You" to –

my loving husband, Tom, Janice Loos, Laura Stoneman, and Writers
By the Bay

You all know why...

The time is now near at hand which must probably determine, whether Americans are to be, Freemen, or Slaves... whether their Houses, and Farms, are to be pillaged and destroyed, and they consigned to a State of Wretchedness from which no human efforts will probably deliver them. The fate of unborn Millions will now depend, under God, on the Courage and Conduct of this army--Our cruel and unrelenting Enemy leaves us no choice but a brave resistance, or the most abject submission...

— *George Washington, July 2, 1776, General Order*

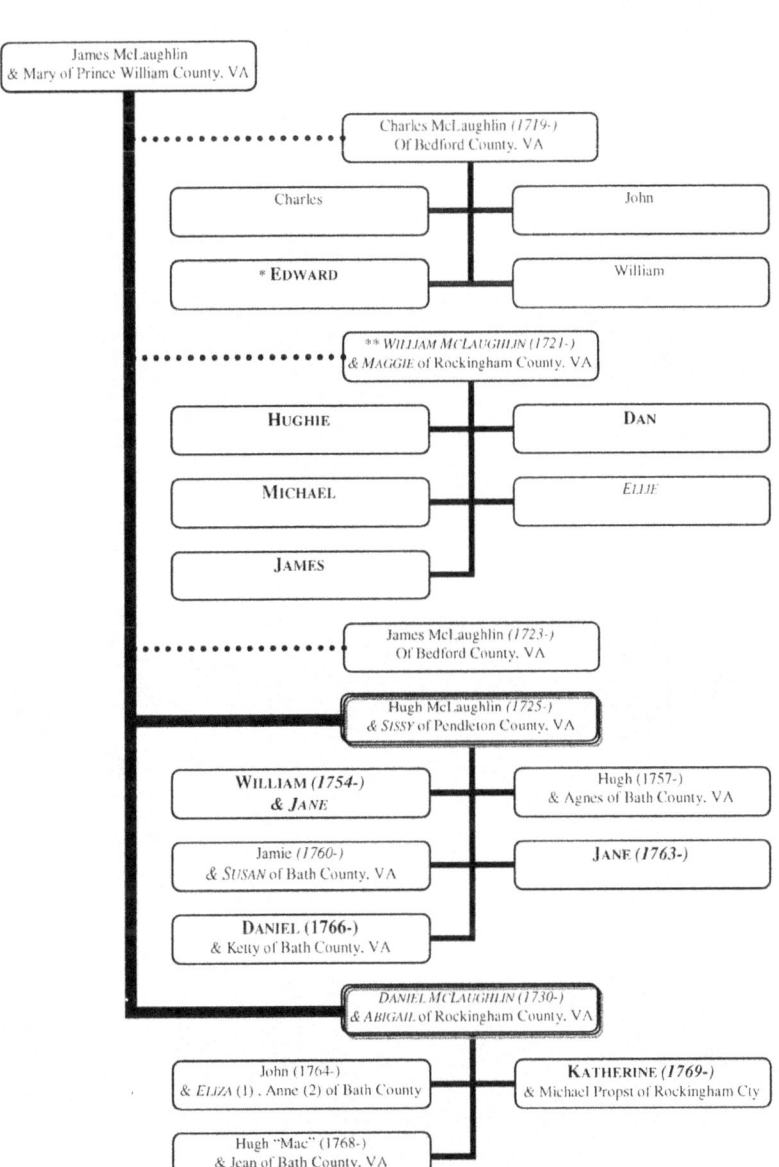

MCLAUGHLIN'S VALLEY FAMILY TREE
* FAMILY RELATIONSHIP UNKNOWN
** FICTIONAL/COMPOSITE CHARACTERS

PROLOGUE

Virginia Coast
September 6, 1743

Five men, on foot and dripping seawater, scrambled through an unkempt autumn garden, an acre or two away from a small bayside plantation. A familiar port town, quiet in the still night, spread out to the north. Before their escape from the Navy's *H.M.S. Cruizer*, in the groaning below-decks, the men had solemnly agreed on stealth and silence. But now a few couldn't hold back anxious laughter as they carelessly crushed tender orange mums under their bare feet and dipped muddy hands in a carved stone fountain.

Only one dared a look back to the inlet, trickling in over a sandbar from the ocean-sized Chesapeake Bay. Hugh McLaughlin, son of James, a tobacco planter from Bull Run in Virginia, had been snatched by the Navy's press gang a year earlier while at the wharf shipping hogsheads of his father's tobacco. He now balanced his weight on a low brick wall and patiently scanned the water. The other four men crossed the bricks and climbed a terraced hill, leading to a dark stand of trees.

All was quiet between them and the shore, where waves slowly lapped.

But beyond the shoreline, under a misty rising moon, a sloop rocked gently in the murky water, just far enough away that the swaying could not be heard over their own exertions.

Once dragged from riverside taverns, crowded wharfs, and merchant vessels to serve the king, there were stolen men among their number, eagerly joined in the running by the disillusioned, the beaten, the scurvied. *His Majesty's Sloop* the *Cruizer* had held them tenuously, desperate to deliver a life of adventure and honor, but instead merely giving sustenance to the essence within the men that demanded all that God provided but earthly lords drained away. And the men ran to grasp God's gifts. Of the soil, of the sea, of their spirit. They sought no less than their own liberty and security.

But the captain would want them back. Not even a pirate vessel, her belly pregnant with a king's ransom, would be closer guarded than a deck full of seasoned and cynical sailors with the fever of liberty. Experienced seamen, they were as valuable cargo to the Navy as the great guns pointed outward from the colonies' coasts, guarding into the night against French invasion. And still, they made good their escape.

For Hugh, this run was born of their last orders. The *Cruizer's* anchors would soon be retrieved and her sails would snap in the wind, to blow them eastward to Spithead, England, after escorting one last ship into the Virginia capes.

Leaving. Back across the choppy, frigid Atlantic to England. *No, Captain.*

Hugh thought of hot, loud, colorful Barbados where he had sailed to this summer, and then of the warm, salty breezes of the Chesapeake. No. He would not leave America, would not cross the unforgiving Atlantic. And so Hugh threw in his lot with George Anderson, Richard Welch, John Bond, and John Mayou—all running and in this escape together.

He turned and followed the rest of the men, leaving his home in Tidewater behind.

Soon he crossed Virginia's Blue Ridge Mountains to settle in the howling wilderness beyond, in search of liberty and security, far out of the Navy's long reach.

PART I:
1772 – 1780

CHAPTER ONE

*Twenty-eight years later; Augusta County in the Valley of Virginia
January 1772*

Fourteen-year-old Hugh McLaughlin thought split oak smelled worse than a pile of dog shit. But he shouldn't have told his sister, Jane. "Doggy shit," she said from behind him in a squeaky brogue. He stopped, glanced back at her and then at the warm cabin they had just left. The door was closed. His mother couldn't have heard, she was busy inside nursing his sick father, but she would whip him with a birch switch if she found out what he had taught Jane. He had to keep her quiet.

His two younger brothers, Jamie and Daniel, passed him by, their footsteps crunching the frozen ground. They bickered with one another as they went. Hugh gave Jamie's wiry blonde head a firm push.

"Get on about the chores," Hugh told them.

He waited impatiently for his sister to catch up, giving her his best hard stare while trying to ignore the smell from the pile of oak logs next to the barn. He was glad it wasn't the middle of summer when the smell would have been baked and wafted his way on a breeze.

"Jane," he said when she reached him, "dinna dare let Mama hear the boy talk I taught you. She'll switch me 'til I'm sore. Understand?"

She nodded, then sneezed and sniffled. He laid his musket on the ground and pulled the hat of her cloak over her red-blonde hair, so like his own, and fastened it around her neck. "Mama doesna need another patient, Jane." He kneeled down to her level. "If you come down sick, who's going ta care for you, I'd like ta be knowing?"

Jane smiled down at him as she wiped the brown wool of her cloak across her pug nose. "I know, Hugh Òg," she said, using the nickname given to him by his Scottish mother, meaning "Hugh the Younger" or

"Hugh Junior." His father was Hugh Mor, or the Elder. Jane pointed at him. "You will."

"I willna," he said gently. Two identical pairs of green-flecked blue eyes stared at each other for a moment. He took her by the hand and they caught up with their brothers, who stood shivering at the barn doors. "Jamie, take Daniel ta the spring and fill these," he said as he handed off two dented brass pots. "I'll keep Jane with me."

Jamie, twelve years old and full of the devil, ran off first, the pot handles tight in his fist. Daniel, half his size, ran after him, shouting, "I want ta fill them. Give me one. Jaamieee!"

They disappeared behind the sagging corncrib.

Hugh and Jane opened the barn doors and he double-stepped over the small gray cat weaving through his feet—a harried, mangy, tired looking cat, desperate to escape her five mewling kittens. He watched her stretched belly sway back and forth as she jumped and ran across the short logs heaped high near the barn.

His father had cut down the oak tree, hit by lightening last summer and grown nearly tall enough to threaten falling on the house. Couldn't let a tree grow tall enough to hit the house. First rule. His father had about thirty "first rules."

But his father wasn't splitting firewood any time soon, and the pile had looked the same for days. It wasn't going to split itself—Hugh had to do it. He didn't like oak, even before their old barn had burned down, but even less after. The new barn was built with oak and the fresh cut smell that had floated around for weeks had reminded him daily why they had to rebuild it.

The first had burned.

No, he thought, rubbing his face. It had been burned—by a ruthless enemy. And that ugly morning Hugh's father had had his long gun in his hands before the rest of the family had even rolled out of bed. With the musket's muzzle, he had busted through the thin oiled skin that covered the window and stood still while Hugh's heart pounded against his ribs. When the gun finally cracked into the silence, Hugh decided it was the loudest sound he had ever heard, forever destroying the peace of his valley.

"Get under the bed," his father had said.

The two oldest children, William and Hugh, ran together to their parents' bed, dropped to the cold floor, knees smarting, and crawled underneath. Hugh could hear Baby Jamie fussing in the middle of the bed above him.

Slowly, the gun smoke dispersed throughout the small room and faded away. In the firelight near the hearth, his mother held her quilt up in front of her chest. Her face and the white ruffled cuffs and neck of her shift was all he could see of her. She was pale.

After his father reloaded, he stared hard at each child peeking out from under the bed. But then his face softened as he winked at his wife. He left the cabin.

Indians!

Hugh wanted to shout it out, maybe his mother would tell him he was feeble-minded, there's no Indians out there. Maybe she would pull him out from under the bed and spank him soundly for saying such a thing. No one said a word.

Maybe it wasn't Indians, he thought, listening to William's deep breathing. Maybe it was the French. He shook his head. No, it was Indians for sure. He had heard from a traveling German minister that all the courageous immigrants to the Valley were nothing more than human shields against the Indians for the "dandy tobacco pickers in Tidewater and the limp-wristed Quakers" in Pennsylvania. The minister didn't know he and William were listening. And he didn't know Hugh's grandfather was a dandy tobacco picker, either.

In the quiet, waiting for his father to return, he struggled not to picture other stories he had overheard about the shields being knocked down. They were tales of wives stumbling around the farm yard, dazed and only half-scalped as their husbands came running from the woods or the riverside, a heartbeat too late to save their families. The wives bled to death before long and the children were gone, captured and dragged along behind the Indian warriors.

He didn't want to be dragged along—he squeezed his eyes tighter—and he didn't want any of that other stuff to happen either. Maybe the French would be better.

When he couldn't endure the images attacking him in his dark hiding place any longer, he sneaked to the window, his mother whispering furiously from behind but not stopping him, and peeked out. His father's three horses galloped by. Plodding behind was their milk cow, swinging her large, panicked head from side to side. A chicken squawked and ran as she passed.

Hugh peered into the dim morning at the naked bird hurrying away, and wasn't sure what he saw could be real. But he knew it was and he became more afraid than ever. The hen really was naked, her every feather having been patiently plucked. Her blood-red comb and waddle lay starkly against light, bare skin. She ran off into the darkness.

His father was back before the sun fully rose. He had run the attackers off—for now. The children watched as he held Mother's hands. "Sissy, we'll have ta get the bairns ta the fort." At her panicked look he added, "We havena another choice..."

Jane squealed from inside the new barn. "Kittens!"

Hugh turned from his black thoughts to watch her skip through the settling dust motes and thought how lucky she was to have never known that morning, long before she was born. Her valley was peaceful. And she wouldn't find out from him that in the scrape of a chunk of flint the peace could be gone forever.

"Get me the pails, Jane. I'll help you milk the cow. Just for today, but dinna dare tell a soul. You ken it isna a man's job. They'll call me 'missy' and no mistake," Hugh warned.

Jane nodded. But first she checked on the kittens, inspecting them each carefully. She giggled at their rough tongues on her chin, but then put them away quickly as their forbidding feline mother dashed back into the barn.

"How did she know?" Jane murmured.

She left them behind the hay, and Hugh saw in her face that she just now remembered her job was to fetch the milk pails.

She stood below the pails hanging high on the edge of the stall, hands on hips. With a snort, she reached up, stretching onto her toes. Her fingers just grazed the bottom of one pail. She hopped and her fist banged the bottom. It swung back and forth.

Hugh sat on a stool in the cramped milking stall, stroked the impatient cow's side and, shaking his head, continued watching his sister.

She jumped again and again, but the pail hung on. Small teeth pulled at her bottom lip. She took off her shoe, and, standing on one foot, threw it at the pail. When it still just swung, clinging stubbornly to the stall, she whirled around—Hugh tried not to laugh out loud—and stepped over her fallen shoe. She grabbed up a wooden-handled hay fork, and finally, after stabbing at the flat bottom of one pail, they both fell to the ground.

She slid her blue-stockinged foot back into her shoe and daintily picked up the pails. She carried one in each hand, carefully, so they wouldn't bang. Hugh smiled. He knew Mama always scolded her that it wasn't ladylike to bang pails around. She delicately placed them at her brother's feet.

Humming softly, she took a small rag doll from her pocket and sat on a nearby stool, rocking the doll on her knees and watching him milk the cow. Soon she began to tell him about her upcoming trip to town. "Da promised me so long ago, it's probably been thirty weeks or more, now." Hugh smiled at her little pout. It had been only a fortnight. "I've havena been ta town ever and everyone else has gone over and over. It isna fair!"

"Jane, do you think it fair that the boys have ta chop wood, haul water, and get the chilblains in the freezing cold, when you dinna have ta?"

She pushed hair out of her eyes and hugged her doll. "He said a shopkeeper just got in so many spools of beautiful ribbon, I can have my choice of colors. Imagine!" she said. She turned to him and opened her blue eyes wide. "Mother has a ribbon, and she said I could put the new ribbon in my best cap." She looked back down at her doll. "Imagine, all alone with Da and a ribbon for my cap, too. I might—"

They both started at loud voices coming from the direction of the spring. Maybe it was just his brothers bickering again, but since he couldn't be sure, he thought he'd best check on them. He had just grabbed his musket, an old Brown Bess his father had given him, when Jamie screamed.

Hugh pointed to a dark corner of the barn. "There, Jane. Now. Dinna come out until I say." He rethought that and added, "But run like the devil's after you if there's smoke."

He sure wished now that he hadn't had Indians on his mind. He stood still for a moment to ready himself. Because it was too late to run for the fort, and their father was too ill to leave his bed, their protection was all up to him. He had the musket. It was his job.

He let out the breath he had held since ordering Jane to the corner and wiped his hands on his breeches. Kicking the door open wide, he rushed out of the barn. The corncrib hid the springhouse. He walked through the yard with his heart in his ears, raising the musket as the squat, stone springhouse came into view. But then he chuckled—though he felt a little weak—and slowly lowered the gun.

Raiding Indians had apparently not caused Jamie's loud scream, as he was now sitting on the ground and calmly pressing his coat sleeve to his bleeding brow.

9

"What happened ta you?" Hugh called out. "And where's Daniel?" His eyes scanned the yard, looking past the undisturbed cabin with the slowly swirling gray smoke clouding the chimney.

Jamie looked up. "He's run off, 'cause he's afraid of me now. That's where he's gone ta. When he comes back, I'm going ta have Da take a switch ta his backside, that's what I'm going ta do," he said in a rush. Jamie lowered his arm and inspected the smear of blood on his sleeve. "That's what I'm going ta do."

"You're no' ta bother him, do you hear? No' Mama, either. What you are going ta do is help me find Daniel and explain yourself as we go." Hugh held out a hand to help his brother to his feet. But he stepped back as Jamie jumped up, his thin arms flailing and his temper high.

"Just like that!" Jamie said, swinging a pot up over his head and back down in a wide arc. "He smacked me for no good cause, just like that, he did. And no good cause,"

"Jamie, he's just a child, he didna—"

Jane. He suddenly remembered he had left her hiding in the barn, likely scared to quaking because of his forgetfulness. He sprinted to the barn, rapped on it and called, "Come on out, Jane, it's safe."

She ran out and threw herself at him, squeezing him around the neck. He wasn't surprised to see that she had been crying, but he didn't make a point of it. Instead, he gently pried her arms away and ordered Jamie to stay with her. These two were safe. That was a start. Now, where on earth had the little one run off to?

"Daniel!"

He waited.

"Daniel!"

There was only silence.

He strode toward a thick stand of trees and brush on the hill behind the springhouse. "Daniel, this isna amusing, do you hear?" he yelled. "Come on out and you willna suffer the switch, but if I have ta search this mountainside for you I'll take it out of your bottom."

"What will Da do ta me, Hugh?" a small, tremulous voice called from up on a winter-barren tree branch above Hugh's head.

Hugh looked up, wondering how he had missed him. A length of thin black hair fell across Daniel's crinkled brow. He felt a little pity for the child, but despite the scared look in the round, babyish face and wide eyes, Hugh replied sternly, "Nobody's bothering Da today, but as for me, I only wish ta speak ta you boy. Come down."

"How?"

"What do you mean 'How'? You got up there like a squirrel you can just get down like one."

"I canna."

"Then you'll have ta jump," Hugh determined. "Tell me when you're ready. Come on now, I'll catch you," he promised as he lifted his arms.

As Daniel's surprisingly solid little boy's frame cut through the air and collided with his brother's, they were both knocked to the hard ground.

Hugh lifted his head and looked at the little boy, sprawled on top of him. "Now what'd you go and do that for?" Hugh asked. He helped Daniel to his feet and retrieved his musket from where he had propped it against the trunk of a scraggly pine. "Well?"

"You said jump." Daniel looked up at him and narrowed his eyes. "And you said you'd catch me."

When they neared Jamie and Jane who were busy filling the last small pot with water, Daniel pointed an accusing finger at his brother. "I dinna want ta work with him."

"You mayhap dinna, but you will. And you also will be explaining how your brother came ta be bleeding out of his head like he is," Hugh said.

"He said Da's going ta die! And I said that was a lie, an awful, mean lie. And he pushed me and said 'it's so', so I knocked him in his head, because something must be wrong in it," Daniel cried.

None of the brothers noticed the frightened look in Jane's wide eyes, but they noticed a few seconds later when she dashed off toward the cabin bawling, "Mama, Mama!"

Hugh rolled his eyes heavenward. Each thread of the tattered family cloth he had been struggling to hold together this morning unraveled. It was too big a job for him alone.

This time it was Daniel that got a smack on the head.

* * *

The crowded bed, stuffed with straw and covered in an old, black bearskin, was really only big enough to fit two children, but it was normally shared by three of Sissy McLaughlin's boys, usually with much squirming, pushing and shoving. Tonight it was shared by four of her children and they were silent.

Had she fed them supper tonight? Afternoon dinner?

She watched them silently from across the one-room cabin. Whenever the wind found its way into the house through the countless chinks, they crept deeper into the fur. Except for Jamie, who had a thin arm sprawled across Jane's face. The tip of her braid spread out through his fingers. Hugh Òg—strong, blonde and handsome like his father—snored suddenly and then quieted.

Did she feed them at tea? Did she make tea?

From the far end of the room the fire popped, and she turned to watch as it crackled and swayed, as if it were led in a slow dance by the howling wind. The shadows it cast showed enormous furniture filling the room. The short pine table next to her stretched out in flickering black tones along the back wall. It overlapped the shadows of four tall posts thrown by the largest bed—her bed in the corner near the fireplace.

Her shelves were nearly hidden in the shadows. One shelf held almost a dozen new candles—she never let her family run out of fresh candles. Below, herbs were strung up to dry. More hung, closed up in cloth bags, in front of the fireplace. She had depended on them to make her husband better, to relieve his fever, to keep him here on Earth with her. So far, they had failed. His fever still raged.

She saw herself stretched along the wall and up onto the ceiling above the table. Her shadow was long and drawn out, eight feet tall. Her dark hair was piled beneath an old mobcap, and in the shadow the heavy brim circled her forehead like a crooked halo. A ghost of a sad smile drifted across her lips. She looked grand and meaningful up there, working diligently at the spinning wheel in her bed jacket. Or was the wheel a harp and the blue striped robe a gauzy gown?

She tilted her halo to the left and kept spinning and watching.

The wheel's soft whirring was interrupted regularly by a louder *whap-whap*, the slap of a warp that had yet to be fixed. Her outstretched arm swayed with each *whap* as she worked to keep the thread taut.

The spinning slowed as she pinched and straightened the thread and paused to look to the bed nearby, where her husband slept. She had tended to him since breakfast, washing the heat away from his large body with cool water, comforting him when he became confused, and then worrying until she lost what little stew she had eaten when he became deathly still.

Had she fed the children stew?

Her husband, Hugh Mor, was even now horribly still and quiet. Earlier today, for just the briefest of moments when she thought he might die, she had considered curling up next to him, closing her eyes, and joining him on his journey into the next world. A chill went through her now.

She put down her work and sat on the edge of the soft bed she had shared with her husband for more than twenty years. It was the same bed where she had given birth to their six children, and where years ago her youngest daughter, just three days old, had died.

She laid her slender hand on his thick arm and was surprised and heartened by the coolness of his skin. The fever was gone.

She rested her head on his chest, where thin blonde hair peeked out the top of his long shirt, to listen to his heartbeat. Every night it lulled her to sleep—a sound no one knew like she did, not even her husband. It was hers and it was private.

What she heard now was not the same. His heartbeat was fast, but weak and quiet, when usually it was slow and strong. She could barely feel him breathing beneath her. *Perhaps this means he's getting better, he's so much cooler, he must be getting well again.* Sissy lay down beside her husband.

CHAPTER TWO

For as long as young Hugh could remember, his dreams caused him to toss and to think longer into the night than his mind had ever intended. Ugly scenes would dance before him for a time, most often haunting him with things he had left undone. A late milking of the cow could cause her to approach him in the night and suddenly she learned to talk plain as his sister, Jane. She would complain long and loud in first Jane's voice then in a strange cow-English that the next day could leave him laughing, but would, in the gauzy dream world, frighten him to a girlish panic. And then he learned to stop fighting them, would assure the phantoms that he had learnt his lesson right and proper, and they congratulated him aplenty for it. They dragged him up out of bed, pulled him impatiently along on their mischief through the inky black of midnight, and dumped him atop the sloping roof of his father's barn. The sun would then shine and there he would sit, perched atop the world, king of the Shenandoah, watching the wonders of life moving below.

This cold winter night he was castigated for nothing—and this the first time ever that had happened—before he looked down on his kingdom, and there he watched his father under the hot sun, moving along the fields of summer wheat bending before him. The plow horse suddenly cupped along behind his father at a good clip, and it looked like a right good harvest was shaping up, although the plow bumped along, following the horse untended, thumping against jagged stones and rocking from side to side. And then the nag's gait slowed and then faltered and then wavered until its front quarters buckled to the ground, the plow broke away, and before the hindquarters also gave out, its ass-end stared up at Hugh. His father turned back to the great beast. His tools were carried tucked in the front of his belt; seemingly every tool from the barn was there—his froe and mallet, a long razor strop, two

15

axes, a smaller hatchet. His father looked up at him for a moment, as hollow-eyed as a black gum stump, and then he spread the tools out on the ground before him and went to his knees beside the horse, wrapping his great arms about the beast.

Hugh scrambled down the roof, working his way like a spider, bumping along on his rear, balancing with his hands, and digging in for traction with his heels until he reached the edge where he was stopped by the girl from last night's dream. Sally, she was, a bold girl from a farm just over the ridge. She had wanted him to put his hands on her last night, whispering her warm breath onto his neck and the hollow of his collarbone and the dip behind his ear. She grabbed at his arm tonight, trying to force him to touch her, but he wanted none of it. He had to get down to his father. She shook his arm with a steely grasp.

"Hugh Òg," she said, "you have ta run for Uncle Daniel."

He opened his eyes and his mother stood over him. Hugh jumped up and Daniel whimpered.

"Hush, children, go back ta sleep, now," his mother said soothingly to the younger children.

Little Jane rubbed her eyes and wetted her lips as she searched through the dimness for the older woman's face. Her lips parted in a wide smile for her mother and she stuck the tip of her tongue through a gap in her teeth. "I lost a tooth, Mama, see?" she said.

"Yes, my baby, I see," she assured her daughter distractedly. Mother grasped Hugh's hand and brought him across the room. Shadows darkened her eyes into deep craters and cut her cheekbones into gullies. Her face scared him. He was as aware of her as he would be of a witch. She didn't seem to notice.

He turned away from her, wanting to go to his father's side, now that he was down from that damnable roof.

"No!" his mother screeched, and pulled on him again. "There'll be no time for that, no' now." In a low voice she said all at once, "If you want ta help your father, go, and take this lantern for your feet. Hurry ta Uncle Daniel and Aunt Abigail and bring them back here. Please, Hugh Òg, I'm frightened and I canna do this. Please, now." Tears dripped from her chin as she stared into his face. She soon pulled him close and rested her head on his shoulder.

He stood woodenly in her embrace and smelled the strong odor of her sweat. It recalled a time, years before, being held in her arms when she was running, carrying him, jostling him. He had been surrounded by the strong and bitter scent then, too, as she held him pressed tightly against her.

There had been a mist hovering over the ground on that long-ago morning, the morning their barn had burned down. So much of it had come back to him today, he wished he could shake it, but the memory took him out of this room and dropped him into the early-morning forest.

He couldn't tell where the smoke from the burning barn ended and the fog began, but the mist thickened and spread as they passed a small stream, winding through the woods. There was no underbrush to block it, just tall, thin pines that left a brown carpeting of needles that rustled as they ran.

When his mother had stopped running, her strong grip on him loosened. He slid down past her swollen belly and rested his face against it. The baby inside shifted. He moved his head and tried to hug her around the legs.

She had gripped his shoulders and looked hard into his face. "Your father only scared them off. Do you understand? They'll be coming back." Her movements jerky, she looked into the woods beyond the half-built fence of the fort, in all directions. "There's more out there."

She turned him around. There was a ladder at his feet that climbed up a house built with the door high off the ground. She sent him up towards a dim room. Soft voices from above grew louder as he climbed.

He stood in the doorway, watched his mother follow and then they waited for his father, carrying Baby Jamie. Behind him was his older brother, William, holding a gun nearly as tall as he was. Soon his father dragged the ladder up after them.

Hugh's mother pulled him by the hand across the room. There were many children there, he never knew so many other children lived in his valley before that day. He stared at them all as he passed. His mother sat on the floor and put him and Jamie on her lap. The mothers and children stayed together, huddled in the middle of the one large room, while fathers and brothers looked out of small holes that they could fit their guns through when the time came.

A little girl in the middle of the room wandered around looking at all of the women, searching for someone. Plaited black hair hung down her back, shorter loose hairs streamed around her face. Small scratches covered her forehead. When she began to cry, Hugh's mother put him

17

off her lap, handed over Jamie to his care, and held the girl in her arms. Instead of rocking him, she stroked the girl's hair and tried to dab at the bleeding scratches with her fingers. He watched his mama start to cry, too, looking at a smear of blood on her thumb.

He would always remember his mama's tears that day, the only other day of his life that he had seen his mother cry. She had left him alone there with the strangers, with no one to hold on to, watching her holding the little girl. He didn't know until much later that that little girl's mama had been the Indian's only victim that day.

But somehow his mother knew, and she had been afraid.

And tonight she was afraid again.

"Mama?" Daniel said sleepily from the bed. She stopped sobbing on Hugh's shoulder and let him go, turning without a word, without answering Daniel. Hugh stared at her back, hunched over and shaking.

He walked to the bed and pushed Daniel's hair out of his eyes. The little boy's breathing deepened and slowed. His mother should be soothing him. Not crying and quaking.

Mothers weren't supposed to be afraid of anything and he didn't want to hide his anger that she would break that rule. He couldn't understand why she would stop acting like a mother again, as she had that day, and rely so heavily on him now. And with his older brother, William, gone from home last summer, Hugh was left as the burden carrier for his parents.

He didn't want the job.

He wanted to tell her, Go get Uncle Daniel yourself. You can go out there in the cold and trip over roots and get scared by the wolves. Leave me here sleeping and dreaming. I could have saved him in that dream.

Instead, he silently took the lamp and candle, set them beside a chair and put on his shoes. He just as silently shrugged on his heavy coat, and holding the lantern and his gun, began toward the door. He paused for only a moment when he heard Jane call sleepily from the bed, "Mama?"

"Yes, dear," his mother said heavily.

"I didna bang the pails today."

* * *

"Sissy, dear, we're here now. Come, let's start some water on to boil," Aunt Abigail said to Hugh's mother as she took her gently by the arm.

Hugh stood next to his uncle and they quietly watched the two women work at the large hearth. As Sissy dejectedly tended to her fire, Abigail went to Hugh Senior's sick bed and sat by his side. She dispassionately looked him over, felt his face, and from all appearances, seemed to sniff the air around his head. She *humphed* and moved heavily to the nearby table, opened a coarse satchel and began carefully sorting out the contents.

"What is she doing?" Hugh asked the older man.

Daniel took his gaze off his brother's bed long enough to reply, "Oh, she's brought her women's remedies, butterfly weed, sassafras root, the like." Daniel dismissed any further questioning as he slowly approached the large four-post bed. His palm rested heavily on a well-worn pine post, one that he keenly recalled helping to hew. He slid his hand slowly along the back of the bedstead, his long fingers patiently searching for what he knew was there.

With a small smile he felt the crude inscription that his brother, Hugh Mor, had made before they pushed the bed into the corner. *I Love Sis*, it said. Confessing shame he never taught Sissy or his children to read or write even that much. Probably thought he had more time. He didn't.

But he thought back to all those years ago, putting this home together. Hugh had grinned sheepishly at Daniel when he was caught scratching Sissy's name into the wood. Without any words passing between them, he had sworn his brother to secrecy. And no one else knew about it, even until today.

It was a small thing really—much too girlish to mention. No, Daniel never said a word about it. They set the bedstead in place, Sissy added a colorful quilt she made herself, never knowing what was carved behind it.

He looked up at Sissy now and smiled sadly at the black hair falling about her face, just a few strands that had escaped her bun. A few more strands curled around her neck and had slipped into the bodice of her dress. She looked tired and thin. To be fair, she was thin to begin with, but little matter, he thought, she's a tough girl. She had never shied away from hard work and her family's needs were always placed firmly first.

But then, looking again, he thought she looked gaunt, not just thin, and complacency and neediness had replaced her usual energy and stubbornness. She worried him, especially the way she stood at the fire and watched with vacant eyes as the shorter and much stouter Abigail commanded the room. Until today, she would have been horrified not to have complete control of her own home and family. But now it seemed she had willingly relinquished it all.

He suddenly felt a new awareness of his brother's wife. Before, she had always been one part dutiful wife, five parts mother, one for each child she bore that had lived. Now he saw her as one part fallible woman, five parts child. And without a doubt, she would be coming to rely on him heavily in the days ahead. Yes, a widow had a hard way to go out here, especially with her only living blood kin, besides her children, unreachable across the ocean.

Never even having removed his soft deerskin coat, he gave his sleeping brother a rough pat on his shoulder, wiped at his own eyes with the palm of his hand, and returned heavily to stand beside the smaller bed across the room.

"You've got them together, then?" he asked Hugh Òg while gently lifting his niece out of bed. He looked over the other children, tiredly shrugging on their coats.

"Little Jane needs her shoes, but we're prepared well enough," Hugh Òg said.

Abigail left the bright heat from the fire behind as she dried her hands on her apron. "That onion poultice should be warm, dear," she said to Sissy. "And add some of Hugh's best whiskey to that tea."

To Daniel she added quietly, "Take them to Maggie and let them get more rest. I ken there's not so much room—but, well, this should be over shortly." The pained look on her husband's face gave her pause, but she continued quickly as she bent at her thick waist, "Little ones, mind your uncle, now, and your mother and I shall send for you shortly." She tried to lead them to the door.

"Shouldna I stay here with the women, Uncle Daniel?" Hugh said. "They could be molested here alone."

"No' likely." Daniel furrowed his brow. "Abigail? Do you know my Abigail, lad? No one would dare ta, no' even the most savage beast. Let's move on." Daniel gently steered him toward the door.

* * *

"I canna take you home, son," Hugh's Uncle Daniel told him.

20

"Damn it, dinna call me son again," Hugh yelled at him.

Daniel leaned across the table and smacked him soundly across the cheek. With his face close to Hugh's he said, "The court is sitting tomorrow, and tomorrow it will be. They've agreed that it's ta be Mr. Hogsett taking you in, boy, now that your own father's gone." Daniel settled back down into his chair and his face softened. "It's as good a plantation as any other ta learn the farming and mending that you need ta be knowing ta move on ta your own plantation."

"I know all the farming and mending I'll be needing. You can tell the court so. I know what they do ta boys once they own you, I've seen enough ta know, just as well. The men around here who've been owned look rather more like they're ancient than only twenty-five or thirty years old. Ready for the grave they are, only steps from it, if they've even lived that long. Oh, I know all about it. And now you want ta send me there—"

"It's no' what I want—"

"No, sir. I'll take Jane and Daniel and Jamie and we can make it together." *And you'll never see us again.* Hugh slipped from the table and stood next to the crackling fireplace, well out of reach of Uncle Daniel's hard palm.

Daniel tiredly rubbed his own face, scraping over a two-day beard. "You willna. Your mother—"

"You'll have ta put me in chains if you want ta leave me on that plantation ta slave, and you'll have the fight of your life for it, I'm sure—but dinna ever mention my mother again, it certainly willna help your cause."

21

CHAPTER THREE

Six years later; Camp Valley Forge, Pennsylvania
Early 1778

The twelve soldiers had built their fireplace squarely over the furnace of hell. While the men snored, it belched the devil's smoke and misfortune into the one-room cabin and Hugh barked out a cough. The bunk creaked and complained beneath him. His old friend and bunkmate, Thomas Gillespy, turned over and rubbed his eyes.

"Could you not do that?" Tom whispered.

After another coughing fit caught him unaware, a few of the other soldiers, resting heavily on bunks lining the walls, shushed him. He groaned as he rolled out of his bed and left the cabin behind, limping out into the cold night.

Just outside the door, still in the flickering light of the fireplace, he looked down at his throbbing feet. Hours before he had wrapped his bloody left foot in thin strips ripped from his only shirt, a linen hunting frock, and now the tattered ends flapped against the frozen mud and snow where earlier he had left gory footprints. Fresh blood blossomed through the dirty cloth.

He shook his head and ripped another ragged fringe from his shirt. Where would he have to go to finally get some rest? Inside he choked on smoke from the crooked fireplace and outside he bled on the ground. For this he had left his valley, where he knew every ridge and river, where, when he was a young boy at least, a welcoming home and hearth was never far away? He followed the drums and fifes and the romance of the Army to this piss-poor station? For what? To be a hero, a martyr, a prince? Or perhaps just a free man? Well, he had accomplished that, at least, by marching into the war. Six long years of servitude were over, but now he had just begun a three-year sentence of duty to the gods of war.

But it hadn't taken the chilblains to bring him down to earth. His delusions of grandeur had died this fall at his first skirmish, the first time he heard a soldier praise the Lord over an enemy's corpse. Now, his frostbitten feet were merely the raindrops that crushed the rotten roof.

"A'mighty—ah God a'mighty," he called out in a thick brogue.

"Who's crying?" questioned a tired voice from the bare doorway.

Hugh was sorry he had been heard. "Ah, Isaac. Only 'tis verra cold and I canna breathe in that room."

He stifled another cough as the tall, thin soldier took a few steps out of the cabin and looked down at his nearly bare feet. "So that I can rest, please, McLaughlin, let me give you my shoes, you look rather pathetic," he said and ducked back in. In a moment he returned and tossed a ragged pair from the doorway.

Hugh deftly caught one shoe and the other hit the ground. He shrugged off his musings and grinned sadly at his new friend's smoke-reddened green eyes, reminding himself they all had the same discomforts.

Isaac was several inches taller than Hugh, one of the few men he had to look up at. He didn't like it. But where Isaac was thin and gangly, Hugh was square and muscular.

He looked up at Isaac now. "And what else you hiding there, Isaac?" He peered into the hut, past the knapsacks and tools hanging along the walls between the bunks, to the men on them covered in ragged clothes and blankets, and shook his head. "Shoes. Who smuggled these inta camp?"

"Who else do you think has the wherewithal to get me what I need in this godforsaken place? M'father. Don't forget m'father," Isaac said and pushed lank black hair out of his face.

"How could I, now? With a name like 'Isaac Moses Hamilton... Hamilton...' what was that bit?"

"Hamilton Jackson Moore, Senior. Oh yes, you wanted to hear the 'Senior' again." Isaac turned and raised his arms out to the dark camp. "Yes, fine young soldiers, whoever can hear and appreciate me, my name is, in fact, not in jest, Isaac Moses Hamilton Jackson Moore, Junior. Does that appease your perverse sense of humor?"

Hugh smiled, pleased with himself, as he lifted a foot to put on a borrowed shoe.

Isaac shook his head. "Goodnight, McLaughlin." He disappeared into the hut, identical to the acres of other huts just built, spreading out over the camp.

The rows of cabins had taken them off the cold ground where before they either slept in tents or merely under boughs of evergreens, tattered blankets or thin clothes. They were finally under shelter, but they were still vulnerable, many were sick, and the British were only twenty miles away to the east in Philadelphia.

To that point of the compass, he saw fires flicker near the perimeter for the guards. Some less-fortunate sentinels, he was sure, shivered alone in the dark, standing on their hats to keep their feet off the frozen mud that could slice into feet, as well he knew. He wiggled his sore toes around in the too-big shoes and wondered if there were a patron saint of shoes or feet that he could offer a thanks to. A moment later Isaac stepped back out.

"Thank you for covering my toes."

"Of course." Isaac waved it away. "This is a bit more inviting, idn't it? A few moments of fresh air might be just the thing, and I think it would be good form of me to relieve you from your pouting," Isaac said.

"Pouting? You think that's what I'm here doing?"

"Oh, yes, I certainly do."

Hugh chuckled. "Well, you could be right." He looked at Isaac critically. "Those shoes on your long, homely feet, just who would they belong ta, knowing I'm busy bloodying yours?"

"Ah, borrowed discreetly as the need showed itself. For the good of the Cause, you know."

"Good of the Cause, yes, I'm familiar." The mention lessened his mood again. Hugh pinched the crooked bridge of his nose between a thick finger and thumb—a longtime habit he hardly noticed anymore—and thought of their commanding officers. They molded and shaped this war, this "Cause."

He glanced to the north, to General Washington's headquarters. He couldn't see much of anything, but up there he knew the icy Schuylkill River rushed past that comfortable stone house and he'd bet it was warm in there tonight. He would give anything to dine in that fine house just once—his stomach turned at the thought. He hadn't eaten well tonight. But Washington's house had plenty of good food and he was damn sure the occupants weren't being choked out by smoke. Ah, well, he didn't want to begrudge them, they had a hard enough job. They all had a hard job. Hurry up and wait, and don't starve doing it, that was the common soldier's mission.

Isaac stamped his feet against the cold and after a few moments of silence said, "I miss my daughters."

"Daughters? You? Did you begin siring at thirteen? Or was it fourteen?"

"Margaret was born five years ago, when I was but twenty-two," Isaac said and blew into his fists. "And Elizabeth—Eliza," he added with a pleased look, "is three."

"And their mother?"

"Why do you ask?" Isaac looked away and tightened his lips. He straightened the thick sleeve of his wool coat.

Why not?

As if he had heard Hugh's thought, Isaac looked back at him, somewhere past his right shoulder, and said, "Now you, good man, what did you leave at home?"

"Captivity. I was a slave back in Virginia. It was my mother's doing."

Isaac's face softened and he was silent for a time. "Well, never apologize for existing, that's what I say. The Creator would take great offense, I should think."

Hugh expected more surprise out of Isaac at his shameful confession, but he had one correction for his friend. "The Lord."

"Our Creator."

Hugh shook his head, tired. "You win."

Isaac clapped him gently on the back. "Reveille will beat soon, my once-servant friend. Perhaps we should at least get our eyelids shut before that wretched sound knocks our asses out of bed."

"Goodnight, Isaac," Hugh said as his friend ducked back into the cramped soldiers' quarters.

Hugh had never spoken of his bonded servitude so easily before. Perhaps a warm house and a good honest day in the fields didn't look so bad a turn now from up here in frozen Pennsylvania. And, really, he had only moved himself from one master—who could beat him or end his life for running away—to another.

They had all discussed it, the soldiers had. Why they were here, what would happen if they ran, what would happen if'n they stayed. Each thought they knew the whys and wherefores better than the next,

26

and the conversation went 'round from one to another. And then they would stop and think on it, spitting on the ground and eyeing each other as they thought. Hugh knew the ones who talked the most and the fastest, using the terms philosopher and thinker before naming dead people like Socrates and Plato as they spouted sayings that made no sense to anyone but themselves, had the ideas of least value to him. Those were the soldiers every bit as unable to read their name—much less Socrates and Plato—as he was. But then the quieter ones would say, But you know—and their eyes would narrow and their brows would furrow—but you know, said they, there's a man who writes, a "Common Sense" it's called, and not the common sense your mother smacked into your head but the kind this man wrote in a pamphlet from Philadelphia and wherein it he tells us —"'Tis not in numbers but in unity that our great strength lies." And then another thoughtful one would add, "Time hath found us," and they both would nod, so you would know they were still speaking of the Common Sense, that it was a writing they both knew. One mention a man named Cicero—Hugh didn't think he had ever heard of Cicero—and said, "Extreme laws, extreme injustice..." There were a few of these, the ones that could read and had done the work of seeing to it that someone had made the good case for freezing and dying on this hill in Pennsylvania, and Hugh would think on their words most of all.

But then there were the quietest ones. He knew that these men would be swayed by no philosopher, no thinker that they had ever heard of, and they were leaving. But nobody ever said they were leaving. There were plenty of takers waiting to run, but like leaving Mama on her deathbed to hie off and get married, the guilt of the thing left them speechless and put a veil over their faces.

The quietest ones were leaving.

Well, he wasn't running, but he could still think of home, and he did. What did he leave in Virginia? What else did he miss, besides a full stomach and a good pair of shoes? He missed... he missed... smiles from girls who didn't want to sell him sex. He missed pettiness... fights that didn't end in death... More than anything, he missed his good humor.

He shrugged his shoulders and his cold, dry hand pushed a strand of blonde hair off of his hot, damp face. Sweat? On a night like this? He touched his face again. Ah, God, it was hot, and then his fingers slid over his cheekbones and he knew they were much sharper than just a few months ago. He thought maybe his chin was, too. It was an older man's face, older than when he had enlisted the summer before, soon after his twentieth birthday. Now he felt like he had one foot in the grave—a sore, bloody foot wrapped up in dirty cloth.

He pitied himself. Pouting, Isaac had said. Aye, good humor was long gone. Confessin' shame. And to be replaced by pity, all for himself, wouldn't do him a bit of good. He hadn't had the worst of it, of the misery this camp could mete out, so he thought instead about some of the poor fellows he had seen around camp who had, and he knew they were starving. He wasn't starving. He was hungry sometimes, disgusted at the rancid food he ate some days, or just plain fed up with bread and water.

What's for dinner?

— Shan't be more than firecakes and water.

Well, then…no meat, no soldier!

And the men who were running had no doubt seen themselves in the faces of the starving ones.

Hugh would not sanction the running and he could not imagine the starving, but he would pray for them all, just the same. He'd even be charitable and add in their commanding officers. He closed his eyes reverently as he was taught when he was a child, readying himself to plead with the Lord—Creator—*Ah, who cares?* The camp swirled around him until he leaned against the hut and prayed.

Please, Lord, help us send those British back ta their little island home, tails down and ears back, and let us all get back ta pettiness.

When he opened his eyes, the world looked the same. Except for one thought, *Never apologize for existing.* He liked that. He liked it a lot. "Thank you, Isaac," he whispered.

He ducked into his quarters just as the first wet snowflakes fell on his shoulders.

CHAPTER FOUR

Strong hands carried Hugh out into the cold. Snow fluttered against his face, melting and dripping paths across his cheeks while soft footfalls, voices, and the sounds of men huffing and groaning floated around him in the dark. Some noises were near, some floating far off. But one expulsion of gruesome breath blasted close by—much too close. He turned his head to the side and was sick. One of the disembodied voices said, "Oh, Jesus..." and Hugh's arm smacked the cold ground.

"Take it up."

"Bast'd vomited on me, Captain. We couldn't find a litter to carry this dead-weight giant on?"

"Now!"

A cold grip seized his right arm again and they carried him on through the night.

Some time later, he didn't know quite what day or what time it was, the darkness was replaced with murky light, and he squinted with burning blue eyes about the room where he had been placed. The rafters above his head were low and freshly hewn and a clean, narrow cot lay next to his. More logs and chinking of clay, sticks and rocks stared back at him from the neighboring wall. In the middle of that wall was a merrily burning fireplace.

A cloying, mocking perfume of death breathed over him when the door opened and closed as an officer left. *So, a hospital's where I've ended up. A cramped room where men come ta stink and wait and die.* He looked around for the source of the smell.

He found it three cots closer to the door. Not far enough to spare him. Not nearly.

There, a very still man, with every essential piece of him looking sunken and depleted, rotted away at black feet exposed by a turned up blanket. Hugh wriggled his feet out from under his own blanket. His toenails were long and dirty, smears of dried blood covered the top of his left foot. But no rot. Thank God.

Behind him a throat cleared and a man said: "Oh, ah, that gentleman is leaving us soon, he is. We've had assurances. I just pray they cut the poor, stinking leg off after they take him, not before."

Hugh grabbed the cot with weak hands, shrugging his shoulders and shifting his legs to turn himself to the sound of the voice. Pain sliced through every muscle. His skin felt as though the fire in the hearth had reached out while he slept and scorched him.

"'Do you do?" the man said, and smiled at him. Crooked brown teeth dangled from thick gums. He was sitting up on his cot, back resting against the wall. In his hands, a short knife hacked absently at a small piece of wood. Shavings dusted his lap.

"Lawson," the man said, introducing himself. "Here from Muhlenberg's Brigade, First Virginia." Lawson nodded at the introduction. "Our hospital is a quarantine now for the smallpox pricking. Those of us who are ill," he said, grinning as if the "ill" were in doubt while pointing to himself and a man in the next cot, "are now taking up your space. I assume you are with Scott's Brigade. You belong here?" The dark-haired Lawson cocked his head to the side and waited for an answer.

After searching the thick mud of his thoughts for a moment, Hugh replied, "Meglakin, Grayson's Regiment." His throat burned.

"McLaughlin, hunh? Have a brother Hugh?" Lawson asked and looked back to his work.

"I am Hugh."

The man looked up, a slow surprise moved across his face. He laid down his whittling. "Shared a tent with a Hugh McLaughlin for a short while, I did. Died early on though, I believe, maybe June or July. Illness if I remember right, wasn't it Robert?" he said and looked to the soldier pretending to doze next to him. When Robert didn't answer, Lawson threw the palm-sized piece of wood at him. The man groaned and opened one eye. "You remember McLaughlin, from the First Virginia, back in the summer?"

"Ah, yeh, shot and killed couple of months ago wadn't he?" Robert was very loud and stringy hair was plastered to his red, flaky pate. He scratched and it snowed onto his blue shirt.

"No, Hugh McLaughlin died early on."

Hugh closed his eyes, tired of hearing he was dead.

But there it was. He was dead, this stinking place was Hell—it had finally escaped up through his cabin's damnable fireplace—and now the minions Beelzebub and Belial taunted him in a long overdue payment for his sins.

"What Hugh? Aren't you Hugh? He said he was Hugh."

"He is Hugh, not that Hugh."

Two-who? Yoo-hoo. Me, Hugh? No you, Hugh. Shut up, shut up, shut up.

He looked at them again. The devil's imps were still talking, but they hadn't grown horns and forked tails. Around them, the room whirled sickeningly. *What Hugh?* He couldn't be dead, he didn't think he was dead, but if he were, there was nothing to be done about it now.

"Oh *Hugh* McLaughlin. No, sorry, only knew Daniel. Daniel McLaughlin from Capn' Moss' Comp'ny," Robert said. He glanced around and continued in a quieter, conspiratorial tone, "Died in a bad way, too."

Hugh didn't think to ask what the bad way was, his feverish mind was stuck on his own image of Daniel's death. Daniel, his baby brother, killed? Killed a "couple of months ago"? They hadn't been together since Daniel was six and he was fourteen. So how old was Daniel now? Wasn't he still a child, too young to be in the war? Eight or twelve or maybe older, just old enough? He counted again and again. Oh, damn this fever.

No, damn the court that took his brother from him when his family fell apart. Damn his mother who had let it happen. He had only wanted to keep him safe and happy and now he was dead.

"How old was this Daniel?" he asked quietly of the two men who were still disputing the finer details of the war, such as who served in which company and various other insignificant points of contention.

Getting no response, Hugh questioned the men again, this time much louder. The effort pounded through his head. The man called Robert blinked his rheumy eyes and quietly said, "About forty, I 'spose, why?"

The question hung in the air as Hugh's head dropped back to the straw mattress in relief and he returned to a still much-needed sleep.

* * *

31

Hugh woke again to see gray morning light slanting in through the one window at the other end of the hospital cabin. A fire popped in the fireplace. Some men laughed, some groaned and pleaded. Cots and bunks creaked under them and sleet pounded on the roof. The window showed nothing but wet winter sky. He wished he knew what else was happening outside these walls.

He had been moved while he slept to a bunk across the cabin, against the long wall. He remembered nothing of it. Another bunk jutted out of the wall above him and an arm hung over the side. The dirty hand swung back and forth in front of him, and then made a fist just as he heard the owner give a hearty laugh. The arm disappeared. Hugh wanted to see more of the room than that hammy fist.

He worked his muscles, expecting pain and getting it. But it wasn't so bad as before. Maybe he wouldn't die so soon after all.

He raised his head and looked around the room. More cots had been crammed in while he slept, all sagging under the weight of soldiers. Bunks lashed together three high lined the walls. They were all filled. No sign of Beelzebub and Belial. What was it they had been telling him? Hugh and Daniel McLaughlin, both dead? He and his brother? Oh, horseshit. Of course not. His cousins, then, Aunt Maggie's sons, Hughie and Dan?

Hugh had enlisted a bare few months after his Cousin Dan had marched out, leaving Maggie holding only her youngest son, Michael, and a flag Dan had made from old scraps. Little John and Katherine, orphaned children of Hugh's Uncle Daniel, had stood quietly on the porch watching him go. They had done the same when his Cousin Hughie left home the January before.

But they had joined the First Virginia. That wasn't the same regiment Beelzebub belonged to. Was it?

No. Certainly must have just been his fever, convincing him he was dead or dying and striking down his brother, too, for good measure.

Dust on the floor stirred as the door suddenly opened. A willowy young woman entered and hung up her brown cloak. She took the shawl from her head and settled it about her shoulders before she picked up a stool in one hand, a satchel in the other, and walked his way.

A hand reached out and grabbed at her coarse calico dress as she picked a path through the cots. She muttered a curse and snatched back the hem. Hugh smiled. He thought she might just swing up her satchel and beat the man with it.

He stopped smiling when he recognized her face, pale and framed by messy red hair. A camp follower. Maybe even one of those used-to-be women who sold themselves to the men for whatever they could get. Why was she here?

He closed his eyes, hoping she would go to one of the other men. He soon heard the stool legs clatter and scritch next to him. And then nothing, until he felt her take his hand and begin wiping him down with a damp cloth.

He looked again when she let go of him. Her red, cracked hands wrung out a rag in the basin of water near his bunk and a trail of droplets glistened on the shaky table. She stroked his arm with the icy cloth, up to his elbow, where she stopped when she realized he was watching her.

She plumped up her thin, colorless lips briefly before she spoke. "You know where you are?"

Sounded like a standard greeting for the ill.

"I'm in a camp hospital."

She pushed her unbound hair out of her face. "Very good." The rag dripped on his grimy shirt. "Are you feeling better?"

"You know how long I've been here?"

"Maybe over a week now, I don't know for sure."

His hand scraped across his chin and he counted up at least five days of growth.

She dipped the rag back into the water. "I see you don't meet my eye very well. You know what I do? Who I am?"

Yes, he did. More than likely that's why she was here, it was probably payday. Whores always came prowling on payday. He didn't say it, but he tried to meet her gaze. She had dark gray eyes, framed by thick lashes. Just last year, he would have thought them beautiful. While he stared into her eyes, her breathing slowed and she wetted her lips. She touched his face with the rag.

He pushed gently on her arm. "Why are you doing that?"

She pushed back. "I thought you might like it—"

He grabbed her wrist.

"A...a shave. I thought you might like a shave."

He let her go. "I'm well enough ta barber myself—when I have a kernel of privacy."

Her face colored and drowned out the sprinkling of freckles across her nose.

Damn.

"Why are you here? Dinna you have a family?" he asked her as she started to stand. He wanted to bite his tongue in half. Why did he insist on carrying trouble around on his back? Someone else's problems were always shifting around there, weighing him down.

And a woman's problems at that. You give them an inch and they go, dragging you in, batting their lashes, pouting their finest pouts. Before long the weight of it all would drop and no one would be there willing to help him. Some might stare or jeer, perhaps tell him how wrong he had shouldered it, *better luck next time*—but help, no.

He had been well-hardened against loading anything else on that didn't directly serve himself. That's when he had joined the war, for so many solid, self-serving reasons, and now he had begun to drop even that responsibility with his illness—now he didn't see himself serving any objective at all, lying on a bunk in the hospital.

But in the end, he was weak. He listened to her prattle on...

She told him that late last year she had married a soldier, and he had brought her here to Valley Forge with him. He died before long in camp, she thought maybe even before the cabins were built.

She touched her lips.

"Oh, yes, that's right," she said, because tents were still up everywhere, and even General Washington was still in a tent, that he had promised to stay in a tent, just like his men, until the cabins were built, even when he had that nice warm house to stay in.

Her husband had told her about his admiration for H'zexcellency, General Washington. But really, she just thought it was a silly thing to do.

But then her soldier died, and she had nowhere to go, so she pitched in even more with the laundering, the nursing, the cooking, and...whatever else she could do, so that no one would suggest that she had to leave.

While she was still speaking, Hugh closed his eyes and told himself he wasn't blatantly dismissing her. She quieted. He heard the rustle of her dress and hoped she was leaving, but then he felt two small hands on his chest, and when he opened his eyes, she was standing over him. She placed a soft kiss on his forehead and told him, "Maybe I'll see you again when you're out of here."

She walked away and slapped at another grabbing hand.

Hugh heard a familiar chuckle and his groan blended into the others all around him.

He sat up, shaky, and threw his numb legs over the side. He saw his feet touch the puncheon floor but didn't feel a thing. He pulled the blanket from his cot, wrapped it around his shoulders and looked up to find Tom Gillespy on an upper bunk along the adjoining wall, about four feet off the ground.

"Looks like you've got yourself a girl," Tom said.

"The kind of girl you'd send me."

"Is that an insult?"

They both stopped to watch a feverish-looking man throw off his blanket, stumble to the door and walk out into the sleet. Nobody seemed to notice.

Hugh looked back to Tom. "I've seen your kind of girl. Ugly as a mud fence after a flood, that's what I've been seeing."

"Looks like you've been seeing the women in your family, then. Where have they been about?"

Hugh narrowed his eyes. "Ah, mon, dinna do that."

"Right." Tom had the humility to sound embarrassed. He knew better than to say something like that, or at least he should. Tom knew the women in Hugh's family had been lost to him a long time ago. Lost as well as if they were dead.

But Hugh didn't want to think about that now.

Instead he tried to smile thinking of the two of them enlisting together in the war, on the same steamy Thursday in July. Owen Kelly had joined them the next day. They had all marched out double-time, young and foolish, from Augusta County, Virginia.

Now, Owen and Tom made Pennsylvania feel a little more like home. He was grateful for that. They knew each other like brothers. Still, Tom stepped in it every now and again. But Hugh was glad to see him.

A sudden, sick chill swept through him. He pulled the blanket tighter around his shoulders. "Anybody else ill?"

"From the hut?"

Hugh nodded. "Owen all right?"

"Fine. Isaac might cause you worry, though. Getting a bit spookier every day."

"Spooky?" *Hugh and Daniel McLaughlin, both dead...* Hugh shook his head. "That's an odd word. How so?"

Tom stretched out on the cot and linked his hands under his head. "Can't really say. Just seems that fellow is trying to catch too many rabbits with the same fist."

CHAPTER FIVE

Inside a wide circle of stones marking off the kitchen area behind the soldiers' huts, a dry pine log popped in the campfire and sent sparks flying into the cold night air. The fire glowed on the faces all around Hugh. Isaac concentrated on pouring lead into his ball mold, while Tom Gillespy threw his arms around in a wild imitation of the new Prussian drillmaster, Major General Frederick William August Baron von Steuben.

Benjamin Jenkins, a large man prone to drunkenness, whipped off his hat to salute Tom, who bowed slightly in return.

"For the difficulty Baron von Steuben had been caused," Tom said, "he cursed all the soldiers, the lot of them."

The wind changed direction and blew smoke from the campfire into Hugh's face. He put down his filled bullet mold and wiped at his stinging eyes.

The smoke didn't stop Tom. He waved it away, pushed dark hair out of his eyes, and continued with his story. "He cursed them in German. He cursed them in French. He even asked an interpreter for a fitting English censure and '*Sacre!*'"—Tom threw his hat to the ground—"'Goddamn de *gaucheries* of dese *badauts*! I can curse dem no more!' was the best he could string together. Can't rightly ignore that." Tom smiled and scooped his hat back up off the ground.

They cried with laughter as they growled with thick Prussian accents, "*Sacre!* I can curse dem no more!"

Hugh watched Isaac wipe tears away from his eyes with the palm of one hand, while the other held his mold. His laughter faded and he snipped the tail off of the cooled metal ball that slipped from his mold, and then deposited the smooth shape into a small leather pouch at his side.

Hugh looked from Isaac's thin fingers down to his own scarred and stubby ones that fumbled over the small tools. He worked better with fleshing and currying knives. He had apprenticed with Master Hogsett since he was fourteen to be a currier, dressing and preparing skins. Of course that, too, was delicate work, but the thick handles of the knives fit his wide palm and his strong arms knew just what pressure to use to turn out the highest quality skins.

While Hugh steadied the ball mold, ready to pour in the liquid metal, he was surprised by small hands coming to rest on his shoulders and the scrape and swish of rough fabric against his back.

"Ah, he's back from in hospital, he is. And is he fine?" a familiar, sultry voice said. The redheaded nurse. Her cold hand slipped across his neck, over his jaw, and up to his forehead. "Well, he's as cool as the evening." Her movements caused the bittersweet smell of perfume and unwashed clothes to drift around him. She leaned closer to his ear. "I'll be at the bake-house tonight."

He bristled at his helpless position of two full hands and an exasperating, cloying woman on his back. Working hurriedly, he filled the mold and laid it on a warm rock.

Benjamin cackled from across the fire. "I wasn't never in hospital, you can come set on, *er*, with me awhile."

Good, she got herself a customer. Hugh relaxed his shoulders, but the grip on them tightened. An ember popped out of the fire and landed at his feet as he reached his freed hands up to remove himself from the woman's grasp. A murmur of voices that had hushed when the man first spoke cautiously started up again and someone chuckled quietly.

"I guess you didn't listen to what I was saying to you, whore."

Hugh's head jerked up as Benjamin again hurled his words across the fire. Then he shrugged. *Probably drunk.* Many said that General Washington would someday order against any spirits entering the camp at all because of men like him, who would cause a disturbance or ruin parade or drill, and thereby drink them all into a dry camp.

With the man's taunt the redhead backed away from the ring of stones around the fire. She turned after a moment and walked away.

"What's wrong? Aren't you a *camp* whore, honey?" Benjamin called to her retreating back and laughed in a high-pitched chortle. He tried to poke a chuckle out of his neighbor with a thick finger. No one laughed.

Benjamin stopped and patiently looked at everyone around the fire. Into the uneasiness of the circle he finally called out to Hugh, "You think you get all the whores to yourself, pretty lady?"

"I think you can stop calling her a whore," Hugh countered without looking at him again, though he knew the man stood up and was possibly walking his way. Hugh reached for his mold, tapped out the ball and snipped it smooth.

He found he had ignored the man much too long when Benjamin's brick fist caught him across his right cheek. Hugh fell to the ground and his head smacked against a jagged rock. Embers flared and sparkled in front of his eyes. He heard a scuffle and a few muffled voices, and then felt a pain swelling in his head that drowned everything else out but his own thoughts.

Sonofabitch threw a cowardly shot.

When Hugh opened his eyes, he saw Isaac standing between him and Benjamin, holding the bigger man back. He wiped bloody grit from his mouth and asked: "What sort of a Devil's hag have you for a mother that she taught you ta fight in such a way?"

"Get your girly ass up off the ground and give me satisfaction," Benjamin shouted.

Hugh was too weak from his long fever to fight the man with his fists, words would have to be his weapon instead. With new resolve, he grasped a hand that Tom offered, pulled himself up, and then slowly straightened his coat. "So, you think I'm womanly, do you? My Aunt Maggie used ta say 'you doth protest too much, methinks.'" Hugh winked at Tom. "Think she got that from Mr. Shakespeare."

"And what does Mr. Shakespeare want to tell me?" Benjamin asked, sounding confident.

"Think on it awhile," Hugh replied.

The man's only comrade whispered loudly, "I think that means that you call him 'girly' because you're afraid you yourself are weak and womanly."

Benjamin shoved the bony Isaac out of his way without effort and cracked Hugh across the cheek again. Hugh's tailbone smacked the ground and blood wept down his face.

Benjamin rubbed his fist. "Will you find it hard to be so cheeky tomorrow with yours all split and swollen? Maybe if I knock out a few of those pretty teeth, the ladies might not swoon o'er your twirling Scots brogue when you give them your Mr. Shakespeare's sonnets. Your girly face isn't much to look at now, anyway."

Hugh struggled to his feet and stood eye to eye with him. He smelled brandy on the man's fetid breath.

"It isna a Scots brogue, you shit, it's the *mere* Irish altogether, so what do you want ta say now?" He wanted to cut off the man's chance to mock his Irish blood first, as many Englishmen and even some Scots did when they called them the *mere* or *wild* Irish. Hugh did have half Scots blood, too, but he'd be damned if he'd let on to this jackanapes.

Isaac picked up a piece of firewood and said to Benjamin, "Back up."

Tom rested his hand on the head of the tomahawk in his belt.

Hugh ignored his friends and stared hard at his opponent, wary of the next punch. He didn't know why he bothered telling Benjamin anything about himself. He had wanted to dance around him with words, shame the man into giving up with his sharper mind, as he was obviously sensitive to slights and slurs. But Hugh had failed. Now his only plan was to knock this big man off of his long legs and onto his ass.

He wasn't sure he had the strength.

Benjamin spread his arms out and laughed. "Ah, Ireland. The land of Popes and fairies—"

Hugh lunged at him and cracked his right fist across Benjamin's jaw. He had no power behind it, the man barely moved backward. Instead, he began to finger his darkly whiskered jaw, then he chuckled unpleasantly.

"Pretty lady, pretty fairy, with that wrist you won't make it through this war alive," Benjamin said, and laughed again. The derisive sound was cut short with a loud thud and a grunt came out of the man before he fell forward.

Isaac stood behind Benjamin, looking pleased with himself and still gripping the length of firewood—long, but not too big around—that he had used to whack him across the back, right below the shoulder blades. Hugh groaned. *Oh, God, right where it hurts like almost no other ta be found.* He nearly felt sorry for the man.

Isaac spat between his feet and narrowed his eyes. "If they're weaker than you, stay off them," he said to Benjamin, who lay curled up and moaning. Isaac's square, dark shoe pushed at Benjamin's leather box that had spilled open when he fell. A handful of white papers lay on the ground. A small tin flask, hidden beneath the layer of cartridges, peeked out of the box. It glimmered in the firelight.

Isaac laughed. "Oh, for the love of God, soldier, stop crying and dust yourself off. Your brandy didn't spill and your lady's long gone, she won't be coming by to give you tea and sympathy."

Hugh felt a needle of guilt at the mention of the camp follower. How many times had she been called "whore" tonight alone? *Camp follower.* Lord, wasn't he a confessing damn shame. He didn't even know her name.

Holding the sore side of his head, he left the groaning Benjamin and the laughing Isaac behind and went to search her out, though he told himself he didn't know quite why. He had a passing thought of enticing her into being their squad's laundress for a few pence. The men would consider that quite a coup. Some of them had rags still threaded together, sufficient enough to be recognized as clothing, right and proper. Put together with their worn haversacks and muskets, their officers might even say they were amply accout'rmented.

Too, the bake-house was as good a place as any to go. Close to the Provost where he was on duty later tonight and clear across camp from where the much stronger Benjamin lay on the ground. He didn't want to be anywhere near when Benjamin got to his feet. But he wouldn't mind meeting up with him again when he got his strength back.

Or maybe he just wanted to see her. Before he could stop himself, he thought of resting his sore head in her lap. He shook it away.

When he finally arrived, the bake-house was warm and bright. He stood on the cramped landing of the porch, out of sight, and sneaked a glance inside. Bread lay on boards around the hearth, rising for the next day, and the smell of the warm, yeasty dough drifted out of the half-open door. His mouth watered painfully.

A burly German barked at the bakers. His hands rested on his hips, at the string of an apron liberally dusted with flour and yellow meal. Hugh felt sick seeing the waste.

The man clapped once, short and loud, and he and the bakers moved to gather around an enormous table, sprinkled with more meal. A woman in a drab gray dress tended the fire behind them, her head covered with a dingy mobcap. She could have been the woman he was looking for, but he thought her waist too thick.

From a hidden corner the redhead appeared dragging a large broom across the floor. She headed for the door and he ducked back as she sent the dirt and crumbs flying out with a flick of the broom. She leaned her head out. Her gray eyes were steely as she said, "You. You came." And then she gasped. "Oh! What happened to your face?" She pulled a stained handkerchief from her waistband and handed it to him.

"Thank you," he said and pressed the cloth to his bleeding cheek.

He suddenly realized her guile was missing. Her thick hair streamed out from under a crooked cap and her pale face glimmered with sweat. She didn't smile or bat her eyelashes—she merely looked annoyed.

Where had the wanton woman gone to?

"Yes?" she prompted when he just stared at her.

No coy looks? No suggestive conversation? She had changed so much he didn't have any idea what to say to her now. He stood there and stared at her freckled nose, feeling like a fool. He found himself surprisingly disappointed by her brusqueness. She didn't want him anymore, it was plain. *Thrown over for a pence—or a dozen bakers?* he thought crudely, spitefully, and felt another niggling of guilt.

She waited another few seconds and then glanced behind her as the German voice grew louder. "In de ovens. Yes," the man said. Another loud clap. "All vight. Enough!"

"I can't stand here any longer," she whispered to him.

Just why had he sought her out to begin with? Or at least what had he told himself to put his feet moving here? Laundress? Silly fancy, his squad didn't have enough coin to offer her. A warm lap to rest in? Her name? Oh yes, that then—Sir Galahad. His perennial, damnable chivalry.

"What is your name?"

She blinked hard and let out a deep breath she had been holding. Her stiff spine relaxed. "That's what you got me standing here for? My name? Very well, Nellie's what they call me." She pushed gently on his shoulder to send him moving as she said, "Go, I have to earn my keep. I have a son in Philadelphia to provide for and this job came first tonight, I don't have time for you now." She looked him over critically. "Pity." She shook her head and a hint of the sparkle he had seen before was back in her eyes.

He smiled sadly and knew then that his guilt wasn't entirely for thinking badly of her—he liked having her wanting him and coming back each time he brushed her aside. But he had gambled and now finally lost, treating her indifferently for his own peacock pride. He had convinced himself she might even need him. She didn't.

"Off with you, before I lose what few pence I got coming to me," she said and shut the door on him.

He leaned against the railing of the porch and crossed his arms against the cold as a new thought came to him. *A son?*

CHAPTER SIX

The morning after the fight, Hugh dragged himself back toward his hut, clear across camp, from a long night on Provost guard duty. He thanked God the officers gave him only twelve-hour duty instead of twenty-four, but then again, they were probably faced with finding very few men who were well enough to serve an entire duty.

On the way to his brigade he stopped to watch the morning drill. Pink fingers of light streaked through the sky over the barely-risen sun.

"*Achtung!*" a crimson-cheeked man shouted across the frozen field.

Hugh had never seen him before. Large, loud, and neatly dressed in a crisp uniform, he owned a bulbous nose even rosier than his cheeks. It could only be Drillmaster von Steuben, the Prussian Tom had told them about last night.

"*Zwei zaehne?*" von Steuben asked.

The men lined up on the field seemed puzzled and stared at another man instead, a tall, slender French officer standing next to von Steuben. In the morning light, his angular face was etched sharply in shadows.

With a smile as he looked over the rows of ragged soldiers in front of him, the Frenchman quickly answered their look with a booming voice. "Baron von Steuben wishes to know how many teeth are left in your head." The tall officer stood silent for a moment and his heavy breaths fogged around his face. No one said a word. He grinned deeper. "He has asked you in German if you have two teeth. *Zwei zaehne*—two teeth, top and bottom." He strode along the front line as he spoke. "That will be enough to tear through your cartridge"—he held up the white paper packed with powder and shot, then ripped the top off with his teeth—"to prime your musket."

A few men burst into laughter at a sheepish, toothless grin from a soldier in the front row. He turned his head this way and that so they could all get a good look.

The interpreter shouted over them, "Again. Right hand to cartridge box! Seize cartridge! Quickly to the mouth!" The men and their drillmaster smoothly demonstrated the current task and moved on to the next. "Prime and shut the pan. Yes, elbow up. Right hand under muzzle."

Men not in training often found any excuse to pass close by this field while carrying out duties and now Hugh knew why. Here among the shouts, stomping feet, and cracks of gun blasts and laughter lived the deepest sense of accomplishment the soldiers had known in many months.

But his aching body urged him back to his hut. Hugh continued on his way across the frozen mud of the field and turned onto the road leading south to Valley Creek. He stopped a few times along the way, sitting on fat tree stumps to catch his breath and rub his legs. Standing sentinel all night had left him exhausted.

He had been released, at his own urging, from that inhospitable hospital nearly a week ago, after being there for over a month. His weak, aching muscles told him he was too rash in leaving and getting back to duty. But then he touched the tender split beneath his eye and thought back to last night. Being beaten hadn't helped him recover either.

Walking on, the rows of huts of his brigade came into view through a sparse stand of trees. He wanted to crawl into bed and wake up some time next week...

"Roll-call!"

Hugh heard the shouts and drums and quickened his step toward the huts. His leg muscles screamed at him but got him there in time to line up in front of his cabin. Six men from the squad were present. The officer marked his book, looked them over again and then moved along to take names from the next hut. After Hugh shrugged off his coat for another soldier to wear on duty, their corporal reached for Hugh's musket, gunworm ready to remove the charge. He looked at the gun critically, turning it over in his hands. "Clean your weapon, Private, and check it in with me at next beating."

Tom Gillespie mocked the self-important swagger of the corporal as he walked away, while Owen Kelly tossed Hugh a tin flint box. "I've heard we get coffee today. Start the fire, I'll find out where the biscuits are hidden," Owen said.

Tom clapped Hugh on the back. "Unless Hugh brought the biscuits home last night from the bake-house."

Owen raised a bushy red eyebrow. "The bake-house, you say?"

"Most certainly. He was last seen planning a rendezvous on its shadowy porch. With no less than our own sweet Nellie."

They both turned and stared at him, twitching smiles on their lips. Hugh lightly pinched the bridge of his nose. "Oh, och! Both of you go ta hell, I'm too tired for this baiting." He walked behind their hut, to the kitchen campfire, and scooped frost-covered kindling out of a box. He tossed back a few wet sticks. Smoke from other campfires drifted on the air, and—damned if Owen wasn't right—he even smelled coffee. He sat on a log next to the soot of last night's fire and dropped the kindling at his feet.

Owen and Tom returned just as the fire began popping and ashes drifted into the air. Owen sat next to Hugh, ran thick fingers through his wild red hair, rewrapped his head in his gray wool scarf, jammed his hat down on his head, and stretched his legs toward the fire. "Ah, my poor frozen toes." He squinted pale-blue eyes at Hugh. "So, are you going to tell us about your lady?"

Hugh stoked the fire and threw on another piece of pine. "She isna my lady."

Tom hung a pot of water over the fire. "She hasn't quite the reputation of a lady at all."

Camp follower. Whore. They were still belittling her. Hugh continued stoking the fire. "She has a son in Philadelphia and she's a widow trying ta make her way the best she can. She wants ta provide for that boy. You both know she's doing better than my own mother ever did. Yes, I'd say she's a lady with no truer sense of the word ta be found."

* * *

Later in the day, after a few hours rest, Hugh sat on his bunk, cleaning his musket. Tom poked his head in the bare doorway. "We are about to practice with the tomahawk. Loser throws in his brandy. Are you coming?"

"Of course."

Hugh snatched up his hatchet and followed Tom along the narrow road passing in front of the regiment. A chilling breeze ruffled Tom's shoulder-length hair. The afternoon sky was thick with smoke from blazing fires, the sun no more than a dim candle smothered by angry clouds.

They stopped at a stand of hardwoods overlooking Valley Creek. John Mote, a soldier from their squad, yanked his tomahawk out of a broad poplar. Owen sat on a stump off to the side. Stones were lined up many yards away from the tree and John walked back to toe the line. He pulled his arm back to throw the hatchet again.

Owen stood up and waved his arms. "No, no, no. Move those stones farther away. Throw like a man for God's sake."

John pushed the rocks with his feet and shook his head. When they were another ten paces away, Owen sat back down, satisfied. John sent his hatchet twirling end over end. It sunk softly into the tree.

Owen called out, "Hugh. On the line."

A light dusting of snow from the night before covered the matting of leaves under the trees. Hugh crunched them walking to the stones just as the sky darkened even more and a brisk wind blew through.

His shoulder ached as he swung the hatchet up and steadied it. He let it go with a good forward motion and the tip slid into the wood just above where John's had hit. He looked over smugly to where Tom stood next to Owen. Far behind them, Isaac leaned against a tree deep in the woods. Isaac watched them all silently and Hugh felt uneasy. Why didn't he just join them?

"Go on, Hugh, take another swing, you're wasting daylight," Owen said.

Hugh pulled his hatchet out and readied it again. Isaac still stood there, watching. Hugh missed on his next throw.

"Down by one," Owen yelled.

Fat snowflakes began blowing around on the wind and Tom's dark hair was dusted by the time he took his place at the rocks. Soon, the snow had picked up until it fell like a curtain hiding them from the world. Tom looked over his shoulder. "If this blizzard keeps up, do I forfeit my losses for my inability to see the damned tree?"

Hugh chuckled. "Nay. You forfeit your winnings for your lack of providence."

When their short burst of laughter died down, Hugh heard hoofbeats clocking on the frozen ground—solid beats of a slow walk. More than two horses, he'd say, but he couldn't see anything up the road in the driving snow. He soon heard creaking leather and low voices. The horses were nearly upon them.

Owen had his hatchet drawn and across his knees. Hugh reached for the sling around his shoulder and then thought of his musket sitting unattended on his bunk. There would be hell to pay if that were found. He pulled the hatchet from his belt. They waited. High black boots were visible first. Then a dark coat over white breeches appeared out of the snow. The officer walked with a spontoon spear lightly scraping the ground with each step. More soldiers on foot followed behind and one lone horse rode beside them. Hugh slid his hatchet back into his belt when he saw the colors of the Pennsylvania line, and then he heard a woman's voice raised in anger.

"Don't grab at me, I can walk on my own," she yelled.

Owen leaned in close and whispered, "What do you suppose they're doing?"

Hugh shook his head and watched the procession materializing out of the snow. More women appeared, each holding tightly to her own cloth-covered bundle and being escorted by a soldier. A few more horses plodded along.

Another woman, wearing a long brown cloak, said, "What do you know of propriety? Leading us out into a blizzard... You hopeless son-of-a-jackdaw, you know nothing about propriety."

Her soldier answered her, "Miss Nellie, the blizzard will only delay your departure. We will wait it out in the next brigade. None of us wishes to march you all the way out of camp in this weather."

"Miss Nellie," Owen whispered.

Hugh caught the flash of red hair peeking out from under the cloak when the woman flicked her head at the soldier's words. Hugh took a few steps forward and Owen grabbed at his arm. Hugh shrugged him off and Nellie turned to face him.

"Did you tell them?" she asked.

He walked close enough to be pierced by her gray eyes. They narrowed and hardened as she stared at him. "Curse and rot you, then," she said as if he had answered her, but she kept her stride and passed him by. Woman after woman followed. Some looked at him curiously, but none gave him a stare furious enough to melt the snow.

Except for her—Nellie, the prostitute, nurse, mother. He strode up the line after her until an officer put out an arm and stopped him firmly. She disappeared ahead of him into the storm.

The officer that had stopped him walked out of line. "Follow me, Private." He started off toward Owen, Tom, and John. Hugh walked slowly behind him.

No more women passed, only a few more horses, these wearing packsaddles. Silence settled in.

The officer looked them over and then walked to the tree marred by hatchets. He ran thick fingers along the grooves. "You will return to your regiment immediately or I will be forced to make note of your flasks of spirits and the gouges in this poplar."

They all saluted him, gratefully. "Yes, Sir."

With a nod, he turned and jogged briskly to catch up with the caravan.

Tom picked up his knapsack as Hugh sat down on the stump. "Did I tell them what?" Hugh asked. No one answered him.

Why were the women being drummed out of camp? What could Nellie have done? And what could he have told anyone to cause this?

He wouldn't admit it to anyone, but he felt something for Nellie. Oh, it wasn't romantic or any nonsense like that. It was something he couldn't quite name. Perhaps a puppy-hearted poet would know better than he.

The look in her eyes just now told him she felt something for him, too—contempt, or worse. It was just as well. Why worry over a woman when he'd do better ta occupy himself with surviving this war?

Watching Owen, Tom, and John walking away, Hugh heard more horses approaching, their pace as slow as the earlier procession. He walked to the road to catch up with his disappearing friends before he was reprimanded again and found that the three men had stopped to let the horses pass. Owen called back to him, "Pick up your step."

Virginia soldiers, two abreast on horseback, passed as he walked. Owen, Tom and John snapped to attention and whisked off their hats. Following their stare, Hugh looked behind him and there appeared more riders. He recognized the tall chestnut horse with the flowing mane and tail as General Washington's horse. The general himself sat atop, dressed in a dark cape. Snow dusted his hat and shoulders. Another officer rode next to him on a large-boned black horse. Hugh swung around and straightened his back, shaken by the sudden appearance.

Washington waved their salutes away and they gratefully put their crumpled hats back on. His cold-reddened face looked weary. "You should be under shelter," he said to them. And then to Hugh, "And you, without even the barest of coats for comfort. Find shelter, soldiers. Get to it." He turned to his companion. "More sick and frostbitten…" He shook his head without finishing and they continued on, apparently more concerned about the health of the soldiers than any rules of troop movement about camp. More of his Virginian guard followed along behind.

Hugh relaxed just before the tall horse slowly wheeled around again in their direction.

The general called out: "You have stayed." They watched him through the driving snow, waiting for him to say more. He looked uncertain and his horse stamped lightly underneath him. "Thank you." He turned and rode away.

CHAPTER SEVEN

Coffee had been a nice surprise that morning. Dry biscuits and a rancid stew of meat, puckered peas, and rice was expected for supper and no one was left disappointed. Hugh picked at the slime on top of the stew with his eating knife. It slid over a gray hunk of meat and caught on the side of the wooden bowl. He flicked it to the ground.

He squinted as he ate, irritated by the sun's glare on the fresh snow. The storm had gone as quickly as it came. Tom stood at the fire across from him, slowly stirring the slop in the pot, as if he thought he could stir long enough that an appetizing portion would somehow rise to the top. His look was hungry, bordering on desperate, while still bargaining for something better. Hugh felt badly for him. Tom made his choice and sat down.

Isaac appeared from the road in front of the cabins and loped toward the fire, crunching an inch of snow from the brief storm under his shoes. He dipped out stew indiscriminately from the pot and sat next to Hugh. "Learned something about the exiled ladies," he said. "Seems if they were found to have questionable ties to Philadelphia they were put out as possible spies." He took off his cocked hat.

"Did they find out about Nellie's son living in Philadelphia?" Hugh asked.

"Perhaps they did." Isaac shrugged his shoulders and shoveled stew into his mouth.

Hugh nodded and pinched the bridge of his nose. Staring at the fire he asked, "And how did you come ta know about her son?"

"Oh, well, I didn't, but I assume that would be as good a reason as any other."

Hugh turned away from Isaac. "Tom!"

Tom looked over to Hugh and wiped his mouth with the sleeve of his coat. "What?"

"Who told you I was meeting with Nellie at the bake-house?"
"Ah... Isaac and John, I believe."
Hugh turned back to Isaac. He was gone.

Over an hour later, Hugh and Owen ambled down the narrow road to their hut. Bright sun slanted in on their left, shining on the rows of nearly empty cabins on their right. Most of the snow had melted away into mud in front of the sun-drenched doorways. It drizzled from the eaves.

Owen shook dice in his hand. Hugh knew Owen was eager to shoot them tonight and win the bottle of brandy he had missed out on earlier today, but he was quickly becoming annoyed with the constant clacking.

A hundred yards away from the cabin, they heard a muffled gunshot and a man's scream. Hugh stopped short for a few seconds and then sprinted down the road toward the sound, nearly tripping on his oversized, pilfered shoes. Owen jogged slower behind him.

The shrieks grew louder as he ran, while casting quick glances in and around the empty cabins, and were nearly deafening when Hugh reached the doorway of their hut. He grabbed the jam and swung himself to a stop.

Isaac sat on his bottom bunk, a musket on the dirt floor at his feet. The smell of burnt gunpowder filled the room. Blood seeped through the fingers of Isaac's large hands, cradling the left side of his head. His screams quieted when he turned his wide green eyes on Hugh, but his mouth still opened and closed, soundlessly. *Like a bloody, hooked fish.*

"What in God's name did you do?" Hugh shouted. He didn't intend to sound cruel, but his heart slammed against his chest and he felt bile biting the back of his throat. "Well?" He went to his bunk and pulled down a shirt hanging from a peg on the wall.

Isaac took his crimson hands away from his head and stared at them. A thin spray of blood pumped from his temple. "I need to be there. I just miss them," he whispered.

"You what?" He couldn't have heard right. Hugh pressed the shirt to Isaac's head. Blood had already thickened in his black hair. Hugh felt slow. His hands shook.

"I checked it for repair. Then I dropped it, cleaning, you know."
Owen walked in. "What the hell?"

Hugh looked at him in the doorway and wondered if he looked as pale as Owen did. "He's shot himself, the simple bastard. Go, run for the captain and be quick about it. He's with the drum major at practice. Go!"

Isaac pushed Hugh's hands away and stood up, swaying. "No!" He sat back down, hard. "No. Please, don't go."

Owen was already gone.

Hugh nudged at the gun with the toe of his shoe, as if it were a snake that may or may not be dead. It moved a few inches across the dirt floor. No hissing, no slithering. His body relaxed. Isaac had a mild wound from an accident, no more.

But acrid smoke still filled his nose.

"You were cleaning a loaded gun, were you?" He finally brought himself to pick up the musket. "And my gun at that." He had left it on his bunk before the snow and never came back for it. Oh, Good Jesus, how could he have been be so stupid?

From under the wadded up shirt, a small trickle of blood still seeped down to Isaac's chin. His eyes were flat and dull. A new anger welled up in Hugh, and he had a brief, uncontrollable image of smacking Isaac across the head with the butt of the gun. It was a sight more disturbing than the one he had first burst in on.

Hugh closed his eyes and tried to control himself, but couldn't stop his rage completely. He felt a clinging vulnerability in Isaac that, frankly, scared him. "What's the matter with you? You stupid, simpering sonofa..." When he opened his eyes, Isaac was staring at the floor.

"I just wanted to clean your gun for you. It was left there," Isaac said, pointing across the cabin to Hugh's bunk, "half done. I thought I would be a friend, like you've been to me."

"I didna leave it loaded." *Did I?*

A new look surfaced in Isaac's eyes that said he didn't.

Heavy footfalls outside the door saved Isaac from another tirade and Hugh lost his chance to find the truth. At least for today. A private from one of the surrounding squads stepped into the room and looked around dispassionately. Two more men stood in the doorway, merely curious.

"We heard a shot and some yelling. You seen anything?" the soldier said to Hugh, and then looked beyond him to Isaac sitting on the bunk. The man grinned over browning teeth. "What were you trying to hit, the shoulder?" Isaac didn't answer and the man nodded, his dark brown eyes creasing with morbid humor. "Yep. The shoulder would maybe get you outta here if'n it was shattered. And maybe only on furlough. Wouldn't hardly push a plow no more, though, would you? Head wound won't get you far." He shook his head. "Gotta think things through better."

The three men left just as Owen returned with Captain Smith. The captain's face was ice hard. He took off his hat and threw it on the floor. "What in God's name happened here?" He looked at Hugh, Owen and then to Isaac again.

Isaac straightened his back. "Sir, I lost control of my gun while cleaning it. I neglected to remove the charge, sir."

Hugh watched the captain kneel on the bunk while Isaac was speaking. Looking for the shot, no doubt. Hugh's shot. He readied himself to be disciplined severely for neglect of his weapon.

Captain Smith picked at the bunk's frame and splinters fell to the mattress. He pulled a short knife from his belt and dug at the wood until the lead ball came free. Standing next to the bed, he bounced the ball in his hand. "You are to have re-instruction from your corporal in proper handling of arms, for three weeks. You will both undoubtedly be brought in for courts-martial."

"Both, sir?" Isaac cast a quick glance at Hugh.

"You, Private, to assess your fitness, and your corporal for his dereliction," the captain said. He removed the bloody shirt from Isaac's head wound and frowned deeper. "Get that treated and bound, immediately."

* * *

It was an accident, nothing more.

Isaac would be bandaged, learn to be more careful with his arms—that would be that. Hugh reached up to pinch his nose and his elbow smacked into Tom, lying next to him on the bunk. "Pardon."

Tom grunted and turned over.

No one had to know that Hugh's gun was the one that went off. That he was suspicious of how—and why—Isaac happened to shoot himself. It was mere suspicion. What good did that do anybody? Better to let the officers find the truth. Yes, that was being a good soldier.

Let the officers find the truth.

CHAPTER EIGHT

Winter had finally slinked away from Camp Valley Forge, utterly defeated; and now the sun of a spring day shone down on thousands of soldiers. Each stood ramrod straight, musket propped smartly against his shoulder. They blanketed the camp's parade ground. General Washington patiently inspected the lines from atop his graceful horse, and for the first time since any of the soldiers could remember, they were exultant. They shouted until their throats ached.

"Long live the King of France!"

General Washington attempted a smile. They had never seen one from this particular man before.

And so again they shouted, "Vive la France!" and "Huzzah! Long live the thirteen united states!"

General Washington had ordered a celebration in honor of the fledgling country's newest ally, France, who had thrown down yet another gauntlet with their historical enemy, now America's enemy, Britain. They had declared the United States independent—independent of the tyranny of George III.

To honor their own accomplishments, as well as the French surprise, an artilleryman was signaled that it was time to step to his weapon and light the powder. Roaring canon fire soon echoed across the field, along the Schuylkill River, and out of camp. An enfilade of musket fire took its place. Slowly, each soldier added to the smoky haze, firing his own musket in turn.

When the thousands of men had finished their running fire, they gave a hearty "Huzzah!"

With Drillmaster Baron von Steuben's training, now they could beat the British back until the French arrived on America's war-torn shores. They felt victory was now written in stone. Their Cause had gained legitimacy abroad. They toasted their impending victories with a celebratory taste of rum.

Hugh swallowed his distaste for the French with a nip of sweet liquor, vowing to leave his old prejudice behind today in favor of a quick, certain victory. He—and most of the men surrounding him—had been children during the French war, and they would all now have to see their old enemy as their new best hope. War made the strangest bedfellows.

He followed along as the buoyant army gradually dispersed amid the songs, shouts, and cheers of the grateful men. Thousands of privates and non-commissioned officers soon streamed down roads and footpaths to their brigades, leaving behind the bright sounds of triumphant fifes and drums.

"Huzzah! Long live General Washington!" called one young private as he missed a footstep, bumped into Hugh, and then caught onto his comrade's shoulder for guidance.

"You, sir, have had more than your allotted gill of rum, sir," Owen said to the man. He didn't get a response. "Four gill of rum have undoubtedly found your empty gut and made an uncomfortable home, sir." Now the drunken private was nearly out of sight. "'Tis likely they should soon be leaving their new home, sir, and returning from whence they came."

"Sir, yes, sir," someone called.

Hugh laughed loudly, although the exchange was little more than mildly amusing. But he was ready to laugh out loud with the least invitation. No one was freezing today. Not many were hungry, no one present was ill and, better still, not one camp hospital was in view. Every man in sight was fully dressed and each and every one of the two-dozen or so in their small group had a pair of shoes.

Hugh supposed others had noticed, too. A red-nosed man to Hugh's right shouted, "Long live the Patriot!"

Hugh and Isaac walked to their hut, while Owen kept on down the road, whistling to himself on his way to assemble for duty.

"A fine day," Hugh said quietly as the two entered the low doorway. "The war is turning this spring, isna it? And without even so much as a skirmish."

"Yes, it is. And it's thankful we are, too, that you're so fit and sound these days," Isaac said. "As for the skirmish, I think I recall...I can't readily name the combatants...but I do believe I stepped into a minor skirmish and saved someone from himself, once upon a time."

Hugh thought of Isaac standing in the firelight holding a length of firewood and smiling at the downed Benjamin.

He dropped onto his bunk and tried to grin at his friend. He couldn't. "I dinna know what you're talking about." He watched Isaac sling his knapsack about his shoulders and straighten his coat.

"It will come to you. By the by, I'm on duty now, so you may have this whole place," Isaac said with a dramatic sweep of his arm, "alone, for the next few moments. Enjoy."

Hugh admired the vibrant colors of Isaac's tailored uniform, a rarity in camp. "You look so like an officer. Why did you no' buy a commission?"

"Distasteful. But I wish I could have bought my way out of court-martial. Such a demeaning process." Isaac shook his head as he straightened his uniform again. His large, light green eyes sparkled as he impishly added "Sir" and then left the room.

Hugh's bed of the last few months was the lowest of the three bunks covering the left wall of the cabin. Above this cramped, moldy, straw-stuffed space that he shared with Tom was the bunk of John Williams and Patrick Boyd, whose collective thrashing about each night in search of comfort never failed to keep everyone else awake.

Owen Kelly and Richard Splender were assigned to the topmost bunk and were usually quiet throughout the night. Isaac, Smith Thompson, Thomas Coleman, Michael Golleher, John Mote, and Ambrose Jones occupied the right wall of the cabin. The top of Isaac and Smith Thompson's bunk was still cracked and splintered.

Along the back wall, between the two rows of bunks, was the smokiest fireplace Hugh had ever had the misfortune of living with. Many of the cabins were built with the fireplace in the east wall, instead of the north wall to the rear as in their hut. That might have been more comfortable, Hugh thought. Confessing shame, but it was too late to worry about that now.

He lay on his bed and tapped his fingers on his chest. He closed his eyes, but sunlight streamed in the bare doorway and over his face. He looked over to Ambrose and John's bunk, nearly reaching the ceiling and hidden in the shadows. No, he didn't want to lay there either. He had only been alone for a few moments and already he was bored. He had duty later and should be resting for it, but he didn't feel like sleeping. He went out the door in search of the rest of his squad, knapsack on his back.

He came across them at an old privy area of their brigade. Owen, Tom, John Mote, and another soldier, a short, blonde stranger, stood at the head of a skeletal black horse sprawled on the ground. Behind them were a mound of dirt, a shallow hole, and three shovels standing with tips sliced into the ground.

"Does a dead horse weigh more than a live one, you think?" Tom asked the others.

"This sorry beast doesn't look to weigh more'n the bag of feed it would have taken to keep her alive to begin with," Owen replied. "But she must still weigh nearly a thousand pounds."

Hugh said, "Looks like a half-tho'sand ta me."

Owen looked up. "Ah, Hugh. Give us a hand burying this stinking nag, will you?"

Hugh lifted his knapsack from off his back and dropped it at his feet. "Send John for more rope and I'll be thinking about it."

John, never much for words, loped off silently.

Hugh walked to the hole and looked in. "What you burying here, a blade of grass?" He grabbed up a shovel and then nodded at the stranger, putting out a hand. "Hugh Meglakin, Private."

The soldier wiped dirt off on his pants and shook his hand firmly. "Steven Hyde, Virginia militia. Just arrived in camp and they put me on this shitty detail while the officers are celebrating at the theater." He quickly continued, "Good God, man, what have you done with those hands to give them such hell?"

Hugh inspected his thick fingers casually, surprised by the blunt question. He'd never considered the hard skin and scars on his hands remarkable; most men worked hard and had the hands to show it. He absently rubbed a finger along a deep groove in his right thumbnail. "Dressing skins isna so tough on the hands," he said, "it's the back that takes the torture."

"A currier, then? Yes, that's tough work. I've seen it done. Get some good skins?"

"Deer's good ta work with, but it's hard ta find. I see more cowhide than anything." The conversation drifted off and Hugh jumped in the hole to shovel more dirt. Tom joined him.

Steven looked over at Owen. "That friend of yours that just came by, Isaac Moore, what's he do to keep himself in new uniforms?"

"Isaac is a gentleman farmer, waiting to take over his father's plantation," Owen said.

"Oh, that sort."

"Good sort," Hugh added without stopping the shovel.

"Good sort, sorry," Steven said. "Well, then, I guess he's improved his temper?"

"His temper, you say?" Owen asked.

"Used to know him in the militia, back early last year. He was always in some fight or another. Got the news in February, and some say he didn't speak to a soul until spring, at that time fistfights were his only conversation. Cap'n didn't take too well to all that disruption. But I don't think Moore much cared."

Tom stopped and leaned on his shovel. "I'm not following you. What news?"

"The news about his wife," Steven replied. "I don't really know the man, hadn't ever passed more than a few words with him, but most of us were told, around the way, when the news came in."

Hugh silently shoveled and recalled conversations he'd had with Isaac over the past few months. He realized now that something always prevented Isaac from talking about his wife.

Well, if Isaac wishes this kept for himself, we certainly shouldna be gossiping like women about the mon.

He was about to say as much to Steven and Owen when he heard, "Lost her in a fire, poor chap. British sacked her father's place tearing through New Jersey, that's all I know that's not speculation."

Hugh slung a shovelful of dirt over his shoulder. What had Isaac said the night of the fight? "If they're weaker than you..."

That's why he never talked about his wife.

A short while later, John returned with the rope and two more soldiers. Hugh pulled himself out of the hole, made at least two feet deeper while he reflected on Isaac's long string of strange behavior.

A familiar, ruddy face caught his eye when he straightened. "Edward!" he said.

His Cousin Edward lunged forward, laughing in surprise, and threw his arm about Hugh's neck. It was a clumsy embrace. "Private Meglagin. Half-aboot across the continent, and here you are, haunting my side. And by God, you're as thin as that dead nag," Edward said.

Talking excitedly together, their brogues thickened.

"Private Meglakin. Didna they tell you there in Virginia that we were starved here this winter? Seeing as you have a bit o' pork still upon your backside, you havena been here long."

"I've just arrived. And we didna know, indeed, aboot the miserable conditions here. For all we hear aboot is the great routing we're giving the lobsterbacks. I've found that isna quite true, either."

"What then aboot the family? How have they come along, I'd like ta be knowing. John? Charles? William?" Hugh named off each of Edward's brothers in turn.

"John's home in Bedford with Father and Mother. Charles and William are both serving together as much as they can, in and oot of regiments like fleas swap their victims. For a few years I've been traveling Augusta County, south of Staunton, most times."

"Staunton, you say. Then you've seen Aunt Maggie! How is the sweet ol' dame?"

"Sorry ta say, she isna quite the same after losing Hughie and Dan last year."

Hugh's chest tightened and his mouth went dry. After a few seconds of silence, he left his cousin behind with a thin excuse, grabbing up his pack and heading to the cabin.

"Hugh!" Edward called once, but Hugh continued on, alone.

He worked no more that day. Instead, he lay on his bunk, cursing the fates that would take two such fine, young men as Dan and Hughie, then imagining the freedom he would feel if he were to leave this encampment and this war behind, creeping past houses neatly to the sides of the road he absconded on, housing families happily ignorant of his plight and his resentment towards them and the Brits and his own officers right now celebrating their future *coup d'etat* with laughter and bright music.

He chewed on the sudden anger he felt at hearing of his cousins' deaths until he fell asleep.

* * *

"I've never felt so strongly that I might die here." Hugh said quietly, looking at the straw ticking poking out of the bed above him.

In the dim firelight, Tom turned and propped himself on an elbow. "Here in camp?"

"Nay, here in the war. 'Tis almost a certainty."

"A stubborn Irishman like you? The enemy would have to get past your dagger-sharp tongue first. I'd say they would surrender."

"Edward brought news that Hughie and Dan are both dead."

"Ah, Hugh, no, don't say. They were such good men."

Hugh glanced at him. "No' around quite long enough ta leave a mark, though, were they?"

"Now that's no way to be talking. *You* are thinking of them, aren't you?"

Hugh threw his legs over the side of the bunk and cradled his head in his hands. "I know what it is now that stinks so badly in this camp. You thought 'twas the privy, but it isna. 'Tis black bitterness, is what it is. It hovers over the camp like smoke from a wildfire."

"Isaac," Tom whispered.

"Aye, and a tho'sand other men just like him." Hugh looked back at him. "When we slipped and slid up this slushy blood-soaked road of soldierin' November last, remember the men hollered, 'No blood, no soldier'?"

"I do."

"That's what was taken from us. Our life's blood. Oh, no' the blood from our feet and our fingers, but the very things that keep us alive. Our families, our dignity. We were abandoned here, as much as our families are still abandoned back home. As if...as if we were toy tin soldiers left forgotten on the floor when the rains dried up and the careless child clambered out inta the muddy yard ta play instead. The citizens are'na grateful. Congress isna grateful."

Tom nodded his head and then lay back down. "They didn't even care enough to send food."

"And they dinna care enough ta get money home ta the families. What are they doing back home? How are the wives getting along?"

Tom shrugged. "They're pushing plows the best they can." He added with a smile, "Women often make exceedingly able husbands, you know. Too, they can appeal to the courts if they're in desperate need. You fearing for your family's welfare, are you?"

"I do wonder how Jane's getting along. And Daniel, too"

"Ah, missing the rascals."

"Aye."

That was a lie. He had no longing for the broken family he left behind. Too much bitterness tagged along with it—and he felt as much abandoned here as he had six years ago when his father died. His mother had destroyed his family by leaving them to the wolves in judges' clothing, so he had a hard time longing for what no longer existed. It was more the idea of family that he missed. A whole and happy family. The one he used to belong to.

He tried to picture it and then thought it strange that he should think now not of his mother or his sister, or even poor Aunt Maggie grieving for her sons, but of the young black-haired girl he met just before leaving Virginia and marching north.

Her father had brought her to the plantation where he toiled nearly unnoticed by the better folk—insignificant, a fixture of the plantation not much different than a field of wheat or a saddle hanging in the stable, and her father had treated him as such.

He was used it. The sting had nearly been worn out of him.

But the little girl had been watching him, and listening, unnoticed, while Hugh and Tom talked of going off to fight. When he finally saw her standing there, staring at him with innocent brown eyes, she said, "Please come home. Don't get hurt." So young—not more than five or six—to already know the dangers that come with war.

He didn't even know her name, only her father's, a one very wealthy Mr. Gwin, an officer in the militia. Captain or Major or some such.

She was what he thought of. Of innocent childhood and a sweet little girl being frightened for a stranger, a servant. It had made him feel like a hero even before his first march.

Now, it only made him smile. That was just as good. Maybe he still had one hand on his old humor.

"Tom?"

Tom's heavy lids fluttered open a crack.

"Do you recall the pretty, dark-haired little girl? Just before we left? The one who knew that men who go ta war get shot. You recall, dinna you?"

Tom's eyes closed. "No."

Hugh lay back down, the worst of his hand wringing over with. The girl convinced him, across all these miles, that he would, stand or fall, fight this war as far as God would allow. There were children at home depending on him to bring peace to their valley again. How could he let them down? For his entire lifetime, war had tread its thick heels across their lands and it had to end. He had to believe that this war would be the death of all wars in America—and so, worth fighting and dying for.

But he wanted a chance to enjoy that peace, too.

He wanted a farm on the banks of Dry River. He wanted a strong wife to give him a son to pass it to. And that was all. He wanted no other responsibilities, no more war, no death, no resentment, no regret. With the exception of war, it was a life that he knew well until he was fourteen. It was the life his father had, before he died.

CHAPTER NINE

New Jersey
June 1778

The scout had done a damn fine job.

The detachment of soldiers had followed his directions and soon found the swollen stream, winding its way through stately trees at the edge of a forest. The water was clear and sparkling and after it left them it rolled through the pastureland of the farm they were about to camp on. It promised some relief from the cloying heat, which effectively answered the crucial question of where to pass the hot night.

The officers, after hurriedly washing off in the stream just before dusk fell, marched as regally as disheveled, road-grime covered men could to the large house at the edge of the pasture. Swords banged against their thighs. Hugh watched some of them straighten their unruly hair as they approached the house.

Theirs was a small detachment traveling light: No wagons, no baggage, no tents. The men were to sleep on their arms, so as to be ready at a moment's notice to march or fight, and they dropped gratefully, wherever was convenient, as they watched their commanding officers approach the white house drenched in the reds and oranges of a setting summer sun. The house, neatly trimmed in black, perfectly symmetrical in every way, and even fenced and landscaped with lilacs and roses, was enough to make any road-weary traveler homesick.

What was worse, the humidity from the day's rain cloaked them all in a smothering blanket of heat. And indifferent to their suffering, summer's creatures sang from deep inside the looming, darkening forest as their biting, bloodsucking cousins attacked the sweating bodies trying to find rest. Hugh found his own place to spread out, under the trees, and he smacked at the mosquitoes while he listened to Owen and

Isaac complain about the heat.

Before full dark fell a few of the lesser officers returned, the rest no doubt invited by the patriot homeowner to a civilized meal in the manor house. The returning officers called out greetings as they strode toward the tree line, as others began to sing in a chesty bass:

Gallants attend, and hear a friend
Trill forth an harmonious ditty:
Strange things I'll tell, which late befell
In Philadelphia City.
'Twas early day, as poets say,
Just when the sun was rising,
A soldier stood, on a log of wood,
And saw a sight surprising.

By the time they reached the bank of the stream, dozens of other laughing voices had joined in:

As in a daze, he stood to gaze,
The truth can't be denied, sir,
He spied a score of kegs, or more,
Come floating down the tide, sir!
A sailor, too, in jerkin blue,
The strange appearance viewing,
First damned his eyes, in great surprise,
Then said some mischief's brewing.

These kegs now hold the rebel's bold,
Packed up like pickled herring:
And they're come down to attack the town
In this new way of ferrying

Singing continued into the night, although unfortunately many of the finest voices dropped out early and opted to sleep instead of reveling. Soon replacing the brigade's lighthearted songs, night sounds settled in with the full darkness, including the occasional owl's call, *Wahu! Huda.* The trickling creek sang faintly in the background.

Far off, the calling owl's large wings soon spread and clapped slowly as it let go of its perch at the edge of the woods to descend on a small, unsuspecting pasture animal. After a silent moment following the swoop of the bird. Isaac continued the story he had been sharing with Hugh and Owen.

"I left my family as helpless as that little rabbit in a countryside full of predators," he confided dramatically, looking up into the trees the owl had returned to.

Owen spit out the blade of grass he had been chewing on and waved at Tom through the trees. He called out, "On my way." Hugh smiled at him but felt badly for Isaac, who had unknowingly chased him off. "Excuse me, please," Owen said to them before he walked away, swinging his knapsack over his shoulder.

When he was gone, Hugh said, "Really, Isaac, I think the owl just caught a mouse, no' a rabbit. See, a rabbit could bolt quicker than any mouse, and it's much ta heavy for another—"

"For the love of God, man," Isaac exploded. "Could this not be fodder for your bloody wit?" He strode away to the edge of the stream.

Hugh regretted his flippant tone immediately, especially as he watched Isaac kneel on the grass, his head low. He decided a solemn apology should be given when his friend returned. *Hugh, you are an utter ass. The man was just confiding in you that his wife was murdered by the enemy because he wasna there ta protect her. An utter ass, Hugh.* He closed his eyes.

When he heard Isaac return a few moments later, he squinted one eye open, surreptitiously watching him to determine his mood. It appeared that his earlier anger had fled. Now his chin was nearly resting on his chest, and in the light from the brilliant moon hanging low in the southern sky, his high, sunburned forehead was furrowed into deep groves.

Hugh was lying on his back, his worn, dirty knapsack under his head, his knees drawn up. He had had to change position more than a few times to avoid the forest's vast root system. Isaac was barely four feet away, his back resting against a massive twin oak tree.

"I ken I'm no' so amusing as I sometimes think I am. And I'm no' so much for thinking before speaking. Now, you were saying?" Hugh prompted.

Instead of an answer, a long, heavy silence settled in and Hugh nearly drifted off to sleep when Isaac said in a low, nearly unrecognizable voice, "I want to know who the bloody bastards are."

"There's no way ta be knowing," Hugh said without opening his eyes.

"I thought of little else the entire, miserable winter. Hell, it haunted me even before. That's why I reenlisted with the Continentals after leaving the militia. Then at Brandywine, I thought I had my chance. I cursed every red-coated bastard I saw, and took two of them out. At least I was doing something. At camp, I had nothing. I could do nothing. I couldn't protect my family; I couldn't feed my family; I couldn't send the British bastards to hell, nothing. But now maybe I'll find the whoresons."

Hugh kept quiet and left his friend to his thoughts. He had never heard this from him before and the stress showing in his face made Hugh more than a little uneasy. A man with a devil riding him could be a danger to himself in so many ways, even in the best of times—this was not the best of times.

"Eliza was hiding in the old stable," Isaac said, staring at the moon. Hugh recalled that Eliza was his youngest daughter. Isaac turned to him. "No one knew. That old place wasn't used any longer. Hell, it even frightened the children, it was so decrepit. But there she chose to hide. Little darling. Did I tell you about her? Yes?

"Well, Peggy, my wife, was frantic for her. Called and screamed and nearly went wild from what her father described. She was convinced our little one was in the flames, perhaps retrieving a doll or such. She died going in to find her. That's the kind of mother she's always been." His voice rose and wavered. "I'll find the bastards." A man lying nearby lifted his arm from across his face to look up at him.

Hugh was worried. They were even now resting from a march on the British. They would catch up to their rearguard in perhaps only a day or two.

They were eager. The winter had been a long and tedious time, but they had learned to fight, and by damn, that was what they were going to do. They would make a fine showing and they were thousands strong. That was the key. They could march and fight before—in ragtag groups of twenty or perhaps as strong as forty, so a few could boast to fight as an entire company, none as an entire brigade.

But they had left that shame behind with their bare feet, sunken bellies and ragged clothing on the training field at Valley Forge. Perhaps now they could run the British off in only a skirmish or two more. Maybe they could even be done with this war before another winter set in, and be sent home to stay. Someday his children could proudly say,

"My father helped win the greatest war in history in 1778." And so could Isaac's daughters. He could only hope that that would slake Isaac's thirst for vengeance.

They were all eager, but none could afford to be rash. He tried to gently broach the subject. "If you fash yourself with it, it could turn out badly. Anger this deep can turn back on you, and vicious at that, dinna doubt, friend," Hugh said.

"You need to smooth out that brogue, Hugh-boy, I can barely understand you," Isaac said, sounding more himself.

"I said—"

"Oh, for the love of God, I heard you, I just think you're a bit too young to be lecturing me about this matter. You're hardly off your mother's bosom, and you're to tell me about the world?"

Isaac's eyes were wide and pleading, reminding him of the day of his accident. Hugh looked off, away from the trees, intending to watch the dancing of the fireflies. Instead, he remembered the blood spraying from Isaac's temple. He put his hands over his face. Why would Isaac try to disable himself to leave the war if he wanted to kill Redcoats? He pinched his nose. *Sometimes a bitter man doesna make sense.*

Hugh had had his own unfortunate experience with bitterness, and it had seemed earned and more than appropriate, too—at the time. Perhaps his pain and Isaac's weren't equal, but he decided to share his own misguided arrows with his grieving friend anyway. That's what he did best—talk. A lot.

"Six years ago my father died," Hugh began.

"My condolences."

Hugh waved his hand in dismissal. "That's just the way," he continued. "After my father died, my mother gave up on us children, my brothers and my sister and me. I should have seen at the time that it was all too much for her. But I didna. She let the court take over our raising and they put me with another family, ta work for them instead of myself and my family, ta sleep at the bottom of their bed on a pallet instead of in my own bed at home."

He thought of the few friends that he made while living there—all manner of slaves—some English, some Irish, quite a few African, most with an easy way about them that made their brutish lives bearable. Much of their time was spent working the fields, and if they didn't talk to each other they would not have much more to listen to than the grunts and groans of their labors, so they filled up these hours with stories—fantastic, complicated stories that would take so long to tell he might wait for days to hear the ending.

He loved good stories. His father used to tell them with great fanfare. He made them up as he went along, Hugh realized as he grew older, but his father was good enough to fool the children when they were young. Now Hugh had picked up the mantle and told ceaseless stories of his own...

"That was, until I had the chance ta fight for our cause of independence, ta make sure my family will be free, no' in bondage as I grew up. Of course, it didna hurt me a bit that I won my own freedom by enlisting." He tried his best to grin. "And orphaned children will still be bound out I suppose, I canna help that. As much as I resented it, the institution could have its place, if more of the masters werena so crooked and brutal. But my children willna live under the tyranny of King George, and that's a salve for my hurt, in a way, so I see what you want ta achieve by finding the men who hurt your family, I do."

He looked at Isaac and saw that he was still listening, so he continued, "However, the way I was withdrawn from my home and family, discarded by my mother...it's just the turn of things now, but then I felt no one had ever been as wronged as I. It was so awfully bitter and lonely, living with a family no' my own, bound ta work for a man who was no' my father year after year. Well, the difference in the then and now is that my pain was fleeting and childish, yours verra true anguish."

"I see, you're attempting validation to defuse my anger, are you?" Isaac said, his mouth grinning, his eyes showing his annoyance.

Hugh realized he had taken a wrong turn. *Oh well.* "Think of it as a fable, a well-crafted one at that. The innocent son, a strapping manchild sent ta live in exile, was a bitter ass, positively as unpredictable as a young lady's heart. Are you inclined ta hear further?" Hugh prompted.

"Would you cease if I said 'nay'?"

"Mayhap," Hugh replied.

"Have your way." Isaac sighed. "But don't be overly bombastic."

The night closed in around them, the moon slowly reaching into the sky. The humidity never lifted. A deep chuckle punctuated low conversation about twenty yards away, where Owen and Tom were bedded down. Snores rumbled closer by.

"Well, a wee, lonely girl from a neighboring farm used ta love this small, mongrel bitch that was really a fine shepherd. When she—the dog mind you—quit herself of a heavy load of pups, the little girl seemed ta never leave the place; her kin little gave her mind and never appeared ta take her in hand. But she was so quiet and respectful, no one denied her. Soon she became no more than a shadow. Unfortunately for her, she became my shadow.

"See, the runt of the bitch's litter soon became her favorite pup. Any plans ta do away with the scruffy thing never came ta pass, because the girl brought food with her every day for the dog. Food that her family could ill afford, I should say. That poor pup got ta about thirty po'nds, and he was likely ta be a handy shepherd, too, like his dam: A fast, low-lying dog.

"Now, about this time, I acquired a new shadow, a young bound boy. Eager he was, that boy. Always with the questions. 'What?' 'Why?' 'Did you know...?' That was his particular favorite, 'Did you know the gestation of a dog is...?' 'Did you know the constellation Libra...?' or 'My father told me all about...did you know?'"

Isaac smiled sadly. "I know the kind."

Hugh continued, "I wasna well at the time, you ken. Oh my body was sound and strong, but my temper wasna so sound.

"This boy and the little girl got ta putting their heads together sometimes. They annoyed me whenever they were about. They especially bugged me when they giggled together, leaning in together and giggling." He shook his head. "That made me mad, and too often. The little girl was the image of my sister Jane and when she would laugh with the boy I was so angry. At my mother, my father, the court, myself. I thought of my sister sleeping on the floor at the foot of her master's bed, like I did, cold and alone. Or of maybe one day when the master got ahold of her like they do sometimes,"—his voice had lowered to a whisper—"you know they take the babies born that way straight out of the mother's arms and sell them."

Hugh shook his head. "Well, anyway, I told the boy once that the little girl's favorite dog went after the lambs and that he had ta shoot it, it was the rule of the plantation, if we didn't follow the rules of the plantation, things could fall apart. This was his test as a farmer." He looked at Isaac. "I assure you, two forlorn children would no' have bothered me nearly as much as giggling children."

Isaac looked at him, in some sort of daze, his eyes not focusing quite on Hugh's. "You said your body was not so strong?"

Hugh stared back at him for a moment, not knowing what to say. He decided on "yes." Isaac nodded and looked as if it meant as much to him as a flea jumping off a squirrel at the top of the tree.

Hugh continued, "Peter, the boy, and Mary Ann, the girl, didna seem ta notice I wanted nothing of their company." *As I'm no' paying mind ta your disinterest.* "They did so much remind me of my kin at home, but they werena, you ken?"

"No."

Hugh crossed his hands over his chest, his fingers drumming reveille. "I see I'm no' helping so much with my..." He lifted his head to look pointedly at Isaac. "What was I no' ta be?"

"Bombastic, you ass."

"Exactly, my bombastic story. So, I'll leave it at that," Hugh said. He shifted position, stretched exaggeratedly and prepared for sleep.

"Oh, finish your fable, but quickly, please. There was a boy. His name was... he did... something?"

Hugh sat up and propped himself against the thick tree trunk. He spent a few moments deciding just how to cut a complex story into only a few more lines; how to convey the burden borne after hurting one to honor another.

Then he wondered why he was putting in the effort. Didn't he tell himself time after time that other people's problems were not his own? Hell, he couldn't even help himself.

He didn't want needy people around him, anyway. They cling to you like lice and drag you down like the smallpox, he thought, so why do this? Why try to save people? They wouldn't be thanking you for it. He decided to stop trying, just end the story and get some sleep.

After swatting at something that had crawled onto him from the tree, he continued in a more solemn tone, "'Twas no' my finest day. Every day should be your finest day, ne'er forget. But this day, well, I convinced the poor hero-worshipping boy—I'm the hero of course—ta shoot the girl's favorite dog, do you remember that part?" Hugh said.

"No. How did you convince him?"

"Told him it went for the lambs, which it didna, but it's got ta go then, no way 'round it."

"True enough. But, did he?"

"What?"

"Fire the bloody gun."

"Of course."

A heavy silence enveloped them until Isaac asked without looking at him, "Was he an accurate shot?"

"Thank God, no. Missed him by a rod."

CHAPTER TEN

In the small hours before sunrise, the soldiers left their heavy packs behind in the camp on high ground above Englishtown, New Jersey. The order had come to move against the enemy. A small advance detachment of six hundred men, they marched through the night and into a steamy dawn, when youngsters out for morning chores stopped to watch them pass on the highway. Behind him, Hugh could hear the heavy plodding of the horses pulling the ammunition wagon and four cannon under the command of Lieutenant Colonel Oswald. "Keep it up!" the commander shouted at regular intervals.

"Huzzah!" Hugh heard a small boy's voice cheer from an orchard on their right. The child, his legs dangling from a thick limb, blanched and quieted when so many soldiers' eyes turned to him.

Within seconds the men shouted back, "Huzzah!" and green apples fell to the ground when the boy shook the branches in excitement. Drums soon told them to double their step.

They reached a stream a few hours after dawn. It cut through a ravine, trickled under a narrow bridge, and the men were drawn to it while they paused to see the artillery safely across to the east side. Officers turned the other way while the men left the ranks and dunked their heads, flicking up sprays of cool water as they shook like dogs.

Through the water dripping off his forehead, Hugh looked at Isaac, squatting next to him and wetting a rag that he pressed to his face. "You could have taken that damnable thick coat off and left it at camp."

"I'm a soldier proud to wear his colors, you find something amiss in that?" Isaac asked.

"No' one officer here would require you ta smother in that thing. We'll let the lobsterbacks roast themselves under orders ta no' even let open one button, but we dinna have ta—"

"Man gone down!"

Hugh and Isaac looked behind them to the back of the ranks, where the shout had sounded from. Though they could see nothing past the hundreds still trudging toward the bridge, they knew what had taken him down. The heat. He was the second to drop this morning, and would not be the last, Hugh was certain. He felt that the temperature must have already reached ninety degrees, and it was rising steadily. Isaac still kept on his coat.

They didn't stay at the stream long. They were told to quicken their step once the cannons had passed. After they crossed the ravine, the land sloped up a hill and they began to climb it, marching smartly, colors held high and bright but barely stirring in the still air.

A horseman who had been riding the flanks suddenly thundered past on Hugh's right, hurrying to Colonel Grayson, not far behind. "Skirmish ahead, sir," the horseman said.

"Numbers?" Grayson asked.

"Handful of militia, twice again as many dragoons and British foot."

An irregular volley suddenly pounded through the quiet woods.

"I said numbers!" Grayson shouted. He pulled out his field glass and rode to the front of the detachment, dust from his horse's hooves swirling. He soon returned and gave orders to display their full force when they reached the clearing ahead.

"Scare the devil out of them," someone shouted.

After that outburst, they silently complied with the colonel's orders, marching and spreading up and out, up and out, until they formed a mere three rows well before they came into view of the skirmishing party over the rise.

Owen marched ahead of Hugh. Isaac and Tom were to his right. And then another soldier caught his attention as he surveyed his surroundings. It was a boy, one company farther to the right. One of the youngest he had seen since enlisting. *No' ripe enough for ta shave. My God.* The boy was doing his own surveying, but not in any tactical way. His eyes made their way to Hugh's, and for a moment, Hugh forgot where he was. He saw a small, frightened child cringing in those eyes and it startled him. There were no enemy approaching them—yet. They were on the offensive. Reportedly, there were no canon pointed at them. So he had yet to feel any real fear for himself; the only fear he felt was for their cause.

They needed this victory. Oh, Congress probably thought they could wait until the French showed up to pursue the Brits, but they had to show they could do this thing alone. And wounds were still too raw from the French war to be overly eager to rely on them. Many of the soldiers had lost brothers or fathers in the fighting of the last war.

He cared little for the way Congress saw their pawns lining up. Every man walking up this hill, appearing into the practically unknown at the edge of a secluded wood, was more important to this nation than any puppet-master, in this country, in France, or in the enemy's. It would be the worst kind of confessing shame to lose even one. Yet, he wondered as he looked around how many of them were already scratched down on Congress's parchment as losses necessary and acceptable for victory?

Still, there was fear so deep in this boy's eyes that Hugh forgot the puppet-masters. If there had been a way, at that moment, for Hugh to snatch this boy, throw him on that big black horse riding the flanks and gallop him home, wherever his home may be, and to his mother, he would have gladly done so. *If only ta stop those blue eyes from haunting me.*

"Quicken your step, make some noise!" came a sudden order, and they did. Within seconds, the militia ahead and taking the pounding gave a cheer and scrambled back over the rise to slip behind the cover of their approach.

Drums rolled and men pressed forward, charging the top of the hill. Once there they found the British dragoons wheeling about, beating a good retreat around their own foot soldiers. The hardened battle masks of the American faces suddenly broke into whoops and hoots at the hasty retreat of the enemy.

They held their first hill! Owen and Tom laughed together, a few jeered obscenely at the fleeing enemy. And Isaac walked, calmly at that, straightaway down the grade of the hill after the Redcoats, alone. After nearly twenty yards, a mottled gray horse bearing a major circled about in front of him, the officer's sword drawn and held down at his side, menacing but not yet threatening.

Owen and Tom forced Hugh's attention away from Isaac with their merriment. Owen grabbed Hugh gently with an arm about the neck and laughed. "Their flying hooves and coat tails are quite a sight, don't you say?"

They moved aside as the artillery passed through, coming to rest at the topmost of the rise, pointed to where the fleeing men had disappeared. Isaac was now back in the ranks.

Not long after, when they were finally ordered to leave the hill, they marched by platoons for two miles without a single halt, the hunt for more Redcoats now deadly serious. They had only met a small skirmishing party at that last hill. The full rearguard of the British forces was still up ahead of them somewhere, and they were marching to find them. The soldiers matched the graveness step-for-step, grimace-for-grimace. Canteens were shifted and hats were straightened as they passed the enemy's last encampment. Campfire remains dotted the sides of their path. Hugh smelled old smoke rising from the warm ashes.

But the human tide moved on. Rank and file, cavalry and flank riders, drummers and fifers in shades of blues and whites and browns and reds, continued rolling along the countryside, winding through rough woods and thicket, climbing hills, crossing ravines, all the while struggling to remain concealed.

Hugh found it odd that the closer they came to the main body of the enemy, the more he thought of Peggy Moore and her daughters. Her small, wide-eyed daughters watching their mother's childhood home enveloped in licking flames, crumbling into black cinders, the loud popping of furniture and shingles soon to be ashes floating through the twilight...their mother trapped inside.

And Aunt Polly, left without her two oldest sons.

The more he thought of the women, the straighter his back became, the more resolute his marching feet. With them in mind, Hugh glanced to the right again at Isaac. Only Tom looked back at him, and, at his puzzled look, Tom shrugged. That damned wool coat, Hugh thought. It had probably suffocated Isaac and dropped him on the ground behind them.

He looked back. Some of the lines had lost stragglers and Isaac was one of them. He walked next to an older man who was limping. Smiling, Isaac was, and chatting as if the two were old acquaintances, casually strolling the avenue. But as he chanced a few more glances back, he noticed Isaac begin to look first this way and then that, his neck craning, and Hugh could imagine his eyes darting as if in a panic. Before long, a rear sergeant importantly approached the two and ordered Isaac to return to the ranks. Hugh turned back to follow the lead of the color bearer's gently swaying flag.

They soon reached the dusty road leading to Monmouth Court-house, far in the distance, and Hugh thought for the first time today just how damned thirsty he was becoming and how the heat of the day was starting to drag on him. But he continued on, drinking from his canteen sparingly. It looked to become a long, hot fighting day.

The road's dry dirt gutter was filled with petals of browning, dis-membered orange lilies, their bald green stalks silently watching the brown and white laced-up breeches pass. Just beyond that point, slowly, the brigades of soldiers streamed out in three different direc-tions—east, northeast and south. Reports came in in sketchy dribs and drabs, and the latest revealed the British hidden by woods, beside the open field near the courthouse.

Hugh's brigade continued on, moving northeast across a small causeway. The march was sluggish, ponderous. They had been much too long without orders and some of the men felt they were marching without purpose. Hugh could sense the same frustration in his captain, and in his colonel, too, whenever he rode through.

Soon they were approaching another detachment of fellow Conti-nentals, along a stand of trees. Hugh smelled burnt gunpowder in the air and heard an occasional musket shot. Commands rapidly circulating among the officers were drowned in the din of high-pitched rattling of summer pests, soldiers' stamping feet, the endless droning of muffled voices. They made hand signals and flailing arm gestures, but advanc-ing troops were left to speculate about what they meant. Busy murmur-ings trickled down the troops.

"They're low on cartridges," someone ahead of Hugh said.

"Who?" Hugh asked.

The man looked back at him. "The men up ahead, they're gathering cartridges from us fresh troops, one per man." A loud volley caught their attention and the man blinked hard. When it was over, he said, "Guess they've enough, now."

They began to march again, now across squishing, soggy ground beside a morass, and Hugh felt a wave of nausea roll over him. The heat had finally asked too much and soon his legs felt unstable and his vision faltered and swam. He tipped his water bottle for a long drink. His head stopped spinning, though the nausea stayed, and he thought he might just be all right. And then he slapped at a bug on the back of his neck. Pain tore through his head like a crushing blow. He had to close his eyes.

In the darkness, his whole world was filled with nothing but the scorching sun and his pounding head. He imagined that he was walking into a blacksmith's forge, heading straight toward the searing heat of the raging fire, coaxed and cajoled by the constant wheezing of the bellows. He could hear the *tamp, tamp, tamp* of the brawny, sweating blacksmith's tools, and from somewhere deep inside the forge, a rib-shaking explosion.

Hugh opened his eyes, and through the sweat dripping into them, watched as smoke encircled a cannon ahead and slowly lifted in the thick air. They stood in a clearing where countless men knelt and fired or stood behind them and fired or stepped back sprightly after lighting the cannon. More American heavy artillery struggled to set up at the edge of the woods and Hugh stiffened as two of the men went down under fire while they labored.

A three-story clapboard house watched over the surrounding fields, and beyond it was the enemy, spanning the far end of the clearing. Closer by, American light horse dotted the forest, stamping while riders checked their arms. After another quick volley, the troops they had come to cover, now depleted of cartridges once more, rushed the enemy's lines, bayonets held out stiffly. The British dragoons fell back and American light horse came out of concealment, thundering past Hugh's left side. The dragoons wheeled back in response, charging full force until the Americans let out another volley backed up by cannon shot. One horseman went down, his horse left to trot off toward the woods.

Hugh tucked his chin to his chest as he ran across the edge of the field. Dirt pelted his feet from raining grapeshot. Before he reached the cover of the woods, a twelve-pounder skidded across the field. It smashed through a soldier's legs and carried them away, leaving him writhing on the open ground. His compatriots soon pulled the bloodied man along.

To Hugh's relief, another American brigade appeared through the trees, pushing across the causeway to the skirmish side of the ravine. From their number, one horse and rider pulled ahead and soon sped along the road. The large, dark horse barreled down on them, frothing when the rider skidded to a halt near Colonel Grayson.

"General Lee has ordered a tighter pincer movement, all troops to surround the enemy. Continue east, sir," the adjutant said loudly to the colonel as he held his mount under a firm grasp. But even before he finished speaking he was contradicted when weary troops in the distance crossed the ravine once again, reforming on the far side. The artillery were also withdrawing.

"We will not advance alone, by God," the colonel responded. "Though we will do our duty to hold this field. You can relay that to General Lee."

After a quick glance behind him at the retreat, the message bearer tersely said "Sir" as he whipped his horse around and galloped back.

Hugh heard the word "retreat" passing back and forth. Quietly at first, questioning and confused, then with more certainty, as if General Lee were there himself, urging them to remove themselves without delay.

By now, most of their backup were steadily shrinking from the fighting. He watched for a moment as more poured through the woods, leaving them, crossing the ravine by the causeway or just scrambling and slipping down the embankment and climbing up the other side.

He quickly dismissed them as his detachment moved forward, just into open field again. He was now on the front line and instructed to ready for fire. He knelt to the ground. The heat of the day settled over him in the ensuing silence. Then he waited, ready, his dark musket burning his hands.

"Aim."

He adjusted his grip and squinted at the line of Redcoats, their broad chests a wall of targets. Across the field the enemy mirrored their movements.

"Fire!"

Hugh felt the rush of debris from the explosion near his face, acrid smoke hung in the air. The gun blasts down the line were nearly as deafening as the earlier cannonade. He quickly reloaded.

The return gunfire was light, three casualties on the front line, and the enemy was soon repulsed, at least a short distance, by the volley. Colonel Grayson shouted back toward the ravine for Colonel Jackson's men to come support their left flank. Colonel Jackson returned that Grayson's lack of artillery made them too vulnerable. Grayson rode the lines impatiently, conferring with his majors, sending messages to the far side of the ravine.

As the men waited for orders they kept a wary eye on the enemy, reforming from their short retreat. The farmhouse between them, a casualty of the latest volley, popped and creaked as flames licked up the sides, passed over the windows and reached for the eaves. British reinforcements streamed along the forest line. Soon the roiling smoke of the blaze hid their number.

Hugh's officers ordered a retreat.

"Battalion! To the right about—face!" They wheeled. "Forward— march!" Hugh stepped heavily into it—a humiliating, honorless retreat. How would they return home victorious heroes if they slithered away like snakes from Saint Patrick?

The abrupt about-face sent Hugh's company to the rear of the battalion. Color-bearers had a difficult time finding their place to lead and men began faltering in step and formation. Soon, entire front platoons broke away just as two of the American light horse stormed through, retreating, slicing their way between the splintering troops.

Isaac ran up to Hugh's side as the riders disappeared in a cloud of dust. "We're turning back?" Isaac looked back to the field at the edge of the woods from where they had retreated.

Hugh kept up his pace and left Isaac a few steps behind.

An iron clasp on his shoulder swung him around and Isaac stared at him hard. "We are not turning back."

They had nearly reached the causeway where the retreat was stopped up like an hourglass. Men began streaming around the sides of it.

Hugh looked at Isaac blankly. "What would you like me ta say?"

Isaac searched out the captain, nearby. "We're turning back?" he repeated. "Sir," he added as an afterthought.

"Yes, Private. Reenter your rank immediately."

"But, if we display the columns, sir, fully—joined with another detachment?" They stared at each other silently for a long moment. "We're not turning back."

The captain seized Isaac's coat sleeve without further argument. Isaac sent his elbow up and out to deflect the grasp. Isaac's gun, before slung across his shoulder, was in his hands in seconds, pointed at the blue sky.

Hugh strode toward Isaac's back. *Ah, by God, he'll be shot by his own captain. That's a fine way ta be getting out of the war.* Instinctively, he shifted his musket and slid open the buckle on his cartridge box. Lifting the flap to settle his hand atop the paper cartridges, he felt the bare block of wood inside, but no more shot. His last reload was the last of his ammunition. Where the hell?

Isaac quickly backed away from them both at a surefooted pace; his musket held securely, but still pointed at no one.

Hugh forgot about his ammunition. "Isaac! You canna convince the whole of the Continental army ta turn and follow you. You willna," he yelled. A small hiccough of fear unfurled in his pounding heart. "Fall inta rank and do your duty."

"Oh, but I am doing my duty, Hugh. 'Dinna doubt,' don't you say? Yes, dinna doubt, friend." He grinned and bowed to Hugh—a sweeping, strange bow, then sprinted away.

"Isaac!"

Isaac kept running. Hugh looked to the captain for help, but Captain Smith had turned his back on him, guiding his troops into the retreat. Hugh would soon be without his company, without his regiment, left to make the decision for himself to run behind enemy lines for Isaac or fall back. Tom and Owen had disappeared into the retreat.

Hugh drank the last of his water and considered his choices. His troops were still in view, but Isaac should have a good lead on him by now. He looked for his half-witted friend. A confused and fractured company about twenty strong pushed past him. Across the open field to the north, clouds of smoke from the merrily burning fire and a sea of stragglers hid any sign of Isaac.

Hugh put his hand back into his cartridge box and fished around, not believing he was without shot. He looked inside. Nothing.

That solved it. He couldn't run into the enemy's arms with no ammunition but what was already loaded in his musket. He jogged toward the fleeing troops, but stopped short when he saw Benjamin Jenkins, the man who had once thrashed him soundly, watching him from the rear of the battalion. The large man calmly patted his cartridge box, shook his head, and turned to join the captain.

He knew in that instant where his shot had gone and that Isaac's cartridge box would be empty, or nearly so, as well, and then a figure in a blue coat caught his eye. The white turned-up tails were flying, the once jaunty, cocked hat missing from the man's black head. It was Isaac, running across the field. *No need for ammunition, that pompous coat is going ta suffocate him in this heat.*

Isaac was not running headlong across the field into the enemy, thank God for small favors, but instead along the safer tree line. Hugh put his full force into the pursuit, every breath a thick gasp, head bent low, arms pumping at his sides. His muscles cramped but he continued

83

running. If Isaac disappeared around the bend where the woods ended, he thought, he would be on his own, Hugh's strength could never hold up against this heat. He looked up to check on his distance.

Ahead, a horseman whipped around the trees and ran his animal through a clump of branches while he was turned about, firing his pistol. The soldier, luckily for him, merely lost his hat. But Isaac was running head on with the horse, and the rider had squandered precious seconds righting himself after being lashed by the trees. Hugh knew there was no time for either to stop. Fate already had her way.

The horse reared up. Its sinuous chest and thick hooves smacked into Isaac and he fell. The animal trampled over him. Horse and rider continued on.

Isaac, splayed on his back, didn't move again. Hugh stared at the sight until his knees buckled and he put a hand to the hot, sandy ground to steady himself.

He heard more riders approaching from behind the trees. Soon he would be trampled too, while swooning like a spinster. He couldn't afford to be missish now. Leaping to his feet with the last bit of strength he thought he could muster, he sprinted to Isaac's body and knelt beside him.

"Isaac," he said in a strangled murmur, "ah, Isaac. What have you done?"

He struggled to raise Isaac into his arms. Slipping his right arm under his friend's knees and his left under his arm and around his shoulder, he tried not to look at Isaac's bloody face. His long body slithered, again and again, back to the ground. Soon Hugh had no strength left. He stood up, breathless, and heard double hoof beats—*full gallop*—growing in size.

He watched the tree line, and through the thin branches he saw more riders, more light horseman or possibly the militia scouts who had been busily reconnoitering the enemy all day, soon to be charging straight toward them. The first horse rounded the bend and Hugh waved his arms and shouted. The rider looked surprised but dodged the patch of ground where Isaac lay.

Then came a second rider's gray mount. He waved and shouted again, but then feeling dirt spray on the back of his legs, he pulled his musket off his shoulder and spun around.

A British soldier stood just over fifty yards away in an orchard on the hill to his left with a musket pointed toward the ground in its priming position, readying to shoot at him again.

Another rider stormed around the trees and dodged Isaac's prone body, as had the last. The sounds of the hoof beats softened.

Hugh dismissed the horses for a moment while he dropped to one knee and took aim at the man on the hill. The other soldier's hand reached for his cartridge box. Hugh now had twenty seconds to make sure it was a perfect shot, if the soldier was skilled. Muffled shouts came from the other side of the ridge and the soldier turned while putting the cartridge to his mouth.

Maybe thirty seconds.

You know your musket, Hugh, he assured himself. She hasna changed. The ball shoots off to the right. Happens every time—he gently moved his barrel a few degrees left and squinted—better happen this time.

He could see tips of British hats now, bobbing behind the soldier, who had turned back to his musket, primed the pan, and was now stuffing the cartridge down the barrel.

The soldier's next move would be to grab his rammer in a sweaty fist.

Hugh squeezed the trigger. He watched as the soldier dropped his rammer, put his hand to his shoulder, and looked behind him again to the hats. At last, he turned in their direction.

Hugh ran and grabbed Isaac from behind, under the arms, and dragged him into the trees. *Please let us disappear, please, God, let us disappear.* One more horseman charged past just as Isaac's heel bumped over a thick poplar root sprinkled with moss where the spreading trees softened the brilliant sunshine. He dropped Isaac a hundred feet deeper into the woods.

He stripped to the waist and pressed his wet white shirt to Isaac's face, although he knew the shirt was not going to help Isaac. He tore Isaac's canteen off its leather straps and poured the last of the water onto the shirt. He held the canteen over his own turned-up face and a warm drop landed on his tongue. He tossed it aside.

Kneeling there amid matted brown leaves, rotting acorn tops, and jagged sticks, he wanted to just remove the shirt from his friend's face. A simple thing, but his hands wouldn't move to do it. He needed to clean him up and check his injuries and do all of the things a fellow soldier was trained to do, was expected to do.

But the face he couldn't bring himself to look directly into while he was first wrestling to get him off of the ground he knew was horribly wrong. His face was just *wrong*, and he felt ashamed for leaving him covered, but he couldn't uncover him. The best he could do was to get him to someone who could help. The enemy knew they were in the woods.

As he thought it, another blast sounded from the field outside the trees.

A stamp and soft whinny drew Hugh's attention. A fellow refugee, the riderless horse from the first downed cavalryman, was patiently waiting, like a good soldier, under a sweeping, low bough at the very edge of the woods; not nearly as deep as Hugh had entered, but far enough to be hidden. He would have to risk their only chance on this horse.

Soon Hugh thanked God the horse was approachable and he was able to get Isaac, in his sticky uniform, across the large animal's back. The shirt fell off Isaac's face. Hugh didn't look.

They left the musket fire behind them as the horse picked its way cautiously through the trees, down the ravine and then slowly struggled up the other side, to the clearing leading to the retreats.

He found his company resting at a fence near the road. The yard of a small house spread out behind them. Tom and Owen, their faces streaked with dirt and sweat, scrambled to their feet and hurried to the horse when they noticed him. Without a word, they grabbed Isaac and slid him gently to the ground.

"Oh, hell!" Owen yelled when they finally had Isaac turned face up.

Hugh still didn't look. While he dismounted, a crowd formed around his fallen friend. They knelt in the road, surrounding him completely and cutting him off from Hugh's view as he skirted them, heading toward his captain.

"Sir," he said when he reached him, "Private Moore is down. He needs a surgeon."

"Take him to the house," the captain said, concern lining his face. He pointed to the house behind them. Hugh turned away, but the captain grabbed his arm. "Here now, soldier. I'm coming with you."

They brought him into the house. Three other men helped Hugh carry him, their faces sunburned, clothes wet and reeking of sweat and burnt gunpowder. As they settled him down in the front hall amid the fluttering of the woman of the house, Hugh had to grab Isaac's shoulders to settle him on the bench. He looked directly into his face, close enough to feel his breath—if Isaac had been breathing. But he felt no stirring at all.

Behind him the group of men murmured, the woman still fluttered, the captain went off for the surgeon, and Hugh stared into Isaac's face. His high forehead was misshapen and black. Below, his closed eyes were discolored, his right jaw dislodged and hanging, most of his teeth missing. Dried blood was everywhere.

The blustery surgeon clattering into the house barely drew Hugh's attention. He felt the man come up beside him, hand him a shirt, and then nudge him out of the way. When Hugh finally looked away from his friend, the surgeon's flyaway white hair and wrinkled, florid face took him aback for a moment. How did this ancient man hope to handle the rigor, the heat of battle, just to rush in and face the demands of stitching the men back together?

Hugh prayed to God for a moment that Isaac was in the most capable hands that could be found.

"Are you whole?" the doctor asked.

Hugh nodded yes and warily watched the old man tug off Isaac's prized coat.

"Good. Return to your troops, they'll be needing you today." He dismissed Hugh, put his fingers on Isaac's neck, and grunted. "Barely," he said.

"Barely, what?" Hugh asked.

"Barely alive." He pointed at the door. "Go on."

Hugh grudgingly rejoined his detachment, moving on with the rest of the retreats until they reached the first deep ravine they had crossed, seemingly years ago, and there they faced the outraged command of General Washington.

"Where go you here, soldiers?" he thundered from atop a frothing horse. Behind him two members of the general's guard grasped a young fifer who had unfortunately led the retreat. He loudly denied his own desertion. Hearing the cries, Hugh's own step slowed. Though they had been warned that the enemy was twenty minutes behind them, perhaps less, General Washington's anger was difficult to run toward fleet-of-foot, and he thought them deserters all, besmirchers of honorable soldiering.

The soldiers overwhelmed the commander in chief with their pleas of innocence, and within seconds his face softened, his tone turned commanding instead of accusing. "There will be no retreat today,"

Washington said. "Prepare yourselves for battle." He dispersed them into the nearby woods, and ordered a ration of rum to be issued to each and all.

They fell to the ground on the forest floor, hundreds of weary men, past the point of caring whether they were to be in rows or in columns, just-this-far from his right hand man, just-that-far from the man in front. They dropped. They coaxed one last drop from their canteens. They prayed on their knees, they prayed sprawled where they lay. They checked their arms, they checked their ammunition.

"I need cartridges," Hugh said to Owen.

"So do I." Owen inspected his musket, not even bothering to glance at Hugh.

The twenty minutes they had left had now counted down to perhaps fifteen. He grabbed Owen by both shoulders. "I didna say I need a reply pulled from your arsehole, I said I need cartridges."

Owen raised his light blue eyes, over horribly sunburned cheeks, to look up at Hugh.

"Yes, now!" Hugh prompted.

"Tom!" Owen called out while fishing around in his shot pouch. "The man needs cartridges."

They both handed over a fist full, reached back in and handed over another. Hugh counted them carefully as he put them in his rigid cartridge box. Two, four, ten. That would have to be enough, he couldn't drain his friends.

He loaded his gun, secured the flap on his box, and looked at the men still streaming into the woods behind them. Soon, Benjamin Jenkins straggled in and collapsed barely inside the tree line. A few men stepped over his feet as they passed. Hugh's anger had found a suitable target.

He waited until the stream of soldiers slowed before he strode over and kicked Benjamin's feet. "Where the hell are my cartridges, you bastard?" He kicked him again as sweat bit and burned his eyes, the toes of his thin shoes thumping and smacking into the meat of the man's thick legs four times, five times.

Benjamin's eyes rolled in Hugh's direction. He looked drunk. "What?" His arm slid off his chest and hit the ground heavily. Underneath was a spreading bloodstain.

While he watched it swallow a wide circle of Benjamin's white shirt, Richard Splender appeared at his side. "Hugh, I've heard they've got Isaac in the hands of that butcher they've been calling a surgeon. Owen says don't look as if he'll come through, is that true?"

Hugh nodded woodenly, pain bit the back of his eyes. He leaned over and swiped the cartridge box from around Benjamin's good arm. "This one needs the surgeon's tender mercies." He hung the box over his shoulder and shrugged. "Or maybe a chaplain. Who cares?"

The wounded man's eyes had closed, his body unnaturally still. Hugh wasted not an ounce of pity on him, at least he died with his rifle in his hands, with his soldiering clothes on. God may even take pity on his black soul for it.

With his soldiering clothes on! No bright coat like Isaac wore and was so damned proud of, of course. But the grime-smeared shirt the man wore was enough to mark him a patriot anyway. How do you like it? he thought as he shook his head listlessly. A man can live a coward's life and still die a patriot, with all the reverence that's due him. He thought of Isaac and wondered if he was still alive, lying there, alone...without his coat—

"Ah, God. Isaac's coat," Hugh said.

Richard gave a half-hearted "Eh?" before they both turned at shouts from the road.

"Huzzah! Huzzah!"

Hugh grabbed Richard's arm before he was lured away. "He's no' wearing his coat! He's no' dying with his coat on! That pompous coat! Dinna you—?"

Another round of cheers cut Hugh off as Richard's attention followed great groups of men hurrying to their feet, pushing past the last men straggling in out of the dusty, sun-drenched highway. Hugh followed behind Richard and he felt a moment's pity for the men who had yet to rest as they turned, too, and followed the huzzahs.

Hugh hung behind, on the tree line, watching the American troops reforming into companies and regiments, lining the road, covering fields and spilling into orchards. Between them rode General Washington, up and down the lines.

"There will be no retreat," Washington called. "You fine men will have this day."

As a wave crashing to shore, a roar of approval, or more likely anticipation, came from the men and moved down the lines toward Hugh.

"You will carry these fields, this highway, these forests. You will have this day," their commander in chief declared.

They had drilled for this day, bled for this day, some had died for this day. But now Hugh hardly gave a damn. Isaac was to die without his coat on—and any moment now, he felt—and he couldn't abide by it. He slipped through the trees as the men offered their fiercest battle cries, rallying for General Washington.

The shouts lessened behind him.

He soon came upon an old pine eaten up with pests to a good distance above his head. A sad looking tree, she was, and he slowed his pace as he neared, seeing a wickedly sharp, barren branch near to his left hand, pointing at him. He threw his palm into it as he walked, impaling a good distance in through the meat of it, found it wasn't quite dead enough to break on him, and that suited his purpose just fine. The pain came with another quick jerk as he pulled it to the right and then off again. When the blood flowed freely he smiled at his work. The old surgeon at the quiet house by the road could fix him up and Hugh would see to it that Isaac died with his coat on.

Then he could go meet the Brits.

By nightfall, the army trained by von Steuben and rallied by Washington had lost sixty-eight men dead, one hundred sixty-one injured, one hundred thirty missing. The survivors held the field. Soon the British slunk away under the mask of darkness, Hugh slept fitfully under an oak tree, and Isaac lay dead in the parlor of a farmhouse, his coat draped across his shoulders.

CHAPTER ELEVEN

Two years later; Charles Town, South Carolina
May 1780

"Corporal? Sir..."

Out of the string of explosions pealing along the streets, one of Hugh's soldiers—a new recruit, the green boy—called out to him. The sounds were muffled.

"Corporal?" the boy repeated. The frantic words wavered high above Hugh's head, which was just now smashed into the rocky ground. Grit and blood laced his tongue, his lips, sealed the breath of precious air out of his nose. Dirt crunched as he gnashed his teeth, struggling to raise his face out of the earth.

No air, no soldier...

He clutched empty air with his free right hand, turning so painfully to reach the back of his head where an unforgiving mass sat still upon him. When his throbbing chest refused any more movement, he let his hand drop back to the ground.

No air, no soldier! No air, no air.

More voices carried to him. "...I see your faded glory, whipping in the breeze. She won't be going back up on this colony again. I'm here to take her down for good."

"Fock you, ya lobstaback bastard!"

There was air. His flag whipped in it. His own soldier hovered above him, could pull him free. A defiant Irishman and a lobsterback bastard stood close enough to lift his head and let him breathe.

Oh, God, why didn't they?

The voices drifted away. The explosions stopped. Hugh no longer felt weight on his head, he didn't feel the ground beneath him. He felt as if he were floating, and then a soul scarring pain dropped him to the ground again.

When he opened his eyes, a brilliant blue sky spread out above him and his burning lungs filled with air. He swiped at the dirt on his face, coughed, and looked beside him. Another soldier stared back at him, a thin trail of blood dribbled across the bridge of his nose and under his right eye. He was dead.

"Corporal, can you get to your feet?" Private Dodson, a young, gangly teenager new to his squad, pulled clumsily on Hugh's arm. The pain that had dulled as he stared at the fallen American soldier burst anew.

"Oh, dinna, dinna," was all Hugh could grit out.

Dodson dropped his arm and stared open-mouthed at the fresh blood blossoming through Hugh's dirty white shirt.

"Shit, you were hit. Shit, shit." Dodson paced and kicked the ground, running his hands through his hair as he cursed. "I thought you were fine and whole, only that dead soldier that landed on you after the magazine blew had you down. Oh, God, Corporal, what do I do?"

Dodson didn't have to do a thing. British soldiers suddenly appeared above Hugh's head, and no matter the pain, they grabbed his arms and dragged him away.

As of this morning, he was one month shy of serving out his three years with the Continentals. One month away from going home for good. Now he was a bleeding prisoner-of-war.

PART II
1780 - 1798

CHAPTER TWELVE

Rockingham County, Virginia
1780

Maggie McLaughlin left the cabin door ajar to welcome any errant cool breeze. The chickens would no doubt wander in, she just hoped they would stay out of the custard cooling on the table.

She stepped into the morning just rising over the mountains and tightened her swollen knuckles around the smooth head of her maple walking stick. It sunk into soft dirt once she reached the base of the porch steps. Colonel, her old shepherd, slinked behind as she walked through the yard.

"Don't snivel and hide. Follow straight out," Maggie said without looking at the dog.

Colonel barked and bounded forward through the wet grass to follow at Maggie's heel. They passed quietly through the foggy morning, over the shorter grasses of the horse paddock, through the skittering, dawning woods, and into a dappled clearing at the edge of the farm. It was the family graveyard.

There, Maggie dropped her walking stick and spread a handful of daisies on the ground. She wiped her handkerchief over a dusting of moss on top of the oldest stone. Ellie, her only daughter, had rested there for thirty years, nearly ten more than Maggie's husband, William.

She turned to her husband's stone and sprinkled curling, dark tobacco leaves over the grave. "Enjoy," she said as she eased herself onto a bench under a spreading dogwood.

"William, the ground's being turned for the corn. James and Michael have given young John quite a bit of help this year. After last summer's harvest turned out so poorly, they couldn't rightly refuse their mother. But those two of our sons are now off again to Staunton."

Maggie gently rubbed her knees and then stood. "As for the war, we've had no word on the fighting in the South, except it's been said that bloody British eyes have turned to Virginia. But I've no doubt the boys will keep the Valley safe, or die trying. You rest well, William. I'll be back on the morrow."

She began to walk back the way she had come. But after retrieving her walking stick, she turned back. She felt old. Simply, painfully old. "I have had other news that I've not brought to you before. Hughie and Dan have already died trying. I'm sorry."

And softly to the dog, "Come, Colonel, the milk cows are waiting." She pointed a finger at the dog. "Yes, I do talk to empty air and I won't hear a thing from a dog about it, either."

CHAPTER THIRTEEN

Newspaper clippings covered the small, worn table under a sputtering candle. They were the only enclosures wrapped in a wax-sealed letter just retrieved from town, but written many weeks ago. Not more than once a month, but usually only a handful of times a year, did anyone in the McLaughlin house bother to town, and the only other post to come for them in over two years was news of her son Hughie's death. A few months later, an officer on furlough rode in to tell her about her second son Dan's wounds and his death.

This mail in front of her had been waiting to be collected for the past three weeks.

Maggie cursed her old eyes while attempting, once again, to read the paper. "'Charles Town, South Carolina. 12th of May, Seventeen Hundred and Eighty.'"

Footsteps fell on the first and third of the three stairs leading up to the porch just outside the doorway. She heard the dog struggling to his feet in greeting, his long nails scrabbling on the wood planks.

"John?" questioned Aunt Maggie's voice from inside the dark house.

John paused outside the open door to remove his soiled boots and hang his hat on the bench under the window. "Yes, Aunt Maggie, and I brought the sweetest drops of honey just for you," he replied as he scratched the old dog's bloated and scabbed belly with his toes. "Fleas," he muttered. He walked past the grizzled, long-muzzled shepherd.

At the table under the front window, his aunt sat in a feeble circle of light from the lone candle. It dimly lit his way around the corner to the kitchen they had just built. Set off from the rest of the house and constructed around the giant hearth that once dominated the one room cabin, it was his aunt's pride.

He set the promised honey on the long oak table surrounded by six sturdy ladder-back chairs. The fire had burned down to glowing embers and that meant he had missed any chance for a hot meal.

"Yes, boy, supper's been over since long before sundown," he heard from the other room. John shook his head and tore a hunk from a cold ham on the table.

"'Beg of you, bring out two more candles from the dresser, we have a post," she continued.

A post! John put the ham in his mouth and wiped his fingers on his pants. He grabbed the candles, brought them to the table, and settled into the chair across from his aunt. She pushed all of the papers in his direction. As she did, he lit the candles and placed them on a spiny holder.

Eager for news, he looked down to see a letter, written in a large scrawl, and two columns of print raggedly ripped from a newspaper. The signature on the letter had a large ink-splotch at the end of the first name. John lifted it toward the light.

"From your Cousin Henry in North Carolina," she said.

He dismissed the letter for the moment to read the newspaper. "'Charles Town, South Carolina. May, Seventeen-Eighty. In light of ... siege began in April ... Lincoln has surrendered the town and—' " he stopped and looked at Maggie. "Five thousand?" he asked loudly.

" 'Five thousand' what, boy?"

"Five thousand patriots surrendered at Charles Town." It was unimaginable.

"Paroled? Exchanged?" Maggie prompted.

John looked back to the newspaper for a few moments. "No."

"Well, then," Maggie said with finality as she eased herself from her chair. At her full height, she barely stood taller than John's head while he was seated, and her dowager hump was lowering her a little every day. Candle in hand, she shuffled off to the porch to dip the dog a bowl of water; his panting was all they had been listening to while they let the unimaginable sink in.

"I don't see Grayson's regiment on this list," John called out.

"There is no 'Grayson's regiment.' Read Henry's letter," floated back in to him.

No Grayson's regiment?

He read.

3rd of June 1780
Dearest Aunt Maggie,

Hope to find you well as cane be expekted. Well I do
not want to be long on Plesantres when I have such
hevy News to report on. Thursday last I came to a
tavern where the News was posted and I was able to
get this paper to you seing as it held a lote of facts
that you mite deem necessary to know. Now I talk'd
a long bit of time with some gentlmin from the tavern
and thim being from south Carolina and bringing up
the News from the big Paper down there I know that
most of what they say is the Truthe, so far as cane be
ditermin'd. Well it seems that Hughs regment is one
that was in that Surrender and that being the Gists
regment and not the Graysons because Graysons is
no more after there was a Smallpox run all among the
Graysons regment. And thank God he was not in the
Tarleton's masacer. I remane,

Your devot'd Nephew,
Henry

So, Cousin Hugh was a prisoner of the British.
While I'm sitting here enjoying honey and ham. John laid the letter
on the table and joined Aunt Maggie on the porch.

"That's foul," he said as he sat next to her on the bench. Maggie
looked up through the offending haze of smoke swirling from her just-
lit pipe and chuckled.

John squeezed his hands together and stared out into the yard. "I'm
signing up," he said after a long silence.

"Well, then."

"I will. I'm going ta."

"I know you will—you're going *ta*. It's *to*, you're aware, not *ta*.
You sound like the rubbish boys up toward the ridge."

"You're not being thoughtful, Aunt Maggie."

"And you're being petulant. If you're mad, say so. Get angry. Shout and holler. Say you're mad straight out. But you say so first, mind you, and then see if you still want to sign up."

John continued to stare into the yard.

"Boy, I do think you serious. If I said 'do not,' would you not?"

"No."

"Well, then," Maggie said again as she tapped out her pipe.

From the stony look on her face, he knew she would try, slyly, in her way, to convince him not to go.

Maggie had taken care of John and his sister, Katherine, for almost six years, after their parents, Daniel and Abigail McLaughlin, died. His younger brother was apprenticed to Master Herdsman on a nearby farm when he turned six, but Maggie saw to it that he was home more often than not. She complained bitterly about the burden of the children at every turn, but they knew she was grateful for their presence. She needed their help, having been a widow for over twenty years, her only two surviving sons grown and gone.

Now, she always insisted she had never received help from anyone—for anything. But soliciting help she was expert in.

Reportedly, she had convinced her parish priest back in Ireland to teach her to read and write when she was a child. In secret, of course, for it was against the law of the Crown for him to do so. A dangerous request to fill, to be sure.

And all of the additions to her one-time one-room cabin had come at the sweat of her neighbors, her nephews and her sons. Yes, she could convince anyone to do anything—and with a smile.

Little matter, she could needle him about it all she wanted, John was still signing up. Will she, nill she, he was going—he didn't need her consent, anyway.

CHAPTER FOURTEEN

The slaughtered hogs were salted and barreled. The winter could see to itself now, John decided, so he pinned this morning as fine as any other to set off from home to volunteer. It helped that he heard Colonel Matthews was encouraging men to do just that today in the common room at the Crab Apple tavern.

From the height of the sun in the clear sky, his trip took a little over three hours. The settlement he was headed for was just across the ford, a-ways up the heavily wooded road, and his excitement grew the closer he came. He wanted to put his heels to his old girl, a small sorrel, just let her have her steam, but he held back—he would look like a hotheaded child if they arrived in a lather. It wouldn't do, and Aunt Maggie might even hear about it. That was to be avoided.

As he guided his mare across the sandbar and trickling water, he pictured the crowds no-doubt already gathered at the tavern. There would be politicians there for sure, ready to shake hands and show their support for the Cause, to make their impression on the enlisting men as the only ones worth voting for once the fighting was done. He would only wonder why they were there shaking hands and not out fighting, anyway—and he would let them know it. He sat straighter in his saddle. He would let them know it.

He was proud to be signing on to Colonel Matthews today. True, he was a senator, himself, but he was a fighting man first. He would let the other politickers know that Matthews had his vote for whatever office he wanted in the future, solid as a post.

John rounded a bend and the town came into view. It was nearly deserted. He had thought the shopkeepers would be busy men by this mid-afternoon, with many villagers gathered in and around the tavern and general store. Their surrounding farms would be dormant and self-reliant on this unusually warm midwinter's day. And besides, sordid gossip, shrewd haggling, and reluctant barter in town needed more tending to than the milk cows at home. But there were only a handful of old men sitting on the benches in front of the tavern.

John stopped his mare just short of their notice and dismounted. "Four shilling and not a penny more..." he heard as he walked her to the hitching post beside the log tavern. He fiddled with her reins longer than he had to, listening for a moment more to their banter.

"With the new money shrinking like it has, you might be in for more than a few pounds for that, instead o' shillings. You might as well promise a fat sow in exchange and be done with it."

"Aye, she's a truth!" a third man said. "And if Morgan loses his hold on the Brits and they storm through here on their devil's way, ravaging and plundering as they go, you might as well burn your Virginia dollars for warmth, for that will be all they'll get ya."

"But our militia boys will be ready for them, by God. Why I seen three or four boys come through here this morn' before you even had your arse out of bed."

"And seeing how only two have come through since then, we've six fighting boys 'tween us and the lobsterbacks. Splendid."

John walked to the front of the tavern, where the men sat. They smiled at him broadly and greeted him "Good day!" He nodded, paused for only a moment in front of the quiet tavern's door, and then headed for the James' general store, his heavy shoes clocking across the wood planked walk.

Old Mr. James looked up and smiled as the bell jingled at the door. "Ah, young John," he said before he turned back distractedly to his account book on the high wood-planked counter. His pink scalp peaked through white hair much more than the last time John was in town.

"Mr. James," he said with a nod as he removed his round-brimmed hat and walked about the store. He brushed his hand across a bolt of blue linsey-woolsey. Straw and felt hats hung above barrels of vinegar and flour along the north wall. A handful of dried ginseng filled a bowl on the counter in the rear where he finally lay down his hat.

Mr. James shielded the writing in the account book from John's view as he put a blotter paper between the pages and then closed it. He laid it down on a desk behind him and looked at John expectantly.

He suddenly wished he needed a whole passel of supplies, maybe some tools, and some dried foodstuffs, too. That might take him a whole hour of bargaining with Mr. James. Instead, he only needed cards—he didn't feel up to bargaining for them—and then he would be free to march up to the recruiter and sign his name.

John cleared the lump from his throat. "Aunt Maggie needs a new pair of cards, sir. Have you got any in?"

"I've got in three pair of carding brushes, son," Mr. James said and bent over the account book. He scratched a note with his stained quill and then asked, "Anything else while I'm in the back?"

"No, sir."

The storekeeper nodded and shuffled along behind the counter, past the small fire snapping in the back-wall fireplace, and into an adjoining room. A moment later he returned with the tools and remarked, "You came all the way from your place for this pair of cards, son?" Then his look warmed. "Or did you hear Colonel Matthews was here today along with his recruiting officer, over in the big room of the ordinary? Well, what're you wasting time over here for?"

John thanked him politely, as he was taught to do, and stepped back outside with the parcel deep in his large coat pocket. The muddy road beside him was quiet as he trudged back the short distance to the tavern where the old men still sat and wished him another good day. He wondered if they still counted him as soldier number seven, or if they had had enough warming rye brandy to count him number eight.

Warm, smoky air rushed at him when he pulled open the door of the dim common room and the smell of cabbage and horse blankets greeted him. He saw it often, but he still marveled that the room was one of the largest he had ever seen that didn't have animals living in it, being about thirty feet square. No one played billiards at the new table that normally sat in the center of the floor—a plank of wood had been straddled across its length to create a makeshift desk instead and it had been pushed across the floor to sit in front of the fireplace at the far end of the room. And there, standing soberly at the side of a young man writing in a large, ornate book, was Colonel Matthews.

John stood silent, halfway between the door and the table, and he hated to admit it, but he trembled just a bit. He had thought to find a raucous mood at the tavern, men singing fight songs or drunken patriotic ditties, perhaps loud stump speeches in front of colorful broadsides.

He was left disappointed.

He heard the clunking of wooden trenchers, throats being cleared, a cough from the back of the room. The grand beginning to this adven-

---

ture that he had anticipated the entire three hours of his trip into town now crumbled into an unremarkable signing of a contract. There was no excitement in the tavern to get caught up in, to carry him forward to the table. The dullness of the room raced his heart. He would just as soon go home and wait to be drafted.

He slowly withdrew from the firelight, edging toward the door, and then a voice from a back corner called out, ending his flight. "John McLaughlin!"

"Sir?" he asked, his gray eyes scanning the dark room. Tables spread out to either side of the door, out of the way of the comings and goings of would-be soldiers. No sconces were burning, the tables were in shadows.

"You can step over here for a moment. Colonel's not going anywhere. Come, sit down," the voice said as a heavy chair scraped across the floor, out from under the table.

As John approached the scarred table, he recognized two of his neighbors. The one hailing him, Samuel Stevens, was a large, boisterous man who lived just south of John on the river.

"How's that old place going out there since Michael left?" Samuel asked. "I hope Maggie and you are getting on well. I'm so sorry about Hughie and Dan and I've been meaning to call out there, just haven't found the time," Samuel said.

"Sir, the family's all fine, and—"

"Boy," Jared, the man on John's left, cut in, "I need to come out to your place to talk to you about that old bull you got there. He's a good-looking animal. You been doing any breeding with that fellow?"

With the man's florid complexion, red-rimmed eyes, and drooping lower lip, John thought he looked as if his face had been freshly burned and just slightly melted.

"Sir, you'll have to talk to my Aunt Maggie, see—"

"Shit, boy, I'm trying to talk to the man of the house about business. You want business or don't you?" Exposing two rotting bottom teeth, his lip hung down, waiting for an answer.

Samuel cut back in again, "Jared, Maggie *is* the man of the house. No offense, John."

"None taken, sir. If you gentlemen will excuse me?" John began to rise out of his uncomfortable chair when a large hand on his arm stopped him.

"John, I wanted to tell you, too, I see you out here signing on today," Samuel said as he motioned to the Colonel, busily shaking hands and encouraging a new recruit. "Your father... he'd be real worried about you, but he'd also be proud to tell us all about what his son's out there doing. I just thought you'd like to know. I'll check in on Maggie and Katherine for you, too, while you're gone."

"Sir, thank you, sir. I..." When he couldn't think of any more words to say, John turned back to the table at the fireplace and, before he again lost his nerve, signed his name in large strokes with the rich, dark ink. The date he wrote was the first of January, 1781. The next column asked his age. He scratched in "16."

* * *

John made it back to his aunt's farm as night was falling. The warmth of the sunny day had been chased away by bone-chilling winds, and in the moonlight, he watched the steam rising from his breath and his horse's jouncing head. He bundled his long wool coat tighter against the mare's sides to trap her warmth.

When he turned off the darkening road along the river and onto the winding lane that would lead him home, a horse and rider bounded forward from the treeline.

"John! I'm so glad you're home," his sister, Katherine, said as she drew her horse up beside him. "I came to the road to wait for you." Her cloak was fastened tightly at her neck, the hood covering thick, dark hair. One small tendril slid down the side of her face and she pushed it back under the gray wool. "We've had news that Cousin William's wife, Jane, is at her time, it's early, too, and I'm apprenticing to the midwife. I wasna home when she came 'round and ...'tis my first birth. John, I can hardly believe it! A baby! Can you see me there safely? I canna go alone."

He laughed at his sister's excited, nonsensical chatter. "Calm down, I'm sure we'll be there in plenty of time. You know, other babies have been born, this isna the first."

As the pair set off together into the cold night, John looked longingly behind him to the road leading home. Aunt Maggie had promised him mashed sweet potatoes for supper. They were sitting there waiting for him.

They turned back onto the road snaking along the river's edge, a one-time buffalo trail cut by migrating herds of the great beasts heading to their pasture in the valley, and then they traveled north the rough three miles to William's small parcel of land.

Once the cabin came into view, John and Katherine, who had been traveling abreast, had to step their mounts gingerly, one by one, across a creaking bridge spanning a small moon-dappled stream in front of the cabin. The shutters on the windows were drawn tight against the night air, but a bright fire could still be seen burning inside through the cracks and uneven shutters.

They dismounted and Katherine threw John her reins and disappeared into the house.

He started walking the horses to shelter when the door opened again. The brawny figure of William McLaughlin stepped out and gently closed the door against the cold. William was a half-score older than John, and although close cousins, they resembled each other not at all. John towered over William and was so lanky that his height weighed down his shoulders. William had his mother's black hair and turned-up nose, John had light brown hair and a long, aquiline nose that never failed to grow more pronounced with each passing year.

Apparently not dissuaded by the cold, William was dressed in his working clothes—long breeches, sooty coarse white shirt, dark and heavy leather vest, a snug knit cap, and no coat. He appeared to be scrutinizing John's attire as well. "Well now, dinna you look no' like a 'Glakin today, man. All in your finery, are you? Was there kirk this morn that I didna know about?" William said. His words clouded in the moonlight as he approached John and took the reins from him.

John glanced down at his best coat. A hint of his only linen cravat peaked through at the neck. "I signed on today with Colonel Matthews, couldna have him show me up, now, could I?"

"Och hone, John! Are you pulling my arse hair? You're going off wi' that man? Ta do what, I'll be asking?" He didn't give John a chance to reply. "He's a senator, for the love of good Jesus, John, a politician." He opened the door to the dark stable. "No, sir. I did my three months a long time since, that's enough for me, if you should be asking." He turned and looked back at John, raising a dark brow. "The British do have my brother Hugh still caged up down there in Carolina, dinna they, though? So, then, you figure it's about your time?"

"I suppose it is."

After they got the horses settled in, John started toward the cabin, a warm fire the only thought in his mind. William sat down and lit a pipe.

"I'm no' going back in there, John," he said quietly.

"Why are you not?"

"You dinna ken what's been happening in that place. It sounds most like a room for the insane, no' a home for my wee wife and me. And it's just the one room, man! No place ta go! I'm no' going in there just yet."

John thought for a quick moment about bundling with the horses, he was so tired and cold, when the shutters flinging open on the nearest side of the cabin surprised him.

"Will! Will M'Glakin, you have a son! Will you be entering the house again or no?" the midwife shouted across the yard.

She didn't have to yell it a second time.

CHAPTER FIFTEEN

Outskirts of Portsmouth, Virginia

The soles of John's shoes lay behind him, stretching out for hundreds of miles on the darkening roads. Thick and new when he first put them on, he thought they would last forever, or at least until he reached the end of his three-month tour of duty.

He winced with each step. For now, he suffered quietly, but he had felt the road on his heels for too many miles to hide his pain long, though it wouldn't do to appeal to Captain Gwin. It would pay better to pray for a rest instead. Hearing distant shouts, John glanced up from looking at his feet and squinted over the heads of the other soldiers marching before him. In a clearing less than a hundred yards away, campfires flickered and blue uniformed men ducked in and out of tents the color of fresh cream.

"Praise God," a smiling young man beside him said.

John couldn't have agreed more.

Captain David Gwin, leading his horse by loose reins, stopped the march and addressed his men. "Through this bog and pine forest is the town of Portsmouth. To the north is the James River. To the northeast, the Chesapeake Bay. Be glad you're here in the winter. This swampland is unbearable in the heat of summer." He looked over the militia, shifting haversacks around on their backs and whispering among themselves. He nodded in the direction of the tents and campfires. "Ahead is the camp in which you will reside indeterminately."

John looked again. Beyond a wide stretch of open parade ground, row after row of tents spread out through the camp, and ashes floated over snapping fires into the early evening sky. The largest marquee, set toward the back, held his attention. A general or two would be in there, he thought, pouring over maps and correspondence, planning a stunning and decisive end to the war.

Captain Gwin swung up onto his horse and steadied her. "When we enter camp, immediately set out to gather firewood. The soldiers already there will have a hot supper ready for you. You do not eat until you've paid them in a return labor. And the stacks of wood you offer had better look ambitious or you will not eat at all."

The man who had praised God lost his smile.

The captain turned his black mount and led the men into camp.

* * *

An aide-de-camp ducked out of the tent and brushed against John's arm. His uniform was crisp and neat, the red facings at his cuff and chest brilliant against the blue coat. Nearly a head shorter than John, he looked up at him with an eyebrow raised, a frown on his thin lips, and passed him by. John straightened his ragged wool coat and crossed his arms over his chest. His hands warmed under his armpits and he waited. It was his second day in camp and already Captain Gwin had summoned him for duty.

He stood alone. A few men brushed down the officers' horses at the tree line nearby and three more men passed them coming out of the pines with armfuls of kindling. Others stoked already blazing breakfast fires. John smelled coffee and burned biscuits.

Was he to serve the captain directly? No corporals? No sergeants? What kind of mission could they be going on alone? He felt a surge of pride that he could be so important.

His captain left the tent next. He rolled a yellowing map in his hands and smiled.

John straightened his spine and swiped off his hat. "Sir."

"McLaughlin." Captain Gwin nodded and then scanned the camp. "The rest?"

"The rest, sir?"

"I've more men than you summoned." He glanced about the camp. "Ah, good," he said, seeing the soldiers tending the horses. Then he frowned. "Why are you not brushing down the team?"

"Is that my mission, Captain?"

"Your mission is food. The camp has nearly depleted its stores and the quartermaster has reported nothing but broken wagons and busted barrels in his supply train." Captain Gwin shook his head. "Bull all you need to know is where Patriot farms are," he tapped the map against his thigh, "and what supplies to gather."

John followed behind the shorter man to the group of soldiers where Captain Gwin spread out the map and gave instructions to a blonde-haired corporal. The other two soldiers stopped working with the horses and watched.

They were considerably older than John. One was graying around the temples and thick around the waist. He looked angry and unapproachable. The other was dark, nearly swarthy, with huge, drooping ears John couldn't help noticing.

The captain turned back to the waiting men. "Private McLaughlin, Corporal Jones, hitch the wagon."

The four soldiers took off within the hour, written passes carefully tucked into their pockets. The graying man, the only one with experience driving a wagon and team of horses, banged along the rutted road at an eager pace. The rest hurried beside on foot.

They walked without a word, and John's thoughts soon turned to Cousin Hugh and how they hadn't had word about him since Henry's letter last summer. He secretly hoped that the Virginia militia would be sent south again to harass the British flanks or even attack the occupying forces in Charles Town.

Aunt Maggie had been right. He felt toothless and bitter every day that Hugh was still a prisoner. He hated the lobsterbacks and he would like nothing more than to crack some of their heads together and take Hugh home.

If he could just get within reaching distance...

It was all he had to offer Aunt Maggie. Her two older sons were dead. He couldn't bring them back.

A few miles out of camp, the men slowed down—John was not alone in limping. Grady Jones shouted for the driver to stop, but the wagon rounded a bend at the fork in the road and continued out of sight. The fork's crooked signs read, "Portsmith" and "Suffolke." The wagon was headed north to Suffolk.

"Should've ridden in the back, after all," Grady said and whipped a rock up the road.

"Doesn't matter," the much older man on John's right said. "We've got the map."

Grady dropped his knapsack at his feet and pulled out the thick, rolled paper. "You're right about that, Peter, you are. Shittin' bastard won't have to wait around for us, but he won't get much in the wagon if he doesn't find the right plantation. 'Course, he'll just as soon resort to pilfering."

Peter agreed.

John felt two pairs of eyes come to rest on him, waiting for his stance. He cleared his throat. "Isn't pilfering forbidden?"

Peter cackled and soon Grady joined in. "He's precious, that he is," Grady said. He chuckled some more and then removed his hat to scratch at his head. Black hair fell forward and covered his drooping, oversized ears.

Thank goodness, John thought. He hadn't been able to stop staring at the huge things since their walk began.

Floppy-ears crinkled his dark brown eyes John's way. "Don't matter if it's forbidden or not to most men when they're hungry or under strict orders to bring back food."

Grady rolled the map and put it away. "Five miles up the road to Portsmouth is the closest plantation. Let's hope they'll borrow us a cart."

The group continued on their way.

After turning on the road to Portsmouth, Corporal Grady Jones began to sing. "Old lady, old lady, don't squander your porridge," he warbled, "your fighting young men are scouting for forage…"

John enjoyed the song, and tried to join in, until the theme of the ditty turned to "young lady" and what the fighting young men needed from her. His face burned to red cinders.

Peter-Long-Ears smacked John with his hat. "What's wrong with you, lad? Scared the devil will find you worthy?"

"Oh, no, sir. I was thinking only of our men down in Charles Town. It's got me feeling out of step."

"Well, I suppose it would, at that. The bungling Benedict Arnold has come and gone through Richmond, so I've heard, but Cornwallis and Bloody Tarleton have not made it as far north as this, though, boy, and with Daniel Morgan worrying their every flank, I'm sure they never will. You needn't worry."

Grady grabbed John's arm. "Look! 'Tis a Loyalist scout coming, alone," he whispered and motioned for them to back into the woods.

"I spoke too soon," Peter said quietly. He knelt behind a thick tree and pulled the gun strap from his shoulder, resting the battered musket across his lap. "I don't see him."

Grady nodded up the road, to another blind bend. "Through the trees. He's disappeared now. Wait." He put his face close to John's, his eyes wide and darting, his breath dreadful. "Boy, you skilled with a knife? Skinned plenty of rabbit, haven't you?"

"Well, yes, sir."

"Then this'll be easy. You're the tallest one here by far. That fellow coming is six-feet, no less." Grady pulled him behind a pine next to the road.

John heard the approaching soldier's gear jangling. He had yet to see him.

Grady pulled a knife from John's belt and whispered again, "Grab him from behind"—Grady's arm jerked around John's neck and lifted his chin—"and get him like a pig. Need to keep it quiet in case he's not alone."

Grady handed John the knife and disappeared.

Sweat trickled down John's cold temple. He wiped it away. Had Grady gone mad? For a brief moment he had thought his officer was going to do away with him in the quiet forest, pulling out that enormous knife and snatching his head back. Now Grady wanted him to do the same to the enemy soldier.

His clothes were as plain as those any other man walking the road may have worn. How did Corporal Grady Jones know the approaching man was the enemy, a Loyalist? How would John know?

He watched with half an eye peering around the tree. The man paused at the bend in the road, a look of uncertainty on his face. He must have heard John's breathing, maybe he could see it fogging in the cold air. Maybe he heard John's heart beating. Or saw his half an eye.

He heard the men whispering behind him. Was that a snigger? He turned his head, careful not to make a sound. They looked back at him expectantly, owl-eyed. He turned back to his assignment.

The so-called loyalist soldier coming their way took a hesitant, limping step forward, and then another, until he was back up to stride. His limp became more pronounced as he walked. A few old leaves clung to his clothes, his hair. Soon, with a hand resting on the hilt of his sword, he passed John by without a glance.

How did Corporal Grady Jones know the departing man was the enemy? John certainly didn't.

A growl came from behind John and the soldier swung around, drawing his sword just as Grady leapt on him, knocking him flat. His sword clattered to the frozen ground, harmless now. Peter came out of the woods next, frowning at John before he knelt on the man's neck and swiped a length of rope around his wrists.

Grady yelled back at him, "Damn it, woman. You've given us away. Hurry down the road to warn us of any others, and follow the order to the letter or I'll tie you to him in the stockade. Now!"

John ran the way the man had come, rounded the bend, and saw nothing. He paused and listened. He heard nothing. He hung his head.

He was not fit to rescue Hugh.

CHAPTER SIXTEEN

Captain David Gwin's daughter Agnes, almost eleven years old and most commonly called Nancy because she thought the shortening of Agnes, "Ag", sounded too much like "Nag" or maybe even "Hag", sat in the light from the fireplace in the front hall, her legs numb and her back sore. Her sister, Polly, had curled up on her lap, cranky because of a cold, and fallen asleep there. Nancy would stay still for as long as she could, but the hard wood bench, enclosed on three sides to keep out the cold seeping into the house, was no place to pass the night.

She was the oldest girl and the oldest of her parents' five children. More of a mother than a sister, really. Her own mother had been thrown into the role of deputy husband the countless times Nancy's father had left them for the war. Now he was gone to some place called Portsmouth.

She hated Portsmouth and never cared to know where it was or who lived there. Someone there would shoot her father. She knew that for a certainty, because men who go away to war get shot. That's just the way the world worked. Didn't mean she couldn't hate it.

Her father was a proud Virginian, a soldier. For as long as she could remember, he would give loud speeches about the freedom of Virginia, about the rights of the "planting class," as he called them, the benefits of a land where men raised the goodness of life for all of the people by getting the most out of the soil. He talked about their governors, Thomas Jefferson and Patrick Henry, every night it had seemed—that they agreed with him, that they should rule this land, not King George—all the while banging his fist on the table, on the rights to freedom of the Virginians and the thirteen states.

The other twelve states, she thought, he had usually added on without much feeling, if at all. His heart lay firmly within the borders of Virginia, that's what her mother said, even though he taught all of his children who were old enough to understand about the colonies they were a part of, not just about Virginia. So Nancy knew her history and her geography very well.

Just not much about that place she hated—Portsmouth.

She had watched her father gallop off to war the last time so many months ago on his black gelding, a light snow covering the ground, Polly already hanging on her skirts like a child on her mother. She had wanted to sneak into the barn and take off, too, on her favorite horse.

Her mother had stood like a stone on their porch steps, leaned on the railing for a short moment, and then herded her children into the warm front hall to start life without Father again until who-knew-when he would return.

But Nancy kept dreaming about that horse. And now with her legs aching and Polly getting heavier and heavier, she added a stream and a field of flowers to that wild ride. She didn't want to grow up to be like her mother, a child hanging off her and a husband to leave her to them. She just wanted to take off by herself and ride and ride and...

She wiped away the heavy webbing of sleep from her eyes when her mother banged in through the front door, a bucket of water in one hand, a basket of eggs in the other. One of Father's old coats hung off her loosely.

"Did you change Jane's diaper cloth, child?" her mother asked of her. She was a small woman and Nancy was growing up to take after her, so everyone said, with smooth, dark hair and warm brown eyes.

Nancy sighed quietly, so her mother would not hear. "Yes, Mother."

Mother set the basket and the pail aside, shrugged off the coat, and came to stand in front of her. She felt Polly's head and smoothed her hair before she lifted the child off Nancy's lap and carried her to the girls' bed across the room.

She soon returned to sit next to Nancy and push the hair out of her eyes, like she had Polly's. "Turn around," she said softly, a hairbrush in her hand. As Mother slowly brushed her long black hair, Nancy closed her eyes.

"When will Father be home?" she asked her mother.

"When he feels his duty is done." Mother stroked her hair again.

She wanted so badly to ask her mother how they would know how her father was faring, but didn't dare. It would worry her and her mother didn't need any more worry—or work. Her mother spent her days at so many extra chores since her father was gone, sometimes she came in at night so tired that Nancy worried she was going to take ill. But she always rose in the morning before any of the children and had the fire, the water, and the breakfast going for yet another morning.

Nancy worried so much about both of her parents, but she had no one else to take her fears to.

Her mother turned her around again and cradled Nancy's face in her hands. "You have had to grow up faster than any girl should. Don't think I have not noticed that. But these times, God willing, will not last forever and I have more confidence in your character and strength than you could possibly imagine and I know that you and I will both weather this storm, together, and be all the stronger for it."

CHAPTER SEVENTEEN

Five months later; Charles Town, South Carolina
22nd of June 1781

"Whereas in pursuance of adequate powers respectively delegated to us to carry into execution...between Captain Cornwallis, on the part of Lieutenant General Earl Cornwallis and Lieutenant Colonel Carrigton, on the part of Major General Greene, for the exchange and relief of prisoners of war, taken in the Southern department... Now public notice is hereby given, that all the above mentioned British and American prisoners, wheresoever they may at present be, are hereby declared to be fully, absolutely, reciprocally exchanged; and such of them as are on parole within the lines of their respective parties, are hereby declared to be released therefrom; and such as are within the towns, garrisons, camps, posts or lines of the powers who captured them, shall be immediately liberated and permitted to pass without restriction to the party to whom they belong.
[Signed]
Edmund M. Hyrne, *Deputy Commissary General prisoners*
James Frazer, *Commissary prisoners*"

They were not released immediately from their imprisonment in Charles Town. Instead, they left in painfully scattered groups.

A mere day before his captors told Hugh he was free he could not have imagined feeling incredible grief at leaving the town without a backward glance. He had been here for over a year, from summer to summer, for more than half of that time on a prison ship in the harbor. It wasn't his home, no, not for a minute. But there were hundreds of faces he was leaving behind, not knowing if they were already gone, or when they would be set free or where they would go.

When the enemy put him to work in the town, so many of his friends and fellow patriots were left behind on the ship. It made him feel like a traitor of the highest order. Though he had known leaving the bowels of that diseased vessel would save his life and he had to take his chance to get out. But the others—waiting their turn to escape the dankness, the sickness and misery below-decks—he didn't want to part from.

The summer sun glinted off the water the day he walked the streets of Charles Town a free man. He watched the ships slowly rocking on the calm water of the harbor. People hurried past him, swinging back into the rhythm of a town still held, but no longer quite so terrorized, by the enemy.

The bustle of the port town had slept long enough, a few residents had returned from exile in the countryside, shopkeepers hung signs outside their doors again. Hugh stared at the boats riding on the water while the clanging and laughing and shouts of renewed spirits carried on behind him. Without him.

Were they all gone? Every soldier? Already walking the roads heading to the thousand ends of America? Or were some still left dying below-decks?

Men slowly gathered on the deck of one ship anchored far off shore, little men from this distance, with one at the bow looking out over the water. Hugh watched, losing interest, as the man moved from the railing. A finely dressed gentleman gently bumped Hugh's shoulder and they exchanged their "pardons" as a flash of white caught his eye, falling from the ship. He heard nothing from the water, he was much too far away, but he knew what the splash sounded like, he knew exactly what bodies thrown overboard sounded like.

But that always happened at night, this was broad day. They couldn't be dumping bodies in plain view of the townspeople, in their harbor, in broad day. Could they?

Why not? They let us die and rot in those boats, why not this?

He clenched his hands into fists and pressed them hard against his thighs. *Because there's an agreement. We have secured an agreement! We're ta leave this place. There's no prisoners left ta dump over.*

He watched the figures on the ship turn away. Soon the deck was empty. The boat continued to rock, unfeeling, pitiless. The normalcy, the silence of the ship's deck, only increased his feelings of horror. He stamped his foot like a child. "We've an agreement! A goddamned agreement signed in rivers of blood, you bastards."

He heard a gasp beside him. He turned and there stood a pale woman in a barrel-skirted blue dress, her parasol lightly shading her wide eyes as they stared at him accusingly. Yes, he had been shouting obscenities, but so what? What here wasn't obscene? He frowned at her and she hurried away.

He walked away from Charles Town, and the pain of abandoning the others lessened with each mile until it was only a dull ache pulsing beneath a wide-open future and he heard the little Gwin girl, far away, saying, "Please come home."

* * *

Before he even left South Carolina, Hugh was ill. Desperately ill, with violent chills, sweats, and a fever that weakened him to the point of delusion. He told the young couple that had taken him in that he had been poisoned, that the Redcoats had dipped the death water from the harbor where they dumped the bodies, and they poisoned him with it before they let him go.

Now he recalled telling them so, as he stood by the whitewashed fence in front of their neat townhouse, dressed in one of the man's old suit of clothes.

Today he was leaving their care.

A slight shake from the ague and the too-small clothes gave him an uncertain look, he knew, but he was firmly in his right mind. Looking back at the house, the drapes tightly closed against the southern heat, he felt ashamed of his earlier hysteria.

But the couple had treated him kindly, fed him, and nursed him through, assuring him he only had malaria, not a "death water" sickness. They had both survived the same within their first two years in America. No matter their assurances, he knew they had gambled with their lives taking him in. He could have been carrying any deadly disease and visited it upon their home.

He wished them a silent farewell and began again on foot. He was ready to see more of this country he had fought for. And then he could go home.

CHAPTER EIGHTEEN

Aunt Maggie cackled, lightly smacked John's cheeks, and fed him goose and early summer berries the first night he was home from Portsmouth.

After the war, he worked his aunt's farm, mastered the art of coopering, watched the green mountains turn to orange, to brown, and then to green again, and wondered whatever became of his cousin Hugh. Four years had passed since his discharge from the militia, when, on a hot day in the summer of 1785, John worried over nearly having passed a deadline on an order for three new barrels and two hogsheads. While his potatoes were sitting in the dark, moist ground and his three-foot high corn waved in an occasional breeze, he was sweltering in the barn workshop, engrossed in crafting a small whiskey barrel. By the middle of the day, he was ready to move his staves and hoops outside—it was time to light a fire in the half-finished oak container.

He stepped out of the dusty barn into the sun and his favorite mare greeted him by stamping from her paddock. She swished her long tail at fat, lazy flies and bit the air with her thick teeth. John didn't think she ever caught any flies, but she tried. He smiled in spite of himself. She was the damnedest thing.

Heavy late-spring rains had left her paddock a vibrant green and delicate white flowers laced the grass in the shade of the barn. On beyond the buildings and newly repaired snake fence where the tall pokeweed grew up and around, a half-dozen or more dark cattle grazed contentedly on the steep hillside.

John pushed up the sleeves of his dirty white shirt and doused his arms with water from a rain barrel. With a rag from his pocket, wetted in the cool water, he wiped the sweat and grime from his face. He looked up when he heard a clatter at the front of the house, but then dismissed it, dried his hands distractedly on his pants, and cursed himself for misplacing his flint box. Returning to the heat of the barn, he swore to continue the rest of the day's work outside.

"John! John!" Katherine suddenly shouted.

He could tell by the pounding beats of her voice that she was running downhill toward him. He looked up as she rounded the corner, grabbed the solid but splintering wooden post and swung around it to slow herself down. He thought her a giddy, full-grown child.

"What's pulled you out of your garden, Kate?" he snapped, feeling too tired for silly games with the women.

His tone stopped her short. With her brown eyes wide and her dark brows high, she said, "Well! Aunt Maggie thought you might like to know we have company, and it looks like they might stay some time." She wrinkled her brow and deepened her voice in mockery. "But I'll tell her you're 'not-ta-be-disturbed'." He could see her struggling not to laugh out loud. She dashed away.

John's long legs quickly overtook her as she tried to outrun him. If she made it to the house before he did, Maggie's disappointment in his comportment would make life unpleasant, to say the least, for a long time to come. He passed Katherine by without a glance, still irritated, and only slowed and composed himself once he arrived at the base of the porch.

His clothes were a mess. Just how important was this visitor anyway?

Having no other real option but to walk through the front of the house, he pushed his long hair back as best he could and straightened his shirt. It'd have to do. Katherine had nearly reached the house.

He heard a deep male voice through the open door at the top of the stairs, punctuated by his aunt's delighted laughter. *She really should be less of a stickler about these things and save us all a lot of trouble.* John straightened his shirt again and entered the house.

In the kitchen, Maggie held her pinner apron away from the fire as she fussed over a pot on the rack sitting on glowing coals in the hearth. She peered at him with dulling brown eyes. "John, it's about time. We have company." She held up a hand as she said, "Ah! Don't bring any dirt in with you from that barnyard."

Hugh looked up at John from the table and grinned his crooked half-smile. His thick legs spread out under the table and dust from his riding boots trailed across the floor.

"She's trying ta force tea on me," Hugh whispered loudly, "could you get me out?"

John smiled brightly and knew Maggie could hear every word. She straightened her back and rubbed her swollen fingers. "Oh, now! Speechless is not a proper greeting for your cousin just come home. Get him out of here if he likes."

* * *

Hugh and John walked beneath the cooler canopy of the trees far from the house, picking up kindling to refill the box. Maggie was in a rush to begin supper, or, more accurately, to begin directing supper. She hadn't done more than putter, or put on the occasional tea, in years. Katherine handled all of the heavy cooking. Maggie directed.

As they walked along, three small pigs darted out from the underbrush ahead of them and ran together down an old narrow animal path leading to a small stream. John could hear the swollen stream bubbling over its smooth stones.

"So, you left Kentucky County. Then where were you off to?" John asked.

"My brother, Will, has spoken so much of the Greenbrier River Valley, I traveled up ta see that part of the country, before dragging myself home. Three fine men I was with were heading ta the Ohio, but I was weary for home."

John watched Hugh as he spoke and thought how changed he was. He had three small pockmarks on his face now, he assumed from the smallpox epidemic that had disbanded Grayson's Regiment. Certainly nothing disfiguring. Women would probably find the marks endearing, and Hugh would see to it that every ounce of pity was wrung out before it was over, John was sure of that. He was a fine-looking, brave warhero. John was more than proud to be his cousin.

And he still had his humor, as wry and obnoxious as before, although his brogue wasn't so heavy as it once was, not nearly as thick as Hugh's brother William still spoke it.

He supposed his own father would have sounded the same as his cousins, but he couldn't seem to pull his father's voice out of the memory pile anymore, not after all the years that had passed. It became a sad link to a loved one, once lost: The sound of their voice.

"Say 'up and about,'" John said.

"Up and about? Why would I say that?"

John smiled. Hugh's brogue had rounded the words to "oop and aboot" and it sounded so warmly familiar.

"How long will you be staying?"

"Oh, I suppose forever. I've already picked out that tree over there ta be buried under, if it's all the same ta you."

* * *

In the pink rays of a dusky twilight, Maggie's house sat peacefully under the only two large shade trees that had been allowed to stand.

Around the large, roughly hewn table inside, a contented, groggy group of adults talked easily; while two small children played quietly on the floor. An infant girl slept in her mother's arms. The afternoon's hearth fire had burned down to ash-covered embers. The room was warm, but comfortable.

"Put that child down, Jane, on my bed if you like, and we'll take these dishes outside," Maggie said kindly after a long silence.

Jane, William's wife, and Katherine each scooped up a toddler, Jane with four-year-old Johnny and the infant Janie, and Katherine with little John's sister Nan, and deposited them in front of the open door, near the porch, to play in the cool breeze. Maggie shuffled along behind.

When she had disappeared from view, John said quietly, "She just wants a smoke of her pipe, not merely the cleaning, don't let her fool you."

His cousins grinned in agreement.

"So this is my brother, Hugh!" William said. "What do you think of my little brother Hugh, John?"

"Oh, he's a fine one, Will, to be sure," John answered, good-naturedly.

Hugh splayed his fingers on the table and stretched tiredly against them. He stood up and stretched again, poured himself more to drink from what was left on the dresser, and looked carefully around the room. Rubbing a hand along the mantle of the hearth and admiring the fine cookware hanging on the wall, he said to John, "You've done an impressive job here."

Turning around in his chair, John replied, "You know Maggie gets what she wants, never doubt."

Hugh nodded and grinned, and then took another long draw from his mug of mead, a specialty drink of Maggie's made with honey from the swarming apiary in the front yard.

William set his mug down heavily in front of Hugh, still standing at the dresser. Hugh stared hard at the back of William's head and then quietly poured him a drink.

"I think I see a problem in you, young John," William said as Hugh was pouring. He quickly moved his large arm aside as the mug, still in Hugh's hand, clattered roughly back to the table in front of him, mead sloshing over the side. "You're a mite bit too hard on old Aunt Maggie, boy. I see it all the time, that I do."

John clenched his jaw and said, "Am I, now?"

"Yes, that you are. I'm tired of seeing it, if you be asking me."

"I dinna believe anyone has been asking you, Will," John said stiffly, his knee bouncing heavily under the table, a mild brogue sneaking in.

"Is this any way ta be seeing me home?" Hugh asked.

John ignored Hugh's halfhearted question. "Will, you don't know what it's like for me here."

"Och hone, John. What 'tis like for you here? What's that about?"

John growled in frustration, threw himself from the table and banged out of the door. The younger children whimpered at the loud sounds and the four-year-old Johnny stared wide-eyed at the adults.

Inside, John heard Hugh say, "Oh, you're a fine one, that you are, Will. Do you intend ta make everyone glad you're moving off away from us all?"

He left the porch and moved through the yard and Hugh was soon by his side, meeting his long gait step for step. "What are your problems, John?" he asked quietly.

"See here, Hugh," John started, raking a hand through his hair, "I know you've been through more than any being should have to suffer. I cannot be a man and complain to you about the absurd at the same time, and face myself in the process."

"That's just no' so. I know men who have been through much worse than I, living and dead." He seemed to lose his thought for a moment, but then he shook his head. "A splinter is a splinter, John, and you shouldna have ta live with them because someone else doesna understand."

"I want a life of my own," John said quickly, staring him in the eye.

Hugh's sudden laughter floated across the yard, and the women looked up at them. He stopped, glanced at John's stricken face, and then leaned over with his hands on his knees and continued laughing deep within his chest. As he stood straight again, he said, "Everyone wants their own life. Be assured, John, you're still a mon. You dinna have ta tear inta William about it, though, and race around the house like a..." He couldn't continue, another spattering of laughter cut him off.

John eventually smiled at himself, and at his cousin's good humor. "Like a thoroughly sotted bull?"

"A drunken bull, excellent!" Hugh mussed John's long hair. "That's it. You've got it."

John warmed to his praise. "A sotted bull who should puke or get off the brandy, eh?"

"Couldna have said it better."

"How about...a steer who knows he's supper?"

"Now you're trying my patience."

As they started back together toward the house, Hugh said, "So get off the brandy, already. What do you want out of this 'life' of your own?"

"I don't know. A home, family?"

"You have a home and family."

John stopped walking. "My *own* home, my *own* family, my own animals, my own crops..." He trailed off with his eyes on his feet. "I at least want to court."

"Oh, well, then. Whom do you want ta spark?" Hugh prompted.

John answered, gritting his teeth, "I don't know, I've never had the opportunity to find a girl to court. Do you see?"

As they were nearly close enough to be heard by the rest of the family, John allowed Hugh to pull him to the back of the house.

"I stopped in a good bit south before I came here, ta see my brother Jamie and his new bride, Susan. My good brother Jamie has decided ta eschew the normal path and set himself up with more horses than he can handle, in my opinion, and he's looking ta breed these horses and somehow still find a way ta feed himself and keep the rain and snow off him at night. What I'm thinking you should do is head down there and save my good brother from himself."

"How would I save him from himself?"

"You could give him a hand, for one thing."

* * *

128

It was time to explain to Aunt Maggie.

William and Jane had taken their children to the only private room in the house, Aunt Maggie's, and all had settled down. Occasionally, a loud snore sounded from the room, the bed and the roping under it would creak, then all was quiet again. Katherine and Hugh had gone to the barn on some pretext and hadn't returned. John wasn't sure if their disappearance showed courtesy or cowardice, but he was grateful either way.

Maggie and John were silently enjoying a comfortable breeze on the porch when Maggie said, "I'm sleepy, John. I'm going in." She leaned over, placed her warm, misshapen hand on his strong brown one, and gave an affectionate shake. "Could you help me?"

"Give me a moment, Aunt Maggie."

"Is there something you want, boy?" she said tiredly, though not unkindly.

He bristled silently at the word "boy." "Aunt Maggie, I'm leaving home," he said in a much sharper tone than the one he had practiced with.

"Well, then," she said.

John lost a bit of his confidence. "I'm on my way to Jamie's down at Back Creek, to try and make my own life there. I'm not happy here, Aunt Maggie, I'm sorry. There's so much work...and no life for me. I..." He sighed. "I need something more than this. The world has to hold more in store for me than this type of meager existence of chronic work and progressing nowhere." Had he gone too far? He couldn't bear to look at Aunt Maggie to find out. "Hugh has agreed to stay on here," he finished. His voice was still sharp; he couldn't seem to change it, and he was no doubt saying much too much, much too unkindly.

"Oh! Well, my now, Hugh's agreed! I'm so glad it's *agreeable* to someone to stay here with the old woman and her meager existence," she said with exaggerated cheer.

This was not going well. John looked off to the barn and thought he could see movement. Then he heard voices. Hugh and Katherine were returning. He could easily have given Hugh a hand sign and they would have returned to the barn... for whatever they had gone for in the first place. But he didn't have the chance—the first blow came as a surprise. "Oh!" John said just before another sharp smack hit him on the back of the head.

"What do you think—" Maggie said as she punched his shoulder, surprisingly hard, next. She winced. "What do you think I've been doing all these years? You? Hard work?" His hair flew up the back of his head and into his face. "Hard work. The neighbors did more work on this place than you will ever realize." She smacked him again.

"Stop hitting me, Aunt Maggie, stop!" he cried in a little boy's voice. He was more shamed than hurt, but he did want her to stop.

"Why? Why do you think I've done this? And don't you say *I* haven't done these things, because I have, boy. In ways that you will never understand, I've done everything for you. The best room next to the hearth, do you think that's for me, boy, just to comfort my old bones? No, that was for you and a beautiful young woman who would be your wife, and that oaken table in there," she pointed a crooked finger to the kitchen of the house, "for your fine children."

John hadn't been able to look at Maggie since her tirade began; he had looked down at his lap at the first smack. He thought it was over until she added with less heat, "You go where you will, John, and you try your hand at making it alone, but I want you to always remember this: The doorway of a great house is mighty slippery."

He considered her cryptic statement, and although he couldn't interpret it, it somehow made him feel smaller than any of her earlier accusations.

As a lone cricket started singing, John looked up and saw that Hugh and Katherine had stopped at the foot of the stairs. They both stared sadly at him and he assumed they were disappointed in his behavior, too. But when John finally mustered the courage to face Maggie, he better realized what Hugh and Katherine were thinking—no one had ever seen Aunt Maggie cry.

CHAPTER NINETEEN

John stopped unhitching the plow and watched Aunt Maggie climb the steps to the porch and disappear into the house. She hadn't said a word to him in days. Not since the night he said he was leaving and she had called him "boy." Over and over again. Under the weight of her subsequent cold shoulder, he had already forgotten his contrition.

The heavy cabin door slammed shut.

"She's concerned about guests shortly ta be arriving, John, is all there is ta it." Hugh came up from behind him and pulled a thick leather strap from around the horse's belly. "Katherine gave me the warning. Aunt Maggie's not speaking ta me, either, I'll have you know. Seems some preparations need ta be made, she requires our help, but she willna deign ta ask us."

John sighed. "What needs doing, then?"

"A preacher's on his way through. Sunday's sermon will be under that sugar tree," Hugh said, motioning to the tall maple shading the dusty lane leading to the barn.

"I suppose we'll need to make room in the stable," John said, rubbing his face. "And I wonder, does she want bird or fresh pork? She will certainly want plenty of weak beer, too, I should think. We'll bring this all together nicely."

"I dinna like the look in your eye."

John smiled. "As well you shouldn't."

* * *

"Don't touch the skin," John whispered.

Hugh backed his hand away from the nicely blackened skin of the goose he slowly turned on the outdoor spit. "What did you do ta it?"

John shrugged. All around them, guests chatted in the yard, more

131

walked up the lane behind them. The traveling preacher, whom everyone had come to see, had been delayed this morning visiting a sick neighbor farther down the river. The sermon would begin as soon as he returned.

John put out a warning hand as Hugh started to settle himself into a chair close by. "No! Don't sit there."

Hugh raised a thick brow and shook his head. "No, John. Dinna say. No' the chair, someone could get hurt."

"It's not as bad as all that."

"'Tis a confessing shame. You're a grown man, you—"

"Who's coming in a carriage, I wonder?" John said.

Hugh turned to follow John's gaze down the dusty road. Visitors on foot stood off to the sides while the two-horse carriage bumped its way along, stirring up more dirt.

"I hav'na a clue," Hugh said. He dismissed the carriage and inspected the chair instead.

John watched him. He wouldn't find anything wrong with the chair. John had merely placed one front leg over a freshly turned piece of ground. As soon as someone sat down it would pitch forward, not enough to hurt anybody, just shake them up.

And a few minutes before he did that, he dusted the cooking goose in soot.

Hugh cocked a questioning brow at him again.

"It's nothing," John told him. If Hugh kept staring at him like a wayward child, he would soon begin to feel like one.

John heard the cabin door close. Aunt Maggie left the porch and started regally toward the arriving carriage, while Katherine, swaying the skirts of her best dress, hurried over to grab his arm. "Come, John. Guests."

The carriage had stopped in front of the barn and John crossed the yard with his sister on his arm to greet the latest arrivals. Two men had left the carriage and now one was giving instructions to the driver. Maggie was already there.

"Widow McLaughlin. It's a pleasure," a handsome, graying man was saying to his aunt as he took her hand.

John admired the man's fine linen shirt and embroidered waistcoat.

"Silver," Katherine whispered, motioning to his shoes. The buckles glimmered in the sunshine.

"Indeed," John whispered back.

Aunt Maggie beamed at the gentleman. "Mr. Hogsett, my niece Katherine McLaughlin."

"Miss McLaughlin. How lovely."

Katherine lowered her gaze appropriately. "Thank you, Sir."

John waited to be introduced, though he already knew who the man was—Hugh's old master.

Mr. Hogsett turned to his companion. "David? May I present to you the ever-gracious Widow McLaughlin? Widow, Captain David Gwin."

"He's polite to a fault, don't you agree?" Captain Gwin said and then nodded in John's direction. "John. You're looking well."

"Thank you, sir. I am well."

Aunt Maggie stepped in front of him. "Sirs, you have traveled rather far. Won't you please rest in the shade and enjoy some refreshment until the service?"

"Certainly," David Gwin said and then turned back to the carriage door. Impatiently, he said to someone in the shadowy inside, "Is the bonnet straight yet, Agnes?"

"It's fine, Father," a young woman's voice answered back. David put out a hand to help his daughter to the ground.

John forgot about being introduced as he watched the delicate young woman of perhaps sixteen years straightening her crumpled skirts. Her face was heart-shaped, a hint of black hair peaked from under her white bonnet. Below, friendly brown eyes welcomed attention, and a playful dimple creased along the corner of her mouth.

He was surprised. He had expected her to leave the carriage simmering, or at the very least bristling, at her father's lack of tact. From John's experience with Katherine, one should never bring attention to a woman's vanity. Not if one wanted to keep his head attached.

"Oh, my! What a beautiful dress." Katherine reached out a hand to her. "May I?"

"Certainly," Captain Gwin's daughter said. "But it's only plain linen." She leaned in to Katherine and said quietly, "It's in the dying."

"You'll have to tell me all about it," Katherine said.

John wouldn't have told a soul, but he admired the fabric as well, a rich red-brown with the look of napped leather. The color was usually the choice of a matron, not a young girl, but she looked stunning anyway, as Katherine had noticed.

Captain Gwin took their attention again when he boomed, "Finery should be reserved for the Lord's day." He turned to his daughter.

"Agnes, I've seen that there are also a few young men of note in atten-
dance. You should not be too bold with them, but gracious and atten-
tive enough to give them the proper impression of your character."

The young woman nodded and her teeth worried at her lower lip for
a moment. "Widow?" she said finally. "May I assist in the kitchen?"

"Of course. Your help would be indispensable, Agnes."

"Call me Nancy, please, Good Widow."

"Nancy it is. Katherine will show you the way."

Katherine introduced John to her new friend quickly, then linked
arms with Nancy and led her away to the cabin. John watched the
young men in the yard watching them go and then two bounded forward as Katherine misstepped, losing her shoe. Laughing, she headed
for the chair he had rigged for someone to tip over.

He now changed his mind about the wisdom of his joke, but it was
too late. His sister was already sitting down, head low, knee up to put
on her shoe. She pitched forward. Blood oozed from her lip when he
finally drew near, feeling so contrite and foolish that he wished he were
a woman so he could cry. A young man down on one knee in the turned
up dirt had a handkerchief at the ready to tend to Katherine's lip.

Before John could reach his sister, Hugh gave his shoulder a solid
shove. He shoved back without thinking.

"I told you no' the chair, John, so help me I did. Now look at your
bonny sister, bleeding and shamed because of your silly tantrum. And
the goose, what—" Hugh's eyes narrowed as he looked beyond John's
shoulder. "John, was that Mr. Hogsett coming down the road earlier?"

John was thrown by Hugh's sudden distraction and he regretted being the one to confirm that Hugh's old master was indeed here. And, in
all likelihood, unavoidable. "Yes. Well—perhaps. Captain Gwin and
his daughter just arrived with Mr. Hogsett. In whose carriage, I don't
know."

Hugh looked at John with his brows drawn down. "I dinna give a
damn whose carriage bounced down the road." But then Hugh's eyes
lost their fire and took on a look of an undecided rabbit. "You said Captain Gwin?"

"That's right."

"And his daughter, as well?"

"Yes. Nancy, I believe. If you will but turn around"—John motioned behind Hugh—"you will be nose to nose with the girl."

Hugh turned to the growing group of young men and women behind him. They were all dressed finely, though some admittedly better than others, for the passing minister's sermon. Katherine had attracted a passel of admirers in the wake of her accident, and more than a few had discovered the beautiful newcomer, Miss Gwin.

She was engrossed in bantering with a tall young man, but when Hugh stared at her long enough, she returned his look and then smiled, blushing.

John looked back to Hugh and was surprised by the even greater change in his cousin. If he had never seen melancholy before, then he surely had now.

"Too much," Hugh said to no one in particular, shaking his head. "Too much." He walked toward the house, shoulders weighed down like a man who had just lost everything. He disappeared inside.

John let him go and turned his attention to his sister, Miss Gwin, and their growing circle of friends. "I thought you ladies were headed to work in the house?"

Hugh closed the door behind him, shutting out the festivity in the yard. He was in no mood for it.

He glanced down at his clothes and grimaced as he rubbed his hand across the light tow-linen shirt. His laced-up breeches were unfashionably long, nearly covering scuffed and worn shoes. He sported no stylish hose, never had. He nearly looked like the servant he had been. Nearly, but not quite. He took a deep breath. *Never apologize for existing.*

When he had first seen Master—*Mister*—Hogsett crossing the yard, Aunt Maggie on his arm, he felt the past decade tumble away. He was no longer a man, one who had proven his worth by fighting—and winning, by God—a long, painful war for his country.

No. Instead, he was an angry boy. One who had lost his home and his family and would never accept his position as a mere servant, owned like a bull or a stallion, and bucking worse than they. Hearing of Captain Gwin was only an additional, irritating reminder of what he had been.

But it was the daughter who had sent his world spinning. Gwin's nameless daughter—she was here, she was real, and not nameless any more. Nancy, John had said. The same delicate heart face he remembered, same glossy dark hair. He had only met her once, but he had carried her memory around like a talisman for the last three long years of the war. Mostly, he had conjured her innocent child's face for comfort while rocking in the packed prison ship, flies lighting on and off the pulp of his ruined chest. It was somewhere no child belonged, but she would never know she was there, in his head, and that she was the one thing that saw him through.

After the war, he thought he could spend every day just happy to be alive and free. And he had succeeded for a while, as he tramped the roads across the country.

And then he came home.

Maybe here he would never forget. Here he would always be known as an owned man, as property.

Just yesterday, it didn't matter what a low station he had filled before he left home all those years ago, or what damage he was left with after the war—the scars on his face and on his body, or the ague. And now it did. Could he live that way forever?

But he had fought for her, that little girl, and here she was. Smiling, beautiful, free.

He silently thanked her and God for seeing him through.

Nancy smiled at the tall young man she just met. John his name was and he doted over his sister's hurt lip, looking as sorry as if he had hurt her himself. His warm gray eyes came back to her again and all at once she felt she had missed something in never having an older brother, or even one close enough to lean on. She had many little sisters and two brothers, the youngest just a baby, so she didn't feel void of family. But while love and loyalty and justice were strong virtues in her house, tenderness and affection were more of a luxury that no one ever seemed to find time for.

John put an arm around his sister's shoulder. "If you do not get to work in the house, we shall have a yard full of guests expiring where they stand ere the preacher returns."

"I see Aunt Maggie's grammar lessons are finally beginning to take hold, John. You sound nearly like a proper gentleman," Katherine said, holding the hand he had draped around her.

John looked embarrassed. He shouldn't have. Nancy was enjoying herself immensely listening to their banter, and she thought a more proper gentleman she had never met.

Katherine glanced around the yard and her look sobered. "Where has Hugh gone off to?"

"In the house," John answered.

"Well, he should be tending the goose."

John's eyes were suddenly the size of saucers. "The goose, yes, of course. Excuse me." He hurried away.

Katherine turned to her. "Have you met my cousin, Hugh? He's only recently returned home after serving in the late war." At a leisurely walk, she led the way to the house.

"But the war's been over—" Nancy said.

"Oh, no,"—Katherine shook her head—"he left in '81. Actually, he was released from a British prison then. But he's just now decided to come home."

From the look of her, Nancy thought perhaps Katherine was a bit infatuated with her cousin, this Hugh she was speaking of.

When they reached the porch, Katherine said, "The shade is much more inviting, don't you agree?"

Sweat trickled down the side of Nancy's temple. "Certainly."

Katherine tried to smile, but the split in her lip seemed to pain her. "We'll have a quick drink before serving everyone else. No one has to know." She opened the door to the small cabin.

About a third the size of her father's house, it was warm and dim inside, very quiet. She smelled wood and yeast and honey and the smoky fireplace. Embers in its hearth burned low, banked for later, and when she fully entered the room and Katherine shut the door behind them Nancy noticed that the fireplace was open straight through to the kitchen on her right. She had never seen that done before. She had to remember to tell her father.

"Give me a moment to tend this and then I'll fetch us something cool," Katherine said as she stoked the cooking fire from the hall side.

Nancy continued to look around the room. A door directly across from her, in the back, was open a crack and through it she could see the edge of a bed covered in a red and blue quilt. A bed jacket hung behind it.

A loft ran along the same back wall. The logs were fresh-cut from the look and smell. Another bright quilt up there caught her eye. A book sat on the end of the bed, the rest of the loft was lost in deep shadows.

Katherine rattled the poker putting it away and Nancy turned. As her new friend hung a kettle of water over the low fire, Nancy was surprised to catch a glimpse of a man's legs through the open fireplace, sitting at the long table in the kitchen. She had thought they were alone.

"You know, Hugh," Katherine said suddenly, "Aunt Maggie will throttle you if she finds you are sitting on your backside with all these people needing attention."

"Oh och, woman. Stop your prattling. I brought up an onion from the cellar, see?"

Nancy couldn't help but chuckle softly as the faceless man, his brogue deep and smooth, held up a scrawny onion for his cousin to witness.

"An onion! I swear, Hugh, honestly."

For reasons Nancy could never have named, her chuckle turned into peals of laughter as the man still proffered the onion, now silently. She bent down to look past the low stones on her side of the hearth. As her breath caught in her throat, her laughter died.

The saddest, most handsome face she had ever seen was looking straight at her, the blue-green eyes not sharing at all in her mirth, but not looking a bit angry at it either. What was eating him was anyone's guess, but it certainly must have been something powerful. She had caught a glimpse of it outside earlier, the first time she noticed him, but then had dismissed it just as quickly, enjoying the rare chance to socialize too much to let it worry her.

But being in here nearly alone with him was all too...intimate. She had never really known what that word meant until now. She felt like she was part of his world and part of his sadness, even though he was a stranger.

He set the onion down on the table, pushed himself back, and walked out of the cabin. She followed him.

His long, thick legs carried him much faster than she could go, down off the porch, skirting the crowded yard. She glanced around. Her father would tan her hide if he saw her practically running after a strange man, but she found that her father hadn't seen her, was in fact deeply involved in discussion with Katherine's brother, John. She also saw Katherine watching her from the porch, amusement on her face. She pointed Nancy to a narrow door on the near side of the barn, just down the hill.

Still stealing glances at her father, she slipped into the dim barn—unnoticed, she hoped. Once the door banged closed behind her, shafts of light sprinkling down from very few gaps in the plank siding and around the door were all she had to see by. She had never known a barn pen to be so dark and she didn't dare move in the strange room until her eyes adjusted. Until then, she listened to horses stamping and whinnying through a wall straight ahead.

Slowly she began to make out the shapes around her. Directly ahead, leaning against the wall the horses were stabled behind, a ladder climbed up to a loft that ran the length of the building. A jumble of tools sat propped in the corner. A froe, a mallet, and a few axes were hanging. Staves of wood lay in low piles on a pallet to her left, nearby was a barrel without a lid. Dark shadows swallowed up the rest of the room.

She didn't hear or see Hugh.

She gently pushed open a door to her right and peeked in. Light flooded that room from the wide-open double doors at either end. A few guests milled around in front of the barn, but her father was nowhere to be seen.

Except for a plow, the floor of the room was empty. Nancy knew this was where they threshed their grains. She imagined Hugh, his light hair tied back as it was today, hard at work here in the late summer, bringing in his wheat or rye. He would be hot, he would probably take his shirt off, and...

What in God's name was wrong with her?

She went back to the doorway of the smaller room, cast one last quick glance around, and then turned to leave the way she had come, hoping to get out unnoticed.

She banged into a broad chest hidden in the shadows before she made it out the door.

It was Hugh's chest, she was certain. She smelled soap in his shirt, a black—or was it blue?—and white checkered gingham, unlaced at the neck, full and loose in the sleeves. But the shirt he wore before, in the house, was white and of a tow-linen that looked to have softened a respectable degree. Somehow, in the time he had disappeared, he had managed to change his clothes, down to his black felt boots.

She had a passing thought that perhaps he hadn't changed his clothes at all, perhaps she was pressed tightly to some other man, skulking about in the barn. She pulled away.

It was Hugh. He gave her his profile when he turned his head to the closed door to her left. His thick blonde hair was now covered in a dark linen kerchief, knotted tightly in the back and flowing down his back.

Quite the pirate.

"So, you've searched out the stable hand, have you, now?" His voice was cold, as much changed as his clothes.

"No. I've searched you out."

"I would like you ta leave."

She didn't pay his gruffness any mind. She watched his eyes, still hard but with some uncertainty filling them, and then his chest, slowly rising and falling beneath his rough shirt.

"Well, I'm a guest here. You have to be nice to me."

"I most certainly dinna."

She smiled. "I'll tattle to your Aunt."

He shrugged.

"You really want me to leave?"

He walked to the door and opened it. Sunlight spilled in. "I do."

"Fine." She walked to the door, waited a moment, and then spun around. He was so close, looking down at her with a soft, unguarded expression. She stretched up onto her toes, kissed his cheek, and then hurried off through the yard.

He watched her go, her thick skirts swaying beneath a tiny waist. Lord, he thought, he could probably completely encircle that waist with his hands. And that fine dress couldn't possibly be as soft as her skin looked—

What was he thinking?

He couldn't touch that girl, Gwin's daughter. And just what the hell was she thinking, anyway? Following him in here like that, nearly stumbling across him in the workshop changing his clothes.

When he had first slammed through the barn door, his only thought had been to make sure he let no one mistake his place by wearing middling clothes—he felt like a workhand, a servant, so he should look like one—and she had caught him at it, coming in as soon as he had swiped off his shirt.

He considered it a great turn of luck that he had stored his clothes in the loft, and was up there changing, hidden in the shadows, when she came in. Or then again, maybe not. Maybe she would have run, screaming into the yard at seeing the horribly twisted skin of his chest and his back, and then he would never have had the misfortune of having her tiny, brazen body pressed against his.

Avoid her for the rest of the day, that was the best advice he could give himself. He closed the door and turned to change back into his good clothes.

Avoid her. Perfect. Now, if he could just stop thinking about her.

CHAPTER TWENTY

Two years later; Augusta County, Virginia, at Back Creek
April 1787

As John emptied the bucket into the trough, he heard Jamie say, "It's a tail." He looked to his cousin, kneeling in the clean hay they had laid out for the birth of the foal. The rest of the stable was lost in shadows from the flickering lantern-light.

Jamie looked up, his face haggard. Wiry blonde hair spiked out around his head, his blue eyes were distant. He wiped his forehead against a broad shoulder. "A damned tail!"

John turned cold at his cousin's words. The horse struggled to her feet and her black tail rode high as she desperately pressed her rump against the stall. "She shouldn't be doing that now, should she?" John asked, watching as milk slowly dripped from her teats.

Jamie stood up and wiped his hands on his breeches, hay stuck to his knees. "She's going ta do what she's going ta do at this point."

John squatted on his haunches, leaned back against the rough planks of the stall, and ran his hands through his hair. The mare soon lay back down near him. He stroked her silky coat and she nickered, blowing dust off the floor. "Can't you turn the foal around?"

"How would you like me ta do that?"

"You're the damned horseman—"

"Dinna yell at me, John." Jamie kneeled down behind the sweating mare and began to work at birthing the foal again.

Within a few moments, John saw her upper lip curl over her thick teeth, her mouth turned pale, her eyes rolled. Water gushed, soaking Jamie's clothes and puddling on the hay-covered floor around his knees.

"Come on, son of a bitch, come on," Jamie grunted.

John moved closer to see just what the hell his cousin was doing to his horse. Jamie's arm was wet and splattered with blood, and when he pushed his hand back into the mare, a dark tail finally sprang from her blood-red opening.

"I dinna think I can do any more, John," Jamie said.

"That can't be right," John said as he lunged forward. "Move."

Jamie jumped up and grunted as his elbow smacked the stall.

John dropped down and reached into her, as Jamie had done. After nearly a year of waiting for this first foal of his very own stable, carefully bred from the finest two horses he could buy, he was not willing to lose it now.

He felt the shape of the foal's rump—so warm—and the silky tail brushed against his arm. He tried to push the rump deeper into the mother, hoping that he could somehow pivot the animal to help the birth along its natural course. But the foal hardly budged and fresh blood seeped out each time he pushed.

"John." Jamie was stroking her poll and forelock with one hand and her cheek with the other. He cradled her head in his large, soiled hands. "John, stop," he said, an icy calm to his words.

"What is the matter with you? I have to get this foal born quickly. I nearly have a leg. Just comfort her."

"John," he said. "John! She's dead. I'm sorry."

John rested his forehead on his arm and let the animal go. "Son of a b—" He ground his teeth. All their efforts had been for nothing. He just couldn't admit it before. They had been at this for almost an hour and she had been laboring for much longer than that. Too much time for any mare to last.

"Bitch!" He snatched a harness from the wall and flung it across the stable. It bounced off the far wall and landed with a quiet thud on the floor in the shadows. His stallion stomped and banged against the east pen, and through the thick logs, John could imagine the spirited animal's nose flaring, his long tail swishing. He was a magnificent animal. "We've got to get the foal."

"The foal's probably gone as well," Jamie said.

John whirled around to look at him. "I can't lose them both."

Jamie sighed noticeably, then said, "Give me your knife."

John touched his waist. He was without his belt or his sheath. "Forgot it."

Jamie looked around for a moment and then left the stable. He returned with a hatchet. John knew it was razor sharp. He had stoned it that morning.

John put up a hand. "No!" The knife would perhaps have been bearable. Not an axe.

Jamie motioned toward the door. "Leave then, I'll do it."

"I'll get it out myself. Just keep that thing away," John warned. He kneeled again and reached in for the foal. When he finally got a grip on the animal, he pulled until his arm shook. He felt the thin leg bone bend and pop. He drew his bloody hand away. *Oh, my God.*

Jamie knelt beside him. "What was that noise?"

John couldn't come up with even one word to describe...

Jamie took his place behind the horse. Within a moment or two he said, "I've got the cord in my hand, but it's stone still." He looked over. "There's no life here."

John got to his feet. "I know."

"What?"

"Snapped its leg. Got nothing, not even a twitch. That's it. It's over."

Jamie laid a blanket across the mare's flank and tail. "You should get some sleep. I'll take care of her first thing." He put an awkward arm about John's shoulder. "Come on."

But John was staring down at the dark horse. He went to her head and stroked her white blaze and straightened her mane. Her eyes were closed.

They picked up their lanterns and soft halos of light swung back and forth as they left the stable and walked into the cool night. They stopped outside of the barn to wash their hands with water from the rain barrel and dried them on dirty pants.

The full moon had already ridden most of the way through the sky while they labored in the stable, and stars winked at them in thick batches wherever they escaped the moon's shine. New leaves filled the few trees in the yard, clustered where no crops grew, and they passed under them as they walked to the cabin.

Inside, they slumped into chairs beside a wobbly table. Nearby, the fire burned low. John stared at the mug of beer he had left on the table, before... "I thought I did everything right."

Jamie sipped from his own mug and then cleared his throat. "You did. Of course you did. You canna control everything. It's nature."

"I should have cut her open earlier. Saved the foal."

Jamie shrugged.

John couldn't understand Jamie's confidence and casual acceptance of the randomness of life and death and loss. Jamie must not see clearly that success meant that you planned properly and trusted in God after that. Why, every prosperous man was moral and just—enlightened even. Wasn't he?

An immoral man could never succeed in the world. God wouldn't allow it.

A man well-satisfied with his lot decided early on what his life would entail and planned for it. He was God-fearing. He worked hard and lived nobly. If he built his life around those virtues, John knew his life would flourish. More than anything, he wanted to be a respected, successful man.

And at the very least he didn't want anyone to find out he was a failure.

But his best mare dead and his foal lost he did not consider happily flourishing. How could he have forgotten his knife at a time like that? "I'll have to plan more carefully for next spring." John rested his forehead on his palm and stared at the table.

"Yes, you can do that, and you can just as easily end up with a breech foal and a dead mare. But it doesna hurt ta plan, of course. All would be lost without planning, you're right."

Jamie stood and clapped John on the shoulder before he crouched down to bank the coals in the fireplace. He refilled his mug of beer, and then John's, and soon sat back down.

"Speaking of planning, John, I thought you were looking for a wife?"

John tried to smile but couldn't. "I've hardly left the place since I came here."

"Well, that will change. I've agreed for the both of us ta give a hand with a barn raising in three days' time at the Gibson's. You will be there?"

"Will there be dancing?" he asked in a flat voice, still staring at the table.

Jamie chuckled. "I'm sure there will be. Just for you if we have ta."

* * *

For the first time since leaving Aunt Maggie's, John finally felt productive. It had been a hot day, but working putting up the barn had been satisfying, and he had met more of his neighbors in this one day than he had in the year and some odd months he had been here. He had to admit, though only to himself, that he had made a mistake spending most of that time cloistered on his farm and trying to make a go of it all alone.

Aunt Maggie had neighbors working at her place year-round, and John found it shameful then to let neighbors with nothing to gain toil and toil at responsibilities that weren't their own. He didn't consider then how good it felt to help someone else, especially when the people that were helped were so appreciative, or perhaps especially because he had never been alone so much in his life.

Today there had even been sincere offers of help to get his own place into good shape, after the men heard what farm he had moved to.

"You move there in the fall or the summer?" one man said after he had sliced his axe into the pale wood, the last cut completing a notch in the end of the log that would cradle another notched log as the side of the barn went up. He laid the axe on the ground and they moved the log for the other workers to put up.

"Fall," John said between grunts.

"That old barn was in damned poor shape. Did she get a new roof to cover your hay?"

"No." He couldn't bring himself to lie, but he hoped the ridicule would be bearable.

The man laughed pleasantly. "Lean winter, hunh?"

Hours later, when they spotted the women coming out of the cabin, carefully balancing food and drink, men took off their hats and threw them into the air. Tools and wood dropped to the ground; two men put down the end of a log they were setting in place; and John wiped his hands, dirty from squeezing mud and straw and rocks together for chinking, on his pants.

A young woman brought him a mug of watery beer. It smelled like old bread and the metal was cold in his hands. "Thank you for being here today," she said.

He smiled at her and drank most of the brew. She was still standing there when he looked up, so he finished off the beer to hand the heavy mug to her. He held it out, and she looked at it, surprised.

"Yes?" she said.

"Aren't you waiting for this?"

"Oh! Yes, I suppose I was," she said, taking the mug and hurrying away.

He watched her skirts sway as she walked. She doubled her steps as another woman her age walked out of the house with more drinks. They put their heads together and the young lady he had been speaking to broke into a dazzling smile.

"My Lord, did you see that?" Jamie said to another man as they walked up to John.

"I did, but I'm not so sure about him." The man slapped John on the back and shook his hand. "You don't even know, do you, young fellow? Well, at least you should know her name is Elizabeth."

When John just stared at him, Jamie laughed and told him to get to the food before it was long gone.

After they had loaded their fill of meat and hunks of cheese into hollowed out crusty hunks of bread, they sat on a log waiting to be put up and rested their bread trenchers on their knees. Women continued to bustle through the yard, seeing to it that all the men were comfortable. John caught the young woman staring at him again and again, and he started to smile.

He was still smiling when he stripped down for bed that night. The cabin was quiet, as it always was. On the nights that he was still awake a few hours after sundown, the deep woods behind his cabin became alive with sounds, and he would stay up listening to them.

The owls were comforting and he would count the beats between their calls. When the leaves on the ground were brittle, he often heard rustling and he tried to determine by the quality of the crunches and skittering just what kind of critter was sneaking around. He usually laid it at the feet of the raccoon, and on moonlit nights he would see the bandit peer out of the dark woods and then slowly creep through the yard.

All too often, a piercing scream broke into the peaceful night, a scream close enough that it could wake him from a sound sleep, and he would lie there and stare into the darkness of the empty cabin and listen for more, unsure whether the scream were real or dream. The sound was of a woman in pain, a mournful woman, and although John knew when fully awake that a wildcat made the noise, it never failed to race his heart when his eyes first fluttered open. It also made him aware that he was completely alone.

It was especially true tonight when he woke to the noise of the wildcats. After the bleariness cleared from his eyes and no further noises disturbed him, he thought of the young woman today, her skirts swaying as she walked through the yard, her efficient way of carrying food and drink and waiting on the men, and the way that she had made him smile. He didn't smile much anymore. And he certainly didn't want to be alone.

CHAPTER TWENTY-ONE

Rockingham County, Virginia

Later that summer, just before the sunset of a warm day, John stood and looked at Aunt Maggie's house. His horse stamped behind him and, when he looked, shook her head. "Wait girl," he told her and looked back to the house.

Nothing had changed. On the outside.

Jamie rode in behind him at a slow walk and John heard the creak of his saddle as he dismounted. They had both been summoned.

On the porch, Hugh's boots were tossed casually next to the door, one standing, one on its side. John walked up and righted the boot and the door swung open.

Hugh's cheeks were covered in days' worth of dark stubble. Under his bright blue-green eyes, purple smudges blended into the lines that deepened when he smiled. "John," Hugh said and nodded. They shook hands firmly.

"Are we too late?"

Hugh nodded.

Jamie sounded heavily on the stairs behind them and Hugh moved to greet his brother with a handshake and an arm around the shoulder. "I'm so sorry," Jamie said.

John walked into the house.

Katherine sat at the small table near the door, her quaking hands sewing on a long white sheet. She looked up at him and swiped at her wet face with the palm of her hand. "In the best room," she said, pointing to Aunt Maggie's bedroom, directly across from the open front door.

The heavy door was closed. It shouldn't have been. He glanced back at Katherine—didn't she know how wrong they were to close her in there, alone?

He pushed on it, and it returned a slow squeak. He leaned against the jam and looked at his Aunt Maggie, laid out under the shuttered window along the back wall. Candles near her flickered. Wilted flowers were carefully spread out around her. She was dead.

Her hands were crossed over her chest and clutched her rosary beads. He hadn't seen them since he was a child. She still had them, had held on to her faith, without a church or a priest, for all these years.

He ran a fingertip across the cold beads and then covered her rigid hands with his. *All these years.* He had always known Aunt Maggie to never let go—of a love, a need, a wish, an obligation, a grudge.

And so he thought she would never die.

He went to his knees beside her and whispered, "Our Father, Who art in Heaven..."

Out on the porch, Hugh clapped Jamie on the back. "Sorry ta have you back home like this, but it's grateful I am ta see you." He couldn't even begin to say how much.

Jamie nodded his head in the direction of John, kneeling at Aunt Maggie's side. "Think he's taking this badly?"

Hugh took a moment to look. He smiled at the broad swath of white shirt where John's waistcoat pulled up from his breeches. His breeches had wandered far enough up his legs to show inches of bare skin.

The boy was lankier than anyone he had ever seen. He looked altogether patrician standing up, nicely turned out in his grieving clothes, but kneeling down he looked like a half-dressed urchin.

Hugh shook his head. "He's a boy giving respect, no more than's due. You thinking something different of it?"

"A boy, is it now?"

Hugh sat on the bench and stretched his legs. "When he's no' so gangly, I'll take it back. Watch that he doesna trip over those long feet before he's out here again. I'll be betting you that he does."

Katherine's sobs floated out the door before it slammed shut.

Jamie sat next to his brother and smacked him with his hat. "Well, Hugh, I think you may have upset her with your irreverence for poor Aunt Maggie. Katherine's a delicate young woman, she knows talking on about such things, it isna fitting the occasion."

"Never once said I wasna an utter horse's ass, now did I?"

"I never did, either."

"No, you probably never did." Hugh turned and looked critically at Jamie. "And what's this about Katherine? When did you form the opinion she was such a delicate young woman? You've hardly seen the chit. She ain't delicate. Beautiful, maybe. I dinna know about delicate."

"Seeing from the way her brother John falls apart at the slightest, thought she would've earned the same earmark."

"Falls apart, you say? All I've seen is he's something of a brat. But falls apart? What's wrong with the boy?"

"Dinna call him a boy—or a brat—it doesna fit you," Jamie chided. "What's wrong with the young man?"

Jamie's dimple crinkled. Hugh tried hard to keep a smile off his own face, it would ruin his joke. Funny how that easy dimple in his brother's face recalled at once a hundred moments of childhood devilry.

Hugh wanted to laugh out loud. And yet, he kept it to himself— Katherine would never understand. But Aunt Maggie would have.

"The last year, John's been catching his feet in the mud no matter what he does." Jamie glanced at the shuttered window behind the bench. "I dinna think he ever realized how much these two women took care of him. He's as lost as a shaky calf. And now Aunt Maggie passing," he shook his head, "this is bad on poor John, that's what I've been thinking."

The door swung open and light dipped across the crooked planks of the porch. John stepped out and sat on the top step, his long legs nearly reaching the ground. He put his hands out behind him on the porch and leaned back, staring into the yard. "Are you going in to pay your respects and pray for the guidance of her soul?" he asked. "Or are you too involved in laughing at me?"

* * *

John found Hugh in the barn late that night, after his sister had gone to bed. "Katherine said you've been ill?"

Hugh got up from where he had been sitting on the floor, a dim lantern at his side. He waved a thick hand. "'Tis the ague." He patted a cow on the rump as he walked to the door. "Go'night ladies." He pushed open the barn door and stood looking out at the moonlit yard. "John, I knew when I was heading here it was a peaceful place ta live, and I wanted ta stay with Aunt Maggie. I thought at first that she might just need somebody ta take care of her. I was worried about her. But that wasna the truth. What I really knew was that she was someone who would never let me down. I wanted her ta take care of me."

They closed up the barn and John followed his cousin through the yard. Hugh glanced back at him. "You appreciate that when the world gets mean. A solid, quiet house, you know? I thought, I could live in a house like that. And that tough old lady was just the one ta make it all right. But I know she needed ta go, John. She was so old and she lived her life in the best way she knew how. She wanted ta go. It's all right." Hugh clapped a thick hand on his shoulder. "She wasna blood, but she mothered us all right well."

John felt small all over again for his disrespect of Aunt Maggie. For a while he forgot that he had only asked Hugh about being ill.

On the first full day spent at his old home again, John woke early to wander around the property, inspect the buildings, the animals, the woodpile. He consoled Katherine. He fidgeted.

It was after a small dinner that no one ate when he decided a section of the fence needed checking one last time. The old bull was out there in the pasture beyond the weathered snake fence. John wondered how many times the old boy had pushed the fence down since he had left home. In the bull's old age, he had become more content to stay close by, hadn't pushed his boundaries much, but in his younger days John had put this fence back together more times than he could count.

The bull's thick body was a deep, dark red and his side was mottled with white that looked like whitewash had splashed on him and then slowly dripped off. His legs were folded up beneath him, but John knew he was still at attention, especially keeping a pink-rimmed eye on the tall man watching him.

From John's view of him in profile, his white and red head was a straight, flat slope starting between his gnarled horns, to the tip of his flared nose. His face was squat and his neck thick. John called out, "You're still here?" The bull turned his head slightly. "Yes, right, where would you go?" He sighed and turned back to the house.

By that evening, more family had arrived. His younger brother, Hugh—or Mac, as he was familiarly called—searched him out in the dim, dusty barn where John was expending his energy mucking out the cramped stalls. The sleeves of his coarse shirt were rolled high; the shirttail in the back hanging outside of his breeches; and just below his rhythmically swaying shoulder blades, he felt sweat adhere the material to his back.

"Always at work, are you?" Mac said.

John spun around, surprised, and then leaned on the wood handle of his fork. Mac looked well. He hadn't seen his brother in over two years and he was surprised by the changes those two years had made. The awkwardness of his teen years had disappeared, John was glad to see that. "You grew into your ears," John said, grinning.

His clothes, if not of the finest linen, were well cut; his light hair shorn to a respectable shoulder length and not worn clubbed back, as John and their cousin Hugh both wore their much longer hair.

They started back toward the house together. In the yard, John washed his arms from the barrel and stamped his feet to loosen the muck; then they sat together on the porch outside of the low murmuring drifting out of the open window and door.

"Katherine is engaged," John said, removing his hat and retying his hair. "She's having a hard time with it. Aunt Maggie's passing, I mean."

"She's to marry Michael Propst, I assume?"

"Yes, she and Michael will take over this old place. Hugh wants to join Jamie and me down at Back Creek as soon as he sees her good and married. I've got to get back down there, too, if I don't want to miss my own wedding."

"My own brother's getting married! How do you like that? And he wasn't even telling anyone." Mac shook John's hand firmly and gave his congratulations. "What's the gem's name?"

"She's Elizabeth, and we hope you'll break away sometime soon to visit with us."

It was a subdued brotherly celebration, as quiet feminine sobs could be heard through the window. Mac turned to look in. "I've yet to go inside. Is she…"

John's hands and eyes worked around the brim of his low hat, crumpling and rolling, and he nodded without looking up at the mention of Aunt Maggie. "She's laid out right and proper, like she wanted. It won't be 'til morning that we'll see her in the ground. You can go on in."

Mac quietly left John alone. A few short moments after he entered the crowded house, the large figure of Samuel Stevens appeared on the porch. John had only spoken to him briefly when he first arrived. Sam roughly, without a word, patted John on the shoulder as he passed by, sounded heavily on the wooden steps and ambled off in the twilight toward his dark sorrel mare. He watched him ride slowly away.

John's knee bounced and bounced and then bounced faster and higher, stopping suddenly as he placed his hands on his knees, cleared his throat, rose up, and entered the house.

* * *

Hugh looked at his Cousin Mac as they balanced the weight of the pine coffin. He thought of the last time he had seen Mac, as a two-year-old peacefully sleeping in Uncle Daniel's bed in a cramped corner of Maggie's cabin. It had been two months to the day after his father died. And once Hugh was sent off the farm, he didn't see Mac again until now—a total of fifteen years.

Today, they each had a rear corner of the box. Michael and James, Maggie's sons, were at the lead, John and Jamie at the sides. Katherine walked a few steps behind with her fiancé by her side.

The family graveyard was on the southwest corner of Maggie's farm and she was being buried beside her husband and her daughter. John and Mac's parents were also resting here. A dogwood that bloomed brilliantly in the spring cast a dappled shade, and small patches of sunlight spilled through on the softly rounded, roughly etched stones. Moss lightly covered one stone that read: "William McLaughlin. 1721 – 1762." Hugh did not remember this man, Maggie's husband, his uncle.

After a few words, they laid Aunt Maggie to rest. They stood and they stared. Katherine cried. When they all felt they could do no more, they left two of their group behind to close the grave.

Hugh watched them work for a moment and then turned to follow the rest of the mourners. Mrs. Stevens linked a thin arm through Katherine's and they walked through the dewy grass. Mr. Stevens stood with Jamie and gestured to the patch of knee-high corn across the field.

In the opposite direction, two women—neither of whom had been in the burial party—both wearing black shawls over their sober dresses, walked along the edge of the woods. The taller woman had streaks of gray in her black hair, the shorter one had gleaming, red-blonde tresses.

Hugh hurried over to Samuel Stevens and Jamie.

Samuel was saying, "Now see, they'll wind around the bottom of those cornstalks—"

"Who are those two women?" Hugh asked his brother.

Jamie turned to where Hugh was pointing and stared at them. His breathing stopped. "Do you think?" he finally said, incredulous.

Hugh nodded as they watched their mother and their sister, Jane, walking away without a word. Jamie started off first.

"Wait," Hugh called and then started to run.

"Jane?" Jamie shouted.

Hugh caught up with him when the women turned around. Sissy McLaughlin put a slender, trembling hand over her mouth and Jane circled her arm around her mother's waist.

"Mother," Hugh said.

She put out a hand, touched his face, and, before he could even think, leaned into his broad chest, burying her ashen face in his shoulder. All he could do was hold her, his arms heavy as they lifted and cradled her thin shoulders. She was so tiny, this enormous piece of his heart was. He had a hard time finding the old anger he had always felt toward her. He couldn't remember just now why he had ever held her little hands responsible for anyone's suffering. What a worthless, childish tantrum his anger had been. What wasted time. He was so sorry.

He let her go and she fell into Jamie's arms.

"Jamie," Jane said, "take Mother over for more time ta say goodbye ta Aunt Maggie. I'd like ta talk with Hugh Òg."

Jamie led their mother back across the field.

"She doesna talk," Jane said as soon as they were out of earshot.

Hugh looked back from watching them go. "What do you mean?"

"I hav'na heard a word pass her lips since I left my bond and came back home. And from what the neighbors say, she hasna spoken a word since we were all taken. I wanted you ta know, before you became upset with her. 'Tis a bit unsettling."

Odd how he always thought of himself as being abandoned, while his sister considered them taken away. He may have just begun to forgive his mother, but he would never forget. A frown took over his face. "And if she doesna talk, who filled your head with the nonsense that we were taken away? Mother sent us off without another thought."

She was unflappable, his little sister. Coolly, her hands went to her hips and she grew an inch in height. "I resent what you're trying ta say. Everyone around this way knows it for the truth, Hugh Òg. The court didna consider a poor widow capable of our proper raising, figured we'd become trouble ta the County unless we were taken in hand. Liberty and security, Da always used ta say. Remember?"

"Yes." He pictured his father's proud grin when he would say those words. His chest tightened. "He said that's what he found in the Valley after he escaped the impress gangs of the King's Navy."

She nodded. "He just never realized it could all be lost for us if he passed early. He was a landless man. A full corn crib and a few sticks of furniture couldna provide us with liberty and security. But he had too much faith in his new home and his neighbors ta ever consider that it would be so. I'm just mightily glad he never knew about our fate. But I suppose we should be grateful we werena given over ta cruel masters."

"Grateful? Were you grateful?"

She narrowed her bright, round eyes at him. "No. Da raised us with too much damnable pride for that. I said I suppose that we *should* be. You're a lackwit of the highest order and I'm about tired of talking at you."

"Are you angry with me, Jane?"

"Of course I am. This nonsense you're spouting..." She shook her head at him. "And how long have you been back now that you couldna find your way ta your mother?"

"Two years."

"Two years. I think you deserve some chiding for two years, Hugh Meglakin." She swatted him on the shoulder and then threw herself into his arms in a spirited embrace. "And this is for coming home whole and handsome. I've missed you terribly."

* * *

The next evening as Katherine made supper, Hugh and Mac sat together at the small table beside the open door. The summer night was heavy and not a breeze stirred.

Mac sifted through papers of Aunt Maggie's in the waning light. "She has a few promissory notes on her neighbors, none greater than a few pounds. And it seems she has balances owed to two shopkeepers. There will also be charges for the crying sale, the whiskey and such," he lifted one more small slip of paper closer to the window. He handed it to Hugh. "Can you make out this name? The second witness on the bottom left there."

Hugh pretended to look at the paper. "No." He handed it back.

Mac shrugged. "Doesn't matter."

"Where did you learn reading and ciphering?" Hugh asked.

Mac put down the papers. "Well, certainly not from Master Herdsman, although I've been with him since I was six. No, Aunt Maggie was a very learned woman. She taught us all when she had us here. Where did you learn? From Aunt Maggie, too?"

"Oh, here and there." Hugh looked out the window. *Just a little lie.*

"You get away from Master Herdsman often?"

"Occasionally."

"I left only rarely from the Hogsett place, generally the Sabbath, and with good reason. After I was there a while, I realized that I could only do the things that they told me I could. Even after a few years when I grew up and became a man as tall as he was, I couldna even leave the plantation if I wanted ta. If I had wanted ta go work for someone else I couldna have done that either." He stopped talking as Katherine walked through the room and out the door. They heard her light footfalls on the steps.

Mac was still watching him, listening intently for the rest of his story. "Yes?" he prompted.

"If my father had still been living, I could have left home if I had wanted ta and done what I wanted. But there, if I left, they would report me ta the court, put me in the big city papers, perhaps, and bring me back ta face my punishment and undoubtedly make me stay longer than I was supposed ta."

Mac's eyes hardened. "Of course they would," Mac said. "And weld an iron collar 'round your neck and burn an *R* in your face for the trouble. So you stayed until when?"

"When I became nineteen years, so many of the boys signed up for the fighting. They took off down the road with their old muskets in their hands." Hugh smiled, thinking of the last time he and his friends were young and simple. "Sometimes great groups of them, but sometimes they were alone. A few mothers cried, but usually they didna, and after I watched enough of those brave men, I finally told Mr. Hogsett what I wanted ta do. I wanted ta be let out of my bond ta go fight in the War. He said him being a patriot, how could he no' let me go and do a great thing? So, I left the farm in July '77"—he thought for a moment—"nearly exactly ten years ago, and became part of Captain Granville Smith's Company, Grayson's Regiment."

"You got out, bless you! And you never had to see him again."

Hugh shrugged. "No' until I came back ta Aunt Maggie's. Didna matter much, though, I'm a free man now."

Katherine came back into the house. Her nose and eyes were red, her hair a little damp around her face, tiny droplets of water sprinkled across her dress. "Supper's ready."

CHAPTER TWENTY-TWO

The wedding ceremony was quiet and sober, and over so quickly John wasn't sure he was actually married. But he was. When they left Elizabeth's father's house, where the wedding took place, it was fully dark, but the couple was eager to spend the first night of their marriage in their own home.

In search of candles, they laughed as they stumbled through the dark into the small cabin where until a few hours ago John lived alone.

"Well, Mrs. McLaughlin, this is a fine way to keep home. You've let the fire burn to ashes and there's no candle at the doorway. Will your father take you back, do you think?"

"Well, Mr. McLaughlin, I've never so much as stepped inside this doorway before today, and well you know it, too. I expect you'll be taking that accusation back."

Lighting a candle, he told her to sit and rest at the small table near the hearth while he restarted the fire that had almost burned out during their wedding ceremony. After seeing it crackling and beginning to catch some of the larger pieces of dry oak he had piled on top, he went back to his wife; kneeled by her side; kissed her tentatively once, twice and then three times; and reluctantly left her to see to the animals that had also been neglected today.

Chickens squawked, piled together into the dark corner, and then settled their ruffled feathers after his feeble light shined on them from the opening of the barn door. "Ladies, next year you get a coop."

His dark, gentle milk cow was complaining loudly, too, and he took a few moments to relieve her suffering.

As he milked he brooded over the quiet happenings of the day. This was not the way his day was supposed to happen. What was supposed to happen was this: His groomsmen, Cousins Daniel, Hugh and Jamie, would have raced to Elizabeth's house for the prize of a bottle of whiskey and kisses of the bride and bridesmaids, the same as they had done at Jamie's wedding. John and his brother Mac would have dressed in their best clothes, and then ridden the most handsome mounts from John's celebrated stable of fine horseflesh to his beautiful girl's home, where Aunt Maggie and Katherine would have already been waiting. They would have craned their necks from the porch when he and Mac came around the bend to see how handsome he looked, and they would have passed the time before the men arrived embarrassing Elizabeth, fussing about how beautiful of a bride she made.

The first mention of a shivaree, when guests made fools of themselves—some of them drunken fools—by loudly serenading the newly married couple, would have been John's signal to take his bride to the privacy of their own home before anyone began demanding an old-fashioned, wedding night disrobing.

But Aunt Maggie was dead; no one from his family had witnessed his wedding... John leaned his forehead into the pungent warmth of his cow's flank and chastised himself for longing for so many things that he could never get back. Now that he finally had a future to look forward to, shouldn't that be his only concern?

"Oh my God, I have a wife."

He jumped up and put the stool back in the corner, running his fingers through his hair and forgiving himself for talking to a cow. "That's exactly what I wanted—a wife. Didn't want to be alone, and now look where I am. Alone."

Properly shamed for neglecting Elizabeth, he quickly secured the barn again before striding to the dim light filling the one small window of his cabin.

But he had company. He could hear horses' hooves clocking and saddles creaking as he neared the house and he wondered why the dog hadn't barked at their approach. Well, whoever it was could wait. He returned to his wife before he let anything else distract him.

She was sleeping. With her head resting on her crossed arms, she was still at the table where he had left her. He smiled at the long, dark hair waving to her lap. He had never seen it out of its tight knot at the back of her head before.

Outside, an off-key serenade broke the silence, thin pots clattered together, the dog began to howl. A feminine giggle broke the song in two. "Hush, dog," the woman said, and the dog obeyed.

When Elizabeth didn't stir, John gently shook her shoulder. She looked up groggily and then smiled at the racket. "A shivaree?" she asked. "Who is it?"

"It must be Jamie and Susan, we'll go out there if you like."

"If I like? They're my new family. Of course we'll go out there, you silly man."

CHAPTER TWENTY-THREE

Later that summer, after Katherine's wedding, Hugh moved in with Jamie and Susan at Back Creek and within a month his nerves were strung as tight as a hide on a curing frame. He needed a farm to lease, any farm. As long as it could shelter his horse, some hay, and a few tools, it would do. He didn't even care if the rain came down on his own head—if his currier's tools and his chestnut mare's food were dry, he would be happy.

On the first day of his search, Hugh had given his tall horse her steam and she had raced along the narrow bridle path between Jamie's and John's, eager as her rider, it seemed, to find her own home. They galloped up to John's small cabin before dawn broke.

At the ruckus and clatter in his yard, John opened his eyes and quietly cursed. Eliza slept soundly next to him and he felt slightly annoyed that she could sleep like that, though almost anything.

In the fireplace next to the bed, last night's banked fire still glowed under the ashes and he could feel a little warmth radiating across the floorboards as he walked past it to the door.

Hugh's easy smile greeted him when he cracked the door a few inches. He wore a tight linen work cap, fingerless gloves, brown wool shirt, and baggy, cream colored trousers. "You said one of the Hamilton's got a farm ta lease. Saddle up, I want ta make it there before the old man's out in the field."

"Most of the valley's not even off the privy yet and you're worried about them already being in the field?" John said. He heard Eliza stirring behind him and he was fairly certain she would scold him for his colorful words when she had him alone. He looked Hugh over again. "You look like a sailor."

"My father was a sailor."

"So?"

"Do you have coffee?" Hugh asked.

"My wife is asleep. Go wait with your horse and I'll be along." John shut the door on him and turned back to Eliza.

She belted her green bed jacket tighter around her waist and looked at him as if to say, *Well?*

"I'll be back before the coffee's cold," he said and kissed her on the cheek.

Hugh waited on agreeing to lease the farm until he could make a quick ride around the property. By late morning the two of them were traveling down the road beside the creek, heading to the farm. When they rode up a narrow, tree lined road, a small barn, about twenty feet by thirty, slightly sagging in the roof and twisted in the posts, greeted them from atop a gentle rise on the north edge of the quiet farm.

In the stillness of the slowly warming morning, the barn was dank when they entered, but Hugh insisted the rafters were sound and it only needed a day's worth of shingles. As Hugh tested the creaking wooden hinges on the barn's double doors, John wondered just what a "day's worth of shingles" consisted of.

On beyond the barn, over a slight grade that eventually sloped steeply to the trickling creek, a stone springhouse rested in the shade of an enormous chestnut tree. Hugh's impatient, thick-legged stride led the way across the yard and John hurried to keep up. After they both ducked into the squat building where high weeds hugged the entryway, Hugh's laughter echoed off the musty walls. "You'll find me in here in the mid of July," he said, noisy water trickling over his fingers. He flicked the cold water at John and ducked back out.

Toward the back of the farm, at the end of a rutted path, was the small, round-log cabin. Two fieldstone steps led to the narrow door. There Hugh and John were both impressed by the iron handle and hinges in place of the usual leather or wooden ones.

"Sturdy," Hugh said as he opened it. But no more comforts lay inside the cabin, except perhaps the thick stone hearth, liberally caked with soot. The floor was bare earth and only one small, cobwebbed window threw light into the damp room. "It's perfect."

John shook his head at his cousin's unbridled optimism, but Hugh paid him no mind, staring off into the yard through the tiny window. "And soon I might like ta buy it outright. Liberty and security, have you thought much about those two of God's gifts?"

"I suppose. But I'd say liberty may be God's gift, while security is man's concern alone."

"Well, now, I may have ta be agreeing with you about that," Hugh said, turning away from the window to face him. "Liberty we have a tenuous hold on now that the war's done. But security?"—he shrugged—"God does provide it in his own way, with the riches of the earth. But we need ta own these clods of dirt and the trees and the fields and the streams and springs, and be able ta work them as we will—else we could lose the limp grasp we have on liberty as well."

John nodded with understanding.

"When someone else owns the sweat of your labor," Hugh continued, "and the bread you're eating, the pallet you sleep on...it's the dream of a tyrant, it is, so tyranny can no' be far behind."

* * *

Within a week, John, Jamie, and Hugh were sweating in the small stand of timber on the edge of the farm, splitting shingles. Hugh assured them that by tonight the roof of the barn would be whole and sound and he wouldn't take them from their own chores to put down a puncheon floor in the cabin.

John didn't believe him. And from the look on Jamie's face, neither did he.

Hugh filled in the silence between the clanging of axes, froes and mallets with a detailed recounting of his time in Charles Town.

"Keeping us confined on the ships—that was stepping far beyond what they had agreed ta. It was promised that we would be kept in the town, no' on those rolling, rocking death sloops. They never kept their word, as gentlemen would, of course. The only exception being their need for craftsmen in town."

Jamie said, "They didna need curriers such as yourself, I assume."

"Those dandies? No, they wanted hordes of tailors for all their god-awful finery. I assume so they could look pretty at their balls and teas. Especially that garish, murdering, English dandy, Bloody Ban Tarleton, with his plumes and his leg hose." He took a critical look at the wood he was working with and then continued, "They needed other craftsmen as well, but I wanted no part of helping them along."

He stopped talking as he placed his blunt froe at a careful angle to the wood's grain and swung forcefully with his maul; he was much more skilled at this than either John or Jamie and a mound of shingles to cover his barn was piling up fast. John and Jamie were just as quickly piling up their own attempted shingles in the kindling box.

"Look here, John," Hugh said. "Pretend this wood's ta be a stave for one o' your barrels, just make it smaller, then it'll be a shingle."

John looked up sharply. "Meanwhile, back in Charles Town..."

"By all means, go at it your own way, good man, just dinna blame me if you lose a finger, or worse."

Jamie sighed. "Continue, please, with your story, Hugh. Leave our fingers ta us."

"Well, I struggled against working for the enemy for months and then one day I awoke in the stinking bowels of that ship for the last time. We were crammed in there, we were. Confessing shame. What does the song say, 'packed up like pickled herring'? Quite right, like pickled herring. And then the man who, just the night before, had been sleeping next ta me—he was dead that morning. Then I noticed his ragged uniform and his filthy hammock, they were moldering. And I looked at myself—moldering just the same. And I say molder no' just because they were falling apart on our bones, but growing things in the always wet heat, eaten up with it, the same as the damp wood all around us. The man had grown mold laying there so long, and so was I. And then that morning—dead." He paused to take another skillful swing and one more shingle was tossed to the pile. "If I had been touched a wee bit by the scurvy, that poor man had been punched full in the face with it." He looked up and wiped sweat away from his eyes.

"After that, I said, 'Hell, yes! I'm a tailor.' I canna tell you that I hadna had enough." His voice wavered and he gave up a small cough, beads of sweat stood out on his face. "Was I a coward? I dinna know. But I got out of that ship, and I wasna tossed over the side in the doing, either. I've got that ta be grateful for." His voice weakened further as he spoke.

They worked quietly for a time, until Hugh said, "Well, hell."

John started a bit when Hugh chucked his tools to the side, trembled a little, suddenly looked weaker, then sat down on the partially cleared forest floor. John looked to Jamie for help, but he stood by, looking on dispassionately. Hugh soon lay flat on his back, groaning.

"He's been having the ague fits here lately," Jamie said. "From a fever he got down there in the Carolina, so he says. It's the swamp fever, that it is. We dinna see much of it here in the highlands. The low-lands and the swamps, they see it. It's common enough. The worst fits seem ta come about in the morning if he's hard at work. He'll be just fine, though the shakes will last awhile."

John sat down next to his cousin, there amid the scattered shingles, tools, stumps and jagged rocks breaking through the ground, and waited for the terrifying episode to end, as Jamie assured him it would. It was something that he had never witnessed before.

CHAPTER TWENTY-FOUR

"Did you do something ta him?" Hugh asked John as they tethered their horses to a weathered post.

They had dismounted in the middle of what was well on its way to becoming a town. Nestled at the foot of Warm Springs mountain and sitting on both sides of a well-traveled wagon road, it boasted a mill, a general store, a growing tavern, a livery barn that ensured a few extra coin for the nearby farmer that offered the stabling or loaning of a horse, a smithy if the horse needed a shoe, and a growing hotel industry serving the visitors of their famous spring baths.

And just now, the gentleman in question was passing out of sight behind the smithy, around a bend in the road leading north.

"He's the commissioner, he is. He had to explain to the court why I refused my taxes when he came 'round. Don't think he's forgiven me quite yet," John replied.

"You, refuse your taxes? Why?"

John looked at Hugh with one eyebrow raised. "What had he done for me?"

Hugh laughed and slapped him on the back. "Quite right," he said. "But dinna think you'll get away with it again."

"If the tithes keep the roads in repair, I won't have to."

In front of the general store, where Hugh was to meet with Tailor Wilson about a job, Hugh and John tapped off their dusty shoes. A neighbor, Anne Gregory, with her young daughter Creacy hiding behind her, stopped them just outside for a polite chat.

"My husband, Joe, is there just across the road," she explained, pointing to a group of men congregating at Mr. Brinkley's tavern. "He likes to be involved in everything, you know. They're planning to expand that little place over there into a grand ordinary. With so many wagons, and even riding and walking families, coming through, travel-

171

ers need a place when they arrive in such a nice valley as we've got here. Why, they might even like to stay. Don't you agree?"

"Yes, ma'am, I certainly do. Perhaps with this location, he can even attract some of the wealthier ones coming to the springs," John replied politely and then gently held her elbow as she stepped off the small step in front of the door. Creacy stayed close behind her mother and hid in the folds of her skirt again as soon as she could.

Over Anne's head, John told Hugh, without words, to disappear inside to his meeting while he had the chance. And then he looked back to her. "Ma'am, I'd like to see what they're up to over there myself. If you don't mind, I'll see you across the street."

Anne Gregory beamed at John. "Such a nice young man!"

They crossed the street.

"Hail, John M'Glakin!" Joe Gregory, a painfully thin, short man—at least from John's lofty height—shouted from the cluttered porch of Brinkley's place as he waved his arms. "Are you running off with my wife?"

John laughed. When they reached the worksite he handed over Joe's wife and daughter. "You know I wouldn't dare steal Mary Gregory's daughter-in-law from her, she wouldn't allow it."

"That's for certain," Joe said.

Anne found one of the wives agreeable to chatting and they disappeared into the house.

John stepped back to get a better look at the place. They had nearly finished setting logs for a second story and he found that a new stone chimney was rising quickly when he wandered around to the side. He tried not to bother the workmen, but he couldn't stop himself from asking questions. No one seemed to mind. But he walked back to the porch when he heard a lively fiddle start up.

A long-time resident of the town and quite popular citizen, Robert Wiley, played, sitting on the edge of the porch where no railing had yet been built. Work stopped. Men wandered down from their scaffolds and ladders to tap their feet to the music and to grab a tankard from the women just leaving the dark inside of the soon-to-be tavern.

Robert stopped playing long enough to say, "Is this your disturbance, John McLaughlin?" Then he smiled. "Ah! Never mind. This bunch is so lazy they'd stop work building a ladder out of hell if the devil served ale."

Next to him, Anne Gregory handed Joe a drink. She looked sideways at Robert, but John could see a smirk on her lips.

Robert winked at her. "No offense, Mrs. Gregory."

"Very little taken."

Robert played again and John bid them all a good day before he walked back to the store. He pushed the heavy door but then stopped short as he heard a deep voice ask, "Did I give you leave to call her familiar?"

John walked fully into the room. Captain Gwin and his daughter, Nancy, stood in the middle of the store. Hugh bristled a few feet away, one clenched hand resting on the brim of an open hogshead, the other crumpling his hat.

"Father!" the young woman hissed. Her face had reddened slightly, but John thought the sharp look in her eyes showed anger, not embarrassment.

Hugh nodded politely to the two, jammed his hat down on his head and said, "Sir. Miss," and walked toward John, the man and woman left behind to stare after him. Hugh's square jaw was set like a vise as he walked out the door, strode to his horse and mounted without a word.

They galloped home to Hugh's cabin still without a word and Jamie was in the yard when they arrived. Guiltily, Jamie said, "I broke my spade," and held up Hugh's.

"Get a blacksmith," Hugh growled.

John guided his horse between the two of them. "Can I ask you about the meeting, or no?"

With his face still set in a mulish grimace, Hugh vigorously rubbed down his mount without looking up. John dismounted, deciding it was best to leave Hugh alone, when he heard, "That damned arrogant man!"

"Mr. Gwin?" John was surprised. He always thought Captain Gwin a fair and honest man, he couldn't imagine a confrontation between the two. "What happened in the short time I was gone?"

"I dared ta speak ta his daughter. That was all."

"Nancy?"

"You see? You call her 'Nancy' as well and I'm sure you would no' suffer the boxed ears for it." He looked pointedly at John. "Why should I?"

"I've no idea."

Hugh unbelted his saddle. "Well he didna approve of that, he made clear. And I'm thinking he didna approve of me approaching her at all. The man doesna like me."

"But you've just met him, hav'na you?" Jamie asked.

Still ignoring his brother, Hugh stopped working and leaned on his horse, looking at John levelly. "It was in the way he looked me over, as if my lacking a waistcoat makes me a rodent's vermin," he said, looking down at his linen hunting shirt, soft now with not much tow left in it, and buckskin breeches. "Well, maybe I could have dressed better ta meet with the tailor about a job. But Wilson didna seem ta mind. I made these clothes myself, he admired them, and they're fine enough for a working man, if I should say. And I'm clean, am I no'?"

"This is all about fishing for compliments, isn't it? Fine," John said with a mock sigh. "You're as fresh as the first lovely rose of summer."

"We've spent too much time together, I'm thinking," Hugh sighed.

Jamie laughed. "Get your swollen yardarm down, Hugh. The young buck didna intend for you ta get that look in your eye with his prose. And, besides, I have other news for you—Owen Kelly should be riding up any minute."

Hugh finally turned to his brother. He smiled. "Why the hell didna you say so before?"

* * *

By sundown, the three men were deep in their cups.

John had gone home to his wife hours before, and Hugh, Jamie, and Owen soon tottered unsteadily near a fire merrily burning stumps that Hugh had decided were in the way of good fields and pastures.

Hugh pushed a piece of charred wood back into the fire with a dirty shovel. "My father used ta say, 'One working boy's a whole boy, two boys are half-a-boy, and three boys—no boy at all.' I figure he was right."

"That's not true," Owen said slowly, his words formed carefully. The firelight shone on his dark red hair as he turned to Jamie. "Your brother and Tom and me did some fine work during the war, and we made three boys."

Hugh grinned sheepishly. "The cabin at Middlebrook was a might bit drier and healthful than the one we put up at Valley Forge. So we did do some learning, 'ventually."

"Was he as much a stubborn horse's arse under fire as he is usually?" Jamie asked.

"Worse," Owen said as he sat down on an unsteady log a few yards from the fire. "When he finally came 'round after taking it in the chest at Charles Town he fought the Brits good."

"No, I didna."

"You were wounded?" Jamie asked, incredulous. "Was it grievous? Why did you never tell anyone?" He turned to Owen, "He told us he came through unscathed. Leave it ta that ornery bastard ta tell stories keeping him only in the finest light."

"Oh, och, enough!" Hugh said, pinching the bridge between his eyes. He didn't feel like talking about the war, but Owen had other ideas.

"Did you tell him about the sniper you picked off at Monmouth?"

Hugh felt his mood fall even further. "He wasna a sniper, just a green young'un who thought I made easy prey."

"He found out differently, though, didn't he?" Owen said through a chuckle. "And, Jamie, your brother caught the eye of quite a few of the ladies when off the battlefield."

"He has the same effect here."

Hugh took another long draw on his bottle, wishing he enjoyed drinking more so that he could get well and thoroughly sotted. "Those were camp ladies, Owen, more suitable ta my station than the ladies about this way."

Owen laughed. "You take yourself much too seriously."

The mention of Monmouth had put Hugh in a foul mood. Within a few moments, Owen seemed to pick up on the trail of Hugh's thoughts.

"Don't tell me you haven't made peace with that day yet."

"Made peace with what? We chased off the lobsters, didna we?"

Owen leveled a serious stare at him. "Isaac didn't make it."

"Who's Isaac?" Jamie asked. He was ignored.

"I know he didna make it. I was there." He sat down on the ground next to Owen's stump. "But he had children ta go home ta. Great fields of tobacco ta go and oversee. Land, huge tracts of it, all his. He had so much ta return ta. And I had so little." He held up his arms to the yard surrounding them. "Look at what I have ta contribute. No land ta call my own. No children. Sick more often than no'."

James and Isaac began to drown him with "hey now—" and "that's not—".

"Oh, quiet, the both of you. He had so much ta contribute ta the world and I had so many chances ta change things for the better."

Jamie walked around the fire and stood before him, his stance rigid.

"If you dare ta say it should have been you ta die and no' this Isaac, I will bloody your damned crooked nose."

Owen waved him away and rested a hand on Hugh's shoulder. "You couldn't have changed anything," he said.

"But shouldna we have known when he wounded himself? He—"

"That was an accident—"

Hugh looked up sharply. "Shouldna someone have done something?!"

Owen rested a heavy hand on Hugh's shoulder. "He was suffering things we couldn't even dream of in our worst nightmares. He knew what he was about and if you hadn't let him do it his own way... He's at peace now and with his wife." He shook his head. "Some pain is just a fate worse than death."

Hugh shook his head back at Owen and stared at him for a long few seconds. "Never."

CHAPTER TWENTY-FIVE

Out of the murky front window of the tailor shop, Hugh watched a handful of passers-by hurrying on their way as a light rain sprinkled down. Brightly colored leaves spun on the wind. Behind him, Tailor Wilson loudly shook out a piece of heavy fabric, capturing his attention, and Hugh turned in time to see him holding up a coat of rich green, the color of wet summer.

"Hugh," Mr. William Wilson said, spreading the coat on a thick pine worktable crowded with spools and pin holders, "this hem is fine, very fine." He lifted the edging up to the lantern light for a closer inspection.

"Is the owner expected shortly?"

Wilson looked up at him with shining green eyes, nearly the shade of the coat. "I'm the owner."

"Then I'm certainly glad, I am, that you find it so satisfactory."

"Well, now, I had no doubt about your work, or I wouldn't have put you on one of my finest possessions."

At a muted knock on the back storeroom door, Wilson left his stool and opened the door. "Here now," he said to his small grandson, taking a bolt of cloth out of the child's hands, "That's as big as you are, Willie-boy. Why are you carrying such a load?"

"To help you, Grandfather. I'm big now," Willie said, grinning a gap-toothed smile.

Hugh ruffled the boy's hair. "I'd say this here is one of your finest possessions, sir. Dinna you agree?"

Willie followed Hugh to the worktable and clambered up onto a stool. "Mr. Glackin, sir. Will you tell me stories again today?"

"I think I have time for one," Hugh said as he began clearing snippets of cloth and thread from the table.

"And only one, Willie. Mr. McLaughlin is finished for the day and is about to leave," Wilson warned his grandson before he left the room. The storeroom door closed quietly behind him.

Hugh smiled at the bright little boy perched on the high stool. "Did I ever tell you about the mountain that my grandfather brought ta America?"

"A mountain, sir? From where was it brought?" Willie looked at Hugh suspiciously. "Only America has mountains."

"Oh, no. There you're wrong." Hugh pulled two apples from his satchel under the table and handed one to Willie. After taking a leisurely bite, giving him time to develop the story, Hugh continued, "Dinna be mistaken, there are lands across the ocean that are studded with great mountains."

Willie smiled. "Across the ocean, bah! Land can't cross the ocean."

"Oh, och! But are you sure about that, Willie? 'Cause I assure you, this valley's walled in with hills brought by the settlers. They've all been a sentimental lot."

Willie hopped off the bench, went to the window and looked out at the mountain range in the distance. "How?" he said finally.

"Tied 'em up with rope and tugged 'em behind their vessels," Hugh said, as if every boy should know as much.

Willie laughed delightedly. "No they didn't!"

Hugh joined in his laughter. He hoped that someday he would have a son and that he would be as much a joy as this youngster.

They quieted the best they could when the door pushed open and rang the bell. Two young women, voices low and serious, walked in out of the rain. They paid Hugh and Willie no mind as they pulled off soggy capes.

"But your father likes him?" one said. Tall and perhaps nineteen years old, she hung her cape over her arm as she talked. Her companion still had her back to Hugh, and he admired her tiny waist and glossy black hair, hopefully unnoticed.

"Well I don't like him. And you know I'm in no hurry to find a husband, anyway. I wouldn't mind waiting just about forever to take those shackling vows. Besides, he's arrogant and thoughtless, too. Why, I wouldn't have him if—" She stopped her tirade abruptly and turned her head to see the rest of the room. When she spied Hugh and Willie watching her, her eyes widened. "Oh!"

"Go ahead," Hugh said, grinning. The smile grew as he recognized her. "Nancy," he added.

She smiled back. "Hugh. It is a pleasure."

"Nany!" her friend said as she touched her arm.

"Mary, I'd like you to meet Mr. Hugh McLaughlin. Hugh, this is my dear friend, Miss Mary Hogsett. She's visiting for the month and we have been having the most wonderful time, haven't we, Mary? The men are making the rounds of the springs. And the hot springs are quite fantastic, too, good for anything that ails you, aren't they, Mary? Why, they've even attracted the notice of the likes of Misters Washington and Jefferson, who've both come to take the waters, and I'm sure many others that I just haven't heard about."

Oh! Nancy thought. Why can't I just stop talking?

Hugh said something quietly to the little boy at the table and watched him disappear into a back room before he walked to them and took Mary by the hand, every bit the gentleman. Nancy let out a relieved sigh. She wasn't even aware she had been holding her breath, nervous over Mary's reaction to him. Although some might not consider Hugh quite their social equal, they were merely utter snobs who surely couldn't last long in their prejudice. This was America for goodness sake, a thoroughly modern country with wholly different ideals than their kin in Europe. And besides, what could Mary possibly find objectionable about this handsome, charming man?

"Miss Hogsett, a pleasure ta see you again."

Nancy's grin broadened and her heart sped up. His brogue was warm honey. Mary couldn't help but be as charmed as she was. She glanced at her friend, but the pleased look she expected was not there. Her face was bland, even a little haughty. When Mary continued in her silence, Nancy offered, "I wasn't aware that you knew each other."

"I used ta work for Miss Hogsett's father."

"Well!" was all she could say as her mind took her back, so many years ago. She had met him there, at the Hogsett farm, and didn't even realize it before. He was a bonded hand and he had been so fearless, talking with another man of going off to war, and it had scared her so badly, thinking that this man she was looking at, that was close enough to touch, was soon going to be dead. She had wanted to cover her ears that day, stomp her feet, and yell, no! no! no! You will not die!

Mary suddenly shook out her coat and said, "I think the rain has let up. We really should go," and Nancy realized they were still standing there, staring at her while her thoughts floated away.

Oh, the heck with Mary anyway. What did she know? "Mary, could you be a dear and tell my father I'll be along shortly. Within the hour at least."

"An hour! How on earth am I—"

"You'll think of something, won't you? I'd like a chance to catch up with Mr. McLaughlin." And then she thought of her father's disapproval of Hugh at the general store weeks before. "And if you could not mention to my father that a man has held me up? I'll tell him about it later."

Mary nodded tersely and left. Poor Mary, Nancy thought as she watched her walk carefully up the side of the muddy street to where the horses were tethered. Perhaps she had spoken a little too boldly. Mary really was a wonderful friend, but her reaction to Hugh took her by surprise, being so completely lacking in her usual graciousness. While she watched, her younger brother, who had escorted them to town, spoke to Mary for a moment, glanced Nancy's way, and then the two rode off.

When she turned back to the room, Hugh had a bulky satchel in his hand. "Are you leaving?" Nancy asked.

"I'm finished here for the day and I've got animals ta tend ta before they knock down their stalls. If you'll excuse me?"

Now what on earth was wrong with him? He had seemed so pleased to see her, she had thrown all caution to the wind to take advantage of it, and now he was walking out on her? Oh, no, he wouldn't. "I think you owe me a few moments, don't you?" Now that didn't come out right.

Hugh smiled and a small dimple appeared in his left cheek. "You are audacious, I'll be giving you that, little girl. And what did you think ta prove by scandalizing your friend there, anyway? That Father willna tell you what ta do?"

"I wasn't trying to scandalize anyone. And, no, Father doesn't tell me what to do."

"I'm thinking he does, otherwise you wouldna have told Mary ta keep me a secret, now would you?"

"Why don't you take me home?" she blurted out, her chin in the air, not willing to let him think the worst of her.

"Take you home? Right up ta your father's door?" He crooked an infuriating blonde brow. "Are you thinking he'll be inviting me in for supper tonight?"

"Fine then!" She snapped her cape and threw it over her shoulders, reaching for the door, relieved to have an out on the insanity she had started.

"No, no. I'll ride you home, never let it be said I am'na a gentleman." He opened the door and chuckled. "After you."

Oh, bloody hell!

They left the wide wagon trail of the town behind and rode the narrower paths to her father's plantation in silence, his thick arms banding her in, front and back, as he guided the horse. When they finally reached the barn, far from the main house, he must have taken pity on her because he stopped, dismounted, and gently lifted her to the ground. She honestly had thought that he would take her straight to the front door as he had threatened.

"Thank you," she whispered.

"Dinna thank me just yet." His stare was made of ice. "The very next time you use me as some type of..."—he pinched the bridge of his nose while he thought and then looked straight at her again—"some type of negative marriage magnet for your father's benefit, you willna be so lucky."

She absolutely would not laugh at his clumsy prose—from the look on his face she would be heartily sorry for it. "Negative marriage magnet? What on earth is that?"

"You know just what I mean, you are'na a stupid girl."

No, she wasn't stupid, she thought as he rode away. She knew exactly what he meant and was certain that he meant just what he said.

* * *

Hugh stayed clear of Nancy Gwin for nearly a month, but he didn't forget about her, hard as he tried. He couldn't shake the feeling that she really didn't care that her station in life was higher than his in the hard, staring eyes of what cultured people called "society." She hadn't cared in the barn, back so long ago at Aunt Maggie's. And though they both knew her father thought him a no-account son of a squatter and perhaps even an undesirable Irish "native"—a prejudice some of the Scots who had settled in Ireland before coming to America clung to so stubbornly—her actions at the tailor shop still said she didn't share her father's feelings.

He had just begun to think that perhaps he should welcome seeing her again, just to test his theory, when Daniel brought news to him that

Mrs. Gwin, the captain's wife and Nancy's mother, had died. Folks from settlements for miles around were turning out for the service.

Hugh dressed carefully the next morning. Mr. Wilson had convinced him not long ago to make himself a waistcoat, and now, as he buttoned it up, he was glad that he hadn't brushed the suggestion off as an extravagance. Struggling to see his reflection in a dull pewter mug, he oiled his thick hair and tied it back tightly while he planned how to keep himself hidden from Nancy's father during the service.

Daniel and Jamie rode up just as he was stepping out of the door into the brisk day and the three rode off within minutes.

At the Gwin's plantation, just over Back Creek Mountain and on the bank of Jackson's River, a crowd had gathered around the minister, a large man with short, dark hair and square face. His rumbling bass carried over the heads of the mourners and throughout the expansive yard, the accent thick and German.

Hugh imagined Nancy in front of the crowd, near the minister, her father and siblings surrounding her, comforting each other.

After a few moments of silence, the minister spoke again, this time in his native language for the benefit of the many in the crowd who could understand little else.

"How long do we have ta stay?" Jamie asked quietly.

"I at least want her ta know I've been here."

"Her?" At Hugh's grin, Jamie said, "Oh, Nancy, of course. Well, there she is."

Hugh looked to the mourners walking across the grass and realized it was too late to worry about keeping hidden from the rest. Seemingly everyone there had spotted them. "Let's ride out."

As they began to swing up, Hugh was surprised to hear a small voice say, "Wait!"

Nancy gathered her skirt up just above her shoes and hurried over to his side. He was further caught by surprise when her small body collided with his and her arms circled his waist.

"I've lost my champion," she whispered into his chest.

He knew the loss that drove her to completely ignore caution, but he was by no means swept up in it as she was. He allowed himself to be leaned on, to be embraced, but he watched the crowd across the yard warily. Too many had stopped to stare.

Something had to be done, and soon, or the poor girl would sorely regret her moment's worth of comfort.

He gently moved her to arm's length and reached for his handkerchief. He wiped it gently across her cheeks, pressed it into her small hand, and patted her shoulder. "Your father must surely need your comfort about now."

She glanced back to where her father was glaring at them. "Men just aren't the same. He loves me, but he doesn't believe in me like she did."

He only winced slightly at the snipe at men. "We convince ourselves of that when we are in pain. It simply isna true. He needs you and he knows he does."

She looked doubtful. "I always thought it was the mother who was left behind to fare alone." She shook her head, then looked up at him shyly. "Do you believe in me?"

He smiled gently. "Without question. Until today when your senses took a short leave, you've been my champion, with no equal."

CHAPTER TWENTY-SIX

One year later, 1788

"Where will your meeting be today, Hugh?" Jamie asked his brother as he and John approached him at the hog pen.

Hugh had rounded up a few of the slippery animals out of the woods, where they had enjoyed a generous mast crop, and now it was time for winter slaughter. John squatted and began fitting a downed rail into place.

"With whom would I be meeting?" Hugh asked in return. He had been removing his heavy wool coat when they arrived and now he draped it over the pen.

"I ken you've been meeting with Gwin's daughter in secret this last month. Have you not?"

Hugh had a brief reprieve from answering his brother when a nearby hog sniffed the coat curiously and tried to pull it off the rail. "Ya!" he yelled at the dark, bristly animal. It sauntered away after giving a small squeal. Hugh looked back to his amused brother and then to John.

"John, did they depose you like this when you went ta see your girl Elizabeth?" Hugh asked.

John continued working on the rails without seeming to hear the question.

Hugh turned back to his brother. "Yes, I have been meeting with Nancy. But for more than a year, so your spying skills are weak ta say the least. And so I will continue. Why do you ask?" Hugh said wearily.

Jamie's dark skin wrinkled between his thick, light eyebrows and the ever-present dimple in his left cheek disappeared. "Because I'd like ta ken what ta say when someone comes about looking for the two of you and asking questions."

"Have they done so?" Hugh asked.

"No."

"Then what's the problem?" He turned back to helping John secure the last section of the pen.

"The secrecy seems ta bother me."

"It's no' your secret."

"Quite right," Jamie conceded. "Thought you might like ta know, however, Daniel's just returned. He's brought with him a fine stud. Maybe you'd like ta see the both of them?"

"You've got Daniel inta your horse schemes, as well, now have you?" Hugh asked.

Jamie's dimple returned. "Oh, he's got an eye for fine horseflesh, that he does. And more nerve than good John here."

John looked up at his cousin and was carefully formulating a reply when he saw Susan riding toward them from the direction of John's cabin. He felt flushed and nervous when he thought of what her galloping out here in the middle of the day meant. She had been spending her days with Elizabeth for a few weeks now, ever since the first false pains of birth labor began.

He wiped his sweating, dirty hands across his pants as she rode up.

"She's started for sure this time, John. Her waters have come," Susan said.

Hugh and Jamie suddenly looked very pink and quickly started back to work.

Winter-barren trees rushed past and disappeared behind them as he and his cousin's wife rode back to Elizabeth. When they entered, she was standing at the end of their bedstead, near the blazing hearth, her hands tightly gripping the knotty-pine foot post. Her white shift was drenched from the waist down, with smaller patches of the thin linen sticking to the skin of her back, and John thought irritably that Susan could at least have seen her cleaned and comfortable before leaving her alone.

"I'm working hard at it John. I think it's going to be soon," Elizabeth said between deep, heavy breaths. "I wanted you to be here."

"Of course, Eliza. I'm here where I want to be and I'm not going anywhere," he assured her. "What do I do?" he asked Susan quietly.

"I sent for the midwife. Be warned—she will look at you a bit strange when you tell her you are going to witness the birth, but Eliza will convince her. She should be here soon. I went to her first. Until then, we wait."

* * *

A light snow drifted through the darkness as John walked about the yard, alone. He had promised Eliza that he would not leave her, but that was so many hours ago he thought he couldn't take anymore. He sat on a low stump, put down his lantern and the whiskey that Jamie had brought to him a few hours before, and turned his haggard face up to the sky. The fat snowflakes rushing toward him held him fascinated for a moment and helped to calm him. He knew she was bleeding more than she should be and that the midwife was a bad liar. But he thanked God that it wasn't a breech.

His beautiful, brave wife was still in there, hard at work, determined to see this child safe and healthy, and he had to believe in her. She was so strong, so much stronger than he...

He felt disgusted with himself when he realized that while he should be supporting her and giving her strength, he was instead taking it from her—he had taken it from her and then walked right out the door with it. When would he stop being so damned selfish? Leaving his cold oak stump and whiskey behind, he returned to the women.

"John! Come here and push her leg up..." the midwife summoned. She corrected him when he touched his wife's leg, "No!" she said. "Right here, in this way, in the same way Susan is, see? Farther, John, really push, she can't do it for herself any longer." She was barely finished speaking when John saw the dark head of his child begin to push through once again, so much closer to being born than it had been before.

"Is it coming this time?" he asked.

"Yes, yes, I think it is."

Eliza smiled at John with the last strength she had left. The midwife expertly guided the baby's head to face down and pulled the shoulders through, one at a time, in only a few more seconds. "Oh, thank God," John said so quietly that only Susan could hear him.

They had a daughter. Eliza looked up, tendrils of thick hair sticking to her face, and said tiredly, "She's Nancy," and promptly fell asleep.

* * *

The tiny person called Nancy kept John up all through the long, cold night with her wails. Her bruised, accusing face was a fiery red and her mouth worked in constant harmony with her fists, forming each syllable of her demands. But Eliza never stirred.

Earlier, the midwife had fussed over her for a long while. She checked and rechecked Eliza's bleeding until she was satisfied that all was normal. Then she assured John that it wouldn't hurt the baby to not eat until her mother woke; that Eliza needed her rest more than Nan needed to nurse.

And then she left. And Susan left. The snow had become heavier as he watched them both trudge out into the storm to ride the short distance to Jamie's cabin. They left him alone with this little demanding stranger who didn't *Oh! Have his nose* or *Ah! Have her chin*. This was a stranger that he didn't recognize in any way. And only he was there to care for her.

They sat together through the long night, both nodding off for a few short moments, but then Nan would recall that she was hungry or angry and they would both be awake again. As the first rays of daylight came up over the wintered mountains in the east, John creaked out of his uncomfortable chair, bounced the baby gently when she started to whimper again, and looked out of the small window covered in a thin, oiled skin. Before last night he would have thrown open the door and greeted the sunrise properly, no matter the season, he was always an early riser, hard at work as soon as the sun chose to light the world. Today he couldn't risk the blast of icy air on his newborn daughter, so he settled for looking out the window.

As far as he could see through the murky skin his land was covered in a deep blanket of snow. He was still staring out when he heard movement across the room and his relief was immeasurable. Elizabeth asked softly to see her daughter.

"You took care of her all through the night?" she asked him as he gently laid the baby beside her. She sat up unsteadily and began rocking the child.

"She was as quiet as a mouse all night. We both slept soundly." His stiff knees ached as he squatted, began stoking the fire against the cold and added the last few pieces of wood that were left in the cabin into the weak flames. He left the smoky fire behind and approached his new family warily. "How are you? What can I do for you?" he asked as he sat beside her on the bed.

"You can help me up."

"Don't get out of bed. You need to rest. I'll take care of everything."

She looked uncomfortable and said quietly, "John, there are things that I must do that I would rather not do in the bed."

He looked at her quizzically for a moment, began to turn pink, and said, "Quite right."

A short time later he had her settled back into bed dressed in a clean, softly colored shift. It was the only one she owned that bunched and ruffled with a drawstring at her neck and about her arms. The baby had finally been sleeping quietly while John fussed over her mother. She awoke now with first a whimper, then a howl at the disturbance on the bed, but Elizabeth was comfortable enough with children that she, with practiced hands, gently removed the child's wrappings to inspect her new girl child.

"John! She's as wet as if you'd put her in the river," she said accusingly, but then her look softened. "There are cloths stacked up over there, in the basket." She pointed across the small room.

He went to retrieve the basket for her and then sat with them on the bed and watched the baby being cleaned. Elizabeth soon sat back, loosened the drawstring around her neck, and pulled the material beneath her breasts. John turned away, embarrassed, as she raised the baby up to nurse.

"We'll be fine alone now. You can go do what you need to."

He did have many things to do that had been neglected, and he thought he might take the short ride to Jamie's place to enlist their help again. As he opened the heavy door, snow that had piled against it poured in onto the floor. He kicked some of it back out again with his dark riding boots and then walked out into the thick, wet drift that threatened to pull the boots off of his feet with each step.

The sun had risen higher into the blue sky, and he was nearly blinded by the brilliance of it on the unending white landscape. He trudged the short distance to the barn and took care of its needs as quickly as he could and then decided against traveling in the thick snow. It was much too slick to risk taking out the horse.

He returned to the house with the small amount of food he gathered up: Some dried fruit, the only three eggs he found in the barn nests, and a small wheel of cheese. His two girls were asleep again when he came in, his boots trailing snow across the floor. He made a few more trips outside, to collect damp wood out of the pile and to scoop buckets of snow to melt at the fire to use for cooking.

Enjoying the quiet, he coaxed some more heat out of the fire, propped his wet boots near the hearth, covered his wife and daughter in the heavy quilt pushed to the bottom of their bed, and then settled back into the same chair he had held his daughter in the night before. He slept with his cold ankles crossed, his stubbly chin resting on his chest.

* * *

Within a week the snow had cleared enough to travel, and John left Elizabeth and Nan in the care of Susan to continue helping Hugh prepare pork for the winter. If the slaughtering had been done, there was still the salting to do, and Hugh would probably sit back and watch John and Jamie have at it for a while if he had done the rest of the work all alone. They were sharing the meat as well as sharing in the labor.

The slaughtering hadn't been finished. John could hear the squeals as he arrived, stepping his way carefully through a few mud patches that had been left on the hills from the melting snow and sliding every once in a while when he wasn't careful.

Jamie came out into the yard with their neighbor, Joe Gregory, and called to John, "Start salting in those barrels over there, we'll have more for you shortly."

John didn't have a smokehouse, he was content to salt his pork and have done with it. Hugh had built one when he moved here, saying he didn't mind the extra work to smoke his meats; he assured John that his hickory and maple hams would be well worth the effort. But the pork needed salting first.

He worked packing the barrels until Jamie, Hugh and Joe had finished scalding, scrubbing and butchering the remaining meat. He stopped for a moment as they came across the yard.

Joe admired and inspected a few of the oak barrels with his work-worn hands. "Hugh said these are your barrels, John. You do fine work."

"Joe has promised ta dress out a few of his fat geese for me," Hugh said, "in exchange for some of my ham."

"They're six times plucked, might be a bit tough," Joe said.

"No matter. Goose and free labor. Told you it was worth it, John," Hugh said. Gore still covered his arms and legs. "Could never stand keeping geese, even for the down," he added, wiping his cheek with his shoulder. He turned a grin on John and said, "So, I hear you have a fine baby girl. Is all well?"

"Mother and baby are fine."

Hugh held out a hand to give his congratulations, but then laughed at himself and took it back when he saw the results of the day's work still splattered on them. "If you like, we'll heat some water ta clean up and have a hot drink inside."

* * *

John spent more time with his wife and child the next week and the days passed slowly. Nan had become contented on her mother's milk and slept more than she was awake, and he had much more time and patience now to admire the fine child. When she was awake, he marveled over the intelligent, light blue eyes that studied his face so intently, and the day she swatted his chin with her fist he laughed with delight and forgot all about the long, hard first night of her arrival.

He was lying on the bed, with the baby nestled warmly in between Elizabeth and himself. Looking up to see if his wife witnessed Nan's latest achievement, he saw that she was watching but her eyes had a feverish, glazed look to them. Her face also looked flushed. He reached across the baby and laid his hand gently on her cheek. She was hot.

"I don't feel at all well," she said. "I'm sorry I didn't say anything before. I think I may just need rest." She closed her eyes and was asleep within a few moments.

She still wasn't well a few days later and had hardly risen from the bed in the meantime.

On a cold, gray afternoon, Elizabeth unsteadily pulled herself out of bed and began to prepare a meal with carrots and potatoes and dried meat that John had brought in. He had planned on making the stew himself, but first he sat down to repair a tool at the table under the meager light coming in from the window. He watched her silently as she cut the vegetables for the already simmering pot. When he saw that she began to shake and become unsteady on her feet, he rose up to guide her back to the bed.

"But John," she argued, "we all need to eat, and everything is going undone. Nan and I have no clean cloths or gowns left; I cannot lie back down." She stopped protesting when she fainted into his arms, and for the first time, he became alarmed.

He wished for a doctor, but the closest they had was the midwife. Terrified of being the only one to care for her, he left her and the baby alone long enough to gather Elizabeth's mother, who hadn't visited since before her daughter had become ill. He sent her younger brother off to fetch the midwife.

When John and her mother returned, Elizabeth was talking to the ceiling. "Get it now! Off with you!" she said.

Her mother turned and said to John, "How long has this fever been going on?" He told her that it had only been a few days, perhaps as many as four, and that sometimes she seemed fine. But then he remembered she had been sick before that, but didn't tell him. He had no idea now of the number of days she was ill.

As his mother-in-law took off her heavy cloak, she explained to him about childbed fever, that many women who had this fever died of their illness. He felt weak as he watched Elizabeth's mother walk to the bed and sit gently beside her daughter.

John fell into a chair near the fire and rested his head in his hands. He tried not to think the worst, but couldn't help himself.

I've taken her life.

Elizabeth's mother stroked her hair, and John watched, powerless, until the midwife arrived. She had no better news for John than Elizabeth's mother did. They had hope, however, that this was merely a less serious illness—one that she could recover from without difficulty. The three stood vigil all through the night, but there was no change for the better, she seemed to just become weaker.

On the dazzlingly brilliant morning that broke after the long night, Elizabeth woke and lucidly asked to see her daughter. Her hair was wildly askew from its plait and her eyes were hollow, but a tenderness settled over her face as she cradled the baby. She smiled warmly at her mother, but she asked to speak to her husband alone.

"You take such good care of us," she said to him as she touched his face and then weakly handed the baby back to him. Her eyes became heavy. "Hold her tightly, John. Don't let go." She closed her eyes and she died.

The tiny person called Nancy kept John up all through the long, cold night with her wails.

CHAPTER TWENTY-SEVEN

John had worn blinders against God's will, replaced it with his own, and Elizabeth had paid the price. He had known—and known well—that it was against the Lord's plan to marry for light, transient reasons, and loneliness was one of the most fleeting emotions he had ever known, and so, nothing to base a holy union on. Now he wanted guidance and he was ready, desperate, to listen. But he heard nothing.

It was late afternoon, five months to the day after Elizabeth's death, and the narrow path he walked on took him farther and farther up the mountain. On the large expanse of deep woods that he and Hugh regularly hunted in, he passed a rock that marked one of his traps, concealed forty paces southwest of the marker. But he wasn't checking his traps, they weren't even set. He was looking for the perfect spot to sit and wait for the Lord to talk to him.

He soon found it behind the pines—a large, moss-covered rock a pebble's throw from an outcropping. As he sat on the rock and looked down, the village spread out before him, though it was mostly hidden by bright spring leaves, and he could just make out the creek down south before it, too, disappeared beneath the canopy of the trees. He had always thought the view that he saw now was God's window on the world. Although down in the valley, under those trees, nothing was so simple and pure, because the raw human experience ruled down there—folks suffering through loss and love and death and betrayal. He hoped the Lord saw more from this view than the tops of the trees and the sparkling water, as he did, because those in the valley sure could use His attention.

He knew he was edging close to blaspheming so he turned his mind to prayer.

A few moments later, an angry hiss from behind brought him out of his brooding prayer. He knew the sound—a feline warning. Cautiously, he moved from the rock the only way he could go, onto the crag. Over the edge of the drop-off, he looked down on a softer slope more than fifty feet below.

The animal hissed again and he turned. The brown-spotted cat now sat atop the turned-up boulder and watched him as he walked to the right as far as he could go. Close to her were three kittens, new and clumsy. Their den was a cleverly concealed hollow under the boulder, protected by brush and trees and somehow he had been allowed to pass it by, but now he was surely refused safe passage back the way he had come.

She was a large female, perhaps twenty pounds or more. Small stripes and large spots covered her darkly, and her stubby tail swished across the stone.

He was stuck. He didn't have a gun with him today, even though he couldn't have brought himself to shoot her anyway—she was a mother. But of course, he could think that because he didn't have a gun.

Before long, the three cubs fell asleep, wrapped one around another, and mother cleaned herself carefully while still protecting against the tall human threat. As John waited and watched for her to relent her position, the warm spring day began growing into a cool autumn-like evening. He had nearly forgotten about the message he had come here for and was still waiting for, to be sent from above.

She hopped from her perch and walked in deliberate circles, once and then twice, around her family. John moved to the left and then tried a step forward. She looked at him and her whiskers twitched slightly, her bright eyes warning him against coming any closer.

He stepped back again. "Stupid message."

With the words still on his lips, a gunshot blasted and the cat fell.

"Damn it, damn it!" he shouted as Hugh rose up from behind the underbrush. He dismissed both his cousin and his better judgment and scrambled over the rock to see where the mother cat had fallen on top of her kittens. They struggled beneath her. She was still.

"What are you doing?" Hugh asked.

John looked up at him through the still swirling smoke of the musket. "Why? Why did you shoot her?"

"The only place you had ta go was down, what would you have me be doing instead? Wrestle the thing ta the ground while you ran? She's a big cat,"—Hugh looked at her—"one that would be getting our chickens afore long, anyway."

"She wasn't..." John shook his head and slipped off the blood spattered rock to stand beside the animals. "There are kittens here. Help me."

Hugh picked his way carefully through the scrub and laid his musket on the rock. "Help you what?"

John had already grabbed the big cat's wide front paws, dragging her off the kittens which squirmed and yowled.

Hugh sat on the rock and stared hard at his cousin. "Has your mind run away from you? What are you going ta do?"

"I'm going to take the kittens."

"And?"

John scooped up a tiny kitten and deposited it in Hugh's lap. "And—I don't know. Would you leave them here to die?"

The tiny cat bobbed its head around weakly and mewled, and Hugh stroked it with a clumsy hand. "Did you sneak up on her giving birth? They're so small."

John had the other two kittens, one in each palm, but he had already started to rethink his rash plan. Just what the hell was he going to do with three bobcat cubs?

"John? Did you notice the mother is still breathing?"

He turned to look at the cat. Her belly moved—slowly, shallowly. "Well, then we'll take her, too."

"Ah, no." Hugh shook his head.

"Your hog pen will do nicely."

"I dinna think you heard me. I said no." Hugh picked up his musket and slipped the strap over his shoulder.

"Give me your catch sack."

"I'm leaving."

John shrugged. "Fine. Leave me your catch sack and whatever else you have, and take these kittens."

Hugh shrugged back and laid his bag down. "If she wakes up and wounds you good, I'm no' nursing you through the fever, understand? ...Good. Now, give them here." He put out his hand. John gave him the cubs and then watched his cousin walk away without another word.

John opened the bag Hugh had left and rooted around, finally coming up with a good length of rope. He swiped it around the cat's legs a few times, all the while watching her whiskers for any sign of stirring.

She didn't move.

He quickly scooped her up in Hugh's catch bag, hardly big enough for four or five good-sized birds or maybe a few fat rabbits, but the cat just barely fit.

His heart thudded as he closed up the mouth of the bag with another swipe of rope. Only when he finally relaxed after having her somewhat secure in the bag did he understand why Hugh had looked at him as if he had grown another head. He laughed at himself. This was idiotic, but he was determined now to see it through.

* * *

"That boy has lost his mind," Jamie said as he stood next to the hog pen turned wildcat den. Through one thick gap in the logs the mother could be seen, lying on her side, impatiently nursing her kittens and ignoring the men—Hugh, Jamie, and Joe Gregory—talking outside.

"Dinna call him a boy, it doesna suit you," Hugh replied, grinning. "He's setting something straight, though, I'm thinking."

"Is he now? What would that be?" Joseph Gregory asked.

"I dinna know exactly, but it's got him occupied and feeling useful. I think we should let it alone."

Hugh knew word had traveled fast when Robert Wiley arrived with his daughter Anne, a petite girl barely out of her teenage years. The wisps of blonde hair framing her face were windswept, her cap crooked, and she spared barely a glance for Hugh or Jamie or Joe as she jumped from her horse and hurried over to the pen.

Robert gave a hearty laugh as he swung down from his own horse behind her. He shook Hugh's hand. "I had to see this for m'self. Never thought you'd really be stupid enough to do such a fool thing as I heard about." He bent down to look into the pen. "Guess I thought wrong."

Hugh found it hard to take offense at anything Robert said. "These here are John's cats. And I dinna think they'll be causing you trouble all the way over on the Jackson River." He turned to his neighbor, Joe Gregory. "But Joe, dinna *you* think ta blame me when they come sneaking around this way later. I'd suggest you keep a close eye on your geese for awhile after we let them go."

All eyes turned when Robert's daughter spoke up. "They're beautiful!" She looked up at Hugh. "Could you tell me the story?"

Robert held out a hand to his daughter. "Anne, I already—"

"I know. I want to hear it again."

Hugh gave Robert a moment to chide his daughter for her impatience, if he was of a mind to. Robert didn't say a word, so Hugh began to recount for her how he had watched from the bushes as John faced off with the cat, dangerously close to the cliff's edge. And then how he had only wrestled for a few moments with the idea of shooting the animal.

Robert grunted. "Sound decision. Shoulda left it behind, too." He looked into the pen again and the cat hissed.

Jamie clapped him on the back. "I was just telling him the same thing. But he seems ta think the poor boy has something ta make up for, what with the passing of his young wife and all."

"He's suffering sorely?" Anne asked and then she blushed. "I'm so sorry—of course he would be. I just never thought…"

Hugh thought her eyes looked a bit misty before she turned back to the cats.

The men talked for a while longer while Anne stayed close to the cats. Hugh didn't hear another hiss from the feisty mother, but he heard Anne whispering something into the pen that he couldn't quite make out, just before her father announced it was time to go.

CHAPTER TWENTY-EIGHT

"Have you spoken to her father about the wedding, then?" John asked Hugh over his shoulder as his scythe caught its upward motion and laid flat the long grass in front of him.

"I have," Hugh said from close behind and then warned, "Keep your motion quick there, or I'll end up hacking that pretty ankle of yours ta pieces," as his own scythe cut a swath. "He ordered me out of his home. But Nancy's a spitfire—she left, too. Workers around the place were watching, that red-haired stable boy, the black men, and the bricklayer, Harris. It'll be quite the gossip." Hugh stopped swinging and rested on the curved handle of his scythe. "But I think they're sympathetic ta my plight. Or maybe they just dinna like Gwin, either."

John, furiously scratching his red, itchy arms, turned to face him. "He's not a bad man, Hugh. Even for all your difficulty. He's a well-respected and successful man—a hero of Guilford Courthouse!—surely he must be just and reasonable. Can you not find a way to make him soften?"

"How can I if even his own daughter canna, I'd like ta be knowing?"

Hoofbeats barged in on their conversation. As they looked to the west, a blinding afternoon sun blazed around the tall figure storming onto the field. John thought of the day Susan had ridden up this way to tell him his wife was giving him a child.

Susan took care of Nan now for the hours of the day that John was working in the fields or in his barn. The rest of the time he took care of the small, always inquisitive, person himself. He knew the neighbors whispered about it. That it was queer and unnatural for a man to live alone with a small girl with no woman in the house, even if the man was the child's father. But many of the women simply looked at him as if they certainly could respect any man with patience and kindness enough to raise such a beautiful and well cared-for child as Nan was.

But this wasn't Susan pulling back the threads of time and telling him Elizabeth's waters had come. It was only Daniel, as they could see when he dismounted and stood in the shade of his large, thick-legged workhorse. He was laughing.

"I'm trying ta be serious about this, but I canna," Daniel said and then laughed again. He sobered long enough to say, "Jamie sent me here for you. His horses are out, at least seven of the beasties. They were last seen cantering happily doon the road ta the Methany's. I told him he's no' as fine a trainer or a carpenter as he believes himself ta be."

Hugh and John exchanged amused grins, took their tools from the field, the large swaths of downed grasses left behind. In the barn they exchanged their scythes for lengths of rope, and mounted John's two gentle riding mares. They rode directly to the Methany's farm and spotted Jamie on foot in their hay field, waving his hat and shouting at the high-strung horses. As they approached, Jamie's barebacked young stallion took off after a mature mare and they disappeared in the direction of the hidden creek.

Archibald Methany, the patriarch of the farm they were invading, rushed from his stone springhouse toward them, waving his own hat and shouting mild curses. The horses were trampling dangerously close to the man's half-acre flax patch and suddenly two of the horses took skittish steps backward into the patch.

Stepping gingerly around the delicate flax plants, John fixed a quick lasso from his length of rope and pulled one mare to his side. The horses had settled now that the stallion had disappeared, and the rest of the runaways came into line nicely.

"Archie, sir, I won't let this happen again," Jamie said, his hat crumpled in his hands, to the man just approaching them.

Archie slid his hand across the flank of a dark chestnut. "Fine animal." He shook Jamie's hand and then looked to his flax patch, not quite grown enough to be pulled up and dried. A good chunk had been trampled. "Don't let it happen again."

Jamie reddened. "Of course not. Thank you, sir, thank you." He turned to John. "Go after the others, would you?"

John followed the flattened grasses toward the creek. Soon the path was lined with brambles and thick, twisting, wild grape. It led into a clearing that was once an orchard where maples and scrub were now crowding the apple trees.

He could hear the horses, but still couldn't see them over the last sharp hill before the creek's edge. He expected them to be casually drinking from the shallow summer stream, standing at a thin, muddy beach along its edge, patiently waiting for someone to round them up and take them home to their broken stable.

What he didn't expect was a young girl, with light hair pushed up under a delicate white cap, feeding the two runaways dried fruit hidden in the pockets under her dark skirt. She was standing near a small patch of wildflowers thriving in the cool dappled sunlight; flowers which she had once been roping together, but now had been left forgotten on the steep bank. She looked up, surprised, when she heard him break a twig with his last step.

"Oh! Sir, I...I. Are these your horses? I didn't know to whom—" she began.

He surprised himself by laughing pleasantly at her stammer. "You're Mrs. Carpenter's little sister, are you not?"

"Yes, sir, Joe married my sister Martha," she said back to him with more confidence, but then lost his gaze as she glanced hurriedly down the creek.

He approached the water's edge and smoothly took hold of the two horses before they could bolt again. Gently he told her, "You can stop calling me 'sir' and begin calling me John. Why, I'm probably only a few years older than you."

"Yes, sir...um, John. I'm eighteen this year."

"Well, I'm only twenty-five, much too young to be a 'sir.' Don't you agree?"

"Of course," she said shyly. "I've wanted to ask you for some months, whatever became of your cats?"

"Cats?" He thought for a moment and then laughed. "How did you know about the cats? Ah—never mind, I'm sure it was the talk of the County."

"I thought it was wonderful." Her voice was soft and sweet.

"The cats scurried into the woods quite some time ago and we have yet to hear from them again, thankfully."

She nodded and smiled and then craned her neck a bit glancing back up north.

When she turned to him again he said, "I'm taking these two back up the road there." John jerked a thumb back the way he had come. He knew her family lived miles away, clear across Back Creek Mountain. She must have been visiting her sister to be all the way over here. "I can pass by Joe Carpenter's to get home, if you would like me to walk you back."

"Oh, no thank you, sir," she said, already forgetting their pact. She glanced again down the narrow, muddy beach of the low summer creek and then blushed as she looked back at him. "I live just on the other side of the ridge. I'll be going home now." She hurried off, raising her skirts only modestly above her shoes as she climbed the bank.

What was she watching for down the creek? he wondered as he led the horses away. And then fierce squeals skipped a beat of his heart. A sudden splash sounded and he hurried back to the creek, where he plunged nearly knee high into the water. He looked north, praying that the scream had nothing whatever to do with Anne Wiley.

Just around a slight bend, John saw a spray of water, and now he could make out low, young voices. Kids at play—must be, he thought. A tree had gone down across the creek near where the splashing grew louder, and another thick tree leaned out precariously from an outcropping at what John knew was a nice cool cove in the creek, about three murky feet deep, even in the summer—a nice place to dip on a hot day and irresistible to the older children.

He stayed and watched for another moment. Under the tree clinging stubbornly to the outcropping, thick roots straggled nearly to the water, and there a formerly hidden teenaged boy grasped on and then pulled himself across the log. John saw a flash of white backside before turning away. He stifled a laugh. Had the innocent-looking Miss Wiley been spying on the bare-ended young men? No wonder she stammered and ran away! And blushing all the while, too...

As soon as John passed the twisting grape beyond the orchard, he felt free to let out a laugh the likes of which he had never enjoyed in his entire life. With water dripping from the cuffs of his long trousers, he walked the horses to Jamie's and thought about the young woman and her peeking and blushing. He chuckled every few feet as he went along.

CHAPTER TWENTY-NINE

Beside a small footpath, just out of sight of Hugh's leased farm, ginseng and ferns grew happily. The dogwoods had already bloomed and withered, and browning white petals carpeted the dirt here and there. The path wound around and led to a clear, trickling stream. On the muddy banks of the stream, animal tracks led to the water and back up again to disappear into the undergrowth. Shallow, pointed raccoon toes crossed one deep, rounded deer print.

Hugh sat on a rock, counting the prints and waiting. He soon heard rustling and looked up to see Nancy carefully picking her way along the path. She smiled at him and he rose up and took her hands.

"Do we go ta him again today?" he asked her.

"No. Nothing's changed."

"We'll change them."

"No. We won't. Father's not going to change his mind, and I'm past giving a damn."

He was surprised at her harsh words.

She smiled sweetly at him. "Let's go riding." She began to pull him toward the path.

"But it has always worried you ta go about together."

"Not anymore. Let's go to the tavern." She pulled him again.

He budged about as far as a bull.

"You think it's a bad idea ta go ta your father's again, but you want ta go ta the tavern? With me? What for, ta order yourself a stiff drink?"

"A stiff drink, yes, that sounds fine. What's in a 'stiff drink'?"

He took her gently by the wrists and drew her to him. "What has happened? The straight answer this time."

Her face fell and she worried at her lower lip. He felt badly for deflating her bluster and bravado. Oh, how he despised that puffed-up, miserable little man.

"I love him, Hugh, I really do," she said, shaking her head. "And I want to obey him and make him proud, and all the things a daughter is supposed to do. But I can't. I can't abide by it. He said plainly that he will not have you as a son-in-law. There now, I've said it."

"Is that it?"

"What do you mean, 'Is that it'?"

"God sake's, Nany, I knew that already. He already told us no. Hell, I even knew that the first time I met you."

She put her hands on his shoulders. "Then why all this? Why have we come this far, just to be pulled apart?"

He saw her blinking back tears, but just as quickly she composed herself and the strength crept back into her face as she stared into his eyes. He took her hand and began to walk her up the path. "Never fear, I've met worse enemies and beat them. And they were trying ta kill me."

She smiled. "Well, don't get too confident. Father still has a rack of muskets, and they ain't rusty, yet."

* * *

"And he's been seen with Captain Gwin's daughter, too, which has that man none too pleased."

"...no wonder, the McLaughlin family *has* mostly been bondsman, obviously not good for much else..."

"...pockmarked slave—that's what they say."

"What who says?" John asked from behind with pretended indifference. He had been standing behind the two women, in the shade of the tavern, for only a few seconds. But he knew what they were about.

The pursed lips of one speaking woman, a bitter Mrs. Beatrice MacDonough, turned on him, her cap tightly drawn about her pale, pinched face. After a moment's glance she straightened her godawful red cape, swished her heavy skirts, took her companion by the arm, and started across the street. The departing look on the guilty face of the companion confirmed what John had assumed—they, too, had seen Hugh, struggling to open the door to the store, his thick arms loaded down with heavy bolts of colorful linen.

It was he they were speaking of.

Why are you cackling biddies walking away? His throat ached as if he had screamed it. He wanted to yell at them, Why don't you speak up now that I've caught you? Say it again to me and defend your reprehensible position.

John's anger only grew as he considered their rich clothes and bible-clutching ways. He had much more he wanted to say.

No, no, silly women, he thought, don't go back down the road and smile at your free family and enjoy your pleasures of liberated life, won by the blood and sweat of that man you mock. How dare you pretend to be important and God-fearing in this county while you deride its most worthy resident. Why, you're not moral at all. You're bitter and ugly...

He had stopped outside of the tavern and was simply staring down the road when Jamie came upon him, having completed the business they had come for.

"Have you found something of interest, John?" he asked, positioning himself beside the much taller John so that he could see what was being stared at.

John didn't look at him. "I've only found an entirely new disrespect for a great many affairs." Slowly, a wry smile crept over his face. "And perhaps a new respect for still others. Tell me something, Jamie."

"Yes?"

"If wealth, prosperity, and even respect can be clutched in a dirty fist by the least among us, are they so worth having?"

"Only if you dinna sell your soul for it all."

* * *

Hugh was finally putting money away to buy land. He wanted to stand in the middle of it and see nothing that wasn't his.

His. What a feeling. What a long time coming.

He could have trudged west across the Alleghenies and squatted on land over there, he supposed, for quite awhile, too, before anyone but the Indians cared to dispute his right to it.

But he wanted the paper. With his name on it. Signed by Governor Randolph. And just let the court try to take away the child of a landowner and bind them out to work. Not his child, no sir. He had no children yet, of course, but he certainly hoped to some day.

Once he found the perfect place and made it his, he would throw down his axe on rich ground and where it landed would be the west corner of his new home. It would be two stories high and a warm, comfortable room would rise up over the kitchen with a cool root cellar below. He would put proper siding on the house before the first year was up, because, if he didn't, somehow it would never get done.

It was tougher going than he had thought it would be. It could take him years to save enough money for the property he dreamed of. One-hundred and twenty dollars for three hundred acres. And that was what his tailoring job was for. But he also enjoyed the hours spent with so many different people, not something that happened regularly working the farm. Harvest time could call for kith and kin to gather, as could putting up a barn or a house. A funeral was better attended than any wedding, and could get more out of hand if the right fellow carrying the right bottle found his way in. But an ordinary day tending the animals and the fields was as solitary a work as Hugh could think of.

In the shop, people surrounded him all the day long, either the occasional customer or some of the Wilson clan, and he could watch and listen to them practically unnoticed. They entertained him unknowingly with their gossip—prolific gossip that, if it were any more out of control, would surely lead someone to court. Who knows, it probably has, he thought.

He could also count on an amusing conflict when patrons entered with their wives. He knew from the moment they arrived who would end up with a wardrobe of his own choosing and who would not.

The wife who entered today did not amuse him. She was a dragon of a woman and Hugh wondered how she hid her leathery wings under that gaudy red cape she wore. Her husband was much smaller than she and he cringed each time fire spewed from her beak. Hugh gave her another long look and decided her lips indeed looked hard and pursed enough to handily crack through the toughest egg.

She was carefully explaining to her husband the merits of each fabric available to make his new coat. She spent many moments admiring a bolt of red broadcloth and then looked at her husband critically. "This fine fabric would simply swallow your skinny body whole, it won't do."

Hugh wanted to scream at him, Refuse ta be talked ta that way, mon. Tell her—tell her now that you refuse. Tell her it's doubtless that's what happened ta her first husband, she no doubt swallowed him whole, and it looked as if the poor bastard were still struggling around her middle. Tell her anything, dinna stand there like an insipid puppy.

But the man didn't hear or heed his silent urging. He meekly said, "Yes, Beatrice."

His wife, however, turned her jaundiced eye on Hugh. "You," she said pointedly, "will not be working with us today. Where is Tailor Wilson?"

Perhaps you swallowed him. Hugh smiled. "He's in the back. I'll have him for you in a moment."

She turned back to the fabric on the table and lifted it with one pasty hand. "Yes. You will."

CHAPTER THIRTY

John tried to cover his head as rain pelted him. When they finally reached Jamie's place, he was relieved to find shelter but still took time to stop and stare. He'd seen it nearly every day for years, but now he admired the small cabin that was a close twin to his own; the earthy chinking between its rough logs was perhaps thicker, the stone chimney a little straighter, but otherwise identical. They were built by the pioneering families, just a generation or two before, people just like his parents and his aunts and uncles, who spent many years working this land, bonded together in their effort to carve out a place in the wilderness. John didn't know their names, but for the first time he realized just how very grateful he was for the careful craftsmanship they left behind that provided his family's home.

They shook some of the rain off their hats and clothes before they could track it in and earn a reproachful look from Susan, who was working over the hearth, the hem of her thick skirt tucked into her waistband. As they entered, she modestly unbound herself and quickly let the dark material fall back to the floor. "Dinner is almost ready," she told them. "John, you can stay if you like."

He gratefully accepted. There was nothing ready at home to feed himself and Nan, and the rain was steadily increasing outside anyway. For a few seconds, a pounding rain washed over the farm. It drove all other noises from the cabin and the three surprised adults looked at the assaulted rafters as if there would be something up there to see, but then it let up to just a modest pelting and they grinned at one another.

"I'm glad you're staying," Susan said.

John went to the bed and checked on his sleeping daughter. He had noticed lately that her light hair had been quickly turning brown and now it almost reached her shoulders. They had encountered their first knot in the fine strands just that morning, but John had brushed it out patiently and then tied on her cap, which was always pulled off before they reached Susan's.

On the bed, Nan's gown had become twisted around her waist and he wondered how she could sleep bound up like that, but then remembered that her mother used to be able to sleep through anything. Thinking that, he reached out to touch her face. "She's hot," he said to Susan, who was working at the table where pork, sweet potatoes, and biscuits with honey were waiting for him.

"I know she is. She's cutting a mouthful of teeth and her nose is running, didn't you notice?"

"No."

"Well, you can check on it yourself when she wakes up. Come and eat, I have to pay off all of that dairy you bring us."

He looked back to Nan and didn't feel as if he could swallow even a pea. Where before he had been admiring the sturdy, healthy child he cared for every day, a child who would grow to be who he wanted her to be, now he saw a fragile, weak child that he was afraid to raise alone, unsure of what tomorrow would bring. She was ill and he had missed all the signs. He had dragged her out of their warm home on a miserable, wet day and left her here while he was out and about, doing things that didn't really matter. He had put her in danger, determined her fate for her, as he had done with her mother.

"John, she really is fine. Come and sit down," he was urged again. He sat with his family and pushed food around on the wooden trencher for a few minutes before he heard Nan stir.

"A-pa?" she said in her uncertain baby-voice.

John went to her and picked her up. "Yes. It's Papa." He felt her gums with the tip of his coarse finger and ignored her grimace and pudgy, smacking hands. Grinning as he felt three teeth bulging their way into her mouth, he walked back to the table. "She does look fine, doesn't she?" He sat down with her on his lap and began to feed her some of the soft sweet potato.

After the meal, the rain had let up its furious downpour and a dull gray sky was all that was left. John and Nan went home. He did as few chores as he could and later they enjoyed the cold supper Susan had sent them home with. They slept off and on through another loud rain, and the next day was Sunday, August 16, 1789.

John awoke that morning to a pounding on the door. It was very late for him to still be abed, but he had lost sleep to Nan's fever and the pain of her new teeth.

A forbidding and very angry David Gwin was at the door. Standing behind him was Jamie, his wavy hair unkempt and deep brown eyes groggy.

"Where is she?" Captain Gwin demanded.

"He's looking for Nancy," Jamie said irritably from around his shoulder.

John looked at Nan wrapped up on the bed and felt a prickly tangle of fear and anger. "You cannot take her away from me."

"*Hugh's* Nancy," Jamie said.

David turned on him with a hard jaw.

John's fear changed to a deep-seated fury, rooted and growing in his pride. He felt it was this man's fault he had any flickering doubt at all about his place in this world and his ability to care for his daughter.

"She's not here," he said, and slammed the door.

When he heard hoof beats slowly lead away from his cabin, he opened the door again, knowing Jamie would still be standing there. His cousin's cheek was sunk deep in his dimple. "Fantastic," was all he said, and still he grinned. He finally laughed and said, "Imagine. If I had done that, I'd still be sitting down ta breakfast."

He let his cousin in the house. "Wonder where Nancy's off to?" John said. He was still shaky.

Jamie stood at the table and ripped a chunk off a loaf of bread lying there. "I know where they've gone."

"They?" John pulled out a chair for his cousin and stoked the fire against the damp chill that had been let in.

Jamie straddled the proffered chair backward to face John at the hearth, put his arms across its heavy back and said, "Hugh and Nancy—left through the night. They've headed up north, up where they've turned the west of Rockingham inta another county, Pendleton it's called now. Nancy's nineteenth birthday is in two days." He took a bite from his bread.

John joined him at the table, irritated with Jamie's way of never getting to the point. Good God, he knew where Pendleton was. "Why have they gone off to Pendleton for her birthday?"

"They're having a wedding on her birthday, that's why."

CHAPTER THIRTY-ONE

Miles into the county of Pendleton, a tavern sat on the bank of a creek just to the side of a well-traveled and rutted road. Before nightfall, Hugh and Nancy stopped in front of the two-story building, the only tavern in the German settlement, and he helped her off her horse. All the belongings they carried with them were stuffed into Hugh's packsaddle.

In the tavern they found that one room was offered for travelers—men only—and that Nancy could go to a widow's home nearby who didn't mind taking in the occasional lone woman border.

The tavern-keeper went to fetch his wife who would walk Nancy to the house, nearly a half-mile away, and Hugh and Nancy held hands and stared at each other while they waited. The man's tired-looking wife soon appeared, and, without a word, motioned for Nancy to follow.

Hugh gave Nancy a quick kiss on the cheek and pressed a cold coin into her palm. "You'll be fine."

Soon, old wood creaked under the weight of Hugh's tattered, worn riding boots as he followed along behind the proprietor up a dark staircase to a small doorway at the top. Inside the room were three narrow beds; personal belongings were piled on top of one, and on another were two men, sleeping.

Under the only window in the room, a chipped basin sat atop a small table and a dingy cloth hung off one corner. The candle on the table had nearly melted down to a stub, and it flickered as he passed it and sat down on the last empty bed. He had hoped to be spared from sharing it, but it had a satchel lying at the foot and he knew its owner would return again at some point in the night. The two would have to squeeze in together to keep from falling off the sides.

After he took off his boots, he lay down and put his hands behind his head and crossed his feet at the ankles. *What in God's name are we doing? What is she doing? Does she even know?*

He thought back to the beginning of it all, when Nancy had knocked on the door of his cabin late last night. It had been raining when he opened it and saw her standing there. Her hair was plaited tightly and it hung over one shoulder, the dark end sneaking out of her cloak where it opened across her chest. Rain dripped off the hood and he could see a misting of it across her face.

He had already bedded down for the night, on a black bearskin rug and a frayed quilt close to a low fire to fight off the dampness that had settled in with the cold rain. Thick lengths of pine yet to be made into a bedstead stood in a far, dark corner of the one room.

She told him, standing there in the rain, "I'm nineteen in a few days. We'll just be married somewhere else. Do you know Moses Henkle? I've heard he would marry us."

"What are you doing here? Are you mad?" His eyes scanned the darkness behind her out the still open door. He pulled her in.

"No, I'm not mad. I'm angry and I've had enough. I know what's best for me, what I want to do, whom I want to marry," she said. She put her small hands on his chest and rose up on her toes to kiss him. Her cold, damp cloak pressed against his bare arms and then against his chest as he drew her close. Rainwater dripped on his toes.

"I dinna have land yet, Nany, somewhere ta give you a home."

"I don't care," she whispered against his neck.

After a moment, he pulled back to look down at her. The dim fire-light flickered in her eyes. They were nearly black, and instead of staring into his, they watched her delicate fingers lightly touch his chest where pockmarks scarred him. The largest was just under his collar-bone. Her fingers were pale against his dark skin.

She traced down the swelling of his chest to a long, twisted, puffed scar. When she had seemed to have her fill of touching his chest, and as her eyes continued their slow perusal of the rest of him, she slid her hands around to his back. He tensed. Waited for her to recoil. What could he say to lessen the shock—and to be honest he would have to guess disgust—she must feel as her hands rippled over the scars across his back?

He could be witty, perhaps, and tell her there were more than ten years of his life that he didn't own that back, but his mind, which he did own, often got the rest of his body in trouble.

She didn't say a word. Neither did he.

Pockmarks, war wounds, and slave stripes. Why on earth would she stand there and keep touching them? She should run, scandalized, not be fascinated. But he warmed, standing there, watching her explore his body with her eyes and soft hands. He didn't want to break her gaze. Even his breathing—slow and shallow—felt like a distraction.

For so many years he had been telling himself he didn't want anyone to need him. Needy, clutching, grabbing—that's what he had been running from. But he had wanted someone to need him all along. Desperately. Someone who would both need him and stand alone at the same time. Someone to be his equal, who was strong enough to be there when he needed her, too. But he had never before known anyone who could fill that place and he could not afford to hope that this girl-barely-turned-woman could be her.

She was brazen with her "let's run away," but was her devotion to a lifelong commitment—to him—simply a mile wide and an inch deep?

Nancy.

She looked up at him when he thought her name, but the moment wasn't broken, as he had feared. Her eyes burned into his and she dropped her cloak to the floor—only her thin, rain sprayed shift covered her, a scandalous state of dress to be sure. She looked as if she were about to speak and he waited to hear what she would say. Her next few words could very well change his whole world.

He had thought her simply impulsive at first, with her assertion that they be married, her father be damned. Perhaps she was acting as a spiteful child, thrilled at her own disobedience.

And he may have been convinced of it had she merely said, "Please, take me away," or even, "I love you." He would have taken her out into the rainy night and placed her firmly on her father's doorstep. He was waiting for the first wrong word, the flighty, fanciful musings of a wistful girl, his first clue of what she was about, and then he would send her away.

But instead she whispered, "I want you," and it had been his undoing. *Why do you?* he thought. But he pushed it away, crushed his mouth to hers, and led her to the bearskin.

In the dimness of the tavern, the side of the bed dipped and Hugh opened his eyes to see a bedraggled man pulling off his shoes. He reeked of brandy—peach brandy he thought.

Hugh turned on his side and closed his eyes, thinking if he weren't careful with this woman he was making his wife he would end up being led around by the nose.

He smiled himself to sleep.

* * *

Nancy let the woman lead her out into the darkening day. She hoped the face she had put on for Hugh's sake had worked and he didn't worry about her. But she could admit to herself that she was a bit scared. Not only of wandering along a gloomy path to bed down in a strange German house, and following behind a mildly hostile woman who may be her only interpreter with the widow—she was also scared of herself.

This crazy plan of hers was all moving so fast, and that had worked well for her up until they parted at the tavern. Now she had all night to anticipate their wedding tomorrow and what it would mean to the rest of their lives.

She squeezed the coin he had handed her. His first step toward taking care of her, as a husband should. Her first step to being dependent on him, as a wife was destined to be. It had already begun.

Oh, she loved him. More than she ever thought she could. But for so many years she had been staunchly opposed to marriage, opposed to relying too greatly on anyone but herself—and her father, to be honest—and now here she was, throwing away the security and strength of her family, and delivering herself into Hugh's arms.

As she thought it, she closed her eyes and imagined those arms around her, his honey-brogue whispering her name, passionately as he had last night.

Her stomach fluttered and she nearly laughed at herself. Why had she just been worried about delivering herself into Hugh's arms? At this moment, she couldn't think of a single reason.

Soon they were approaching a squat, windowless cabin, and the tavern-keeper's wife turned sharply on her heel. "Here you are," the woman said, and started back the way they had come.

"Wait!" Nancy called.

The woman turned.

"You are not leaving me here this way. I insist you at least secure me the accommodations that were promised at the ordinary."

"You what?"

Nancy heard *You vhat?* She sighed. "I need you. I do not know German."

The miserable little woman clucked haughtily and went back to knock on the door. An elderly woman answered and they talked for a few moments in the familiar tongue that Nancy had never learned more than a few words of. They turned and stared at her.

"You the English?" the owner asked, her voice brusque, but her eyes friendly. She was a small, ancient woman with thin hair wisping out of a gray cap. Her brown dress was crisp and neat, her apron dazzlingly white.

Nancy nodded and walked to the door and the woman waved away the tavern owner's wife, who walked off into the evening. The older woman put a hand on Nancy's arm. "You come. I take care of you, make you fat, get you sleep." She smiled. "Soon you be a wife and then you do all the work."

CHAPTER THIRTY-TWO

John thought that he would like to learn the fiddle.

As he listened to Cousin Daniel's bow weaving over the strings, a cool breeze swept across the threshing floor of the barn. He stood against the wall, watching with a crooked smile while dozens of square, dark shoes lost their inhibitions and twisted and turned, and as many chaffed, worn hands clapped to the strings' swift rhythm of "Red-Haired Boy."

Cousin Daniel was everybody's favorite fiddle player, and he played with a spark that caused some of the older women to whisper about the devil and dangerous bargains.

Hugh and Nancy had returned a week before, and a celebration had been Jamie's idea. The idea to keep the elopement and clandestine marriage quiet was Susan's. "They should be allowed to manage this in their own way," was all she told the men.

They had come together at Jamie's place early to prepare, and now two young pigs were turning on spits over a low fire and a constant parade of food had found its way in with the guests. The dancing neighbors had been trickling in for hours now, the adults all excited by the idea of a brief reprieve from their tedious, never-ending work days, while the young ones, of every age from ten to twenty, played and teased their way through the husking of mounds of corn.

Berries had been plentiful this year, and a great variety of treats had been made with the sweet fruits. John had carried little Nan to the table covered in food and was letting her pick a sweet when he spied Jamie at the stable. Archibald Methany, the neighbor whose flax patch Jamie's wayward creatures had trampled, soon appeared at Jamie's side. He dropped a couple lengths of thick wood siding onto a pile nearby. When a sudden hammering resounded through the yard, more than a few people stopped to stare.

John shook his head. *What…Jamie?* At his own brother's wedding party, no less... "Let's go pull them by the ear," he whispered to Nan.

As he drew near, John could hear one horse, probably the chestnut stallion, he thought, kick at his stall. He shook his head and smiled at his cousin's pitiable expression. Archie, hammer in hand, apparently aided him in his endeavor.

"Says he has an appreciable interest in shoring up the stable," Jamie sheepishly said of Archie's help.

"You have a yardful," John reminded him, "must you do these repairs now?"

Jamie waved him away.

Robert Wiley and Joe Gregory hailed him before he went more than a few feet. The two had taken over seeing to the roasting pigs after one tending woman's skirt caught fire in a breeze that passed through earlier. A flurry of hands had smacked at her, but the smoldering spot was small and went out easily. Of course, it could have been worse. She gladly turned the job over to someone else.

Robert's family was nowhere to be seen, but Joe's wife and mother were comfortably seated nearby where the men were working, and his young children played and chased one another in the waning light.

"Ah, John!" Joe said with pleasure as he approached the fire. He reached out and shook John's hand firmly. "How did they come about marrying with all the strenuous objection aboondin'?" Joe said in a thick brogue to rival his Cousin William's own. He was gesturing to Hugh and Nancy, just arriving in the yard from John's cabin, walking slowly, hand-in-hand.

"They went off to Pendleton, that's as much as I know."

Joe nodded absently and excused himself to speak with Hugh.

Robert laughed quietly as he departed and said, "If he wants to know, he'll find out." His voice was low and deep; and the deliberate way he had of speaking put John at ease. It gave Robert an air of confidence that spread all around him.

John had made a habit of carefully collecting and then hoarding the details of any demeanor that would bring him closer to issuing the proper carriage of a successful, confident man. Today he was collecting the cadence of a confident man's voice. Robert was well respected by one and all.

He listened to Robert talk to Joe's mother. "Mrs. Mary, you appear in need of a drink, what can I do for you?" He walked to her side and squatted beside her to better hear her low voice. John smiled to see her pleasure in being singled out for attention by Robert. It worked. Doubtless it was the voice. She adored him. After speaking for a few moments, they motioned to John.

"Let me see that lovely child, John," Mary Gregory said as he approached them.

John obliged her and was grateful that Nan was comfortable enough with strangers that he could safely set her down on the woman's lap, without fear that she would cry.

Mary began to sing a peaceful cradlesong to Nan and rocked her gently. She stopped to tell John, "You men go on about your business, now. We ladies have our own to attend to." Continuing her song, she turned back to Nan.

John's daughter waved happily at her father with a pudgy hand and dimpled wrist as he began to walk away. He scrunched up his face and made her laugh, but looked away as Robert told him, "Only a few here know those two ran off to be married—as of now. Within a few hours, maybe less, the whole gathering will be talking about it. And a lot of it won't be pleasant. It will be over in the next valley tomorrow. Gossip's a vicious thing."

He stopped walking and faced John. "The reason I tell you this is so you know most of us don't wish anything but a fine life for Hugh— he's a worthy neighbor. But that gossip's a vicious thing." He shook his head. "It's just that some people around here have their way of doing things. Now, I don't agree with their way of thinking. Take my daughter, Martha. I couldn't be prouder of her match with Joe Carpenter, don't matter a continental that he used to slave for someone else. Better for my daughter a man with a free mind than a free body." He smiled at John. "Though I'm sure Joe's mighty glad his body's as free as his mind these days."

John listened quietly as the older man spoke and felt that a weighty blanket was settling over him. Robert was no doubt understating the situation—he wasn't one for light talk. If he took the time to say something, it was serious...

"There they are," Robert said and grinned crookedly as a handsome group of young men and women joined them. James Wiley, Robert's son, was in the lead. "James, you can take over this fire. This spit here needs to be turned."

"James," John said politely and shook his hand. Behind him were

Joe Carpenter and his young wife Martha, Robert's daughter. He greeted them both warmly and then smiled as he recognized another latecomer, the young girl he had met at the creek.

"John," Robert said, "this is my daughter, Anne. I don't believe the two of you have met."

"Yes, sir,"—he stumbled when Anne stared at him with her eyebrows raised—"I mean…no, sir," he told Robert. "Miss Anne, it's a pleasure," he said, taking her hand.

She smiled at him and winked when her father turned his head.

"Come, John, let's wish these two long lives and prosperity, shall we?" Robert asked, motioning to Hugh and Nancy, who were about to join the other laughing couples in a whirling reel on the makeshift dance-floor.

* * *

He smelled of soap and she breathed it in deeply, again.

"Are you smelling me, woman?" Hugh asked as he leaned away and looked down at her.

His smiling blue-green eyes reflected the light from the bonfire outside the barn. She looked around to see who was watching them and then, relieved that they were dancing unnoticed, upped herself onto her toes to kiss him furtively. He put a steel grasp around her waist and deepened the kiss until Nancy thought she would burn to cinders. He pressed his hard body against hers, melding them together. That's when she stopped caring whether they had an audience and that most of the guests would think their behavior improper. Only when he let her go did she consider the stares and the sniffs and the guffaws of the few people that stopped dancing to watch them and what they could do to her standing with her neighbors.

Her face on fire, she whispered to Hugh, "It's scandalous."

"Ta hell with them," he whispered back and led her safely through the twirling couples and into the cooling evening air. She followed behind him as he strode around to the side of the barn and laughed despite herself at his stealthy glances about the yard, mocking any prying eyes that might watch them go.

He took her by the hand and led her past the horse paddock to a moonlit clearing at the edge of the woods where a path wound about to the creek, well hidden from the party.

They sat on the damp ground and she knew Hugh wished he had a coat to spread out for his new wife to sit on. He crossed his legs and reached over to her waist. "Sit on my lap."

"Do we have to go back?" she said as she settled comfortably across his legs.

"Never."

"I wonder what they'll say?"

"Who cares?" he said. "Look, Nany. At the beetles scurrying." He chuckled.

Two fat beetles had wandered together out of the grass and onto the dirt path. They veered off in two different directions.

Hugh chuckled again and whispered. "They just did it."

Nancy turned and looked at him, surprised. "Did what?"

"You know," he said with a devilish look. "Now the man beetle has ta hurry home ta his wife before he's caught."

Nancy doubled over with laughter. What on earth would possess him to say such a thing? As soon as she had recovered sufficiently, she asked, "Does the woman beetle have a husband?"

"No."

"Oh, unfair!" she said, swatting his arm.

He kissed her until her head spun.

"Are you ready ta go back?" he asked after they had sat in silence for a long few moments.

She drew a deep breath and said, "I suppose."

Back at the barn, Robert Wiley and his own fiddle had joined with Daniel in supplying the music and now they had the dancers in a line reel, twirling and spinning. Eyes bright, Daniel motioned for Hugh and Nancy to join them. They jumped in when the men and women were again lined up, facing each other.

The woman closest to Nancy said something she couldn't quite hear over the music, the clapping, and the calls. She glanced up at her for a moment, being nearly a head shorter. She couldn't quite recall her name.

As she clapped to the music, forgetting about the woman beside her, she caught a glimpse of Hugh laughing as he stepped out of time just before she walked out to spin with a man diagonal from her.

The woman who was attempting to talk to her soon twirled by her and said, "So he has his talents, does he?" They passed behind their partners and then met again. "Now I understand. It has been all the wonder."

Violet, that was her name. Nancy didn't trust the tone of the woman's voice. She felt the derision dripping off each word and wished she would keep her opinions to herself. The woman looked at her slowly, callously, appraisingly. She felt like a heifer at market.

Nothing good was going to come of this.

The couples began to twirl again, one man and one woman at a time, while the others looked on, clapping and stomping, waiting their turn. It was now time for Hugh to pair off with Violet.

Please let that snippy woman keep her mouth shut, Nancy thought.

It appeared that she did, though she clearly pressed herself harder against Hugh than she had to. But that mattered little to Nancy, since she had never been one to give in to jealousy of any type. And she had a sinking feeling that perhaps she had more to fear from the woman than a crude attempt at a pass at her husband.

When the women were again shoulder to shoulder, Nancy felt a hand brush across her hip. Violet looked at her innocently and reached out again to flick away a dried up jumble of grass, stuck to her dress from when Nancy had momentarily sat on the ground with Hugh earlier.

She turned to face Violet. "What is it that you want?" They had eyes on them now. "Well?" She wanted to stamp her foot. "Tell me now or keep your mouth shut in the future."

Hugh quickly took Nancy by the arm and steered her, again, through the dancers. She heard him laughing by the time they reached the moonlit yard. He hugged her hard. "I'll just have ta wonder for now how far you'd go ta defend me." He drew back. "That was for me, wasna it?"

She nodded.

He smiled down at her. "My pint-sized general."

CHAPTER THIRTY-THREE

Cold enough again for winter slaughter, John thought wearily, and then rose out of bed knowing that today he would have to push himself to walk the short distance to Hugh and Nancy's. Thankfully, he only had himself and the animals to care for this morning, having left his daughter in the care of Susan this week after considering the unseasonably frigid weather too much for his little girl, one year old just the week before, to be out and traveling so much.

He was also glad she wasn't here last night to see him lose his mind.

Yesterday, his wife had been dead for one year. To celebrate Nan's birthday one week and mourn his wife's death the next...it was too much for him, and so, he knew, the way the rest of his years would continue. The whole room reminded him of it as he looked around—the overturned table, clothes strewn about, the broken earthenware cups from Aunt Maggie's.

He suddenly remembered back, so many years ago it seemed, scraping together a few coins to buy those cups at her estate sale. He smiled painfully. What a childish ass he was becoming.

He threw back the fraying quilt and woolen blankets that covered his bed and shivered at the cold. Only dark coals and light ash greeted him from the fireplace across the room and he sighed, cursing himself for letting the fire die down. He dressed warmly before leaving the bed, then stoked the sooty remnants of the evening's fire. A few live embers finally gleamed up at him and he threw on some kindling.

He dragged a cold, hard chair to the hearth to sit on. Glancing about, he saw no wood but for a few pieces of kindling at his feet. Chunks of bark and dirt spread out where the firewood should be. He rested, elbows on knees, chin on hands, and stared at the sticks deep in the stone hearth. Soon small, colorful flames licked around their ends, slowly swallowing them. But moments later, forgotten and untended, the fledgling fire sputtered.

With a large, callused palm, he wiped warm tears off his cheeks and stoked the fire again, tossing in the last of his kindling, some fresh pine splinters. Sap popped and sizzled as he stood up and arched his long back. He hung a small kettle of water on the hooked end of the metal arm from inside the hearth. It creaked as he pushed it back over the fire.

He righted the scarred, heavy table up from lying on its side and retrieved the long-legged iron trivet from under his bed. He returned it to the peg beside the hearth. It was still swinging back and forth on the wall as he began to gather his clothing from the floor. A few pieces were covered in soot from the fireside ash bucket, turned on its side near the table.

After he threw the handful of clothes onto a shelf, he looked about the room and decided he was satisfied with the job he had done. Only the ashes from the bucket and shards of the cups on the floor all about the front of the cupboard were left. He could sweep it all up later.

He left the cabin behind and crunched a fresh carpeting of leaves with his thick heels as he strode toward the barn, where his animals lowed and whinnied. He cared for them as quickly as he could and then returned to the slowly warming house with an armful of pungent split oak. As he opened the door, a head of wavy blonde hair looked up at him from the far corner near the hearth, and John took a step back, struggling not to lose his stack of wood.

"Hugh?! Where did you come from?" he said angrily as he steadied his load with his left knee and then closed the door with his right shoe's scuffed heel. With the door closed, a dim patch of light thrown from the murky window rippled across Hugh's legs, covered in heavy gray wool. His dark riding boots crossed at the ankle in the shadows.

"What?" Hugh murmured.

John dropped the oak by the hearth, each piece thundering against the floorboards and then settling askew after their clumsy descent.

Hugh looked up from his position on the floor, his blue-green eyes rheumy. "I hate oak."

"Are you drunk?" John asked mildly.

"No," Hugh answered and sat quietly—if unsteadily—staring at him. "John, what do you think of the world?"

"I don't know," John told him, shrugging off his long wool coat. He sat on the chair near the hearth and pitched small pieces of oak onto the fire. Sparks hit the floor and darkened into cold ash. "But I do know that you do not drink to excess, and to do so with the sun barely risen *you* must have taken a strong position about the world, most likely just last evening."

Hugh nodded thoughtfully as he ran thick fingers, partially covered by the hemmed sleeve of his green napped-flannel shirt, across the floor's puncheon slabs. John watched him struggle with a response.

"On occasion they need you—on occasion they dinna," Hugh said. He waved a hand dismissively.

John stood and checked the pot of water he had left over the fire and dumped in a scoop of hulled corn, soaking in water from the night before. "Who are they?"

"The world, John. Follow me. The world asks from you, takes from you, sometimes they give you a little, and then they desert you just when the bill needs paying for it all."

"What on earth are you talking about?"

"I make her weep. Of all the things I want for her, that isna one of them."

"You mean you make Nancy weep?"

"Yes. You're following me, thank you."

"Hugh, I don't believe it is you that makes her weep."

"Of course it is I that make her weep. I am the one that took her from her fine home and her dapper gray mare. That horse is worth as much as Jamie's entire stable."

John sat down at the table, exasperated. "You believe the loss of her horse makes her weep? Is this what she tells you?"

Hugh looked trapped by logic. "Of course not. I suppose that was a bit much. I dinna know what it is I've done."

"Does she weep all of the hours of the day?" John asked with one thin brow raised.

"No' at all. We're making a good start together, and she should be wanting for nothing. Still, I canna give her all that her father once did. It just is...that at sometimes, late at night when she should be sleeping, she cries."

Pockmarked slave—that's what they say... John gave a quick jerk of his head, as if that would shake up his thoughts, and returned to sit by his cousin on the floor, knees aching as he bent them. Their backs rested unevenly against the thick logs and chinking. He watched Hugh running a short, thick finger up and back, up and back, along a dent in his nail that distorted the shape of that thumb.

"I'm a worthy man, aren't I, John?"

"Yes. You are that." John knew now that he must have been drinking to ask such a vulnerable question, wholly out of character. And just when did Hugh start looking to John for answers? It had always been the other way around.

Hugh's head bobbed up, swaying a little. "What in God's name happened here?"

"Just an accident. It's nothing."

"Nothing my arse. Looks like you had quite a tantrum, my boy." He smiled. "Or were you drunk last night, as well?"

John bristled. "You know I don't drink."

"Pity," Hugh said. "And stop using that Robert Wiley voice, it doesna suit you."

"There's no talking to you, do you know that?"

Hugh grinned. "I've been told that before. I've also been told something that might be of interest ta you, John, so listen carefully." His grin gone, he reached out and held John's face in a firm grip. "Never apologize for existing. Did you hear that?"

"Yes, I think I did."

Hugh let go of him. "Good. Then clean this place up and put things behind you."

They sat together on the floor, unmoving for many quiet moments until John rose to check his hominy. He grimaced at such a bland breakfast. He had eaten almost nothing else all week and he had no honey to sweeten it. He stirred the thickening gruel in the pot and looked back to Hugh, intending to invite him to sit down to breakfast, but he was asleep, the dark stubble on his chin resting on his green shirt, his thick hair partially hiding his face.

Covering him with the top quilt from the bed, John went back to stoke the fire and ladle out his breakfast. He sat down at the table, with pale, badly cooked hominy gruel staring up at him from the wooden bowl, and ripped off a piece of dry bread from the loaf on the table.

As he ate, he thought of Aunt Maggie's warning—*The doorway of a great house is mighty slippery.*

He watched his tattered quilt rising and falling over Hugh's broad chest and thought, Is this what she had in mind? He felt that he might never know. Oddly, that brought him a small bit of comfort.

Within a few hours, Hugh roused himself from his undignified position on John's floor and he was more his old self, if a little crumpled.

John was amazed that just a short sleep could restore him.

Before long, they set off to entice their hogs out of the woods, as they had planned yesterday. They rode along, silently jouncing atop their mounts, each breath fogging in the cold air, and John thought about the work ahead of them. He knew field corn could work to get the hogs, if it outdid the appeal of the mast crop of chestnuts and acorns. But if the beasts had gone wild enough, they might have to bring in the dog.

Hugh surprised him out of his thoughts as he picked up his speed from a leisurely three beats to two, and, then, as his horse entered a full gallop on the narrow road, Hugh laid a firm pressure against the mare's neck. She leaned into the turn. He took her down a sparsely wooded hillside and splashed across a small stream that fed the creek.

John hurried his pace to catch up. Ahead of him, Hugh took a path that led out into the open pastureland that made up much of this small pocket of the valley.

Cutting into the pasture before them was the lazy creek, birthed in the high mountains. The land was rich and dark along its course.

Hugh and his horse leaned in again and wound to the left about, behind John, and then to the left about again, completely encircling him. Hugh laughed. Turning up dirt clods under his horse's hooves, he continued on toward the water. John raced after him, thinking that his binge of earlier must not have been so bad after all.

A good portion of the creek's edge was lined by enormous rocks, farmed from the pasture and dumped at the water's edge, thrusting into the water. Hugh slowed as he guided his horse around them, looking for a place to cross. He soon found a wide break and stepped the mare in. The sun-sparkled water coursed around the stones, splashed to the horses' dark stifles and forearms, rained back down, and continued to its rendezvous with other mountain streams.

John followed Hugh across the creek, the spraying water cold on his legs, and soon they reached a broad, wagon-rutted road that led into the mountains, gradually growing larger ahead of them. As they reached the first slope, Hugh disappeared as the road snaked slowly up through the winter trees, the grade low and easy.

John felt the crispness of the day against his face in the uneven shade of the pines and the nearly barren oaks and poplars as he started up the mountain. He heard skittering in the dry leaves beside the road and smelled must from the damp, dead carpeting all around.

Rounding a bend, John found Hugh off his horse and walking her slowly, the dark leather reins loose in his hand. Brown snow birds hopped out of his path.

"We're not to be finding our hogs here, I think," John said as he dismounted and began to walk beside him.

"I'm aware, but I thought a diversion might help me be of clearer mind before going home."

"These troubles you're having, they're making you not want to go home?"

"No' the way it sounds when you say it, no. Nancy's a beautiful woman and I never mind going home ta her," he said with a grin. He laughed when John blushed. "You have ta stop being so prudish and serious." He tightened his long coat about his chest. "You look green when you even catch us in a kiss. We do that often, you know."

"Alright, you've made your point. I'll paint on a smile at your crudity until I am able to withstand it as everyday talk."

"Crudity? Just how long were you in the war? Doubtful that you were able ta pass a night with that many fellows and no' hear what you must have considered outright vulgarity. Well," he said, shaking his head in mock gravity, "Aunt Maggie did a job on you. Confessing shame." As Hugh had always been able to do, he made John laugh at himself and graciously accept his harassment. "You need those blinders off, as well, ta see the lust in the eye o' little Miss Wiley, with it pushing her ta your side at every opportunity."

John started to protest Hugh's choice of words, and then stopped himself when he knew Hugh would only laugh it off and make him look foolish again. "Another point well-taken. Robert's daughter is a pleasant young woman, I've noticed that."

"'Pleasant young woman.' Oh, we do have some work ta do on you, John. That we do."

"Are you ready to go home yet?" John asked, trying not to bristle noticeably at his teasing.

"No. I'm leading us ta the headwaters up here a ways. I'd like ta sit and watch the spring bubbling out of the hill a while. Are you willing ta come along?"

"Do I have a choice?"

"No' particularly."

They had to cross over a downed pine when they reached the beginning of the stream. A matting of leaves and sticks lined the muddy outlet of the spring trickling onto the cold hillside. John did not find it a particularly breathtaking spot.

He followed behind as Hugh lifted himself onto upturned boulders near the head of the stream and then sat down, legs dangling over the side. The valley spread out below them in a wrinkled, patchwork quilt. Now he understood what drew Hugh here.

A few wooly cows and sheep dotted the hillsides. John thought them brave to leave their warm shelters behind. The shallow creek wandered along. On its banks, quiet cabins squatted, wisps of white swirling from the chimneys. It reminded him of the view he had sought out the day Hugh shot the bobcat.

"She gets ta you, doesna she?" Hugh asked.

The cat? "Who?"

"Anne Wiley."

"No. Why do you think so?"

"You've begun ta bristle lately whenever she comes near."

John shrugged. "She's infuriating." *And seemingly always around.*

Hugh laughed. "Why? Because she enjoys life and you dinna?"

"Aah, enough." He put up a hand and looked over at his cousin. Hugh's cheeks had reddened in the brisk wind. Wiry red-blonde hair blew into his face. John turned away to watch a wagon pulled by a thick horse bounce along the road below. "You think I don't enjoy life?"

"I dinna think you do, no. But I think you could." Hugh pulled a thin leather strap from his coat pocket and tied back his hair. "Little Miss Anne would make a good mother. And a good wife."

"I already tried marrying. And for my stupidity, Eliza died."

"You didna do that. God did. And no' because you did anything wrong."

"God did?" John shook his head. "We have more control over life than that."

"No. In this you're just along for the ride—because, John, everything you are talking about is in the past. Your future you can shape—if only in a rudimentary way, perhaps, but shape it you can. But no' your past. You aren'a a mystic. Do you think God is so cruel, ta make Eliza pay for your mistake?"

Yes. "No."

"You hav'na made one meaningful decision since she died, do you know that, you jackass? And dinna bring up that bobcat ta me. I thought she would help, so I indulged you for a time. More the fool, I. Do you think ta do nothing more with your life because you may actually make a misstep? Let us consider you are right, John, that no decisions made mean that you can never again make a wrong one." Hugh stared at him for a short while and then his brow wrinkled. "I would still be a servant if I subscribed ta your rules, never ta move forward. Would you like ta see that?"

John waved a dismissive hand. "What wrong decisions did you make?"

"None. And neither did you."

"I did. I married her so I wouldn't be lonely. I married her to take care of me." There, he said it.

"Then you are doomed," Hugh said gravely. "Nan is doomed. I can see it in her future. She is the product of a deceitful, Godless union."

Gritting his teeth, John pivoted the way they had come and jumped off the rock. He strode toward the horses, but stopped after a few yards and swung around to face Hugh again, not willing to let that cocky sonofabitch get the last word. He clenched his fists, not knowing what he would do with them, but itching to hit someone, something. "Oh, you are a heartless bastard, Hugh. I am not speaking of my daughter. She is no part of this."

Hugh cocked an infuriating brow. "Isna she?"

"I'm a good father, you'll see. My daughter will pay no debt I owe."

"'A good father. Splendid. But will that be enough? Is that enough for Nan?" Hugh turned his back on him.

"Completely," John said.

Hugh sat quietly for a time before he looked to him again. "There's quite a bit of smoke coming from the valley. The trees over there. Look."

John pulled himself back onto the rock and looked to the woods past the open pasture. "The creek should carry that smoke down with it, away from us. Must be a large fire."

Their homes were beyond the trees.

Together they jumped off of the rocks and vaulted the downed pine. The bark scraped John's hand. He ignored the sting as he grabbed his reins and swung onto his startled horse. Hugh took off ahead of him. Only half-concerned of a dangerous meeting between his mount's flying hooves and any traveler unfortunate enough to be in the way, John wheeled around and galloped down the winding road.

They kept up a reckless pace until they first arrived at Jamie's house. The yard and buildings sat quiet. Smoke deepened and bit at their eyes as they whipped around and took the road farther south. Even a thunderous gallop behind them scarcely grabbed their attention away from the roiling haze, but the rider, Archibald Methany, quickly caught up with them, his leather fire bucket banging against his knee.

"John, I think it's coming from your place. Joe's not far behind," Archie yelled. All three quickly rounded the turn taking them to John's cabin.

As his farm came into view, the smoke thickened.

Suddenly, Jamie was there in front of them, frantically running from the creek, one fire bucket in each hand. Water sloshed from their stretched, pitched black insides. "Ho!" he yelled as they almost ran him down. More water spilled onto his shoes as he stopped short.

Five more men ran past, buckets in hand.

"Where's Nancy?" John yelled at Jamie as he jumped off his horse.

"Your Nancy is home safe with Susan."

Relieved at the news, John looked at his cabin for the first time since he stormed up the road. Half the roof had already collapsed, the chimney was charred and broken, but the worst of it appeared to be out now. Only a few scattered flames around the place were left and they billowed thick smoke each time someone threw water.

"Hugh's Nancy is over there, making smoke," Jamie said and motioned his head toward the house. "She made it here before anyone." They both glanced at the house as a rafter cracked and gave way, crashing to the floor inside. Jamie blinked and wiped at his face. "You'll have her ta thank if there's anything left of your place."

John stood still, staring at the house.

Hugh brushed past him as he ran across the dooryard, snaked his thick arm about his wife's tiny waist, scooped her up like a kicking rag doll, and carried her out of the smoke.

* * *

John tucked his daughter in the best he could on Hugh and Nancy's cold floor. An old bearskin rug was her pallet, placed just far enough away from the hearth to decrease the danger of catching fire. Watching her sleeping there, John thought he would forever be wary of how vulnerable they were to the indiscriminate destruction of fire. *To indis-*

criminate destruction... They had had just about enough of that.

Their home was in shambles; the entire roof burned, and what shingles didn't drift away in the wind fell in upon most of their belongings. But most rafters were stable, if charred. A few small fires did some minor damage inside, but most of it was just drenched with water, and he was confident that most of their possessions could be saved.

He had gathered up a box of Eliza's old clothes—the dress she wore at their wedding, her one frilly chemise—and he sat next to it now in the light from the hearth, running a hand across the soft fabrics. He hadn't been able to bear leaving them alone there with the smoke and the soot. His belongings he couldn't have cared less about.

His neighbors had saved his home—really, Nancy saved his home. He looked at her now, dressed modestly in her shift, robe, and cap, and curled up sleeping exhaustedly on the small bed in the corner. A few moments before, she had slid a puffy loaf of bread in the dark pit of the baking oven next to the hearth, sealed the door, and collapsed into bed.

Even with Hugh's disapproval bearing down on her today, she had looked pleased with herself. She had been a mess when Hugh swung her around and deposited her a safe distance from the fire—her hair had streamed out of its tight bun and her clothes were wet and sooty, but she was smiling when she told them proudly, "I think it's out." Hugh shook his head and stared at her with disbelief, one hand over his mouth. John wasn't sure whether he was hiding a smile or holding back curses, but he was abnormally silent either way.

He thought of the faces of the people that had come, unselfishly, to his aid today: Their plain, lined faces smeared with grime, and their plain, heavy clothes wet and stained with soot. He had always considered himself different from them—going somewhere different and being something different. He had run away from Aunt Maggie for just that reason. He had thought that staying in the same place would mean he had given up, he had failed. Though how hard had he really been trying to grow and move ahead? Hugh had pointed out that he had been doing exactly nothing anyway but steeping in his own misery. He had also designed countless plans about the kind of man he wanted to be: how to speak, how to work, how to get along...and how to grieve endlessly. He had borrowed mannerisms and ideals from every "successful" man he knew. All he was left holding was a futile litany of platitudes.

And now he saw that he was—fundamentally—no different, that his face was plain and lined and his clothes were plain and heavy, and he suddenly realized that he had every reason to be proud of being a part of their community.

Maybe even damned lucky they let him in.

The doorway to a great house is mighty slippery, he thought, feeling that he may be just beginning to understand. He grinned and then walked out onto the narrow front steps. He spotted Hugh resting on a bench in the shadows of the yard and John decided to join him. He heard a muffled conversation from the bench, and after a few steps, he could see two pairs of legs in the meager light thrown from the window. They were crossed casually, identically, at the ankle.

Drawing closer, John was surprised to see his brother sitting on the bench, too.

Hugh stood up. "Your brother Hugh—oh, sorry, he reminded me he's been called Mac now for many a year, as if there's something wrong with the name," he said with a wink. "Anyway, your brother has fine timing, that he does, John. He was thinking of staying with you for a spell. Fate doesna seem ta be working in his favor."

John's younger brother stood up while their cousin was talking and embraced John with youthful exuberance in a firm, back-slapping hug. "I'm out of my bond, John. Left my *master* firmly behind," Mac said with a mixture of relief and resentment.

He had served a neighboring cooper from Cook's Creek since he was six years old and John hadn't even considered that the time was near for him to be let go. And he was thinking that now, as of today, he had nothing to offer his younger brother when Mac said, "Hugh told me of the trouble you've had, I'm mightily sorry."

"It really hasn't been such a bad day as that," John said, and Hugh and Mac looked at him quizzically. He broke into a broad grin that was unlike his usually dour demeanor.

Hugh told Mac in a quiet aside, "It must be the shock speaking."

"I've heard some about you today, as well, Hugh," Mac said.

"Yes? And what would that be?" he asked, smiling.

Mac sat back down upon the empty bench and spread his arms about the backrest. "At a tavern I stopped in at today in the next valley, said you had stolen off with a wealthy man's daughter. I thought, that's the way, Hugh, get them before they get you."

"Now, that's no' the way of it…" Hugh began.

Mac leaned forward to say heatedly, "Och hone, Hugh, you don't have to be explaining it to me. I think it's a good lump to give them sitting high on their plantations. For one of those—those that they're so proud to own and dictate about—to mix with their own laird's blood; it's a fine way, it is." Mac settled back again, looking pleased with his deductions.

"Nancy is no' a lump," Hugh said, attempting to defend his wife and the "why"s of their marriage.

Mac chuckled sardonically at Hugh's unfortunate choice of words.

Hugh dismissed him as he said, "John, have a good evening, I'll see you on the morrow and I hope the bearskin will be comfortable for you and your daughter. Mac can sleep in the barn wherever there's room."

Mac jerked his chin to Hugh's departing back. "Now, who pissed in his hominy?"

John laughed and shook his head. "I think you did."

* * *

The sounds of clanking and banging woke John, and he squinted at the sunlight streaming in, rolling and dipping across each floorboard from the open door. His daughter was up and about, busily walking between two heavy chairs near the table, while Nancy was coaxing an unresponsive fire into cooking their breakfast.

John watched the little girl for a moment, unsteady on her fat, square feet, as she let go of one chair and toddled the few steps to the next. Large, dark shoes appeared behind her in the doorway and John barely had time to think before his coat was thrown at him.

"Get up, John. I've got two fat hogs already, while you've been abed," Hugh said.

"Where's Mac?" John asked him as he pushed back the blankets and shrugged on the coat.

Hugh came to the table, leaned across and kissed his wife. Embarrassed, John looked down at his clothes, straightening them just to have something to do but watch the happy couple. His trousers were wrinkled, but clean; fine enough for meeting the hogs, he supposed. John looked back to Hugh. "Well? Is he here?"

Without ever taking his eyes off Nancy, Hugh replied, "I hav'na seen him, and if you be asking me, I'd like ta wait awhile before I do again."

As Nancy walked away from the table, she swished her skirts a little for her husband's benefit before pulling the sealed door off the hearth oven and carefully removing the crusty loaf she had put in last night. John was uncomfortable all over again. Hugh grinned at him.

Leaving the warm smell of fresh bread behind, John followed Hugh to the bear-proof hog pen where two dark and bristly sows were rooting around with their fat snouts in the slop that Hugh had thrown to them. The top of the sturdy pen lay to the far side.

One beady-eyed creature looked up at John, the top of her snout covered in dirt. She had one light splotch on the left nostril and another covering half of her weak chin. Each side of her mouth dripped with white goop. She looked healthy, the mast crop must have been a bumper.

Jamie walked over from the barn, wiping his hands on a dirty handkerchief. "Up and about are you, now, John? Good ta see," he said. "By the by, your brother spent last evening on little Nan's bed at our home—he said something about too many steaming piles at Hugh's, wha'ever that means." Jamie scratched his wire-haired head in the time-honored expression of the perplexed. "Wants me ta tell you he and Daniel are ta be in the woods today, splitting you some shingles. I went by the place, 'tis no longer smoldering. I think you'll be alright." He slapped John on the back and scooped up tinder from the box nearby. Next to a stack of firewood, a cauldron of water was waiting to be heated for scalding the hogs after slaughter.

Hugh leaned against the pen and told John, "You go, see what you can do ta take care of your home. I know you dinna want ta leave Nan, but maybe it will get you off my floor sooner than expected."

Gratefully, he left them and started off for his cabin on foot, a crisp breeze against his face reddening his cheeks and his thick, straight nose. His thoughts tumbled around as he walked along the deserted road, his long arms swinging at his sides.

Entering the clearing that ended in his ruined home, he lost all the faith he had found last night. He tightened his jaw and looked straight ahead as he passed the lonely carved fieldstone standing at the edge of the woods. He didn't care to think about anything this morning, and whatever feelings of guilt Elizabeth's grave conjured up he tried to stuff away, back in the shadowy niches where memories were safely stored, cluttered alongside ideas and worries, for a better day. He didn't need another reminder right now of how everything he touched went to wrack and ruin.

The cabin was enough for today.

It greeted him crookedly, debris strewn all about. His blankets and some of Nan's gowns were clinging to the low branches of a nearby young maple tree and he grinned a painful grin at the unknown person's efforts. The lighter colored fabrics showed faint smudges of soot, as if a hurried attempt had been made to wash the damage out of them. His hand slowly touched and stirred each of the soggy survivors as he walked past them, drawn to the chimney.

It was made of fieldstone chinked with mud up to a decent height above his head, then of small logs and more thick mud chinking rising up and above the missing roof. The top of the wooden chimney was charred and broken, and he expected he would find some of its remains inside the hearth and likely swept across his floor in the deluge of water pouring down after it.

Without another thought he raised his heavy shoe and kicked the jagged fieldstone. It hurt. He kicked it again and a small part of it fell away, the mud chinking disintegrating at the boreholes of bees long-since dead. Picking up the chunk of offending stone, he hurled it at the log wall and it bounced off and landed back on the ground. It lay there and mocked him.

A flash of white from the trees behind the cabin grabbed his attention, but when he turned his head in that direction there was nothing but a swaying hemlock bough that covered the entrance to a footpath leading into the woods and up a steep hillside. He blinked, rubbed his face tiredly, looked back at the house for a moment, and then forgot about the chimney and crossed the short distance between himself and the dark woods.

Dense thickets of white thorn at its edge formed an impenetrable barrier, but outside of the rugged footpath they had been hacked apart and trampled down many years ago. He pushed aside the bough as he walked a few yards onto the secluded path. The ground under the massive evergreen was rich and soft, even in the cold, and it was covered in a thick carpeting of brown needles. No undergrowth grew up in the dense shade of the tree.

Farther ahead, a short and spindly birch cowered under a towering chestnut. Moss grew about them and covered a lonely, jagged rock upturned on the forest floor. The path led around the rock and veered to the left, where the grade of the hill became steeper.

He rounded the bend and found the flash of white sitting on a tree stump not more than a few feet away from him. It was the bonnet of Anne Wiley and she looked up at him from under the lacy edging with large eyes. He never knew they were green.

"What are you doing? Why are you sneaking about my place?" he said sharply and her green eyes narrowed in return. "Does your father know you sneak off alone as you do? I'm sure he would not approve of you putting yourself in danger. A frivolous, frivolous girl..."

"He told me about the fire. I just wanted to—"

"Enough!" He took a few steps closer to her and stared down at her hard. "Were you the one who hung the clothes on the tree?" He didn't wait for her answer. "Don't. Touch. My. Belongings!"

"I thought I could help," she told him as she stood up and gave him her back. She started along the path leading farther up the hill.

"I didn't ask for your help," he called out to her.

"I know," trailed out behind her. He watched her blue skirt swish beneath her tiny waist, cinched by a tight bodice of striped blues and whites. Her thick, white chemise was ruffled at the neck, where it barely rose up out of the bodice, and at the wrists, over which she carried a light hooded cloak that she soon shook out and wrapped about herself before she disappeared around another bend.

She was actually walking away. She didn't apologize, she didn't accept anything he had to say to her. She just brushed off his harsh words and walked away. He had never even sought her out, not once, she was just always there.

How do you like that? he thought. She's running me like a deer into a thicket, there every time I turn around.

Whenever I need her. Maybe that wasn't such a bad emotion to have. Just because he wouldn't marry out of selfish need didn't mean he couldn't move forward with a friendship.

He sprinted to the bend, and when he could see her again, he called out, "I could have told you all about the fire when I called on you."

"I didn't ask you to call on me." She didn't look back.

"I know," he said as she continued out of sight where she couldn't see his smile.

CHAPTER THIRTY-FOUR

"He's my cousin, but I'm glad he's out of here, I am."

"Someone might hear you saying a mean thing like that," Nancy said. She pulled her shift down over her head and reached for her bodice.

Hugh grabbed it first. "You agree with me, dinna you?"

When she answered "yes" he tossed the bodice at her. "I knew you were as rotten as the rest of us, you just pretend you're not."

He watched her tighten the laces and the stiff garment squeezed her around the ribs.

"It's just my raising." She looked up and appeared to be ready to say something more, but she stopped short. "What?"

"You were saying?" Hugh said.

"No, no. That face. Why do you look so sour?"

He turned and left, grabbing his coat on the way. He stood outside of the door for a few moments and when she didn't follow him he began feeling silly for actually waiting for her.

So, instead, he threw himself into splitting firewood on a broad poplar stump beside the house and ignored the tightening in his chest and then the coughing that came after it.

It was just her raising.

A smooth stroke fell into a split at the top and a good-sized piece of white oak cracked down the middle, some of the bark broke off in chunks and fell to the stump.

While he worked, he had sufficient time to brood. He worried over her constantly, felt sick that she would cry over their life together, and felt contempt for the man who brought it all on so unnecessarily. And just when would she finally come outside and talk to him anyway?

The axe head swung effortlessly at the ground like a needle swings north and he dropped the smooth handle. His thick fingers pulled the two pieces of wood apart and strands of the grain clung to one another until they were pulled free. He hefted the axe and swung again and again and it was quartered. He picked a splintered piece up off the stump and his hand shook, and then he gathered the others off the ground and threw them into the growing pile. He gave one last shaky swing and the tip of the axe head sunk deep into the stump and he left it there while he sat down.

It was coming on again—he could feel the whole-body tremors starting. The coldness of the ground seeped through his breeches, and he raised up his knees, crossed his arms across them and put down his head. His entire body began to quake and he wondered just when God was going to decide that he had had enough. He had had enough. Ever since the war the ague just kept coming, and he just kept getting weaker.

His feeble voice floated through the empty yard, "I will no' be Sisyphus and struggle for eternity. What am I paying for?"

Nancy found him folded up about himself and she went to her knees beside him. How long he had been laying there, his warmth seeping into the ground, she didn't know, but she pulled her coat wide and they lay together. He trembled on and on. She took him inside when the sun was high and they curled up on the bed together while the sun climbed back down the sky.

When the pouring sweats started, Nancy brought him a bowl with cool water and sat by his side on the bed, but what she didn't understand, he thought, was that he was cold, he didn't want the water. Nobody seemed to understand this disease, and it made his dread all the greater. Maybe it would be best for her if she *were* regretting their marriage. He took the bowl from her and set it aside, then held her gently by the wrists and looked into her face. "I know you've been crying in the night."

"I have."

"What do we do?"

"Nothing. It's over."

"What's over?" There it was—he had lost her. John was wrong. His head began to throb and his vision blurred on the sides of his eyes. He closed them.

"Hugh?" Her voice was thick and flat, troubled.

"What's over?"

She took her hands away from him and he opened his eyes again, saw the pain in her eyes, and thought how foolish he must have sounded, *weeping over her horse.*

"The baby—"

"The baby? I—"

"Shut up." She grabbed his wrists as he had grabbed hers. "We were going to have a baby. It was very early, but a baby all the same. Gone as quickly as it came. I'm sorry. But now that I've gotten past most of the disappointment, I'm as confident as ever we'll fill this house up with children. It just won't be this time."

* * *

When Nancy awoke, Hugh was already gone to town. Groggy, at first she couldn't think of why he had gone. She stretched and yawned.

Oh, court day. Gone until tomorrow.

She smiled as she dressed, thinking of how amusing court day was to her, yet how serious the men took it. The same cases would be carried over month to month to month. Arguing over three pounds. For a year—or more.

The bright fire popped, Hugh had seen to it before he left. There was also water warming just out of reach of the flames. She smiled again at his thoughtfulness and sat at the table to brush her long hair. Her smile faded a bit as she thought about Hugh's latest attack of the ague. She hoped he was up to the trip. Well, he would know better than she, at least she had to hope that were true.

As for her, today, she was going to take advantage of being alone by neglecting washday. Gladly. Trudging up and back to the spring house for laundry water she could well do without. Oh, the fire to heat the cauldron was built close enough to the spring house, just at the top of the hill above the spring—a full seventy-three and one-half steps from the new porch Hugh had put on the cabin—and above the creek snaking around the edge of their farm. But the spring was on a mild hill, as springs tended to be, so the water had to be lugged and dragged and cursed up to level ground and she swore every time that she would rather pound those boiling clothes all day than drag that ice-cold, slip-sloshing water even ten feet. Of course, her hands didn't agree with that at the end of those days. They were chapped and cracked from the pounding and wringing. And when she had pinned the last frozen shirt and the final stiff handkerchief on the line, her raw hands told her angrily that for her misuse of them they would refuse to obey her for the rest of the day, not much more than misshapen claws until they recovered.

Yes, she would much rather be visiting with friends, or picking her way through the quiet hills, looking for sassafras or chinquapins or chestnuts.

Hugh had said Jamie was riding out with him today, so Susan was alone, too. She soon decided to ride over there and spend the day with her. A basket sitting near the door held swatches of an old dress, they could add them to Susan's quilt, she thought, as she wound and pinned her long hair on the back of her head. She was looking forward to the quiet day, to putting her chores aside to visit with another woman.

Hearing the dog barking in the yard, she threw on a shawl and walked outside, squinting in the sun, to see a man dismounting near the fence at the barn. He threw his horse's reins over the rail and started up the beaten path to the house. He was a peddler from the look of the bulging packsaddle on his swayback horse. She was almost glad Hugh wasn't here so she didn't have to invite the man in, entertain him, put him up for however long he wanted to stay... My goodness, when did she become so discourteous?

"Good morning," the man called when he saw her.

"Good morning," she returned.

He was very slight, even his hair was thin. It was mostly gone from the top of his head, but made up for it in the back where it lay well past his shoulders. He smiled at her widely and showed quite a few dark spots where teeth were missing.

Turning back to his horse, he rummaged through the nearest pack and brought a handful of goods back to her. "If you have a moment, I've here some fancy perfume that I just knew while coming this way the lady of the house might enjoy." He unwrapped a bit of dark felt and held out a delicate bottle that was actually an exquisite looking bit of glass. Pulling the small top off, he held it out for her to smell.

"No thank you, sir. There's nothing that I need today." A light flowery smell came from the open bottle.

He put the perfume in one of his numerous coat pockets. Another small satchel held a large silver hair comb and he held that out to her.

"Again, no thank you," she said.

"I do have a few tools that your husband or your father might be interested in. Could I speak with him for a few moments?"

"My husband, ah, he's, ah, right back there in the woods. Gathering chinquapins." Damn, he'd never believe that. *Yes sir, that's right, gathering them up in his apron.*

"Your husband?" His eyes lit up and she didn't like it at all.

"Yes, sir, my husband. I'm going inside now, sir. Please do have a good day." She turned and began to walk back to the cabin.

"Ma'am? A moment, please."

She whirled back around, her hands spread out to her sides. "There's nothing that we need. Good luck to you for the rest of the day."

"I don't think Hugh is in the woods, ma'am, in all fairness."

Hugh...how?

"And just who is Hugh, sir?" She could feel her heart beating.

He took a step closer to her. "Your husband."

"No. You have the wrong farm. Good day." She walked toward the house as quickly as she could without looking panicked.

She was halfway into the cabin, trying to slip through the door and close it on him, but he was there, stopping her with a bony hand. She pushed the door harder, lost some ground, and then threw her elbow into his chest. She hit something small and hard, the man grunted, and then she could smell it. The perfume. Nancy's taut nerves let her down, she started to laugh.

He grabbed her arm, pulled her back outside, and smacked her in the face harder than a man his size should have been able to. Her ear rang. "I think you have it wrong, ma'am." He pinned her against the wall of the cabin. "I had cause to run into your husband today and spoke to him for a moment, too. Arrogant fellow. But the real talk started after he headed off."

His chapped lips looked as if they might split apart, they stretched so tight when he smiled. He grabbed her breasts, jammed a bony knee between her legs. She felt sick. "Oh, I know what kind of lady you are. And your husband is not out back, he's gone to the courthouse. Don't think he could make it back today, so I think we'll—"

He stopped when they heard a horse approaching. She looked over his shoulder to see Susan stopped between them and the barn, at the end of the footpath to the house. She slowly raised Jamie's gun up to her shoulder. The man's eyes bulged out over his sunken cheeks and

Nancy was so relieved her knees threatened to buckle.

She held her breath while she waited for Susan to act.

"Get back on your horse, sir," Susan called.

The man looked from one woman to the other and back again, as if undecided. Could Susan manage to shoot the filthy man and miss her? She had to get away before he decided to test Susan's mettle, but he was blocking too much of the door for her to slip back inside.

Too, he still held a fistful of her dress bunched tightly in his greasy claw. He looked at her now with an awful grin pulling up the sides of his awful mouth. His grip on her dress tightened, pinching her skin, and she winced under the pain. He had made up his mind.

"I don't like wasting my husband's shot on useless jackasses, sir, but I will. Get back on your horse," Susan called.

Nancy waited until he looked back one more time, then spent all the weight she had sending her knee into his groin. When he let go, she jumped off the open end of the porch, landed wrong and ended up hard on her knees.

"You can shoot him now, Susan," she yelled as she scrambled to her feet. If her head didn't hurt so badly, Nancy would have laughed again as the man rose from his knees, still cupping the front of his breeches, and limped back the way he had come, his odd, bowlegged gait turning him from a monster to a weasel within a few feet. He pulled himself onto his horse and rode away without looking at the two women again.

Susan's brave face fell as she leapt from her horse and ran to her side. "What did he do to you?" She held Nancy's chin in her hand and turned her head to look at her cheek. "Lord, there's already a purple lump. It's not gonna be pretty." She looked her up and down. "Anything else?"

"No."

"Do you want to cry?" She made an odd, pinched face.

Nancy tried to smile, but winced instead. "No. I want to kill the bastard."

Susan grinned back at her. "We're gentlewomen. Perhaps we should merely wound him."

"I've an idea where."

They went into the house and Nancy laid the wooden plank across the iron lock, barring anyone else from entering. After she tried pulling on the door and it stuck tight, she said, "Why would he risk something like that?" Although she asked, she knew the answer already.

Susan put an arm around her shoulder, leading her to the table. "I don't know, and I don't want to know that grotesque little man's mind."

"You do know, don't you? As well as I do? I can see it in your face. Vicious gossip, that's what it is. He must have heard it. Gossip from those who don't have anything better going than to begrudge other people their own happiness. Some say I stepped out of bounds marrying Hugh, but I'm happy with my decision. And that's all it takes for someone to want to bring me down. That peddler thinks I have no standing in these parts anymore, they say I married a slave. So what does that make me? A woman of the manor? Hardly. To them, more likely a villein—a serf—and that's what someone led him to believe, so then he's free to—"

"Nancy, I don't know anyone who would—"

"Oh, don't you? And you know it's true, too. If I were a miserable, long-suffering wife, those same people would be here praying with me, helping me with chores, bringing me stew and wanting all the sordid details so they could pray about it some more at home. We wouldn't be talking about this now if Hugh beat me once in a while—oh, don't looked so shocked. That would satisfy them, a couple of bruises. And you know that, too. Well, I disappointed them, and for that I'm going to have to pay. Or so they think."

Susan went to the pot of warm water and dipped some into a bowl. "Here, sit down and I'll clean up your face."

"Why? Is it bleeding?"

"No. But it's something to do. Better than this talk we're having."

Nancy took the bowl from her and set it down. Putting her hands on the table, she leaned over it to say, "You ride up here ready to shoot a man, and you're uncomfortable talking about this?"

When Susan didn't answer, she continued, "Well, it's easy to remedy. I go to those responsible, say my piece, and this ends. Today."

* * *

Susan appeared to only accompany her grudgingly. They set off after breakfast, Susan keeping hold of her musket, and Nancy leading the way boldly. The road they followed wound through the valley and into the next and this is where Nancy expected to find her prey.

They cantered slowly into the yard, their horses having been ridden much farther and faster than they were used to. "Give them a good rub-down, will you? I'll be right back," Nancy said.

She walked to the door of the house, a two-story log structure covered in whitewashed weatherboarding. It wasn't as big as her father's, but one look and she could tell the family was on the rise. Or at least hoped to be.

After rapping on the door, a young girl answered. "Yes?"

Nancy bent down to her level and said sweetly, "Miss, is Mrs. MacDonough home?"

The surprised girl shut the door and a few seconds later, the pinched and peaked face of Beatrice MacDonough opened it again. "Is there something that you require, Mrs. McLaughlin?"

"There certainly is, dear Mrs. MacDonough. Would you let me in please?"

The woman looked behind her uncertainly for a moment and Nancy heard a soft womanly voice in the room.

Nancy tried to crane her neck around the door to peek in. "Oh! So sorry to have bothered you when you're with company, but this really will only take a moment." She pushed on the door and Mrs. Mac-Donough acquiesced and let her into the room, bristling noticeably.

Three more women were sitting at the table just inside the door. They white-knuckled their prayer books, an old gilded-edged bible open on the table between them, bulging satchels sat at their feet. One looked at her with condescension, maybe even hate, in her eyes. Nancy stared back at her until she looked away. The screaming paradox of the room was suffocating.

"Are you having a meeting?" Nancy said with as much sweetness as she could muster. "Well, this is so rude of me."

Now two of the women, faces as pinched as the sour Mrs. Mac-Donough's, stared at her with growing animosity. Nancy didn't know them, never wanted to, but she named them Meg and Peg anyway.

But the third, an exceptionally dainty white-haired woman, Mrs. Butler, with a kind face as rippled as the river, stood and walked over to take her hand. "My dear Mrs. McLaughlin, so nice to see you again. Such a beautiful young woman, isn't she, ladies?" She turned to her companions and their affirmative sounds were pointedly lacking in sincerity. The elderly woman seemed not to notice. "You are most definitely welcome here, come sit down. And my, you've hurt your face."

She touched Nancy's face lightly with cold fingertips. "Beatrice, dear, something in your satchel for bruising? Yes? Could you fetch it for the dear girl?"

She felt all of the steam she had built up slowly leaving her as the woman gently led her to a chair. She stopped her before she could get her into the trap, for that's what she considered it to be. Oh, the woman seemed to be genuinely gracious and pleased to have her here. But if Nancy sat down, she knew what she had come for would be lost.

"Thank you so much, but I really only need to speak to Mrs. Mac-Donough for a moment, privately."

"Well, of course." She turned to Mrs. MacDonough. "Beatrice, we'll certainly excuse you for a moment while you attend to her."

Beatrice MacDonough's face reddened as she said, "Thank you, I'll only be a moment. Please continue with your reading while I'm gone."

Once the two were outside and the door closed, Nancy turned on her. Quietly she said, "Do you see my face?"

"Of course I do, I'm not blind, dear."

"And do you know who my husband is?" Nancy stood a little taller.

"Of course I do, I'm not blind, dear."

"Very amusing. I know that it is you and a few other biddies who have been talking about things you have no right to—oh, you can close your mouth, dear, I only called you a biddy. No less than is deserved."

She looked away from the woman for a moment and checked on Susan who was leading the horses around in a slow walk.

When she looked back at Beatrice the woman had her arms clasped across her chest.

"If you're quite finished…"

"Not hardly," Nancy answered. "I'm sure you do know who my husband is, and I'm also quite sure that you've had much to say about it. And that has led me to look the way I do today," she said, touching her tender cheekbone. Nancy's anger caused her to feel bolder and she drew herself up. The balance of power on the porch suddenly shifted completely to her. Beatrice shrank under her patronizing stare and then mumbled something about the herbs inside.

"Never mind that," Nancy said. "But I will give you some advice, and that is you will want to be more prudent in the future when you speak my name or that of my husband, because I will tell you this only once. Are you listening? Good. My husband is an opponent to be wary of, you see, he served many years in the late war, and in the dark of the nights of the soldiers' many victories, do you know what they did? Not many do."

Beatrice only shook her head. Good, she was cowed. There was no one on this side of the door to back her up. Did no one ever stand up to this woman? Nancy thought it was a pity that she had been left unchecked for this long and she wondered how many people this woman had sliced with her malicious tongue.

Quickly deciding to say anything she had to to make the biggest impression possible on this woman, she said in a whisper, "They roasted and ate their enemies. Oh, indeed, it was gruesome. But, such is war." She didn't care if Beatrice knew it was far-fetched, she was only here to make a point. She ignored a niggling twinge of blasphemy when she thought it was turning into a parable Jesus himself would be proud of. Getting on with it she asked, "Do you know what you are, dear?" Beatrice shook her head again. "You are the enemy."

After staring at the miserable woman pointedly for a few quiet seconds, Nancy opened the door and pleasantly called to the only worthwhile woman inside, "Good day to you, Mrs. Butler."

"Good day, dear," the older woman called back.

Beatrice scurried into the house and shut the door.

CHAPTER THIRTY-FIVE

The men had been riding since just before sunrise, traveling east and winding about the valleys, hoping to then keep a steady pace farther north, to the courthouse. The early morning road was dotted with travelers, mostly on foot—they called out greetings as they passed. Hugh and Daniel were at the head of the caravan, trailing horses behind them. Mac and Jamie brought up the rear.

Jamie and Daniel hoped to sell most of their horses today somewhere in the crowds gathered in front of the courthouse, taverns, and merchants' shops. Hugh and Mac left the brothers behind to hawk and haggle and they headed to the tavern.

Mac watched with narrowed eyes a young slave boy following along behind a well-dressed man just leaving the tavern as they were entering. The man tipped his hat in their direction as he passed. Hugh wondered what the pair, perfect strangers, had done to raise Mac's ire, but he was afraid he already knew.

"And you married into them," Mac said.

"And that pleased you, as I recall," Hugh returned.

They passed four square tables—three occupied by men with drinks—lit by a smoky fireplace in the left wall. In the cold shadows to the right of the door, more scattered tables sat empty.

No food had been served yet, but Hugh could smell yeast and beef and onions coming from the direction of the kitchen as they passed the fireplace.

Hugh stared at Mac for a moment. "We need boarding for the night and so do our horses, I suggest that's what we start doing."

"But if your wife—"

"Dinna bait me. Sit down and wait." Hugh left Mac behind and looked for the proprietor to work out boarding and pasture for at least four of their horses. He hoped his brothers would sell off the rest before tomorrow.

Why Mac came along on this trip, he didn't know. He wished he had stayed home. He made Hugh uncomfortable with his constant watching of everyone. Categorizing them, pronouncing judgments and just punishments. He never stopped.

He was especially tired of hearing about Nancy and her family. Did Mac see her family gathered around Hugh's supper table? No, never once. Why couldn't he leave it alone? Damn Mac and his bitterness, anyway. He didn't want to hear any more.

After talking to the tavern-keeper, he found that Mac had disappeared while he was gone. A grateful Hugh sat alone at a table, slowly sipping a strong rye brandy. Mac joined him again before he could enjoy much of it.

In his coat pocket, he fingered an ivory comb he had bought for Nancy from a peddler in the Jackson valley. An unpleasant little man, he remembered. But soon it was forgotten, his attention turning to Mac's bristling as he placed his drink on the table and sat down.

The tavern grew louder and more crowded as trenchers were carried out to the tables. On the far side of the room, a buxom woman in a low-cut chemise, tight red bodice and green skirt leaned over the tables and lit fat candles. Hugh wished Mac would notice her and leave him alone.

He didn't.

Mac cleared his throat. "I'm going to apologize, but first I wish to be heard."

Hugh nodded. "Fair enough."

"It is my feeling that, in the sight of God, anyone who is part of the ownership of another man is fit, without further cause or recourse, only for Hell."

"What does this have ta do with Nancy?"

"But the sins of the father—"

"Oh, for heaven's sake, that's the kind of thinking that got *us* put inta the damnable slave shackles."

Mac stared at him blankly for a moment. "But—"

Hugh waved away his *buts*. "God forgives sin, Mac."

Mac rose from the table. "No." He banged a quiet fist on the wood. "He doesn't."

"Well, then we are at a deadlock."

Close behind him, Daniel's voice rose over Hugh's husky one. "Hugh! I hope you've only paid ta stable four horses."

"I have," Hugh said.

Mac stormed away from the table and Daniel took his seat.

At Daniel's surprised look, Hugh said, "Never mind him. What did you find?"

"We've sold all of the horses, the gentleman is on his way in ta sign the note. It appears we came all this way only ta sell the animals ta a neighbor, but you do what you do."

Jamie found them a few moments later with Mac trailing behind, and indeed, it was their neighbor, Jack Berry, who was there, prepared to sign the promissory note.

"Good day," Jack said brusquely and motioned to someone across the room.

The owner of the tavern waved them over.

"Follow me, gentlemen," Jack said.

He led them through the hot, sooty kitchen and up a narrow flight of stairs. They crowded into a small room. The owner set a candle on a cluttered desk along the near wall and it wavered as he left, closing the door. With him went the heat and light, and the clanging and chatter from downstairs.

Hugh walked to the far end of the room and glanced out the dusky window. The sun had nearly set. The squat, wooden courthouse across the street sat quiet, jurors and complainants and defendants gone. A man in a tattered coat led a horse along the road and disappeared from view.

"What have we decided on?" Daniel asked.

Hugh turned back to the room.

"Twelve pounds for the mares, fourteen for the stallion," Jamie said.

Jack took a seat at the desk, and in a neat hand, wrote the promissory note on a small slip of paper. He handed it to Daniel for approval. Daniel, as incapable of reading as Hugh was, shrugged and handed it to Jamie. Jamie handed it to Mac.

Mac considered it for a moment. "Twelve for the mares, fourteen for the stallion. It's all there."

"Are you transporting them back south?" Jamie said to Jack.

"No."

"Fifteen for the stallion, then."

"Done."

Mac handed him the paper and he changed it and signed it with a flourish. Mac came forward to the desk to sign as a witness.

"And now you, Hugh," Jack said. He turned to Hugh and handed him the stained quill. "We need one more witness."

Hugh stood for a moment, hand poised over the dark desk, and his thumb smeared the whorl on Mac's "Hugh". Mac took the pen back. "My apologies," he said, and added a "J" and an "r" to the end of his name to distinguish his signature from Hugh's.

Hugh was indecisive for a moment longer. He could try to imitate Mac's signature, but he didn't. Mac could pity him his ignorance or not, he didn't care. He signed it with an "X", the quill clamped in an uncomfortable fist.

Mac stared at him for a long moment before Jack took over again and wrote while speaking. "Hugh McLaughlin, Senior—His Mark. Very good." He shook everyone's hand before he left the room and motioned for them to follow him into the noisy common room once more. Waiting there on the table were at least a dozen glasses filled with dark liquid.

Jack smiled widely. "Let's drink."

* * *

"I know what it is, Nancy."

"You're mistaken."

Hugh pulled Nancy's hand away from her face and kissed her fingertips. She smiled and laid her hand on the table, next to the comb he had just given her as a gift from his trip.

"This mark here," he said and touched her cheek gently, "and this mark here are clearly from two fingers, there's even—" He looked closer and furrows deepened between his eyes. "There's a scratch from a fingernail, as well. Why would you want ta be telling me different?"

The rest of the men filed into Hugh's cabin. "Sweet Lord, what happened ta you?" Daniel said. He dropped an armful of leather horse tack on the floor and walked over to Nancy.

"It was an accident."

"No it's wasna, that's a handprint sure as sunshine," Daniel said and looked at Hugh. "What are you going ta do?"

"There's nothing ta be done—yet. She willna tell me anything."

Daniel nodded his head and picked up the straps of leather. He looked at her, sitting at the table—large, tired men surrounding her. "Dinna be foolish, Nancy." After staring at Hugh for a long moment, he left and Jamie followed behind him.

Mac remained, standing in the doorway. Their shoulders brushed as Hugh walked past him out the door and said, "I'll help you get your gear together."

Once they were most of the way through the yard, Mac said, "I'm leaving, but you don't have to be running me off out of fear for Nancy."

"I'm not—"

Mac put up a hand. "Quite right, perhaps fear is the wrong word. I'm aware that I've spoken harshly in the past. But someone would hit that woman…" He shook his head. "No one should hit a woman, Hugh. Let me know what needs be done."

Mac swung onto the back of his horse and lightly snapped the reins. Hugh watched him slowly guide her around the curving hill and he disappeared.

* * *

The day after Hugh's trip, Hugh and Nancy still had not resolved their argument of *Who hit you?—I wasn't hit*, so there was no one for Hugh to lash out at.

He blamed himself instead.

I shouldna have left her alone. Never once did he believe he should not have married her. If he believed in God at all, he believed He had held out this special woman for him.

"Who hit you?"

"I wasn't hit."

"Damn it, Nany." Hugh pinched the bridge of his nose. "It's my responsibility ta take care of you, ta give you my protection. How can I do that now if you willna allow it?"

She took his arms and put them around her waist, they lay there like leaden weights. "No, tighter." He squeezed her and she said, "Now stop your frowning and kiss me hello. You've been home all these hours, and no proper kiss has been forthcoming. I think you're indeed becoming derelict in your duties." He kissed her long and tenderly. When she again looked into his eyes, she asked him, "Tell me about your trip."

"No. Who hit you?" He pressed a finger to her lips. "Dinna say it."

She grabbed his finger in a small fist and said, "Very well. A…vagrant came upon me while I was defenseless." Her choice of the word "defenseless" made him angry with himself again. "What he intended, I don't know, but Susan scared him off with a musket. He smacked my face before he ran off."

"I'll find the constable," he said, already heading for the door.

She grabbed his arm. "Please, no. I don't wish for anyone else to know about this. Please?"

He sighed and ran his fingers through his hair. Grabbing his gun from where he had propped it beside the door, he said, "Follow me."

He spent the rest of the day teaching her to be comfortable with the heavy musket. She learned to prime the pan, what the frizzen was for, how to pull the rammer out backhanded. They practiced with loose powder from the horn first, and then, a holdover from the war, cartridges that he made himself and kept ready to use at a moment's notice. A dying, girdled shagbark hickory was her target. Its barren limbs reached into the waning light. She squeezed the trigger and the gun jumped in her hands. Hugh saw bits of the thin, curled bark chip and pelt the ground a few feet away.

"Did I hit it?" she asked.

"On center."

She already held another white paper packet in her hand. It was nearly his last cartridge. "Show me how to spit it right this time." She ripped the paper apart with her teeth and spit. It stuck to her lip. He picked it off and laughed.

"You canna keep ripping my cartridges open. You'll just have ta practice with the little paper we have left."

"But spitting it is the most important part."

"Why is that?"

She looked at him as if he were a child. "If I can rip and spit like a man, I can scare them off before I even have to shoot."

The next day, Hugh searched out the constable and put him on alert about a vagrant attacking vulnerable women. He was told no one else had reported any such vagrant. Hugh swore loudly once he was alone. The bastard had gotten away.

CHAPTER THIRTY-SIX

One year later; Augusta County Virginia
Fall, 1790

Little Nan giggled as she chased the chickens. The day before she had been beside herself with joy when she found a fluffy black chicken feather and now she was clumsily chasing the flock, trying to get a handful more.

John watched her as he set fire in a new barrel in front of the barn. He had just stepped back from lighting the inside when he saw her chasing the rooster.

"Nan! No rooster, no. Leave him alone. Nan!" He sprinted across the yard when she didn't listen and nearly reached her when the rooster, in an angry flap, jumped up and spurred her tender face.

John scooped her into his arms just as she caught her breath and started to wail.

"Oh, baby girl, don't cry. We'll clean up your pretty face." He absently scooped water from the rain barrel and flung it into the half-finished hogshead as he hurried past, carrying Nan to the house.

He set her on the table and gently cleaned her face. The scratch down her cheek was swelling into an angry welt and he felt badly for her, she had been so happy and proud of herself only moments ago. He pushed aside a small feeling of guilt. He was so unbelievably tired of the feeling.

"Youse good Papa," Nan said as he soothed her hurt.

John laughed and Nan smiled back at him. "Yes." John picked her up off the table and hugged her tightly. "Yes, I am."

A good father. He had never heard three more important words in his life.

Not a needy man, nor a lonely man. And now, he realized, only a failure if he continued to pass up on the life Hugh had told him he could have, the life Anne Wiley had shown him over and over he could have. He would finally go and see her, today. That is, if she would even consider him after all of the grief he had given her. But he had a feeling she would. He had been considering proposing to Anne for some time now, and this seemed to be the sign he was looking for.

He could see Hugh's infuriating grin right now, and could hear him saying, Told you she got to you, lackwit. John smiled as he thought of just how he could convince Hugh this wasn't any of his doing.

He set Nan back down and stared at her for a long few moments, until she fidgeted. "Come along, baby girl, we are going to make ourselves a family."

"We family," Nan asserted.

"Yes, we are."

John and Nan walked up to the Wiley home shortly before the dinner hour. A flurry of children greeted him, and their older siblings, some nearly as old as John, quickly quieted them and led them away. Their mother was standing at the door, wiping her hands on her apron. She smiled at John and then ushered the children into the house.

Robert walked up from the woodpile. "John. What brings you out here today?" Bark stuck to his trousers and shirt cuffs and peppered his shoes.

"I'm here to see Anne, sir."

"Not until after dinner."

"I'll come back," John said. The yard cleared as everyone settled in for dinner and he and Nan stood there alone, as they always were, staring at a house full of another family going on without them. His confidence completely fled him, he was on a fool's errand. "How stupid," he murmured. "What a dimwitted ox you are, John."

"Youse not ox, Papa."

He smiled. "You'll learn." He turned, holding Nan by the hand, and they left.

They had only gone a few dozen yards when he heard light footfalls on the road behind him. He whirled around, knowing who it would be—Anne. He studied her as she hurried toward him. A light blue skirt swirled around slender ankles, her tousled blonde head barely reached his chest. Her cheeks bloomed under bright green eyes that smiled up at him. Never had he known someone to be so bubbling over with life. His spine stiffened as it always did.

"You never do listen to your father, do you?"

She put her hands out for Nan and the toddler reached back for her. Anne swung her up onto a slim hip. "I listen when I need to."

"I think—and he probably does too—that you need a husband to keep you in line."

Anne nuzzled Nan's cheek. "Aw. You have a scratch."

"Shicken," Nan said.

"A chicken? My heavens. Bad chicken, hunh?"

Nan nodded. "Dim ox, too."

Fine. They needed her. He wanted her. God would have to be satisfied with that. "I think I should be that husband."

CHAPTER THIRTY-SEVEN

November, 1790

Hugh watched Nancy bending over the bed where she had just laid down their baby, Jane, born a few months before. He warmed as he watched her, fussing over the child in the firelight—warmed enough to wish that she would hurry back to the table.

Yards of rich blue fabric sat before him and it had been his intention, much to her delight, to make her a fine dress for John's upcoming wedding. Of course, he was simply a man's tailor and had no real idea of just what women's apparel entailed. But how hard could it be, really?

If he started tonight, however, as they had planned, it could prove to be incredibly difficult indeed. She was still showing him her softly rounded backside, so clearly defined under her tight bed jacket. When she finally did turn to him, he had decided firmly that tonight definitely would not do, he couldn't possibly keep his mind—or his hands—on tailoring a proper set of clothes.

"I think I would like it cut to about here," she said, resting her hand above her breasts, "and the waist should dart here, here and here. Hugh? Are you listening?"

"Of course, I'm just planning how ta pin this contraption. You know I've never done this before."

Her smile was brilliant. "It'll be beautiful, I just know it."

He sighed. "Let's get started."

After she stripped down to her shift and moved closer to the fire, Hugh moved behind her and circled his hands about her waist.

"What are you doing?" she asked.

"Measuring your waist, what else?"

"That's not—"

He turned her around and quieted her with a kiss before he confessed, "I canna do this tonight. I'd draw blood, fumbling with the pins and scissors. Will you forgive me?"

"How about you pretend instead?"

He grinned. "Show me."

"Well," she began, "like I said, the bodice would start about here." She put his hands above her swollen breasts. "A very tight waist would be just right," she said as she slid his hands down her waist and around to the small of her back. "With a dart here—" She squealed as he left her grip and squeezed her backside.

"You are a cruel woman," he told her before he kissed her again.

* * *

Hugh, Daniel, Jamie, and Mac let John pull ahead of them. The mottled-gray horse swished her black tail as John dug his heels into her side and flicked her reins. Hugh smiled at the breeches pulling startlingly high up his legs. He had made John the suit of clothes for today, John's wedding day, carefully measuring the impossibly long legs, but damned if he still didn't look like a gangly urchin.

But he had grown into a bold man—at last—high riding breeches or no. He had even confessed to Hugh recently that he saw himself coming out on top from now onward. Quite a change little Miss Wiley had wrought.

John disappeared around a bend in the road heading to Robert Wiley's farm. Hugh turned to his brothers and his cousin and grinned before snapping his own reins and galloping ahead. Farther ahead Anne's brother James leaned, legs crossed and thick coat closed tight, against the fence closing in the barren corn field just past the barn. He held out a dark bottle. A nice bit of warming whiskey if Hugh was lucky. He could already feel it heating his belly.

He heard the rest of the men closing in on him, clocking on the frozen ground, as ahead of him, John pulled close to his soon-to-be brother-in-law and swiped the bottle from him. He wheeled his horse about and raised the whiskey in the air.

A cloud of steam surrounded Hugh as his horse nickered and snorted when he pulled her to a stop at the fence. He swung to the ground. "James," he said, returning the younger man's cold steel handshake.

"He's an eager one, idn't he?" James asked.

Hugh glanced at John, his gray eyes bright above wind chapped cheeks, laughing and passing the prized bottle to Mac. "Aye, he is. He won the kiss, so I'm certain he's wondering where Anne is about in order ta claim his prize." He looked back to James, a dark-haired man a half-head shorter and somewhat slimmer than he. "Dinna blush so."

"Just the cold."

"Of course it is. So where *is* your lovely sister? Shouldna she have been out here ta prize the bottle ta the young buck?"

James glanced around and then grinned. "She's about somewhere. It may take her quite a while to join us." He shook his head and held up a hand as Hugh, concern knitting his brow, started to question him. "As I'm sure you've noticed, my sister isn't hardly a normal girl. The other women have been helping her for days with her latest scheme and"—a chuckle broke him off for a few seconds—"well, you'll see."

Hugh and James turned at clatter and laughter from the porch, far across the yard. A gaggle of ladies in their finery, more lace than Hugh had seen in his life, gathered at the railing. One blonde head stood out far above the others, walking quite clumsily. The blonde had the height of a man, a tall man, but he wore a dress.

Anne's practical joke? A man dressed in the bride's clothing? For John's sake, he hoped the man wasn't too ugly.

A cold breeze picked up and swirled smoke from the chimney through the yard between the men and the women. The laughter from the porch broke off into occasional giggles as John walked to them through the wispy smoke, but he had gone only ten or twelve steps before Jamie whistled and ran to him. They whispered for a few seconds.

And then Hugh saw what Jamie must have. The tall man dressed in wedding finery was no man—but the bride. He laughed long and hard.

James leaned in, "Told you."

John suddenly ran for the porch, lifted Anne until she was good head above him and then gently set her back down. For the first time ever, they stood eye to eye.

And, to think, once they had both thought a cat was what would mend his soul.

CHAPTER THIRTY-EIGHT

Six years later: Bath County, Virginia

Bath County was six years old. The Act of Assembly creating the county, one broken off from Augusta, was passed on December 14, 1790. With this act, Bath's political borders were struck in such a way that the residents were at once walled in together by great ridges and rivers to the east and west and separated by them throughout the interior.

Walker's Mountain, Sideling Hill, and Mill Mountain, running north to south as the eastern boundary, formed a nearly impenetrable barrier. In the view of one standing on a high mountain crest in the interior, gazing east, these ridges appeared to work together, to support one another, as the elaborate fortification of a medieval town, castle and keep would have presented itself to invaders laying siege hundreds of years before. Although, an observant scout may have found small breaks in this rampart, such as the notch at Panther Gap, which welcomed pioneers who settled the southeast valley of Bath at the Cowpasture River.

The view was little different to the west, still valleys dotted with wrinkled, treeless pastures passing into corrugated, sloping foothills passing into forested foothills that climbed into magnificent, densely forested ridges cresting and rolling beyond the beyond until they were swallowed in the fog of distance. Passing through this fog one would have found the western border of Bath winding along the Greenbrier River in the form of the mountains Droop and Greenbrier.

Passes, gaps, bottoms, knobs, levels, blazes, and fords—all different names for ways open to man and beast to snake around these barriers of rock and water and pass from valley to valley, where small settlements were pocketed. And when Bath formed officially and put the hub of political activity at Warm Springs, nestled between Valley and Warm Springs Mountains, this was, indeed, where all roads would want to lead.

Even six years later, there still was no courthouse in Warm Springs, although that didn't stop the endless flow of official County business. The first McLaughlin marriage in Bath was of Hugh "Mac" McLaughlin and Jean Wiley, Anne's sister, in 1792. The Baptist minister, George Guthrie, solemnized their vows. Daniel McLaughlin and Katherine Cleek were married by George Guthrie three years later.

In the spring of 1797, northwest of Warm Springs and over Back Creek Mountain, Hugh's land had been cleared for the year's crops. The soil of previous plantings was weak and therefore abandoned, and trees covering new, fertile land had been cut, rolled and burned in the clearing or used for firewood. The land was ready for new fields of corn, wheat, and flax, while potatoes, both white and sweet, would grow buried in the dark earth this summer. The old kitchen garden could be used one more year, and there Nancy would toil over onions and parsnips, beans and turnips.

In late winter and early spring, the ague had struck Hugh so viciously that Nancy feared for his life. By the end of his labors at clearing his land, he was so weakened that a cough, caught from his daughter, little Jane, had laid him in his bed most hours of the day for nearly a fortnight. The virtue of mutual aid coming naturally to them, family and friends had trailed endlessly across his farm through the season— helping with planting, and mending tools and fences.

On days that Hugh would enter his barn and find a new axe handle or repaired stall, or while walking to the springhouse, find new rails on the kitchen garden fence, he would clatter into the house, sit heavily at the table, and tell Nancy to stop them from working on his place. She would tell him it was all work from her hands and then see him back into bed.

Spring had turned unusually warm on the day Mac and Nancy were planting corn. The sun slanted onto her back and the rays felt as if they would burn a hole through her rough tow–linen dress if she didn't move often enough. The pointed toes of her shoes dug into the planting hills they had mounded after long hours of plowing. The earth was rich and moist and the corn sank easily into the hills as they both sowed along the row.

Mac's straw hat shaded his eyes when he turned to speak to her, but she saw them soon fire and his jaw set firmly. She turned and looked behind her.

Her father was on a large black horse, his pace slow. Behind him trailed two African men on foot. Slaves. She knew what they were about before she even had to speak to her father. He was going to set these two men here to put the crops in, and perhaps he even considered this a twisted olive branch. She hoped she was mistaken.

She held up a dirt-smeared hand to Mac and said, "Wait," before she rushed over to where her father was now dismounting. He handed his reins to the nearest man and removed his hat.

"Father," she said, and reached up to kiss his cheek. It was the first word she had spoken to him in many years.

He accepted her greeting brusquely. Peering about the grounds, he said, "You have quarters?"

Of course there's no slave quarter. "No, Father."

"Well, they will not mind a pallet. How many rooms have you?" He brushed road dust off of his pants with his hat as he waited for her answer.

"One room. Two beds. He's not going to accept them."

He looked up sharply. "In what sort of condition is he to not accept my assistance? I see you here working,"—he motioned with his hat to the dirt stains on her dress—"so I ask instead, what sort of man is he to put you in the fields? A lady does not hoe and plant. She oversees. She spins and sews and mothers. Where is he about?"

He began to stride to the cabin.

She froze for a moment as she thought in despair of the confrontation his footsteps were leading to. "Father, wait!"

He looked at her with a brow that had withstood years of willful children.

"I'll accept, with gratitude," she said. *Please leave.*

"Of course you will."

Mac began walking toward them.

Her father disregarded him and let his daughter lead him back to his horse. "Sam, Nathaniel, you have your instructions," he said to the two men as he took the reins from one. Receiving a nod and a "Yes, sir" in reply, he rode away.

They stared at her, the three of them. Nathaniel, looking about forty, maybe forty-five, with short salt-and-pepper hair, stood tall and straight, waiting for instruction. Sam was nearly half his age, his attention was elsewhere. Mac's temper hadn't lessened in the slightest.

"Let's get to work," she said and turned back to the mounds of dirt waiting for corn. She stuffed her hand in her pocket to grab more kernels and assumed the men followed behind her. But soon, Mac and his horse flew by them, down the road, the same as her father had left moments before.

"Thank you, Lord," she whispered as she watched him disappear. Two clashes avoided—the next would soon be walking out of the cabin door.

"Missus Agnes?"

She looked up at the sound of her given name—yes, she was "Missus Agnes" now and she had a farm to work, a child to care for. "Those pails over there, gather them up," she said to Sam. And to Nathaniel, "You will find the plow just inside the doors of the barn, horses in the stable. Let's get some more earth turned here."

* * *

Hugh woke, coughing, for the second time today. The first had been before dawn, and although his ear and the whole side of his face was thumping and pounding, he had felt well enough to stoke the fire to have it ready for the breakfast hour.

He had shuffled out into the cool spring morning to gather an armload of wood and saw the first breaks of pink fingering through the dark sky. Inside, he started the water to heating and looked at his wife sleeping soundly. The smells of coffee and ham would fill the room and eggs would be boiling merrily before she woke.

She was so exhausted—she shouldn't have to take up his plow, his shovel or axe. And he would tell her so, again, as he served her breakfast.

When he returned from collecting eggs and a slab of ham, the first rays of daylight were slanting in the window. The rich smell of coffee greeted him. He thought, even if she wakes now, it's a fine start to a day. But she never stirred while he cooked the simple breakfast and was still curled up against the cool logs of the wall when he sat on the bed, a plate of food for her held in his hand.

He coughed again. The food jiggled around on the plate and he set it on the bed and turned away to muffle the barking. Each cough ripped at his throat and a horrible, sick taste rose up in the back of his mouth.

He felt a hand on his shoulder.

"We'll eat and then you should lie down again, just for a short while," Nancy said behind him.

"Of course not. A beautiful day is rising out there, and there's many a row that needs plowing and hoeing, and well you know it."

They moved to the table and she poured him hot coffee.

"Breathe in the steam, it will help break up that rattling."

He wrapped his hands around the mug. "You also know I've been neglecting my tailoring, I canna do so much longer."

"You're right, of course. But I'm very tired, perhaps we can lie back down until Jane rises."

Now, when he woke for the second time, Nancy and Jane were both gone from the cabin. He rubbed the stubble on his chin and rested his warm palm on his aching ear. There was corn to put in today and from the look of the fire in the hearth and the light coming in from the window he had missed more than a few hours of daylight already.

He sat while another cough racked his bruised chest, and once recovered he moved to put on his shoes.

Outside, his wife was in the new field, two blacks at her side, planting the corn. Jane was chasing the dog at the side of the cabin, and while he watched, the dog looped around and trotted back the way he had run, toward Nancy again. Jane followed.

"Where did they come from?" he said to Nancy when he reached her.

She didn't look up. "My father brought them a short while ago." She sowed the next kernel.

"And he thinks me incapable why?"

"I don't know. But I have accepted, not gratefully, and I'm surely not beholden, but I accepted nonetheless."

"You knew I wouldna accept, and still we have them here?" The "them" in question never broke from their labor or looked at the quietly quarreling couple. But Hugh knew they were not deaf and could perfectly understand that he was being thoroughly bested by his wife.

He took her by the arm and walked to the front of the cabin where Jane had finally caught the dog and was now sitting propped against his panting stomach, running her fingers through the dirt.

"You know I dinna condone the institution. I dinna have slaves, Nancy."

"You still don't. These are my father's men, although I'd say they are newly acquired by him, so perhaps he intends to leave them here indefinitely. But little matter, let them put in the crops and we shall send them back. You're under no obligation."

"Under no obligation? If they've only been here but a few moments I'm already under more obligation than I could possibly want."

She stiffened her back and drew him out of Jane's hearing. "You could, quite literally, work yourself to death this spring, do you realize that? Is that what you want for Jane, for me? Do you want to leave us like the poor Widow Kelly?"

Oh, he hated her quick tongue. She didn't cut with it, she was not a shrew or a harpy, but she could have him turned around and bound before he could even think. He was never left with wind in his sails. And he had thought himself quick-witted before he married her.

But he did know that something else had grabbed her wit away from her, and that there was more she had yet to confess, because otherwise she would not have argued with him in front of others. She knew better than to shame him that way, so there was more that had her shaken. And to throw the death of his old friend, Owen Kelly, up at him was especially out of character for her. He had been dead less than a year, and she knew he was still raw about it.

Yes, something was eating at her. He would dearly love to know what that thing was.

CHAPTER THIRTY-NINE

"Paying those men for their labor is not enough."

Nancy and Jane had stopped just outside the cabin door when she heard Mac's voice raised in anger.

"It will have ta be." Hugh sounded tired.

"A pittance, most likely."

She peered around the doorway, fully expecting to be caught at it, but hoping not to. The men didn't notice her. Hugh was sitting at the table, nearly with his back to her. His legs stretched out to the side of the table, crossed at the ankles. Mac stood at the hearth, his hand on the sooty mantle. He appeared to be studying the glowing coals. She ducked back and told Jane to be very quiet.

"You can free them," Mac said, his voice hopeful.

"They are no' mine ta free."

"Is this the best you can offer to save a fellow human's life and liberty? Do you understand the obligation we have to protect our weak or injured brothers? Even if we invite harm to ourselves?"

She heard a clatter at the table and a chair scrape across the floorboards. "Then you free them," Hugh said.

Mac laughed shortly, not a pleasant sound. "Yes, of course, 'they are not mine to free.' You're very clever. Again I ask, are you afraid to put yourself up to save another's life and liberty? The obligation of being a man?"

"Obligation," Hugh said slowly. Nancy imagined him closing his eyes and pinching the bridge of his nose. "Yes, that's a fine word. It's incredibly noble, selfless. But no, I, the piss-poor squatter, merely a crude jackanapes, I know nothing about the obligation, Mac. I've only a wife and child ta care for, and I'm ta do so in this sorry condition I'm left with."

Outside, Nancy chewed on her lip and watched Jane draw in the dirt at the foot of the stairs. And, of course, she strained her ears, listening. Mac was pushing him into a corner, and he didn't seem to hear or heed the warning of mounting frustration in Hugh's voice.

Her husband continued, "Yes, my obligation has been ta serve our country for the last twenty years, for the life and liberty that you speak of so eloquently, and I fear I will continue ta do so until they lay me in the ground. Where were you, Mac, in the years of our Lord 1775 through 1783?" Silence greeted the question. "I thought so." She heard an ugly sneer rising in his voice. "More obligation? No, thank you. I've none I owe ta you, you bastard, nor ta those dark-faced men out there."

Nancy closed her eyes. There it was—his impotence, his anger, finally led him to goad Mac to get out of the corner. *God, please, just let Mac recognize it, too.*

The silence held while she prayed, but no longer. She heard the meaty smack of fist against flesh and wood cracking and she swung Jane into her arms and ran back to the barn, her milk pails left sitting next to the open cabin door.

* * *

Daniel's wife Katherine was rocking her infant daughter to sleep when Nancy came into the house. The little girl wore a simple, thin gown and her short black hair tufted about her head. Her heart-shaped mouth was slack, and when Nancy approached and touched her fingers her lips quivered a bit and then went slack again.

Katherine mouthed the words, "Let me tuck her in."

At thirty-three, Katherine was six years older than Nancy and a much taller woman. Everyone called her Ketty. A mass of light brown hair tumbled down her back and her middle was still thickened from the weight of the child born only a week before. She shuffled across the floor and into the one room separated from the rest of the house. When she had the child comfortable and quiet she eased herself back across the room and into a chair at the table.

"Dan told me about the fight," Katherine said. "But all he knows is Hugh got the worst of it. Are you alright?"

"Oh, yes, I'm fine. Hugh's face is pretty broken up, but he'll be fine, too."

Just then Daniel entered the room and Nancy felt relief flood through her. She had been waiting to talk to him. Somehow she was certain that he could make things right.

Perhaps except for Hugh's illness…and probably Mac's crusade…he couldn't possibly help work the farm any more than he already had this year. Too, he couldn't protect her from her guilt. It was her own and it was perfectly clear—if she had just not taken her father's slaves against her husband's wishes there would have been no fight with Mac and Hugh wouldn't stare at her out of that one dark puffy eye.

What in God's name was Daniel going to make right for her? To add to that, he and Hugh would probably both be angry with her for bringing her husband's troubles out of the house anyway.

"How's my brother?" he asked her and leaned down to kiss his wife on the head.

"Ornery."

"That's a truth." He sat on a chair near the wall cupboard and began to change from his shoes to his old, worn boots. "What's the problem going with those two?"

"Which two?" Nancy asked

A dimple in his cheek appeared. He looked as devilish as Jamie. "Exactly. Hugh and whomever. Mac and whomever. There's always a problem. Who knows? So, with Mac and Hugh, what happened?" He looked to Nancy for an answer to his earlier question.

"My father brought two of his men over to put in the crops." She stopped, not sure how much to say.

Daniel had a ready reply anyway, she didn't reveal too much after all. "How bad was the fray between your father and Hugh?"

"There was no fray. I took the slaves and sent him off." Nancy bit at a painful hangnail.

"And Hugh didna know? Didna get ta say 'nay'?"

"No, he didn't."

He shook his head. "That's all it would take. Both Hugh and Mac spitting mad about it, I gather?"

She nodded in return.

"They canna even agree when they agree. The two shouldna be allowed ta pass any time together. Do try ta keep them apart, will you?" He pulled on his second boot and then stood to grab a wide-brimmed hat from a peg near the cupboard.

Nancy felt more guilt than ever.

Katherine had busied herself while they spoke with mending from her basket and now she held a shift that had begun to lose a hem. She looked up at the two of them and said, "I don't think they'll be asking to see each other for quite awhile, it shouldn't be a problem."

Daniel chuckled. "Wrong. Between Hugh, who always has ta answer everything, and Mac, who always demands an answer, this isna over."

Nancy felt her mood sink when she realized Daniel was right, he was exactly right—the two were not near being satisfied. Watching him walk out the door, she thought, *Isn't over until when?*

* * *

For days after talking to Daniel, Nancy avoided her home as much as she could. She did her chores and then visited with Ketty and her new daughter, or walked with Jane through the fields and woods and streams. No matter where she went, the season's warm winds carried the scent of late spring flowers. Brilliant white canopies of dogwoods dotted the hillsides.

She sat under one now, upon a gently sloping hill where the hogs had taken out all the underbrush and made pasture for the cows, who, when they were around, kept it closely cropped. But she and her daughter were alone now; the cows were grazing higher in the hills, there being no calves this spring to keep them closer to home.

Even when they wandered off, they returned often to the waterhole at the top of the pasture. Some days they came down and nosed around at the barn and stable as if to ask, "Anything good here?" But soon enough they would swing their heads and tails, moving back into the hills. Hugh brought them back early in the fall and they stayed, contented, until the next spring when they were turned back out, to go where they would.

Under the tree, Nancy wrapped her arms about her knees, drawn up to her chest. Cold morning dew seeped through her thin dress. Her unbound hair whipped in the wind and thick strands fell into her face and she impatiently tucked it back behind her ear as she watched Hugh, Nate, and Sam working in the field.

Jane was busy beside her pulling the tiny petals off each dandelion she picked and gently placing the bald stalks in a pile. "I'm makin' dinner," she told her mother.

"I can't wait to taste it."

"Oh, no, Mama. It's not for you. It's for Papa. It's goin' to make him so he doesn't fall down anymore."

Nancy took her eyes off the three men and looked at her daughter. "He fell down?" Her hair whipped into her face again.

Jane guarded her treasure carefully from the wind as she said, "Sure. And he hurt his face."

"Did Papa tell you he fell down and hurt his face?"

"No. But that's how I hurt my face, Mama." She pointed to a small scar on her chin.

Nancy ran a gentle finger over her daughter's scar. "Of course, I remember now." She turned back to the men, and watched them again. When the wind wasn't blowing their voices away from her, she could hear the deep tones. Now and again she would hear laughter.

She knew Hugh was paying them money to work that he could hardly afford. And he was barely working them any harder than he was himself, perhaps only an hour or two more a day.

He could live with looking like a fool for giving them money he didn't have to, but he could not live thinking himself a hypocrite. She could hear him saying the words as if he were beside her.

He was going to look foolish, too, when it came time to send these men home with money lining their pockets. Did he think that was the way things worked? That these men earned their own money, they could jingle it around in their pockets and have no one question them about it?

She blushed at her own unkind thought and immediately felt ashamed of herself for thinking it. Of course he was not foolish. Just because someone would think him a fool didn't mean he was one. He would be the first to tell her that.

But even so, she was beginning to suspect something terrible of herself, of why she didn't want her father and her husband to meet the day that he brought the men.

One part of it was pure and simple cowardice. A large part. That— and she was afraid her father would make Hugh look foolish.

But so what? If he didn't care—so what? Because it might have made her see him in a different light? Could it? Was her love so shallow? Or had all these years of battling down opinion worn it all out of her?

She felt sick of her own company and wished she could get away. She closed her eyes and told herself when she opened them she would see the world in a new light.

It had been one of her favorite childhood games, competing against her playmates over who could create the most upside down world once their eyes opened.

Today it was not a game. She would close her eyes, open them again and the grass would not be blue and the sky green, but instead the scales would fall away from her eyes and her clever, strong, smiling husband would reappear.

With her eyes closed, she felt the ghost of Hugh's hard chest against her back and his arms around her waist as they sat on this hill long ago, imagining their new home, their new land. He had said, "But never will I find anything finer than holding you. I'm so glad I came home, like you told me ta." He had never spoken before of the first time they had met. She thought it may have been a childhood dream, she was so small at the time.

The tall, handsome man she had been frightened for had come home. For her. He had remembered her.

She opened her eyes.

CHAPTER FORTY

Dry earth drifted through Hugh's fingers and a light wind carried it away.

A drought would ruin them.

He said a quick prayer for the corn withering before him, then stood up and slapped his hat at one dusty knee.

Nathaniel still knelt, his long fingers breaking up the hard soil around the corn. "It's tearing up the leaves as they push through. They ain't going to make it. We just got 'em in too late." His sharply angled eyes squinted even more into the sun from under the brim of his straw hat as he looked up. "You thinking you want your coin back from us? I might be inclined, but Sam's already spent his, in his head if nothing else."

The older man spoke in a deep voice, drawing out his words and pronouncing each carefully, a steady ox beside Hugh's careless, stallion-like banter.

"You earned it. You keep it." Hugh really didn't expect them to be able to keep the money after they returned to Gwin's place. Although he wanted them to, and he would have Nancy write up a letter to free them from the charge of theft. But every shilling was well spent if Gwin knew where it came from. If he were to hold it in his hand and know that Hugh McLaughlin had put it there.

And he knew the old, greedy goat would take it, too.

He motioned for Nate to follow him to the barn. "We've got more work ta do, you and me. The watering pond in the pasture's dried up."

"I've never been up the high pasture way before. But the rocks on the creek bed're a little closer to the eye today."

Hugh looked at him sideways as they walked. The man had the strangest way of putting things.

He heard his horses nickering in the stable as he reached the double-doors, and he silently cursed Sam for neglecting them. They should have been pastured hours ago.

The stable was hot. And it stank, pure and simple. Hugh threw the double-doors open wide and then strode through, passing an empty cow pen and three enclosed horse stalls on his left, to the other end, flinging open the pasture door, too. The horses knocked and banged as he came through.

Sam, who was supposed to be mucking the stalls, was nowhere to be seen. Maybe the man had run off. Well, if he had, Hugh wished him Godspeed.

Just inside the front doors, Nate sniffed and grimaced. "I told that boy to get his back bent, he's making a fistful of money for cheating." He shook his head. "He don't listen for a lick." Sounding a short grunt of disapproval, he took off his straw hat and hung it on the end of a stall. The rough linen kerchief around his head was streaked with sweat and he swiped it off and mopped his face with it.

"Dinna call him a boy. Grown men dinna much like that, now do they?"

"Me, sir? Never gave it much thought, one way or t'other. I've been called that all my life." Nate led the mottled gelding out of the first stall and sent him into the pasture. He lumbered back for the next horse.

"We're taking the mares, leave them." Hugh peered into the water trough along the back wall. Bits of hay floated in an inch of thick, dirty water. "On second thought, turn them out for a drink."

Hugh picked up a shovel from the back corner, and when Nate walked back in from turning out the horses, a piebald and a tall chestnut, he jerked his chin at a hayfork propped against the wall. "We'll make quick work of this."

His shovel scraped across the floor of the pen as Nate went up the ladder for fresh straw. As he worked, he thought about John and his bobbing Adam's apple as he struggled with the umbrage churning up over the word "boy." He chuckled and wiped his face.

Nate soon shuffled back toward the last stall, a thin trail of hay fluttering to the ground behind him.

Hugh pitched another heavy shovel-full of soiled bedding out the door and turned back to Nate. "My cousin John would stare down a rushing boar if it called him 'boy'. Never did occur ta me ta protest being called 'boy' when I wasna one, either. But it was pointed out ta me long ago that using words of respect when you approach someone commands a certain respect of its own, so keep it in mind."

Nate nodded and pulled some fresh hay off his fork with a thinning shoe. He leaned on the wood handle and his sharp eyes glinted at Hugh in the dusty stall. "I think you're about right. It's good to know."

Hugh smiled. "I suspect Sam will soon feel the same way. But he'll take notice of his idle hands, I assure you, when he gets no pay and no supper tonight."

Nate grunted again as he spread hay for the piebald. "I'm supposing he will, too."

When the stable was clean enough, Hugh motioned to the chestnut in the paddock, a spirited animal he had just bought from Jamie's shrinking stable. "Saddle her up, we're riding out. I'll take the piebald."

"You want me to ride your brother's horse, sir?"

Hugh took a firm tone. "My horse now, so enough with the questions. Saddle up."

They rode out under a sun blazing straight overhead. Clouds rolled in to the north. In the northwest, the pasture high on a hill above the farm was empty, but the two men started up the dusty path, hoping to find the cows wandered up behind the trees higher toward the ridge.

When they reached the pasture, they saw the water hole from a small spring usually trickling from the hillside was muddy and trampled. He barely gave it a glance as he rode past to the steeper path up the side of the mountain.

"Looks like they were here at least yesterday," Nate called out. He was on foot in the pasture, leading his horse by the reins and kicking at a pile of dung.

Hugh started up the trail winding through the trees. Each dry spring he passed was choked with cracked mud and twigs and dead leaves. He turned to look back at Nate when he heard the other horse behind him. "Usually quite a spring coming from near that chestnut tree, see there?"

"Dry as a rock, sir."

Sir.

He wanted to tell Nate that you call your father "sir," your officers, perhaps a constable, but never another field worker. But that wasn't the way. Just now he was the older man's father, officer, and constable.

Along with the dust they were stirring, he spit out the sudden bad taste in his mouth.

"Family?" Hugh asked as the horses pulled and slipped their way up a sharp incline.

279

Leaning back far in his saddle, Nate looked at him long and silently. A deep breath later, "Everybody's got family."

Hugh tipped his hat and grinned.

Reaching the ridge, they headed north to a wagon road curving and spiraling back down to the valley below. Few springs were running along the way, thin streams were dry.

"Dry as a rock," Nate repeated, and then Hugh saw the day darken. Smoky clouds rolled in. He felt the first breeze on his face. Rain. Oh, thank God.

Nearing the valley, Hugh led the way through a sprawling pasture dotted with apple trees and matted with brown grass. The horses crunched and clocked across the rocks of a dry streambed that cut through it.

He kept moving, but was already convinced they might as well head back, none of his cows were going to turn up this far out of the way.

Not even fifty yards beyond, fat drops of rain splattered on their hats. When the wind picked up, it sprayed their faces.

"Good news, sir," Nathaniel said.

"Yes. That it is." Hugh took off his hat as the wind loosened it and turned his face to the sky. Rain ran into his hair and down his neck. Still head back and eyes closed, he said, "Best head back south. We'll ride along the creek and take the trails home. Quicker."

They pulled their reins and wheeled around as the uneven spattering and their horses' hooves stirred up the dirt. Hugh smelled hot earth rising on the steamy air.

"I have a family," Nate offered after a long stretch of silence.

"Good ta hear."

"Now you, sir."

"You know my family, Nate. Other than them, my parents have both passed on, God rest 'em, and my sister has moved off ta the West somewhere."

"Somewhere, sir?"

"The 'sir'—ah, never mind." Hugh shifted in the saddle as the horses pulled a grade. The rain picked up. "I havena known much of my sister and mother for many, many years. My choice. Straited circumstances." He waved it away.

"I don't quite see, begging pardon, the sense in that, sir. I've got a mother somewhere, too, God-willing—but lost to me. Not my choice."

Hugh knew he shouldn't have stood for Nate's impertinence, but he was deserving of it. He let it pass. For now.

"And pardon me again for sayin' so, sir, but I hope you don't let those same 'straited circumstances' keep you ignoring Miss Agnes any longer, she's as strong a wife as any I seen—"

"Enough!"

"Yes, sir."

The day darkened. Hugh kept a closer eye on the mountainside sloping up to their right. If he weren't mindful, he would miss the landmark they needed to follow up to the ridge to bypass the narrow gorge ahead.

As they rode along, he began to regret Nate's new silence. "So, you were telling me about your family?"

"Yes, I was," he said. "Besides my mother, I've got no one. I would have had siblings, like you, but mama said smallpox ended that," Nate said.

Hugh looked to him. "They died of the smallpox?"

"No, sir. She just couldn't have any more after the sickness attacked her."

That was a personal, bold statement—and many would call it heresy. His mother would never have spoken to him about something so delicate. But Hugh chewed on it a while. So many years with Nancy—and one child. He still wore the scars from his battle with smallpox. It may just be true.

"Sounds like a sharp woman. Where did your mother get her ideas?"

"My father was a freeman, his father was a medicine man."

"Indian?"

"Cherokee."

Hugh looked over at him. Why hadn't he noticed before? The eyes, the cheeks. An Indian under his roof all this time? *I'll be damned.*

The sky darkened more with the storm just before the first distant roll of thunder sounded. Hugh looked ahead and thought he could see the landmark he was searching for—an enormous rock ledge, pointing east out of the craggy slope high above their heads.

Hugh pointed, arm extended through the fat drops. The wind picked up and he had to raise his voice over the whistling past their ears. "We need ta travel behind that rock, winding ta the southwest. The trail's narrow, but it'll get us ta the ridge."

Nate smiled, something he didn't often do. "I'll be mightily glad to make it home, outta this storm."

Hugh watched the rain drizzling from the brim of Nate's hat and felt ashamed of his indifference to the man's dignity. He had yet to tell him he was being returned tomorrow, like borrowed pieces of property so often were, and now he was calling it home.

Och, home. An offhand word used now and then ta mean little more than where you lay your head out of the rain.

It didn't help him feel any better.

By now the rain was slanting on them in sheets and Hugh lost sight of his landmark. He could hear the water churning in the creek, rippling over a pair of dark rock shelves.

Ahead, where runnels of water poured down the path unimpeded and barely skimmed over the dry earth, Nate had already taken the lead and started up the hill to the ledge. Hugh would have just passed it by, completely unaware. This time he appreciated Nate's cheekiness.

The mare ahead of him slid a few feet as Hugh's own horse struggled up the steep slope. He slacked off a bit to give the chestnut more room to get her footing, rain pelting his hat and drizzling into his shirt as he waited, but when Nate had nearly disappeared ahead of him, he urged on his own piebald.

Behind the ledge, the path curved to the left and the horses were more surefooted on the easier grade. Even so, the path ahead grew dark and murky, and he began just following Nate's light straw hat as it bobbed along in front of him. If the hat flew off in the weather, Hugh thought, he might not see him at all.

The path weaved about as it rose to the ridge and halfway there suddenly became wider and rougher than Hugh remembered. The horses struggled on the rocks that were grinding and sliding beneath their hooves.

Behind them, thunder crashed on the heels of lightening, giving him a few seconds of sight, but he couldn't place just where they were. His horse skittered a bit and he patted her neck.

He heard some rushing water, and then recalled the stream that poured down near here, to the north. It told him they might be off some from the path, but they were still heading toward the ridge.

As he bounced along, he thought of the water trails he had seen earlier skittering effortlessly across the surface of the dry land and it worried him. He pictured his crops and the dusty earth they were growing in, and he could almost see his soil being carried away in muddy rivulets to the creek.

The plants needed a gentle rain, not a deluge. It could destroy them. Hugh wiped his wet sleeve across his face and then Nate's hat dropped just as the chestnut slid again. Her rump slammed into Hugh's mount, who whinnied and slipped and slid. She bucked, gathering her footing. Soon she faltered again and then lowered her head as she dug in.

Thunder cracked and she bucked one more time and sent him through the air. His shoulder hit something unmoving and rough bark scraped his face before he landed hard on the ground.

At first he didn't move, just felt the soggy ground giving way under his shoulder, a stick poking him in the back, rain still spattering. With a groan, he picked up his head, threw the stick into the darkening day, and felt his shoulder. He was in one piece—the air was knocked out of him and his cheek hurt, but otherwise he was fine—except that he was alone.

He only heard water rushing past, so close to where he lay. And every second the gurgling and churning grew louder. Beyond that was silence. He moved his hand across the ground and water bubbled across his fingers.

It was a right regular stream of flowing water, growing deeper and wider just while his hand rested there.

Damn! Of all the greenhorn things. Wandering up a dry stream-bed...

When a few more seconds passed and he still heard nothing, he scrambled to his feet.

"Nate!"

He listened. Nothing. "Shit." The stream grew to cover his foot and he backed up. "Nate!"

Brush behind him rustled and then Nate was there, suddenly, standing sharply at attention, thick reins in his hand. He handed them over. The chestnut and piebald were restless behind him.

"Your horse, sir. She slid for awhile, then bolted, scared. I got her back for you. And here's your hat." He held out the muddy hat to him. Hugh took it and watched him.

In the meager light, rain glimmered on Nate's skin, his eyes looked somewhere past Hugh's shoulder, he held his jaw clenched tight. He hadn't seen a more rigid stance in a man since Valley Forge. The squared shoulders, tall neck and straight back put Nate at a few inches taller than Hugh. And he looked fighting mad, defiant even.

Hugh nodded at him. "You hurt?"

"No, sir." He still wasn't looking at him.

"Good. Get up on that horse and we'll ride out." Hugh put his hat on, swung into the saddle and glanced back, expecting Nate to follow. But he was still standing there, motionless. "Is there a problem?" He sounded harsher than he meant to.

Nate's eyes snapped from staring off vaguely and met Hugh's. His stance became less certain. "I'd like to know what's to happen before getting it."

"Before getting what?"

"My punishment."

"In God's name, punishment for what?"

Nate's head bent a little and rain spilled out of the brim. "For taking the lead, out of my place, and putting the horses in danger."

He wasn't about to coddle him like a child. "Just get on the damn horse so we'll be out of the rain the sooner."

He didn't see Nate smile or even look relieved, but he felt some of the tension melt away as the man mounted the horse and followed along behind.

Hugh was glad Nate didn't grovel with him, or even apologize. It took spirit not to cower in the face of danger, and they both knew Hugh had an obscene amount of power over him and Sam. He didn't like it.

Maybe he wasn't sorry to see him go.

Out of my place. He knew the feeling. That's what his defiant look must have been about, it was saying he hadn't committed a wrong, but knew he would get knocked down all the same and he was powerless against it.

The man had courage.

* * *

Nancy was waiting in the doorway when they reached the cabin. She held a lantern high and a dim circle of light spilled into the yard. A soft rain still fell. Hugh left Nate to see to the horses, and he slapped his piebald on the rump to send her going. Nancy was glad to see his good mood and his handsome, smiling face.

"Sam herded in the cattle just before the storm," she offered.

He answered her with a grunt.

Rainwater dripped from his pants as he walked into the room and it ran off the hat he held in his hand. Jane sat at the table, waiting for her mother to finish combing out her hair for bed, and Nancy felt a pang of envy as she watched him bend down and kiss the girl soundly on the head.

"My girl waited up for me I'm glad ta see."

He used to say "my girls."

They avoided each other now, and she couldn't seem to find a way out of it. He was still kind to her, but he dodged her as much as she did him. They used to sit together into the night and point out the stars and talk, they used to take Jane for walks, or he would watch her carding wool as he repaired his tools. But now he walked out whenever she walked in.

"I'm taking them back tomorrow," he told her.

The slaves. Was that it? Had she shamed him beyond repair that day? But he couldn't know her secret thoughts, that she had been so close to being ashamed of him, that she had lost her faith in him, for just those few moments.

She didn't know how she could love him so much and still have doubted him. But she had.

He sat down to take off his boots. "Yes," he said, as if in answer to an unasked question, "I've spent enough coin on that foolishness."

Tears suddenly sprang up in her eyes. "I'm sorry, don't you know that?" she yelled.

Hugh looked surprised by her outburst. "Dinna yell in front of the girl."

Now she was a bad mother.

"That's alright, Mama, I'm mad at Papa, too." They both looked at Jane. "He put dirt and rain all over the floor for you to clean up, and he's just plain mean."

"Jane! Don't you say such a thing about your father. You apologize. Now."

Jane's face crumpled and tears to rival her mother's swelled in her eyes.

Hugh put his boots back on. He kissed his daughter again and then said to Nancy, "Let's go." He grabbed her hand and pulled her out the door.

As soon as she was fully outside, she found herself surrounded by him, enveloped in him. His lips covered hers painfully, a sweet pain that made her want to cry again. His wet clothes were molded against his hard body and she felt his warmth seeping through to her, touching every part of her. Her body screamed to get closer, closer, urged on by a runaway passion, sparked after being denied his touch for so long.

She thought she would slide to the ground when he loosened his hold on her. He slowly searched her face and then asked huskily, "Do you know how very fine you are in my eyes, Nany?"

All was forgiven.

CHAPTER FORTY-ONE

One year later; Bath County, Virginia
5ᵗʰ of June, 1798

The sound of milk hitting the pail in long bursts filled Nancy's ears. Just after dawn, the day was already warming quickly and she stopped milking long enough to wipe her hand absently across her brow, although she wasn't sweating yet. She thought over the day's chores as she put the pails aside and led the cow out of the rear of the barn.

She was surprised into stopping on her way back to fetch the pails by the sight of Hugh hard at work in a corner across from the cow's pen. He was without his shirt. The thin linen one he usually worked in was laid across the box next to him.

She stood quietly by and watched him in the light from the high window as he turned and tightened the corners of the curing table. Each time he did so, thick muscles banded across his forearm, and his upper arm and chest muscles would swell. She gave a silent prayer of thanksgiving that he looked so much stronger than at this time last year.

She really should have moved on, the morning was wasting, but she didn't want to stop watching him—he was just too handsome. The early light laid shadows across his face that defined the already sharp angles of his thick brows, not-quite-straight nose, and strong jaw. And since he hadn't shaved yet that morning, dark stubble on his jaw, much darker than his long hair, added even more depth to the planes of his face.

"I know you're watching me, you canna hide yourself," he said without looking up at her. His smoky voice quivered in her stomach.

"Have you been sitting here, half-dressed, waiting for me like a spider?" she asked him.

"You look like the spider ta me, watching and waiting in the shadows for me ta shake your web." As he spoke, he was striding toward her, and now he grabbed her around her waist and pulled her close.

She arched her back to look up at him and, not least of all, to press herself closer. Her small hands rested on his chest, and she enjoyed the smooth warmth of him as she slid her arms under his and around to his hard back.

They stood that way quietly as a few moments passed. "I've something for you. Come see," he said huskily, grabbing her hand and leading her to the north end of the barn, where a wide door led out to the horses' paddock and stairs rose into the warm shadows of the hayloft. They startled a dark, striped chicken that darted around the corner. With a squawk, the bird just as quickly turned and raced back out again.

They scampered like children up the narrow steps. Nancy giggled and looked behind them as if they might be caught at something improper, although no one had a reason to be near, and she had left Jane sleeping peacefully in the house.

Once hidden in the hayloft and on her hands and knees, she felt around in the murky light for her husband, laughing. "Where..." she began, but then screeched as he grabbed her under her arms and brought her down on top of him, reclining in the sweet, soft, nearly depleted hay stores. As she felt the large, strong body under hers, she knew what the "something" was that he had promised her...

Later in the morning she stood grinning and stirring porridge over the hearth as Jane swept the floor behind her. Hugh came in the door and she heard him shuffle toward the table. His usual absentminded banging and stomping were missing and she turned to see if something was wrong.

He sat heavily at the table, sweat beading on his pale face.

"Has it warmed up so much?" she asked.

The morning had promised to turn into a steamy afternoon, but the air still felt comfortable to her, even working over the hearth. And then she noticed a slight shake. Another ague fit? "Is your stomach upset this time?" They didn't even have to mention the ague for him to know what she meant. They regularly talked in half-sentences and riddles about his illness when Jane was listening.

"No," he answered.

She moved to pour him a cup of cold buttermilk.

"Thank you," he said as she put it before him. "I dinna know how much longer I can stand this."

She understood his feelings but shushed and waved a hand at him. Jane was standing nearby. "Why don't you eat and then lie down?"

"No," he said, and then drank down the rest of the milk with a steadying hand. "I have a few shingles ta replace on the roof. More rain's coming."

She came to rest her hands on his shoulders and kiss his head. "Be careful. And if you hear any thunder, any little rumble, you come right down. Understand me?"

He chuckled weakly. "Yes, General." He shuffled back to the door, but paused in front of Jane, who had stopped sweeping to listen to her parents talk. He chucked her gently under the chin. "You can get back ta work now, little one."

Nancy dished out porridge for her daughter. She sat across from her and listened to the sounds of Hugh pounding on the roof, but soon began daydreaming about the trip they had taken the day before to see a plot of land that Hugh wanted to buy. Impatience had him wound tight. She knew he had been tossing and turning at night, sleepless with worry that the land would be stolen out from under him, snatched out of his grasp. He had waited so long and she knew it weighed on him. But the survey had been done and the warrant issued, so now all that was left to do was present it to court so the governor could legalize the ownership. Soon he could breathe again. He had waited so long.

"Mama?" Jane was looking behind Nancy, toward the open window in the rear wall of the house.

"Yes?" Nancy said after she glanced at the window. The laurels were blooming.

"I saw an angel fall."

"Did it have wings?"

"No." Jane took another spoonful of breakfast.

Nancy listened for more sounds from the roof. Everything was quiet.

"Why do you think the angel fell?"

Jane shrugged. "Maybe it's sick."

At once Nancy's throat ached, her body turned cold. Sick. *Sick.* Hugh was sick. Shaking. Unsteady.

She knocked her chair over as she jumped to her feet and ran to the window.

* * *

Mac's yard was quiet when John cantered in on his old mare. The land sprawled east, sloping up from Jackson's River. Mac had settled here when he married Robert Wiley's daughter, Jean. John lived on a neighboring farm, and on beyond that was the sprawling plantation of Captain David Gwin.

Hugh and Nancy still lived close to Daniel and Ketty, a few miles across Back Creek Mountain. But now there wasn't much good soil left for farming on his small plot, and just lately he had been eyeing a fertile tract of land down the creek. Jamie and Susan had packed up and taken off west this spring into the God-forsaken wilderness out that way, probably never to be heard from again, John thought.

Mac's dark, short-haired mutt scrambled from its post in front of the barn door and ran at him, barking furiously. As the dog drew closer, she lowered her front legs and head to the ground, and, rump in the air, growled, and then started barking again as she finally reached him.

John's mare, a calm old girl, stood her ground peacefully. Wincing from his eternally stiff knees as he swung his leg from around the saddle and landed on the ground, John sternly told the dog to "sit." When she obeyed, he pulled a short piece of jerky from his pocket, threw it across the yard, and told her to "run." She knew the game; they played it every time he came.

Mac's light blond head poked around the heavy door of the barn and he told John to go on in the house and wait for him, he'd be in shortly. When John turned to walk the worn path to the house, the dog was back again and waging her thick tail.

"I have nothing else for you, Lady," he told her as he put out two empty hands and then patted her on the side of her barrel-chest. She barked at him again and ran off, a chicken catching her eye.

He watched her race away. She looked as if she might lose her footing when the white and black striped chicken darted right and ran among a thick carpeting of mayapples; but although she threw a few dirt clods with her paws, she just made the sharp turn and they continued out of sight. *She won't know what to do with it when she catches it.* He chuckled at a squawk from behind the tall pile of firewood.

He stamped his feet before knocking on the door and then heard the muffled voice of Jean tell him to come in.

"Lady's after the chickens," he said as he entered.

"She wouldn't know what to do with them if she caught every one," his sister-in-law told him. She looked at him strangely when he just grinned broadly.

Mac had married Jean Wiley, Anne's younger sister, two years after John and Anne's wedding, where they first met. Theirs had been a tempestuous marriage, to say the least. Jean had the patience of Job and the will of Abraham, and everybody knew it. Except Mac. He was woefully oblivious to every coarse word he uttered, every toe he stepped upon, every convention he broke.

And now he was constable—*oh, dear Lord*. Mac didn't know it, but the court was forced to stop sending him to serve summonses. They never had so much trouble getting people into court as when they had been served by Hugh "Mac" McLaughlin. But he fiercely loved the people closest to him, and that included his wife, his two young children, and his brother. No matter the cost to himself, he was very good to them. John considered that an accurate measure of a man's worth.

Mac's children, three-year-old Nancy and two-year-old Robert were napping on a trundle bed brought out from under their parents'. The quilt from the larger bed was crumpled at the foot and the straw mattress sagged deeply in the middle.

Robert sighed in his sleep.

"Sit down at the table, John. I'll pour you some beer," Jean said.

The large table filled the middle of the cabin, surrounded by four sturdy chairs. Trenchers from breakfast were piled at the near end and a heap of papers filled the other. John quietly pulled out a chair for himself. A slip of paper on the chair fluttered to the floor. He picked it up, laid it on the pile on the table, and smiled warmly at Jean's flushed, hot face as she placed a cup of beer on the table for him. She turned back to her fire where she was working at the mid-afternoon's dinner.

He glanced down at the dark beer, lifted it to his mouth, and looked back up at Jean at the hearth. She had a bare backside. He almost dropped the large cup before he had tasted a sip. *Poor Jean, she's so tired*. He shook his head.

She had forgotten to let her skirt and her shift out of her waistband where she had tucked them in for safety while working around the blazing fire in the hearth. He hadn't noticed before, because she had left her pinner apron in front and only pulled up the heavy material at each side and tucked it in behind her hips.

He was torn, thinking of what he could do, something he could say, when the door opened and Mac, with heavy feet, stomped into the room. The moment was lost.

"Quiet!" she hissed, and waved her hand at him, "the children." He continued loudly across the room and she handed him a mug when he reached her. "And those shoes...I don't want goose manure in my house," she whispered furiously, waved at him again and turned back to her fire.

Mac looked at her for a moment, and then grinned until his face appeared to split in half. "My dear, your ass is hanging out."

John rested his head on an outstretched arm on the table. He slowly shook his head. *How has anybody managed to survive in this house?*

When he looked up only a moment later, Mac was still grinning, but staring at the open door. Jean was gone. "Aren't you going after her?" John asked his brother.

"Why for? Ketty's out there with Daniel, with them just arriving. I'm sure the women will find themselves talking on about something else, especially with Ketty so heavy with this child. They do so like to talk on and on about those types of things. By the by, how's your Anne coming along?" Mac sat at the table across from John as he was speaking.

"It'll be just a few more months now from the looks of her growing belly."

"Oh, that's fine, just fine." Mac's rough red hand touched the pile of papers and he said quietly, "There she is." He was holding the small slip of paper John had picked up off the floor.

"There who is?" John asked.

His nephew, Robert, stirred on the trundle bed, and the men both paused for a moment to look at the children. Robert had flung a thin arm across his sister's face, but neither of them stirred again. John rose up quietly to pour himself more of the weak beer Jean had left on the dresser near the stone hearth, before she had run out of the door, humiliated.

"If you would?" Mac said as he turned and handed John his cup from the table. John nodded and took the cup. "Got a note on John Green and Thomas Wilson. Seven pounds, some odd pence," he continued. "Thank you," he told John as he took the cup and set it down, away from the papers.

John settled back onto the chair across from him, stretched his long legs out to the side of the table, and crossed them at the ankles.

"So you're looking for to get paid, now?" John asked, disinterested, and thought that Daniel should be coming to look for them any moment.

The three men were meeting here before starting a trip up to the next county, the shopkeeper up there always gave them the best prices on their goods. John had honey and wax in his saddlebags to get rid of and in a few months he should have a good crop of ginseng coming out of the wooded hillside. Ketty, Daniel's wife, had been busy with hat making now that she was near the end of her pregnancy. And Mac claimed to be searching for a very special die for his blacksmith shop, but they knew he just wanted an opportunity to hone his bartering skills.

"Don't want to lose this note. No, certainly don't. Oh, they paid me for it alright, but if they don't look sharp," he paused to look at the open doorway and then again to John, "I'll make them pay it again."

"Why do you keep hold of a paid note?" John asked, irritated with Mac's scheming.

Mac went to the door and closed it. Propped behind it was a long, dark rifle. "This old gun here I bought from Jonathan Pullins and I gave him a note for six pounds. He took the note from me and assigned it to Green and Wilson. Now, I paid the six pounds one day at their store," he continued as he sat back down. "But when I did, Green said the note was lost or misplaced," he said, waving his hand, "so it couldn't be found at the time. So I intend to hold on," Hugh said as he put the note back with his papers, "to this note. I know they've done me dirty."

'*Done me dirty,*' *alright,* John thought wearily, *someone is always doing Mac dirty.*

"Daniel! Daniel!" They could hear the plaintive screeching, wailing, like the screams of wildcats at dusk, coming from just outside the closed door. John and Mac looked at each other, scrambled to their feet, and after Mac grabbed his gun, they burst out into the muddy yard. Daniel was already throwing himself onto his big-boned horse, the fringes on his hunting shirt bouncing. His horse whinnied in protest before wet, dark dirt flew from her hooves and they were gone.

Hugh's horse patiently grazed on a tall tuft of grass beside the snake fence, while his wife was in Ketty's arms, sobbing. Jean had a hand on her arm and was also holding Hugh and Nancy's young daughter by the hand; and now she bent to the little girl's level, whispered to her, and gently brushed her light hair out of her eyes.

Mac's wife soon straightened her back, struggled with her composure for a moment, her face by turns regal and pale, and then she walked toward them, unsteadily. "Hugh's fallen."

Both men immediately started for the stable, and Jean followed after them. "I don't know if he was ill, like last year, but Nancy said he was going up to fix some of the roof..."

They rode off before hearing the rest. Her long skirts swung along the muddy ground as they thundered around her and out sight. Two sets of double beats rumbled from the soft ground, and a brilliant cluster of laurel waved where they passed.

Only a few neighbors passed them on the mountain passes leading to Hugh's farm. On one dark stretch of road leading away from Back Creek, stately hardwoods walled them in on either side—darkly, fully leafed and busy with the chatter of squirrels. John wanted to stop in the road, stop time right here in the middle of the road and listen to the squirrels. He couldn't see the cabin yet. This was where he wanted to stay.

As Mac pulled ahead of him, John's mare pranced and scraped, eager to catch up. John felt sick but gave his horse a soft *y'up* and lightly snapped the reins. She gratefully bounded forward.

He closed his eyes and let his horse lead him. He remembered a younger Hugh, a few days before his wedding to Anne, measuring and pinning him for a new pair of breeches for his wedding. Hugh had insisted on making him an impressive costume for the day.

"You've got ta get rid of these god-awful rags, I'll have you know," Hugh had said, "or that beautiful girl will run screaming from ya and straight back ta her father."

Lost in memory, he sees Hugh's thick fingers whisking along the seams, improbable fingers for the delicate work of tailoring. His head, under a mass of wavy light hair clubbed back with a dark leather thong, is bent low.

John opened his eyes and guided his horse around the treeline and onto his cousin's farm. The hot green smell of summer grew as he walked his horse up the wagon path leading to the barn. Hugh's fields sloped up into the hills beyond. The turned earth was dark and rich, the damp smell hinting of burials and vigils and eulogies drowned out by women's wails.

Closing his eyes, John sees Hugh's grin as he looks up from his work. Young William Wilson, Tailor Wilson's grandson, listens intently to the men's war stories. No doubt exaggerating for the boy, Hugh talks about Monmouth courthouse and the action there that day. "'Twas mayhem from the word go," he says. "But the lobsterbacks finally got the routing they richly deserved."

Lowing of cattle brought him back from his reverie. Seven deep red and white cows grazed contentedly in the patchy sunshine up on the hillside. Two more with calves haunting their sides stood at the fence near the road. One mother closest to John looked up from her meal as they passed by and watched him with soulful eyes. Her crimped and rumpled horns were down-turned. She was nearly pure white, with a spattering of red around her ears. Her mouth churned round and her pale lips smacked, grinding the long grass.

He would give anything to be a witless beast. Just for this one day.

But soon, in a tailor shop in town, surrounded by bolts of broadcloth and snippets of linen, John sees Hugh's pride swell when young William asks about George Washington at Monmouth.

"Ah! He rode in on his fine horse, he did, after exchanging the one he wore out on his dash ta save us all. The heat was fantastic, but General Washington was cool and, like always, never showed discomfort. But he shook the trees and birds took flight when he called old General Lee a 'damned poltroon' for retreating in such shame."

John heard whinnying beyond the lowing cattle. A chestnut mare and her colt greeted him from Hugh's stable, a separate pen of the barn. A large saddle hung inside, out of view. John didn't have to go in the barn to know this. It just was. Hugh's third horse, a thick, powerful stallion, grazed in the paddock and seemed to not even notice their arrival.

They passed the barn.

Daniel's horse stood impatiently beside the house. Lathered and stomping, she swished her dark tail. Beside her was another, smaller horse belonging to Hugh's neighbor, Osbourne Hamilton. She showed her teeth and then chomped at the curious gelding. He shied away.

John closed his eyes and sees Hugh wink at him and turn back to his audience. Young William scrapes a stool across the floor and perches on it waiting for Hugh to continue. Hugh's eyes crinkle in his dark face.

From behind the cabin, a bellow of rage broke the silence. The bellow turned to grunting, at first sounding like a man groaning under an enormous weight, but it became louder and darker, until it was a guttural, animal sound.

John and Mac threw themselves off their mounts and left their reins dangling, swinging. Their legs were wooden, their arms stiff at their sides as they strode around to the back of the cabin. Osbourne sat on the ground, his back against the house, his head in his hands. Daniel was on his knees in the tall, wet grass. His hands struggled at a jagged rock poking out of the ground. Lanky dark hair fell around his face.

The rock was tinged with red and Hugh was sprawled unnaturally nearby. His dog lay there, stretched out next to him, patiently waiting for him to get up.

And then John sees Hugh laughing and telling young William, "That's right. A 'damned poltroon!' But the men shouted *huzzah!* as General Washington walked that horse up and down the lines and told us we would have that day."

Daniel dug at the soft ground around the rock, loosening the hold of the earth with his fingers. John watched Mac walk past Daniel and kneel at Hugh's side, and then he moved along the same ground and knelt, too.

At the same time, he watches Hugh artfully tell the eager young William that they even took the day from the towering British grenadiers.

Mac gently reached out and touched Hugh's bent neck and then, just as gently, closed his sightless blue-green eyes. Daniel pulled the rock free and hurled it into the laurel thicket, cursing, while the dog's ears pricked and his head turned to the sound.

Staying by Hugh's side, but leaving Daniel and the dog far behind, John enjoys Hugh's newfound dignity as he says again, "Washington told us we would have that day. And we did."

Young William beams. "Tell me more, sir."

It is the hero homecoming that Hugh had long been denied.

PART III
1798-1801

CHAPTER FORTY-TWO

After the men rode off from Mac's place, Ketty gently rocked her back and forth, back and forth. Nancy felt sick with it, as if she were riding endlessly on the water. Her flat stomach pressed into Ketty's swollen one. She could feel the hardness of it, unyielding and lopsided, and then she felt the child squirm. She pulled away.

"Jane. Oh, Jane!" she said as she wiped at her face and turned bleary brown eyes to the yard. Her horse was still grazing happily, her dark brown saddle not even askew.

Not even askew.

The face of Mac's wife swam into view. She held Nancy's daughter by the hand.

She walked toward them.

"Mama," the little girl said and stepped back. "Mama! I don't like the way you look," she cried, and dashed away to the house.

"Jane!" Nancy called.

Mac's wife took her by the arm again, but she yanked herself out of the grasp and marched toward the open door of the house. Before she reached it her daughter dashed back out and buried herself in her mother's skirt. Nancy rocked and stroked the child's hair and made soothing sounds to calm her.

When Jane's breathing evened and finally lost the rhythmic hic-coughing left over from her sobs, Nancy gently led her to their horse and they both mounted, Jane seated snugly between the saddle's pom-mel and her mother. They left at a slow walk, and Ketty and Jean stood like sentinels, watching them pass.

Their pace never quickened as they took the deserted road home. Passing a well-cleared piece of land, she caught a glimpse of a far-off mountain ridge draped in mists, each drop of vapor rolling and swirling around the softly textured face and masking the round, green summits.

She looked to the road ahead.

As they arrived at the farm, Daniel, his lank black hair falling around his pale face, came out of the barn and lifted Jane off the horse. He carried her into the cabin while Nancy led the mare to the barn.

Once inside, before the cramped stall, she worked to loosen the heavy saddle and then threw it over the closest railing. The colt, recently graduated from wobbliness, skittered away from the loud thump and creaking leather. His chestnut mother pushed at him with her dark nose.

She left them where they were, didn't bother to rub down the mare. Daniel opened the door and the strange sunlight of an impending rainstorm poured in on her, it was difficult to make out his face in the halo behind him.

"Jane's settled down on her bed. Here, I'll take these," he said gently as he approached the stalls and took over care of the horses. He led the chestnut out to the paddock.

In the light, dust motes stirred through the warm, pungent air and settled back to the floor. Hugh had mucked the stalls in the coolness after yesterday's light rain, and his fork was still propped in the shadows of the corner.

She walked through to the other pen, where tools were kept in a cramped corner. His plow irons, hoe, and shovel plow were just inside the doorway. His axes, froe, and maul were held along the far wall, propped by rough wooden pegs. A large, shuttered window was cut into the wall next to them.

There was a stool against the wall, below the axes, and propped beside that was an old wheel. Across from the plows was his curing table, the light from the window poured directly in on it in the morning.

It was in shadows now. He hadn't dressed a skin since Nancy couldn't remember when, but now a nice deerskin was stretched taut between its four wooden sides. His tools were neatly laid out on a box near the table—sleeker, fleshing, and currying knives. Small barrels of tallow and oil sat on the floor beside the box. He had been in here just this morning, before...after the sun had broken through the trees.

Still staring at his curing table in the shadows, she pressed a hand to her flat stomach and thought about another baby. All these years and only one child had been gifted to them. Their families and their neighbors had easily born three, four—sometimes five or six—children in the last ten years.

That wasn't to be for them, and they had known it for many years. But now she felt that perhaps they had this final chance to share another child—she really could be carrying her husband's child at this moment and it excited her because he always longed for another child, a strong, handsome son. And then, like painfully stumbling into heavy furniture in the dark, she realized that he was not here with her to share it.

He would never be here with her again.

She had forgotten for a fleeting and painless moment that anything had happened to Hugh—*What a selfish, fiendish thing to do*, she thought, and knew then that there still was no baby, no strong and handsome son, and that there never would be.

She let Daniel guide her back into the house after he found her still standing and staring at the empty room and the silent tools. She wondered where her husband was, but didn't ask. Instead she lay down next to her sleeping daughter in the darkening room, the one room of the sparse, orderly cabin. The lone room that had a small window cut in the back especially for her to see the blooming laurel hugging each other in thickets so dense and beautiful no one dared to cut them down.

The darkening room sheltered them from the rain clouds beginning to roil over their heads, steadily reaching and grasping to cover the sun that had just been shining peacefully. She pulled the woolen blanket about herself and Jane and pressed her body tightly against the small child with thin hair and spindly limbs askew and a cloying stickiness steadily rose in the cabin with the impending storm. But she didn't care. The rain would soon wash it away.

She closed her eyes.

Daniel opened the door slowly, quietly. She turned in the bed to face him, and could hear the rain splattering on the ground behind him. The wind and rain picked up even while he was standing there and she could hear it begin to pelt against the roof. He closed the door and walked to the side of the bed, a trail of water following along behind. "We...we're bringing him in in a few moments."

"Of course. What else would you do?"

He didn't respond, but began stoking the embers in the hearth, threw in some kindling, and then waited until the time was right to carefully stack small pieces of aged oak atop the hissing, colorful flames. She turned to face the wall and listened to his careful movements: A scrape of a chair, a clank of a pot, the screech of the pothook—his movements backdropped by the rain pounding the roof above her head and plunging in runnels to the ground outside.

She soon smelled the sweet mint of sassafras tea and felt herself beginning to cry. It was the smell of bad times, of illness or insecurity of health, the tea of comfort, of strengthening. She didn't want it. He brought it to her bedside.

She wiped at her face, turned to him, and looked into his pale eyes. They were tired. Around them, his face was both pallid and ruddy. Although his skin was not so much different from his brothers', his striking black hair did not fit his complexion and just now it made him nearly look sickly.

"Perhaps you should stay with Ketty tonight," he said as he handed her the warm mug.

She just stared at him and he finally set it on the floor.

"No, you asinine man. This is my home and I'm not leaving him here, alone." She had to yank the blanket out from beneath him to sit up fully, and Jane stirred at the disturbance. "Run away...do you think I would run away? Do you expect me to run away?" She pushed at him to move and felt his cold, sodden clothes. "Oh, for heaven's sake," she mumbled, and pulled a sheet from the nearby shelf and began to wrap it around his shoulders. Fussing around him for only a moment, she stopped and leaned her forehead against his wet hair. "What am I going to do?" she whispered, more to herself than to Daniel.

He pulled an arm from under the sheet and it encircled her small waist, the other held her hand, and the door opened. They both looked to the door. With rain dripping off their hats, down their shoulders, and onto the floor, John and Mac entered the house.

"We're bringing your husband in," Mac said flatly.

Daniel rose and started across the room, while John turned back to Mac. He towered over him. "What in the hell is the matter with you?"

"What?" Mac said. "What does she care? Look at her there. Draped all over him."

"It's fine. It's fine." Nancy said to the men as her daughter sat up in the bed and looked around, confused.

John pushed Mac on the shoulder.

"Stop it!" she shrieked. She breathed slowly and calmed her voice. "I said it's fine. Just... what you were saying about Hugh—wait on that, not right now," she said and motioned to Jane. She turned her back on the men, picked up the mug of tea, and gave it to her daughter. "I want you to have a few sips and then lie back down, little one."

A furious whispering kept up behind her while she smoothed Jane's hair and watched her small fingers tightly gripping the fat mug.

"Can you stay with me?" Jane asked in a whisper, peering shyly at the large men poking each other and gesturing wildly while still trying to speak quietly.

Nancy turned back to curl up with her daughter again. She covered them both up, held Jane close to her, closed her eyes, and after a short while, she listened.

She heard someone pull out a chair and sit down.

"I've got the tools," John said. "I can work through the night tonight and have a box by the morn."

"And who would you elect to stay here for the night? Daniel?" Mac questioned.

"And what if I did stay here, Mac?" Nancy heard Daniel ask. "Are you thinkin' something improper aboot that?" She lay very still waiting for Mac's answer, her body readying itself to leap from the bed if it had to.

John answered instead. "It's no time to argue about pittances when Hugh is waiting barely under shelter out there in the downpour. It's a miserable state of things."

Nancy's shoulders relaxed and her grip on Jane lightened.

John continued, "I'll have enough daylight tomorrow to work on the box. I will stay here—I'm sure Anne and the children will be fine without me. Please tell them where I am as you pass is all I ask." She knew it was he that then pushed his chair out and walked heavily across the floor. The others followed.

As she heard the door hinges creak, the loud spattering of the rain increased and its fresh smell rushed in with the cool wind. When they returned, she left the bed carefully, without disturbing Jane, and stood by, one small hand folded on her chest, as they brought in her husband.

John and Daniel carried him gingerly on a thick six-foot-length of board, stained with age, splintered and warped. Mac carried a box in each hand; she recognized them from the workspace in the barn. Hugh had placed his currier's tools on one of them that morning.

Mac set the boxes beneath the window in the back of the room. The other men set Hugh carefully upon the boxes. His clothes were damp and raindrops glimmered on his face.

A thick smoke of silence filled the room and she felt as if it would choke her. They stared at each other until Mac and Daniel left. The rain had slowed to a mere drizzle by the time they walked out of the door.

"You can get back to bed," John said gently, "if that's what you need to do now. I can take care of things tonight." He sounded uncomfortable with saying anything at all.

Maybe he felt his presence here was improper, too.

She tore her eyes away from Hugh. "He's not shaved, John. He would hate it, wouldn't he, if he were to be remembered like this?"

John nodded and said, "I'll give you time." He left the family alone.

She gathered his box of razors, a basin of water, and on a whim, her only cake of lilac soap. In the circle of dim firelight from the hearth, she stood by him for a silent moment before she tended him. All she could see was her sleeping husband, as comfortable and natural as he had looked this morning before rising. But, as she carefully stroked his cheeks with the razor, her eyes traveled again and again to the tinge of red in his hair. Her bottom jaw felt locked into place and it ached terribly when she finally picked up the sheet from the bottom of the bed where Daniel had dropped it and began to dry his clean-shaven face.

What else could she do to tend him? She didn't want to leave his side. She pulled over a chair, sat down, and held his hand. It was soft and cooler than it should have been. She put her head on his chest and could smell his wet clothes as she closed her eyes and whispered to him. "I was wrong about not wanting to marry. I know you heard me that day, back at Wilson's." She smiled. "And I just bet you set your cap for me at that moment. You could never turn down a challenge, could you? Well, I'll let you in on something. I never knew before I met you that girls these days don't have to marry because it's a sober duty, they have to marry because they're desperately in love. What a shame it would have been, too, had you never shown me the difference. Do you know you've left so many of us better than we were found? John certainly had some starch in him today, ordering the troops to line up quite nicely, you would have been right proud of him. And I might dare to say you had a hand in bringing out that starch, perhaps in more than in just John, even. Quite an admirable job to embark on, much less carry out. We all love you quite fiercely, Hugh, I hope you've always known that."

But tears came as the low fire danced behind her eyelids, fluttering with the tears that spilled through them. "But what a cruel farce it is to tease such love from me, let me warm in it, only to wrench it away."

CHAPTER FORTY-THREE

A trembling roll of thunder woke her. The room was dark, but Nancy could feel the soft bed beneath her and could hear her daughter snoring lightly against her shoulder. A feeble glow in the hearth shed light barely beyond its border, just enough to glint across the shovel and poker and tongs hanging just outside the stonework.

Another crack of thunder came upon a brilliant flash of lightning. The room appeared for a heartbeat, showing that Jane's bed was empty. On the next flash, she saw John stretched out peacefully on the floor.

Relieved that they weren't alone, she swung her legs out of the bed, tucked Jane back in, and felt around for her shoes. She slipped them on, the buckles loose and hanging, put a bed jacket on over her clothes, and stumbled out the door and into the dark rain.

It sprayed her face and trickled into her shoes. *Where am I going?* A low moan came from her throat and she ran in the direction of the barn. As she threw open the large door, another flaming crack came from the sky and she heard a limb snap in the woods nearby, the sound of falling going on and on, shaking leaves and crashing through other branches until it came to rest.

Inside the barn, her mare's hooves clattered on the floor. Nancy fumbled through the dark for her saddle, still hanging over the rail. It slipped through her wet hands and, surprised, she stumbled painfully into the hard stall. She left the saddle where it lay and raced out of the barn, not even pausing to close the door.

Mud pulled at her ill-fitting shoes and she slid, but did not stop. She ran only a short distance with her heart before her head told her she had to slow and put her hands out to feel her way along.

The night was black, and not even shapes or shadows were visible to guide her. She inched along, slowly, reaching and sliding, down the steady grade that took her to the road. She knew she had to turn north when the grade ran out and that she could go nearly in a straight line until another sharp rise signaled her approach to the narrow mountain pass into the next valley.

No one who knew these mountains would expect her to try to stumble over one in the dark. It wasn't done. She was alone. She had no weapon, no one waiting for her on the other side.

Insane? Maybe she was. But what, at this moment, wasn't insane? She stilled, peering into the dark—thinking, grieving—knowing that she could never make it. She shouldn't even try. Finally, nearly convinced to feel her way home, she leaned against a low bank, her hand sinking softly into the moss and mud, and heard a snort. A hot velvet nose nudged her arm.

Her mare. She stroked her wet mane and fleetingly considered the secret minds of animals, their empathy, in some ways so much stronger than that of man, and her eyes welled while she hiked up her skirt and swung onto the barebacked animal. Gripping fistfuls of her old chestnut's mane, she let the horse carry her slowly away across the mountain.

When the rain finally let up to an annoying smattering, she began to make out shapes around her. There were trees to her left. She could see the forms of high limbs reaching out over her head. What she had thought was a gentle, inconsistent rain for the last mile or so, she knew now had been the leftovers, dripping off the dark leaves. She led her mount across the road and traveled beside a grassy bank half as high as the mare's flank and a field spread beyond that—stretching across an immense fertile plane in the valley that was envied by farmers for many miles around. It was the beginning of her father's plantation.

She dismounted, but kept a soft hand on her horse's mane.

Once the grade steepened, the bank dipped and disappeared as a narrow tree-lined road cut into it. She held out a hand and felt the wet, cool bank as it began to dip and her feet slipped into last year's leaves piled up in the gutter as she rounded the bend. They slid up, grasping at her, and she could feel the damp coldness of one sticking to her leg and coming to rest inside of her open shoe.

She straightened her clothes as she walked the familiar winding road, her horse gently plodding along beside her. She felt her hair. It hung in thick, curling ropes down her back and over her shoulders. She reached in her pockets for a cap, but they were empty. Tightening her bed jacket about her chest against a damp wind, she trudged on.

When the tree line ended, she knew that the barn would begin to peek around a corner, a little more and a little more, until a traveler was facing it full on. And there it was.

The road continued past the barn, which sat on a thick stone foundation, and then on to the stables. She felt her way into the long, low building, heard the horses stir at her intrusion, the stable-hand sleepily say, "Eh?" She left her mare in his bewildered care.

Beside the stables, a narrow path threaded into the gently rising hills. She passed it. Upon a slope on the other side of the road stood the silent springhouse—she smiled sadly as she smelled the familiar nose-tickling must and earthy decay.

And then the main house came into view.

There she sat on the wet ground, unconcerned with the mud or sticks or whatever else she might sit upon, pulled her knees up to her chest, and stared at the dark, looming house.

There was a soft glow from two windows to the left of the front door, and she wondered who was awake at this late hour. The room darkened while she watched, and she scrambled to her feet and sprinted to the porch. "Father?" she called. She pounded on the door and waited a few heartbeats. No one answered.

She stepped back and stared and waited again.

Before long, she found herself screeching, "Open the damned door!" She pounded on it again. "Father! Father?" A new sound escaped her throat, a piercing "*Eeee...*" She took off her shoe and began to pound its heel on the door instead of her sore palm.

The door creaked open a small distance and a dark head cautiously peered outside. The man held up a lantern. It threw light and shadow all about the wide porch. "Master Gwin gave me permission to take you home, if'n your husband isn't out there with you."

Her jaw tightened and her hands balled into fists. "No, my husband isn't out here with me. You see, my husband is dead." There, it was said.

The man's eyes grew wide and he quietly closed the door. She waited again. A moment later the door reopened, the same face appeared. "I told him what you said. He says I'm still to take you home."

"Just close that door. Nobody's escorting me home. Does he think...?" She raised her voice as she leaned closer to the door. "Does he think I can't make it home on my own? Well, I came here on my damned own and I will sure as hell make it home on my damned own."

She raised her voice again. "That's right, Father! I said damned AND hell, both of them, in one crude sentence. Isn't that what you thought I'd do? Turn crude and poor and raise babies up on my own. Well, there you are. I've served it all up to you"— she dropped down to her knees—"on my hands and knees." She whispered to the large-eyed man still watching her from the door, "Tell him I'm on my knees. Go on, tell him."

He didn't argue with her. He turned and said, "Yes, sir, she's on her knees, for sure."

Nancy stood. "As for raising up babies, I have one daughter, her name is Jane. She's seven years old. You know where she lives. Good-bye, Father."

CHAPTER FORTY-FOUR

Voices woke Nancy. Dappled, early morning sunlight peeked into the room. The miserable rain had finally ended.

She looked up from her bed and found John busy at the hearth. His clothes and his hair were both rumpled and he smiled crookedly at Jane, standing next to him. The top of her light head barely reached past his waist. He was ladling something out of a pot for her as she stood by with a wooden bowl.

God love him. How strong and perfect he had grown in the last few years. Damn near a bundle of nerves when she first met him, the last decade had hewn him into a right solid support beam for his family, and now she supposed he would do his best to look after her, too, she now having no other family herself. She must try to lighten his impending burden.

She threw back the heavy blankets from the bed, felt the coolness of the morning on her damp clothes and looked down at her grimy bed jacket. Strewn on the floor were her shoes, covered in mud and bits of old leaves. Color rose in her cheeks as she thought about last night. She shook her head.

To heck with her father. She had all she needed right here.

When Nancy glanced up again, Jane stood motionless at the table, one finger curled in the hair across her shoulder and one thumb in her mouth. John set her bowl down on the table and turned back to the fire. Jane stared at her father on his rough pallet.

At some point, John must have wrapped him in a sheet. And there he was, wrapped in white except for his face, his skin having taken on a strange, dark hue; but he still looked as if he were only sleeping.

But Jane was too old to be fooled by any idea such as that. She knew what things were about.

"Have you tasted your hominy, yet, Jane?" John asked from the hearth.

Woodenly, she pulled the thumb from her mouth and picked up a spoonful of corn. Nancy watched the spoon stop at her lips, it quavered just a bit. Before Nancy fully recognized that Jane's face was changing color, a stream of dark yellow water flew from her daughter's mouth and onto the table. Thick hominy fell from the spoon.

"Oh, Mama, I'm sorry," she wailed and tears coursed down her face.

"Sweet girl, don't cry, it's not your fault." Nancy grabbed a washrag from a basin on the dresser. The water was frigid and she tried to squeeze some warmth into the rag with her fist. She knelt down to her daughter's level and wiped off her chin.

"Nancy, I didn't realize, I should have known—" John started.

"Now don't you go apologizing, too. So many things are wrong and they aren't anyone's fault."

John strode across the room, grabbed up his hat from beside the door, and told her, "I'm going home to start work on...some things. You'll be alright?"

"We'll be just fine," she assured him, and he left.

Nancy and Jane worked silently at cleaning up and neither of them tried to eat any more of John's hominy. Finally, Nancy could stand the silence no more and she said to her daughter, "Would you like to talk to him?"

Jane closed her eyes, and the dark lashes fanning her cheeks fluttered as the little muscles all around them quivered and squeezed.

"Would you like to talk to me?"

Her eyes squeezed tighter.

"Well, then. Would you like to talk to Treat, instead?" Nancy had found Jane more than once talking over her problems with Hugh's stallion—always through the fence, however, because Hugh thought the stallion too unpredictable to be completely trusted with a child.

Jane didn't open her eyes, but she nodded her head slowly, yes, and held out a hand to her mother. Holding her small, cold hand, Nancy led her voluntarily blind little daughter to the bed, lifted her under her arms, and set her on the bed. She slid her scuffed and worn shoes onto her bare feet, and then sat down to slip on her own shoes. On their way out, she handed Jane a clean pail hanging from a peg beside the door.

They walked out into the warming air, washed clean by the days of rain, and Jane let go of her hand and ran to the barn. Their dark brown dog bounded after her from his post next to the house. Jane turned when she reached the tall barn doors and the dog sat at her side. They both stared at Nancy until she reached them and swung open the door. As Jane ran ahead, Nancy looked straight at the small of her daughter's back and passed by Hugh's workspace. To the left of the central corridor, where the horses were stalled, the stallion stamped and whinnied. The mares were both quiet, but soon she heard the *tock, tock* of their heavy hooves and she knew they, too, were excited by the sudden intrusion.

She worked in the barn while the sun climbed in the sky and warm breezes coursed through the open doors and across the farm and carried the dampness away.

Leaving the empty cow's pen to fetch water for the horses, she caught a glimpse of Jane leaning on the stallion's closed half-door, looking in at him. She listened for a moment.

"Papa's not coming back," Jane whispered. "But I'll take care of you, Treat. I just don't know where Papa will sleep tonight. Who will take care of him? Who will be there when he needs something or if he gets sick again?"

Nancy jumped when the dog barked, letting her know someone was approaching. She wiped at her eyes and went to gather Jane. Before they left the barn, she looked down at her clothes and felt her hair. Both were bedraggled and dirty, and she felt a knot at the back of her thick hair. When she glanced down at Jane, she felt ashamed that her daughter looked no better. She shook her head. *What do I care? Poor time for judging.* She took Jane's hand and they went out to greet whoever was approaching.

It was everyone she could think of that might possibly have reason to be there. *And they think they're all being helpful.* She straightened her back, squared her shoulders, and walked boldly out to the horses.

Daniel had already dismounted and was lifting his wife off the horse. When she was on the ground, she waved him away. He immediately came to Nancy's side, held her hand, and kissed her cheek. "Dinna serve them, dinna look after them, let them do for you," he whispered as his face was close to hers. He smelled of lye and smoke and she could see that his hair had been washed and carefully combed and clubbed, without any oils put in to weigh down the already slick black strands.

It struck her then that this was an *event. Like a traveling show or more like a church day?* she wondered. During an event you walked through the day purposefully from start to finish, you had a role—everyone had a role—and you played it, nearly like an actor, and it served the day's purpose.

And Hugh's role was to be dead?

His death, too, served a purpose in the event of today?

They came at her and they spoke at her, trying their best to comfort her, and she was strong. She led the processional to the front door of her home, entered into the constricting room, and the women began to weep as one. Faces hidden behind handkerchiefs said, "Just so peaceful..." and "You would never know..."

Little Jane stood amidst the swaying skirts and heavy shoes and fluttering hands, looking up and then around, nearly lost in the group of tall mourners. Nancy took her by the hand and pulled her tightly against her skirt, and then turned her around and led her back outside once again, one hand gently pressing onto her back.

Draped in brilliant June sunshine, Ketty was sitting on a rough bench across the yard playing finger games with a troop of laughing youngsters spread out on the damp ground surrounding her. For the occasion, the children were dressed in the best their parents had to offer—for the boys, round brimmed straw or felt hats and clean shirts; for the girls, dazzlingly clean bonnets and darkly colored skirts. Nancy thought them handsome children.

Ketty's smile stayed in place as she looked up at Nancy and Jane leaving the house, but it became aged and knowing—*and peaceful?*—and then just as smoothly broadened again for the children who swayed and bounced on wet knees and clamored for her attention. Nancy felt a profound change happen in her in that seconds-long glance.

Ketty knew something of the event and the annoying chatter and cloying sweetness. *Something I can hold.* Nancy was drawn to her, and felt tears in her eyes as she gave in and sat down next to her.

"Don't let them treat you like glass," Ketty whispered to her. "And don't give them any reason to, either. You know what needs be doing much better than they. And if you don't do it, you'll never be at peace."

Daniel came out of the door and started in their direction. Ketty shooed him. As they watched him turn away, she leaned closer. "The men, they can take time to grieve, they can stumble and they can even fall, women will always be there to catch them. But we need to pick up and go along, twice as strong, twice as sharp as the men." She put an arm around Nancy's shoulder.

Nancy felt tears well up again when she realized Ketty had nothing more for her.

Twice as strong. *Twice as strong.* She saw Hugh's thick arms hitching plows, splitting wood, threshing grains. And it was his dream that they should work their own land. *Strong.*

She started hesitantly, "Tell me the story again. The land, and Daniel, and Alex Campbell."

Ketty cocked her head a bit, her brows knitted. Then she smiled. "I told him absolutely no sale. That land he tried to sell is a third mine and no one can take it from me. The courts drew up the papers after Daniel and Alex worked it all out between them, but there was never anything those men could do without my say-so. A woman needs a good piece of land, Nany."

"The court helped you tell Daniel no?"

"They would if he didn't listen to me. Of course, they have to. You're not worried that a woman can't get land or hold on to it, are you?"

"No. I can do it."

"That's what Hugh wanted most of all. And if anyone can do it, it will be you."

CHAPTER FORTY-FIVE

"He said I was his champion," Nancy told John.

In her quiet cabin, they sat at the table late in the night. Today had been the burial on the far north end of John's farm. Nancy was grateful to him for giving Hugh a permanent resting place, one where she would never be a trespasser coming to visit her husband.

"His champion, hunh? Well, then—so you were," he said.

"No. I was a coward."

"Everyone's a coward now and again, that's no shame."

Nancy felt a smile for the first time in what seemed years. "Confessin' shame."

John smiled back, his gray eyes tired. "It seems to me we all get bogged down in what Hugh pointed out is no more than apologizing just for existing. Sometimes we do what we shouldn't, and then go on, ruining the rest of our lives over it. It took me quite a while to see his words for what they were—permission to carry on." He settled back in his chair. "And what's this? A coward? He never once gave me the idea you were a coward. He couldn't abide by them, so he would have put you on notice, make no mistake."

"But I—"

"Don't confess to me." John rested his large hand on hers. "He said once you saved his life."

"When did I?"

"Didn't say. But you couldn't have been more than seventeen when he told me that." His brow crinkled in thought. "He may have even mentioned the war, but I can't remember clearly so many years later. But now see yourself, a slip of a girl, and saving that lumbering ox's life. I ask you, is that a coward?"

The door squeaked open and Anne slipped in the door. Her pregnant frame was light and her face impish even after four children. "He's still there. And has now asked for coffee," she said to John as she sat at the table and took Nancy's hands, rubbing them absently.

John sighed and pushed his chair back. He stoked dim coals in the hearth and asked his wife, "Did you get it out of him."

"No."

She enjoyed Anne's comforting hands but stiffened at the conversation. Who was out there? And how long were these two going to riddle it out around her?

"I suppose I will take his coffee to him and get a clear answer this time," John said.

She was near to screaming. "John. Stop dancing. Who is outside of my home and what does he want?" She held up a hand as he started to answer. "What do you *think* he wants?"

"I intend to find out."

John walked out into the warm night, closing the door behind him. His annoyance grew with each step. Nancy did not need his brother's self-indulgence tonight. Not tonight.

Mac had settled into a chair blocking the road in to the farm, directly in front of the barn, close to sundown. A fat candle in a tin lantern sat next to the chair, casting a dim uneven light. With his musket balanced across his thighs, he stared down the road.

He looked like a deranged guard dog.

John clapped him lightly on the shoulder and handed him a mug of warm coffee. "What do you see down the way, Mac?"

"Not a thing, yet." He continued to stare, even while taking a long draw on the mug.

John squatted onto his haunches next to the chair. "I've got to ask you, for the last time, just what the hell you're doing here."

"Just looking out for Jane."

"Hugh's Jane?"

Mac nodded. "I go every which way with my temper, John. Like a damn bull pulled off his tether with cows all around."

John smiled at the thought.

"But not Hugh." Mac shifted the musket and stretched his legs, setting his mug on the ground. "And I gave him one hell of a time." He stared straight ahead.

"He enjoyed a good debate as much as the next."

"Ah, no, he didn't. He wanted to spend the rest of his life in peace, seeing one thing down the road"—he pointed ahead into the inky night—"and heading right for it. A safe family. A contented one."

"And you're looking for...?"

"Someone nosing about, looking to take his child. They'll call her an orphan. An orphan of a poor man."

Ah, of course. "Well, I don't think Hugh could appreciate anyone's effort more just about now. But no one's coming, Mac. To boot, you're the constable. They'd give you the job."

Mac finally looked at him. "They wouldn't ask for me, a cousin, to come around, lackwit." At the sound of a horse plodding down the road, he raised his gun up and hopped out of his seat.

John put a hand on his arm. "Put the damned thing away. Have you turned into the lackwit?"

"Hail, John!" came a call out of the night. The horse drew closer. He soon recognized Nancy's father.

"Captain Gwin," John said in a whisper. He debated whether Mac's fears had just been realized or not. They would find out soon enough.

Mac set his jaw in a firm line, propped his musket against the chair, and rolled up his shirtsleeves. "That piece of..." And then he stopped and looked at John for a long moment. The hard edge soon slid away from his face, his shoulders slumped. After a few seconds of grumbling to himself, he turned to Nancy's father, just swinging down from his horse. "Captain Gwin. Good evening," Mac conceded.

"Good evening, Constable," the captain replied.

Mac sat back down and resettled the gun across his knees.

Gwin shook John's hand. "Where is my daughter?"

John straightened his back so that he rose a good six inches over the older man. "Sir, I'll have to ask your intention." Gwin looked surprised. John couldn't blame him, he did sound a bit callous. So be it. "Nancy has been through quite a time, as you can imagine. I cannot allow her more upset, with all due respect."

"I'm glad to hear it, then. Finally, someone is taking her interests to heart."

"Excuse me?" It was nearly a roar. He could credit a long list of influences that now kept his hands from reaching across the short space separating the two of them—a short space that was in fact as wide as the most fertile plains in the valley—and ripping out the arrogant stuffing from the man. Aunt Maggie's raising had shaped him into a man who knew his place as subordinate to no one, so he need not rely on violence to assert his position as the beasts of the wild tended to do. But most importantly, Hugh had made sure that he cared not a whit that the world had other ideas for him.

He took one menacing step forward and asked calmly, "What the hell does that mean?"

Gwin smiled slowly and with about as much confident warmth as a glass of brandy. "I was right," he said. "You'll do just fine."

He rode away.

CHAPTER FORTY-SIX

Three years later
Fall, 1801

Early evening was settling in, the sun less than an hour from dipping behind the Alleghenies. Jane worked at the table, weaving white oak splits in and out of one other, half done with the basket. It was her second this week.

Nancy admired her daughter's handiwork before turning back to the paper in her hands. From the sunlight still streaming in the window behind her, she read aloud: "James Monroe, Esquire, Governor of the Commonwealth of Virginia to all to whom these presents shall come, greeting... Unto Nany McLaughlin a certain tract or parcel of land containing one hundred acres by survey... on the east side of Back Creek... adjacent James Hamilton... chestnut oak on a hill... to the said Nany McLaughlin and his heirs forever." She looked up at Jane. *His* heirs? Ah, hell, what difference does it make? "At Richmond on the fifteenth day of August... One thousand eight hundred and one."

Jane clapped. "Huzzah! When do we go?"

Nancy set the thick paper on the table and pulled over a basket filled with dark wool. "Depends on how much time Cousin John and Uncle Daniel can spare to help us make a home there." Actually, she had put off asking anyone for help. For one, she was loathe to beg; for two, she liked owning the new land but didn't particularly wish to move there.

It was part of Jane's nature to be eager for new experiences, but Nancy was keenly aware of what she was giving up and what she was gaining in leaving this farm. Hers was a choice between Hugh's memory and his dreams.

In the three years since his death, this leased farm had continued on, decaying slowly day by day. The soil was weak, but she loved every clod of it. The buildings were falling apart without his care, but she hated to have even one shingle, one single post, replaced. She felt Hugh drifting away from her in the smoke and embers of each rotten board they burned.

And now, as she drew fluffs of wool through the sharp-toothed carding paddles, she thought over the work ahead of her. At this moment, her new farmland—Hugh's new farmland—sat nearly untouched, covered in trees and rocks, waiting to be built. That was a bit too much to plan for right now. Her work here was enough.

Hanging in bags on the far wall was the ginseng she and Jane had dug. That would fetch her hefty coin in Pendleton. So too would the jars of honey and beeswax that nearly covered the side table next to the open door. She would soon add that income to what was left of Hugh's savings, wrapped in an old cloth sack and tucked carefully into the deep chest next to her bed. She had used most of it for the land and what was left she was saving to get her started off well on the new plantation, if and when she decided to go.

Still pulling the paddles, she looked to the table, trying to judge just how many coins the goods there might bring her. Most merchants would want to give her credit at the store or a promissory note in payment, but she wanted the metal—always had, she thought as she watched a pair of lazy flies pick their way across the jars and then test the cloth covering her warm apple pie.

Voices floated in through the open door, surprising Nancy out of her musing. She put down the cards and walked to the door. Jane followed. Outside, Daniel strode through the yard heading for the porch, a dark-haired young man by his side.

"You're out and about on a fine day," she called.

Daniel smiled brightly. "Aye, a fine day it is at that."

The young man gave her a polite nod, but hung back some when Daniel joined her on the porch.

Daniel took off his hat and tossed it onto the bench as he sat down. "Nany, this fine young man is in a way and would surely like ta have the chance ta talk with you."

At the side of the porch, the young man in question had dismissed them and gone down on one knee, intent on shimmying a loose stone of the foundation. He pounded it back tight with a firm crack of his palm.

Daniel chuckled. "My nephew John, Will's oldest son. They've recently moved back ta the county—hav'na been around this way for nearly a dozen years. And he's looking for work, if you hav'na guessed."

The young man swiped off his hat and squinted up at Nancy. "People mostly call me Jock, ma'am." He glanced around. "I can fix anything."

She smiled and walked down the steps. "I'm sure you can." She reached out her hand to him, Hugh's nephew, and drew him out into the yard, walking toward a patch of corn across from the house. "Tell me something about why you're so eager."

Jock looked to Daniel for a moment, uncertain. Daniel nodded for him to go on and left them alone to talk, taking Jane back into the house.

"Well, ma'am, I could just as easy take off and work a little piece of land for myself, no trouble."

"But you're not," she prompted.

"I have an infant brother, just seven months old now, and my father has taken ill, ma'am, quite ill and I can't leave them all, not now." He looked for a second as if he had really stepped in it. He stammered. "But I can work both farms, I can, really. My brother William will stay behind, see, to help out, but they need coin—"

Nancy put a hand on his arm to stop him from explaining. "I'm so sorry to hear about your father." She was already planning a trip, well overdue, to extend her goodwill.

"Thank you."

She brightened her tone. "So you're the one named for Cousin John, born the night he signed up for the militia, as the story went."

He nodded. "So I've heard."

"And you have a brother, William, you say. And I recall a sister, Nancy?"

Jock fidgeted with his hat, but he smiled. "That's right. And another little girl squirt, Jane. And of course, the baby." He knelt as he spoke and straightened a rail in the snake fence around the corn.

"A baby brother, you said. And his name?"

"Oh, ah, Hugh, ma'am."

Nancy curled her fist against her heart and her belly fluttered a bit. "That's lovely." She wished for something more striking to say to him, but nothing came to her but a flood of feeling no words could carry.

Jock hopped back up and Nancy chuckled at his energy. She turned to walk back to the house and invited him to join her.

"I was thinking," he said as they walked, "I could get to work on your spring house. I noticed the stone crumbling and some water spilling out. I could certainly rebuild that wall, and—"

"Stop, Jock." Nancy held up a hand as they reached the steps to the porch. "No need to fix this farm, we're moving to a new one."

His face crumpled. "Oh. Is it far away?"

"Only down the creek a few miles." She looked toward the trickling creek just beyond the field, where it snaked around close to the house. It lay past the crumbling springhouse...*seventy-three and one-half steps from the porch.* "Do you think you could help me build a plantation from the ground up, young Jock, with plenty of room to grow? It will need to prove itself the most profitable plantation in the county. What do you think?"

He dazzled her with his smile. "I can do that."

"It's agreed, then. Go on in and help yourself to some pie."

He bounded up the steps and disappeared inside.

She looked around at the quiet yard, the corn yet to bring in, the hay, the bees. It all kept her going—if only just—and some neighbors had wondered aloud why she would bother leaving the place to start over. On occasion, she thought the same thing. Felling trees, rolling rocks, and building barns was no work for a slip of a woman and an eleven-year-old girl. But then again, in some ways, neither was mending or knitting. She had never feared hard work, she never turned away a challenge, but even with the help of the thick-boned horses she owned, pulling logs the weight of a dozen men she simply could not do, not alone at least.

Though today, because of a new boy-child named Hugh that needed caring for, she had a man's shoulder and back, he wanted to work for coin and *that* she had, thanks to her husband's hard work and foresight and her frugality.

A sudden spray of laughter floated from the house and she smiled and thought, A shoulder, a back—and boundless enthusiasm that may prove catching.

The corn swayed as she took a last look around. She knew now that a choice between Hugh's dream and his memory was not really hers to make. His memory could hold its own. His dreams now needed the tending. Two McLaughlin children christened "Hugh" had come into this world since his death—John and Anne's son, born soon after the accident, and now this child... Living testaments to his honor, to carry

322

his name to future generations. No more than infants, they shouted to the world that there was no dark shroud over his worth as a free man, or the worth of his family—which she knew he had secretly feared all his days—no shame tied round his memory that would keep him hidden away from the future.

Free men they all were now, with pride, liberty of spirit, security of land. Hugh's family finally had all that he had fought and bled for. The McLaughlins now owned their piece of this valley.

"Rest well, Hugh," she whispered, "but I'll expect no less than you be there at the Gate to greet me proper when my own work is done."

She enjoyed the cooling breeze for only a moment as she moved up the stairs, the men's voices carrying out through the yard as she opened the door. Then all was quiet again as it banged shut.

AFTERWARD

I took my father for granted. I think most children do, so it's not that shameful. But it is a shame--one I regret more every day.

Although to my benefit, I did listen patiently, sometimes painfully, to all of his stories. And he had a lot of them.

My father, James Lee Gray McLaughlin, loved to stretch the truth, the harmless type of stretching. He spoke of the Philippines in WWII in an easy way—nothing too heavy—but, of course, we kids had seen all the graphic pictures of the war hidden in his top dresser drawer under the neatly folded handkerchiefs. Nothing easy and light was portrayed in those dog-eared, yellowed photographs.

He also told us tale after tale about growing up during the depression in coal mining and logging country. Nothing new to kids of the kids of the depression: "I had no shoes. Well, to be fair, sometimes I had a left one and my brother had the right. We walked ten miles to school, seven days a week, in the snow, each with the one shoe, up-hill..." Well, you know.

But he never once mentioned the names "Hugh and Nancy McLaughlin." I found those names more than ten years after my father's passing, and about 150 years after Nancy McLaughlin's passing. But at the same time that Hugh and Nancy charmed me beyond belief, caused me to write this book, and kindled an interest in family history that I'm sure will never be sated, I felt profoundly sad that my father would never know them.

On my first step upon the path to finding Hugh and Nancy I pulled out and dusted off the endless snippets of family lore, most of it tall-tale built on tall-tale. My great-grandparents were immigrants, so my Uncle Pete claimed. Wrong. They fled the famine. Wrong. The McLaughlins were once kings in Ireland. Well, that one's right, surprisingly enough. But still, not much help there. At that time, my interest in family history was still just mild curiosity.

It wasn't until I finally dug my fingers into the oldest, coldest, hardest facts that I was fascinated. Of course, my more practical side just said, *A nicely drawn and framed family tree makes a really nice Christmas gift.*

Still, I was inspired by the humanity of these faceless names that make up a formal pedigree when I came across this passage in a Pocahontas County, West Virginia, history book, first printed in 1901:

> He [John McLaughlin (1764-1838)] pointed out a spot overlooking his dwelling that is well nigh inaccessible, and gave positive orders to have his body buried there. He seemed to abhor the idea of being trampled upon... A more unique burial scene was never witnessed in that region. The pallbearers on their knees and holding to the bushes and rocks with one hand and the coffin handles with the other, and the procession following on all fours, composed a scene the like of which may never be witnessed while the world stands. Here an illustration of the ruling passion strong in death.[1]

I had found my fourth great-grandfather, John McLaughlin. He's still there, in Highland County, Virginia, overlooking his property, keeping watch.

I learned that he was a soldier in the Revolutionary War and a close contemporary to Hugh McLaughlin. Another John (Jock) McLaughlin (ca. 1780-1845), also a great-grandfather, was a major of militia. My father's love of American history was not wasted on me.

I continued searching, and before long, a year had passed.

I spent so much time in research that I became completely absorbed in the lives I saw unfolding in front of me. Each new piece of evidence was an integral part of someone's life and I held it in my hands. What would it mean, I thought, if I were to stuff it in a file folder and just

---

[1] Price, William T. *Historical Sketches of Pocahontas County*. Heritage: Bowie, Maryland, 1990

move on to the next challenge?

There was no satisfaction in that. I wanted to write it all down, to tell the story, and that's what I began to do.

I first wrote this book with only the facts, no assumptions, with the intention of breathing life into men and women whose habits, speech, laughter and tears have all been lost to time. Trying to revive people who, in their own way, played a part in the creation of these great United States, who touched and tasted and lived our history. I found I couldn't do them justice.

Wait, I thought, what about fiction? It's been done before. But wouldn't it be wrong to put a book out there, mostly based on my own wild opinions, about people I've come to care for so much?

I continued my research.

"They ran away to be married." When I read that comment in the ancient, smeared court record I was struggling to decipher, I wanted to jump and whoop and tell someone, "I knew it!" But it was 1 A.M. Sadly, I had to wait until people woke to spread the news. But, while I sat there alone I tried to put myself back in 1789, the year Hugh and Nancy "ran away." What would cause a couple in that era to travel out of their own region--which was surrounded by rugged mountains and rivers every which way--and away from their families, just to get married? Parental objection? Societal objection? Probably both. I was assuming again.

But as I put more pieces of the puzzle together, I found that time after time my assumptions were right. That's when I realized I could not leave this story written in the bare-bones (boring) fashion I'd started out with. But I was torn.

I could have told you that I felt strongly that they ran away together, and they did. And I know that her father absolutely did not approve and I believe I can tell you why. But I didn't have proof (and still don't) so I couldn't include it. Unless I wanted to spend half of your time and mine explaining, "This could have... This may have... This probably..." ad nauseam. I thought then of just packing away the mounds of paper, full of names and dates and court documents.

But I couldn't do it. I didn't want to abandon these generations of spirited people, all of who, even if some in only the smallest way, contributed to my father's spirit--and my own. I found their *own* spirits aren't dead; their hopes, their fears and their love continue today in the countless people whose lives they've changed or created. They reach out across the years, the decades and the centuries and touch you. And maybe even encourage you to write a book.

And that's the only way to know them, from the feelings they bring to you. That's something that cannot be shared through a name and birth and death dates on an otherwise blank sheet of paper.

It's the feeling I had, standing alone in my great-grandparents' private graveyard for the first time, two states and three hundred miles from my home. Standing reverently away from the sunken old burial sites--to which, one hundred years before, mourners had quietly and solemnly entrusted their loved ones. One stone's etching grabbed my heart: *We've Lost Our Little Sister.*

I lost myself there to imagination. It wasn't hard to do. The day was still and clear and very bright. Not a car passed, and not a house was in sight. Delicate summer wildflowers wound themselves into the old barbed wire fence. Sadly ironic in afterthought, I picked a lily for baby Lillie's grave.

The entire view is mountainous: Just gentle slope after gentle slope. This is the scene that greeted them every day. Soft peaks lost in the mists on a rainy summer morning or blazing with bright yellows and reds on a cool fall afternoon. And all still here for us to witness.

Glorious. Peaceful. God's Mountain.

That's when I heard the low, very ghostly sound of the century-old train whistle echo down the river. The same, far-away train has serenaded that tranquil spot since my great-grandfather, James N. McLaughlin, was laid to rest.

I felt transported.

That's the power I want to return to them. The power to make us feel, even though they have been physically gone for one hundred--or two hundred--years.

Because I can't take everyone for an afternoon in the mountains for the same experience, I wanted to recreate it all for you. *In their time.* So, I compromised.

Consequently, this is a work of fiction. Fiction fleshing out the bones of exhaustively researched and documented facts. Some characters are solely products of my imagination—call them "composite characters" perhaps—but I would never put real people into situations they could not have encountered and I've tried to be faithful to every known fact. I have taken it upon myself in the novel, however, to determine family relationships, motives and whatever it is that fits in the void of missing years.

To any residents or historians of the beautiful counties I have written about—I hope you can please forgive any liberties I have taken with geography, etc., whether inadvertent or intentional.

This is one more humble contribution to my family's heritage. I am my father's daughter, spinning lore and telling tales. Just carrying on a well-loved family tradition.

—J.M.K.

Joan Kay lives in the beautiful Chesapeake Bay country of southern Maryland with her husband and four children. A dedicated researcher, she's excited to be sharing her family history with you and will continue tirelessly—even while buried under mounds of paperwork—sorting through the records of America's fabulous past to do just that. She looks forward to bringing more of the McLaughlin family to life for readers soon. She can be reached at JoanMcLKay@aol.com.